Like Snow We Fall

AYLA DADE

sourcebooks
casablanca

Copyright © 2021, 2025 by Penguin Random House Verlagsgruppe
Cover and internal design © 2025 by Sourcebooks
Cover design by Casey Moses
Cover image © Subbotina Anna/Shutterstock
Internal design by Laura Boren/Sourcebooks

Sourcebooks and the colophon are registered trademarks of Sourcebooks.

All rights reserved. No part of this book may be reproduced in any form or by any electronic or mechanical means including information storage and retrieval systems—except in the case of brief quotations embodied in critical articles or reviews—without permission in writing from its publisher, Sourcebooks.

No part of this book may be used or reproduced in any manner for the purpose of training artificial intelligence technologies or systems.

Originally published as *Like Snow We Fall* (Winter Dreams #1) by Ayla Dade, © 2021 by Penguin Verlag, a division of Penguin Random House Verlagsgruppe GmbH, München, Germany. Translated from German by Alexander Booth.

The characters and events portrayed in this book are fictitious or are used fictitiously. Any similarity to real persons, living or dead, is purely coincidental and not intended by the author.

All brand names and product names used in this book are trademarks, registered trademarks, or trade names of their respective holders. Sourcebooks is not associated with any product or vendor in this book.

Published by Sourcebooks Casablanca, an imprint of Sourcebooks
1935 Brookdale RD, Naperville, IL 60563-2773
(630) 961-3900
sourcebooks.com

Originally published as *Like Snow We Fall* (Winter Dreams #1) in 2021 in Germany by Penguin Verlag, an imprint of Penguin Random House Verlagsgruppe. This edition issued based on the paperback edition published in 2021 in Germany by Penguin Verlag, an imprint of Penguin Random House Verlagsgruppe.

Cataloging-in-Publication Data is on file with the Library of Congress.

Printed and bound in the United States of America.
VP 10 9 8 7 6 5 4 3 2 1

For my father,
who gifted me the art of storytelling—
a spark that became a fire in my chest.
Without you, I wouldn't be here.
I'm not just living my dream.
I'm living it for both of us.

You never got the chance to chase your dreams.
Violence stole your potential before the world could see it.
But with every word I write,
I carry you forward.
You live in every page,
in every line,
in every place my stories travel to.

You are my quiet compass,
my invisible wing.
And when the world sees me—
they see us both.
We're flying up there together, Daddy.

"You are not alone. You are seen. I am with you. You are not alone."

—Shonda Rhimes

1
Still Waters Run Deep

PAISLEY

MY STOMACH IS GROWLING. IT'S IMPOSSIBLE *NOT* TO HEAR it in the silence, but no one looks over. It's right before dawn; most of the people in the bus are still asleep.

I carefully bend forward to dig my smartphone out of my bag without waking up the person next to me. Over the last sixteen hours, we've hardly exchanged a word. His shabby pinstripe suit—which seems about two sizes too large—suggests that he's a businessman. Maybe not the most *successful* businessman. I mean, this Minneapolis to Aspen bus isn't exactly the epitome of comfort.

But it's good enough for me. It's bringing me farther. Taking me away.

To safety.

My bag falls back into the footwell when the bus jerks over a bump. I glance at my phone. 7:17 a.m. It can't be much longer. My stomach is full of butterflies, and they've made it all the way to my fingertips. When I lean forward to try and peep through the yellowed bus curtains, the window fogs up. Warm streetlights shine across rippling snow. Rows of little cabins, one after the other, here and there a lighted window. My glance wanders farther, across the snowy roofs toward a tall, white bell tower.

It'll be a new beginning. A leap into the unknown. I'll be on my own, but that doesn't bother me at all.

It's always been that way. And always will.

Above our heads, the ceiling lights flicker on before casting their butter-yellow glow throughout the bus. After two more curves, the loudspeaker begins to crackle, and the driver's monotone voice comes through. "In a few minutes we'll be reaching Aspen. This is the last stop. Please get off the bus, and remember to take your belongings with you. Thank you."

With a deep sigh, I pick my ice skates up off the floor, press them to my chest, and look out the window. Before me, Aspen's snow-covered peaks tower into the sky as if trying to reach the clouds.

So, this is it. My new home. The opportunity of a lifetime.

The bus stops and the doors open. Cold air slams into my face as I shoulder my jute bag, dig my fingers into the white leather of my skates, and step out into the open air behind the few other passengers. The snow crunches beneath my winter boots.

Between the wildly whirling flakes here and there, I can make out individual streetlights. The air is pure and clear. It smells of freedom. Peace. Aspen is exactly what I imagined it would be.

Magical.

Strands of my blond hair tickle my cheek as I tug my woolen cap farther down over my ears and begin to stomp through the snow. My stomach starts growling again. It's got to be at least a day since I've eaten anything. Most recently, before…

No. I'm not going to think about it. It's over. I refuse to allow this venom to poison my happiness and ruin it like a drop of oil in clean water.

The white sky is streaked with pink to announce the breaking day. Now I can see rows of little cabins across the middle of the mountains as if they'd just sprung out of Santa's village.

A light to my right draws my attention. It's coming from a building on the corner. Behind the large windows, an attractive woman is standing in front of a long counter, pushing cupcakes into a bakery display case.

Cupcakes… My mouth begins to water. My legs start moving before I can even put together my next thought.

A bell above the door rings when I step inside and shut out the cold behind me. I am enveloped by wonderful smells. I close my eyes for a second and take a deep breath. Then I take a look around.

Red and black upholstered barstools alternate in front of the counter; some of the leather is cracked, and I can see the yellow foam underneath. Along the wall by the windows, there are a number of red upholstered booths with white tables in between. Crooked red letters above the old-fashioned jukebox tell me the name of the place: *Kate's Diner*.

It's breakfast time. I can smell pancakes, blueberries, and cinnamon. Chocolate, almonds, and honey. More, more, more—there's just so much, and it's so heavenly I could never really take it all in, no matter how long I tried to define the smells.

And coffee. I can smell coffee.

The flickering pink neon sign behind the counter—*hotdogs, hamburgers, milkshakes*—tells me that the menu changes according to the time of day.

I hear the door close behind me. My eyes flit across the pictures on the walls. One of them is a view of the city lit up at night. The lights look like fires surrounded by the snowy mountains that flank Aspen like a protective wall. The other pictures are full of…

Pigeons. Of every stripe and at all moments. One of them has colorful feathers. Another one is featured close-up, fixing its yellow eyes straight into the camera. And yet another one, head held high, is crouching next to…a petite pile of its business. With the words, "Be like a pigeon—don't lose your shit!" written above it.

"Hey, sweetheart." The thin woman with the polka-dotted

apron smiles at me. Her eyes are the same warm chocolate brown as her cupcakes. The soles of her white canvas shoes make a delicate sound with every step she takes across the black-and-white tiled floor toward me. "How can I make your morning sweeter? You look like you could use an extra scoop of sugar."

"Coffee," I stammer. "And…scrambled eggs. Please."

My heart is in my throat. I'm nervous. It's been a long time since I've met any unbiased people. People who don't know a thing about me. Although I know this woman has never seen me before, I can't shake the unnerving feeling that she can read me.

Before ending up at the home for girls, I grew up in a trailer park outside of Minneapolis. It was a small place. Not a lot of people. Everyone knew everyone else. The kids knew who they were allowed to play with and who they were supposed to avoid. I was one of the latter. A trailer roach. That's what they called us.

Blurry images flash before my mind's eye. Parents dragging their kids past the fence around our community. Scratching my head with tiny fingers only to discover a louse under my nail a few seconds later. Mom on her knees in front of a guy I didn't know, pants around his ankles, laughing that seven-year-old me had caught her.

And, finally, my skinny thighs, which I stared at when I sat down on the thin mattress at the home for the first time.

I'm torn out of my thoughts when the woman with the apron clucks, "Scrambled eggs? You can't be from around here."

A smile tugs at my lips. "How so?" I pull off my cap, sit down in one of the red booths, and hang my jacket and skates over the back. "What's wrong with scrambled eggs?"

"Nothing. The folks in Aspen just don't eat them here."

"Why not?"

"Believe me, sweetheart." She goes behind the counter and pours coffee into a big mug. "Once you get a taste of my chocolate pancakes, scrambled eggs will seem like nothing."

"Inviting," I grin. "Well, let's have some of those famous pancakes, then."

The woman puts the steaming mug down in front of me and shoots me a winning smile. "You won't regret it." She twirls around and disappears behind a door that must lead into the kitchen. In between the sounds from the radio, I can hear the rattle of pots and pans, and, a little bit later, the sizzle of hot oil.

I knead my fingers and wait. In the meantime, the pinkish wisps in the sky outside have vanished. But I see a lot more people on the streets of Aspen, packed tight into their coats, trudging through the snow. With a sigh, I pull my smartphone out of my bag and scroll through my photos.

The laughing faces of my girlfriends beam back at me. In almost every shot we're on the ice, wearing our training outfits. We were hardly ever anywhere else. After high school, the ice rink defined my everyday life. From morning to night.

I swipe to the next picture and suddenly feel an invisible hand grab hold of my heart and squeeze. Kaya's blue eyes sparkle back at me. Our heads are next to each other on the ice; individual strands have come loose from our buns. We're laughing about something that belongs to a moment long since passed.

I remember that day. It was shortly after the regional championships. One of the few days I can think back to with happiness.

The image before my eyes grows blurry. I swallow. Kaya was my best friend. *Is* my best friend. And she has no idea where I am. She has no idea what's happened.

No one does.

A plate slides into my field of vision and lands in front of me on the table. I abruptly toss my smartphone back into my bag and sit up.

"Thanks a lot," I say.

The woman smiles. Her eyes shoot across my face and stop just a moment too long at that place they shouldn't. I lower my head and dwell on my pancakes.

It feels like an eternity before she starts moving again and disappears behind her counter. "I'm Kate, by the way," she says.

I shove a forkful of pancake into my mouth and feel like crying with pleasure. "Paisley," I manage, my mouth full.

Kate nods. She opens the lid of a can containing a batch of baked cookies and sprinkles them with powdered sugar. "Are you here visiting someone or just passing through?"

I've already polished off half of my pancakes, but it's not nearly enough. My stomach cries out for more. "No, I…" I swallow and clear my throat. "I just moved here."

Kate looks surprised. "Like that? That doesn't happen all that often in Aspen." She tilts her head and sizes up my jute bag. "And you're an ice-skater?"

I choke on my pancake. "How…"

"Your skates." Kate nods toward my bundle, tied together at the laces. "Wasn't tough to guess."

"Oh. Right." I take a gulp of coffee before adding, "I was given a place at iSkate Aspen."

"Well, now! Then you must be good. They only take the best." Kate snatches a cookie before closing the can and placing it back next to the cupcakes. "My daughter skates there, too."

The last forkful of pancake disappears in my mouth. I quickly swallow it down while Kate continues to observe me with big eyes. "Your daughter?"

"Gwen. You've got to be around the same age." She points at me with her half-eaten cookie. "Twenty?"

"Twenty-one," I correct her. Then frown. "Do your pancakes have some kind of 'forever young' powder in them or something? I'd like to get me some of that, too."

Kate laughs. Crumbs tumble onto the countertop when she takes another bite of her cookie. "I became a mom pretty young. At seventeen. But if I come across anything like that, I'll be sure to let you know."

The bell rings, announcing a customer.

"Shit, is it cold outside." A young man with a huge sports bag knocks snow off his boots onto the tiles. Which is followed by further flakes when he rubs his gloved hands together.

"Morning, Wyatt," Kate says. She's already moving to fill up a to-go cup with coffee. "You're late today."

"Yeah, I overslept." The guy takes the cup, places two singles on the countertop, and pours so much sugar into his coffee that I seriously have to wonder whether it's a kind of cure-all for the town. "Went a bit late last night." He pushes the top down onto his cup. "Should probably take it down a notch."

Kate raises an eyebrow. "You say that at least three times a week when you show up here in the mornings."

Wyatt grins. His features are frighteningly attractive, and I'd bet he's one of those guys who is all too aware of it.

"Truth. What can I say? You only live once." He lifts his cup in goodbye and shuffles toward the door. His bag grazes my skates. Two crossed hockey sticks sewn into the side pocket.

Ah ha. Hockey player.

"Best steer clear of his parties," Kate says once Wyatt has left the diner. "Or you can kiss your dream goodbye before even thinking of the word *Olympics*."

I swish my coffee around and watch the dark liquid moisten the ceramic. "Competitive sports and parties don't go together."

"Oh, don't let Knox hear you say that."

With a wrinkled brow, I lift my eyes. "Knox?"

"He should be showing up any second," she responds and points to the coffee machine she is filling up.

"Another hockey player?"

"Not entirely." A mysterious smile appears at the corners of her mouth. "Knox is a snowboarder."

Before the last syllable of her words fades, the bell rings again. A wide-shouldered guy with cropped brown hair steps into the diner.

The first thing he looks at is me. His eyes bore directly into mine. They are large and green; I've never seen a green as bright. The white sky outside turns his pupils into pinheads, and I feel like I've been blinded by the color of his irises.

He turns away first. Snowflakes fall from his hair and land on his black down jacket. His feet are tucked into warm Panama Jacks.

"Thanks, Kate," he says while—surprise!—pouring three packets of sugar into his coffee. He rubs his other hand across his face.

"Tired, Knox?" she asks bemusedly.

"That's not the right expression at all. No idea how I'm supposed to survive the day."

"Maybe by deciding to go to bed a little earlier tonight?"

"Kate." Knox breaks into an incredulous grin. One of the disarming kinds. One of the kinds that make women weak. "Please."

She waves her hand through the air. "It's all right. Now take your coffee and get out of here! With your bloodshot eyes, you'll scare off all my customers."

Knox draws a fake punch. "I've got the face of an angel. Say I've got the face of an angel, Kate."

"If angels look like their daily bread consists of shots, well, yeah. You've got the face of an angel."

He laughs, pays for his coffee, and makes his way to the door. Once again his eyes graze mine. The carefree look there a second ago is gone, and now it's hard to gauge what they're saying. He looks like he's judging me for something. Before I can interpret his features any further, though, he's out the door.

"Well, *that* was Knox," Kate says superfluously. "You should steer clear of him even more than Wyatt's parties."

"What do you mean?" I ask, my fingers gripping the large coffee cup. "What's up with him?"

Kate looks to the door where just a few seconds ago he disappeared. "The question, my dear, is what's *not* up with him. Women, scandals, stress… Knox takes it all. He's a good guy, but…" She sighs. "Snowboarding doesn't seem to be helping him find the right path."

For a while we're both silent, while in my head the image of his piercing green eyes continues to whirr. Eventually I sigh, too, and dig my wallet out of my jute bag. "Thank you for your wonderful pancakes. What do I owe you?"

Kate shakes her head. "Put your money away, dear. Today breakfast's on me." She smiles. "Welcome to Aspen."

2
When Eyes Meet

PAISLEY

IT SMELLS LIKE WOOD. THAT'S THE FIRST THING THAT crosses my mind when I open the door to Ruth's B&B.

And, indeed, the walls of the little house are completely paneled in wood. There's a fire crackling next to a sitting area with chintz chairs and a brown leather sofa. In one of the chairs sits a woman with graying hair, knitting. She looks up as I come in and scatter the snow I've brought with me across the thick carpet.

"You look completely frozen," she says. "Frozen and skinny."

"Umm…" Are all the people in Aspen this direct? "I'd like a room if you have any. Just for a few days!" I add quickly when deep furrows break across the woman's brow. "I mean, I hope. It…It could turn into more."

"Girl, what are you doing to me?" She slowly gets to her feet, but not without heaving a deep sigh. "Don't you know it's high season?"

"High season?"

The woman steps behind the counter to leaf through her reservation book. "It's winter. Aspen's ski resorts have been booked out for months. And now all the world's in town to see our Knox at the regional championships." She raises her eyes and looks at me. "You're not another one of them, are you?"

"One of them?"

"His groupies."

"Oh. No." With a vindicating smile I lift my skates. "iSkate Aspen wants me. I don't have anywhere to stay yet." *And I've got enough savings for one month, tops.* "I don't need a lot of room. Just a bed. Or... I mean, I'd be happy to sleep on a couch. Doesn't matter. The main thing is that I..."

"Good God, no." With her head she points at the sitting area. "That thing sinks deeper than a capsized ship. You wanna destroy your back?"

"I..."

"Let's have a look," she mutters, leafs through another page, and runs her finger down the list of reservations. My shoulders sink with every deepening wrinkle on her forehead. "Nope, not a chance."

I feel a lump in my throat. My fingers hurt from digging them into the leather of my skates. I ease up. "Okay, well...not a big deal. Could you, however, tell me where the next B&B is, maybe?"

A sympathetic expression appears on her face. "Everything's going to be booked."

A feeling of panic begins to spread throughout my body. Panic mixed with hopelessness. I mean, what am I supposed to do? A sense of futility takes my breath away.

It's my life. Over and over it's my life that puts me into these situations. Normal people just don't hit the road like me. Normal people plan and are prepared, have more things with them, more than just a few pieces of clothing, sanitary products, and ice skates.

Normal people aren't as confused as me. Haven't had as shitty a life as me.

"It'll be okay," I stammer. My voice seems thin. "Maybe I'll find something outside of town."

The woman frowns. Her lips form a thin line. "Give me a

minute, okay? You can wait by the fire. There's some chocolate in the dish on the table."

The floorboards under the carpet groan as she makes her way to the end of the counter and disappears behind a door. A heavy silence comes over me, giving my thoughts too much space.

I wish she hadn't gone. I wish she'd just continued talking with me. Then I wouldn't have to confront my fear of where to go. Where I'm supposed to sleep tonight.

The couch really does sink when I sit down. I am greeted by the smells of old leather and cinnamon candles.

For a while I just listen to the fire and the clock ticking above it before I hear the owner's steps again. She appears behind the counter, phone still at her ear. "Of course I'm taking my vitamins. All good. Love you, too, sweetheart." There's a smile on her lips as she puts the phone back down. "That was my daughter, Aria. She's studying in Rhode Island. At Brown…"

"Oh, wow. That's…really good." I rub the tips of my boots together and wonder why she's telling me. What am I waiting around for? "You must really miss her."

"I do." She sighs again. She casts a glance at the phone, drums her fingers on the counter, then walks over to me. I notice she's limping. "Aria is full of life. She's such a positive person. Sees the best in everything and… You haven't tried the chocolate?"

"Oh!" Surprised by her quick change of topic, I sit up with a start. "No, I…"

"You're missing out. Here, take a whole handful and put it in your pocket. The nougat balls are the best in Aspen!" Before I can say anything, she's tipped half the bowl into my jute bag. "Hard to believe how little you've got with you. If Aria were to get a look at you, she'd die. Well, better for you." She shrugs. "Less to carry to your room."

"My room?"

"Why I called my daughter. She's fine with you sleeping in her old room. But beware: for years Aria's sworn a marten's been up to all manners of mischief under the floorboards." Her eyes twinkle. "I can't let you freeze to death out on the streets of Aspen. What kind of headline would that be? And in high season of all things!"

"Oh my God." My knees begin to tremble in thanks as I spring up from the couch and reach for the woman's hands. "You're saving my life. Really. God... Thank you! I don't know how to thank you."

She runs her hand through the air. "Find the marten."

I let out a laugh. It sounds wild and raw, not like me at all. But after the last twenty-four hours, it doesn't surprise me whatsoever.

"I'll lure it with your chocolate," I say, making my way behind her. "My name's Paisley, by the way."

"Ruth. Be careful with this step here; it creaks. This here is the floor with the guestrooms, and through this door," we came to a dark wooden door with a brass handle at the end of the hall, "you'll come to where we live." Ruth hands me a key before turning her own in the lock. We step into a corridor decorated with bright-colored pictures. She points to a log ladder at the end of the hall. "Up there is where your room will be for the next little while if you're up for a work exchange? I don't like to rent in the family quarters but I can use the help. High season, like I said. It's yours as long as you need it. You can help me with the food and the guestrooms. When something opens up downstairs, we can switch to a rental if you want. Whatever you want to do."

My heart is pounding even though we're only talking about a room. But, for me, it feels like a milestone. Another step I'm taking into my life, the one that *I* want, the one that *I'm* creating.

"Thank you," I say again, yet I feel as if it's not enough. "I'd love to help out with the guests. At the moment... I'd really like that."

Ruth smiles. "Of course, sweetheart. And stop thanking me all the time. Here in Aspen, we help one another. Get used to it."

I'd rather not. Getting used to something means becoming careless. And carelessness can lead to horrible things.

Horrible, horrible, horrible.

I shake my head to chase off the images. I smile at Ruth instead. "And would you happen to know where I might be able to find a more permanent job?"

Ruth runs her fingers through her graying hair. "Let me think. A few après-ski bars downtown and on the slopes are looking for help. Maybe you'll get lucky at Woody's, too. That's our local supermarket. And, hmm, hold on a sec…" She tilts her head. "You're a figure skater. In shape, right?"

I nod.

"Then you can give the southern slope a try. The young up-and-comers need an endurance coach. Well, no idea if they still do, but you can give it a shot."

"Thank…"

Ruth lifts her hand to interrupt. "Don't you even finish." Instead of letting her hand sink back down, however, she keeps it there. The amused look in her eyes disappears and turns sad. Her fingers caress the soft skin next to my right eye and wipe the strands of hair out of my face—a soft, comforting gesture, but I flinch as if she'd hit me.

"You're safe here," she says softly. "In Aspen you're safe."

I hardly took a moment to inspect my new temporary room. All I noticed was a dream of rustic wood furniture, string lights, and a whole mess of decorations before I jumped into the shower and hurried back out the door.

Ruth's map of the slopes in hand, I step out of the little bus that took me right to Snowmass Mountain. I study the colorful image with all its descriptions until I find the little symbol of the Aspen Ski & Snowboard School.

"Hey!" I hear a voice call out next to me. I look up and into the face of an older man whose dark beard looks almost white from all the snow. He points to the gondola. "You want to come along?"

I stomp through the snow toward him. "Will that take me to the Aspen Ski & Snowboard School?"

"Of course. Hop off at the second station; you'll be right there."

"Perfect. Oh, God, I've never been in such a thing. Can it crash?"

The guy opens the door for me and takes my money. He shrugs. "Sure. But I've never seen it happen."

"Reassuring," I mumble, one leg already inside. "And generally speaking? I mean, statistically? How safe is…"

The door shuts. Great.

As soon as the gondola begins to move, I begin to feel queasy. I wouldn't say I suffer from a fear of heights, but…the thing creaks. And creaking things a couple of hundred feet in the air are suspicious. The same reason I've always considered people getting onto a Ferris wheel with big smiles on their faces to be masochists.

I clutch the cold bench and try not to think about whether my body would ever be found in the mass of snow before my limbs would be covered by frostbite. But, paradoxically, the higher the gondola climbs, the more my heartbeat slows.

It's the view that causes my fear to stop. Aspen's mountains are just so beautiful. They don't leave any room for negative feelings.

Without really being aware of it, I press my hand to the cool windowpane and observe the horizon. Maybe it's up there, in the snow-covered summits, where I'll lose my head and find my soul.

The sky above me, the earth below me, and in the middle: peace.

Stepping out at the second station, I promptly sink up to my shins in snow. Within seconds my jeans are soaked, and I decide to get myself a pair of snowpants as soon as possible. Maybe off eBay.

At present, I'm completely at a loss. In the distance I can hear children laughing and words being shouted, but I can't see anyone. All I see is a mass of snow and, far below, the rooftops of Aspen's houses.

"Okay," I murmur and look at the blackboard, which has a

picture like the one on my map; this one here is clearer and larger. "You'll manage, Paisley. Let's have a look."

It takes a few minutes, but then I slowly manage to find my way through the crazy labyrinth of colors, symbols, and lines.

My jeans are happy to have me trudge through the heavy snow for only five minutes until I finally—*finally!*—reach the right slope.

Before me people are bustling about in thick snowsuits—*what I wouldn't give for one of those!*—the kids making their first moves on their skis and snowboards. Before stepping onto the packed snow of the slope and approaching the closest teenager, I slowly shake the white wetness from my jeans and boots. He's got a snowboard under his arm and is about to disappear in the other direction.

"Hey!" I raise my hand and wave, like I'm some kind of missing person who's just been found. He doesn't hear me. I gasp and call out once more. "Hey! Over here! Yeah, I'm the one who just yelled!" I'm breathing quickly by the time I finally reach him. Beneath his helmet I can see the tips of brown hair. It looks like he's got that Justin Bieber cut that's been out of style for years now.

"You know your way around here?"

Underneath the bright sky I can see that he's blushing. His cheeks and forehead are dotted with big pimples; he must have just entered puberty. "Yo," he mutters, without looking at me. His bindings seem to be far more interesting than I am.

"Right. Can you bring me to whoever's in charge around here?"

He nods, turns, and tramps off without saying another word. I wade after him, carefully avoiding two kids who otherwise would have taken off my legs.

"Him," the boy says. But before I can make out who he means, he's gone.

With a sigh, I gaze out across the slope. Colorful snowsuits galore. All alike. Everyone is yelling over one another, laughing, children screeching with joy. It's impossible to recognize anyone here, especially if I don't even know who I'm looking for and…

"What are *you* doing here?"

I blink. The guy who's suddenly in front of me, I know him. I'd recognize those eyes anywhere.

It's Knox, the snowboarder.

3
Sorry for the People I Hurt While I Was Hurting

Knox

At Kate's earlier, I noticed the swelling in the girl's face. I couldn't tell then if it had to do with the dim light, but I didn't want to take a closer look, either. To be honest, I'd overslept, was hungover, and didn't want to concern myself with anything beyond my aching head.

But what I thought I saw earlier this morning couldn't be any clearer now. The swelling is red, if not already turning green. Whatever the cause, it's clear it didn't happen all that long ago.

With her huge glacier-blue eyes, she stared at me like she's seeing a ghost. Her lips are open just a hair, and in the bright sunlight I can see a thin white scar on her jaw. I let my eyes wander down her petite frame and have to keep from laughing when I see her jeans, wet to the knees. As she still hasn't uttered a word, I wave my hand in front of her face. "Hello? You okay?"

She quickly blinks a few times before batting my hand away as if it were an annoying fly. The corners of my mouth twitch again.

"Stop. I'm looking for someone."

"Up 'til now without all that much success, am I right?"

She casts me an angry glance, then turns away to continue staring casually into the distance.

I take a breath. "You know, I'd really love to leave you standing here to get whacked by a skier, but unfortunately that would fall within my realm of responsibility. So…" I make a sweeping gesture with my arms toward the side slope. "Would you care to continue your search over there?"

"This is…" She stops midsentence before closing her eyes, then she looks up at the sky. Slowly, she turns back to me. "Your responsibility?"

"Yeah. Responsibility. You familiar with the word? I can put it in other terms if you'd like." I nonchalantly tilt my head. "Morals. Sense of duty. Conscience. Accountability. Obliga—"

"I'm not dumb!"

"Oh. That's good. Who are you then?"

"What?"

"Your name." I grin. "You got one, don't you? I'm Knox, by the way."

"I know. You don't need to know my name."

Odd. The crabbier she gets, the more interesting I find her.

She takes a deep breath, as if she had to arm herself for something, then says, "If you're responsible for all this, then maybe you can help me."

I laugh, plant my snowboard into the ground, and lean my arm on it. "You want my help without telling me your name?" I put on a theatrically skeptical face. "Didn't anyone ever tell you not to trust strangers?"

She gasps for air as if I'd offended her and takes two steps back. She looks at me for a moment, her blue eyes so big I feel as if I could disappear inside them.

"Of course," she counters coolly. "They did. There's just one problem."

"And what would that be?"

She doesn't bat an eye. "It's not strangers who are the problem. But those you think you know."

I don't often lose the power of speech. In fact, I'm usually pretty articulate. Quick. I always know what to say. But right now, I have no idea. Right now, I'm simply standing in front of her, staring into her eyes and wondering who on earth this girl is.

"If you'll excuse me," she adds, taking off in the opposite direction. "You're stealing time I don't have."

"Wait." I rub a hand across my face before following her. "Hey, wait up." I grab her arm to get her to stop. Wrong move. With a power I wouldn't have expected her delicate body to possess, she tears her arm away only to punch me in the chest a second later. In spite of myself, I stagger a few steps back.

"Don't touch me!" she hisses.

I raise my hands in a conciliatory way. "I'm sorry. Really. I just wanted…" With a sigh, I let them sink back down. "Tell me how I can help."

"You can help by leaving me alone." She stomps off, her head barely missing a snowboard a tourist had draped under their arm.

"Come on." This time I'm smarter. Instead of grabbing her, I take a pair of large steps, circle her, and put myself in front of her. "Don't be so stubborn. You want something; I can probably help. If you don't have any time, continuing to skulk about the slopes without any plan isn't the most effective path."

For a moment, she just stares at me angrily. But I am far too busy with watching how the light makes the blue of her eyes shine to let it bother me.

Eventually, she shifts her weight from one leg to the other and seems to get that I'm right. "Good. Someone told me that the up-and-comers need an endurance trainer."

"And?"

"And I'm looking for the person who's in charge."

"What do you mean?"

"I don't think I need to discuss that with you."

I crack a grin. "I think you do."

"Ah. Sure. Just because you're Knox, the sought-after snowboarder, you think everything revolves around you. Got it. But let me tell you something." She takes a step toward me. Her face is now much closer to mine. Only now do I notice her right eye is streaked with burst vessels. "I'm not like all those other girls who will kiss your feet. I don't care what you want or what you don't want. Your charm leaves me cold. So, if you want to help me, just tell me where I can find the person responsible for those kids."

Holy cow. This girl's got a temper. I like it.

"Feet are nasty," I counter. "Why would I want someone…"

"Knox."

I raise a corner of my mouth. "Well. He's standing right in front of you."

She screws up her eyes before looking to either side of me. Once she sees the kids on their boards and skis, she turns back to me. "Real funny, Knox."

I grin. "Don't you think it's unfair that you know my name, but I don't know yours?"

"No."

I have to laugh. "Okay. Maybe you'll tell me when I inform you that I'm the one who's responsible for the up-and-comers."

Surprise is written all over her face. "You can't be for real."

"As real as I'm standing right in front of you."

She closes her eyes for a moment before turning her head to the side and looking into the distance. "That was obvious."

"Come out with it. Do you know anyone who wants to train the little daredevils? But I'm warning you: there's no commission for the middleman."

She doesn't laugh. Instead, she just looks at me, expressionless, and chews on the inside of her cheek while appearing to think. Eventually she says, "I want the job."

At first, I think I've misheard her. But when she doesn't say anything else, I slowly realize that she's serious. I let out a big laugh. "No, you don't want to do that."

"Oh, wow. You're really getting on my nerves, you know?"

"Then why are you still here?"

Her eyes flash. "Because I need the job. I'm serious. Why do you say 'no'?"

A kid on a snowboard is coming right toward us. I carefully raise my hand and urge her to the side. She flinches again but doesn't punch me a second time.

"Well…" My eyes sweep from her face to her feet and back. "You're really delicate. The kids are primarily boys hitting puberty. Really stressful. They say a lot of dumb shit, are demanding, and you've got to act like an authoritarian. You look like they'd run over you at the first opportunity."

Her nostrils flare. "That's sexist. Just because I'm not a dude doesn't mean I can't assert myself."

"Maybe so. All the same…" Unsure, I suck in my lower lip and run my teeth across it. "You know about training?"

She raises her chin. "I'm a figure skater at iSkate."

That changes everything. From one second to the next.

A figure skater.

It's like those words have taken my breath away. Here I am, stiff as a board, my feet stuck into the snow, but I feel totally unstable. As if the ground beneath me might disappear, casting me into the abyss, without any security at all, unconscious, or maybe not, which would be even worse, much, much worse. I'd feel everything, the pain welling back up, the heat, the cold, the heat, the cold rushing through my body and inflaming my nerves to the extreme.

"Hello?" Her voice seems far away; it's riddled with a rustling, and I can't tell if it is real or just in my head. There's a rustling and it's loud, it's roaring, maybe shouting, no idea, but it's loud, so loud that I can't stand it. Just her voice; it's barely there, a distant, dull sound, as if coming from shore, and I was out there, real deep beneath the water. "Is, umm, everything okay?"

I gasp for breath. With the memories the word has brought up, I feel bile making its way up into my throat.

A figure skater.

"There's no job for you," I stammer. I'm dizzy. The brightly colored snowsuits of the people around us turn into a single mosaic.

"Umm. Okaaay. And why not?"

"Because."

She crosses her arms across her chest. "Do you already have someone? I'm better. I can prove it. Give me a chance. A test. I'll show you that I can train the up-and-comers. I *am* assertive."

My eyes flit to the swelling in her face and stay put. She notices. Of course she does. That is exactly what I aimed to achieve. I know that it isn't right. I know that she'll think I'm the biggest asshole in the United States. Maybe I am; who knows? But at the moment I don't see any other way of keeping her at a distance.

A figure skater.

"I doubt it."

She gasps. The shock in her face is deep. A blaze that's impossible to miss fills her large eyes.

I can't say that it doesn't affect me.

"You're obnoxious, Knox." Her expression is full of disgust. She shakes her head. "Repellent." And with that, she turns and goes.

All the sounds around me fade into the background.

I don't know how much longer I stand there, watching her go. I only know that I'm still there once she has long disappeared from sight.

4
Lost Boy

PAISLEY

I WAKE UP TEN MINUTES BEFORE MY ALARM RINGS. My stomach is tingling, and my heart is racing. It feels just like when I have an event; it's just that today doesn't have anything to do with a medal.

Today is my first official day at iSkate. I'm going to sign my contract. A contract watched over by the sword of Damocles from the very beginning, waiting for me to do myself in.

Don't think about it, Paisley.

The lilac-scented sheets rustle as I turn onto my side. I ball the pillow together to bury my face and allow my quivering breaths to die down. I kick the comforter to the end of the bed, swing myself up, and turn on the lamp on the nightstand.

It's early. Shortly before six. Between the slats of the window blinds, I can see the moonlight illuminating the dancing snowflakes, as if the sky was their stage. They remind me of myself, bringing back images from long ago. I see myself as a child, with a dazzling smile, in a cheap, secondhand figure-skating dress, following my first ever public ice dance. Every step was accompanied by a kind of magic that only I could see.

And that magic has remained. It's my constant companion. The power that drives me forward. My best friend. The voice within me that courses through my veins with its prickly whispers and settles in my heart. The voice that tells me I have to fight if I don't want to lose the magic.

I've got to hold onto it. And that's why I don't give up. That's why I'm here.

With a soft swish the slat falls back into place when I pull back my hand and nervously make my way through the room to pull my training tights out of my bag. They're underneath my other things, which is why I spontaneously decide to sort the few pieces in Aria's spacious wardrobe.

I open the doors and stop short. Either Ruth's daughter forgot a few things or…she's a shopaholic. The pieces inside don't exactly give the impression that their owner is on the other side of the country. There is hardly any space for my few things, and, ultimately, they end up in a disordered bundle between Aria's shirts, hoodies, and tops. A miserable sight.

I'm about to close the door again when I notice a pair of Asics. I hesitate a moment before finally bending over and having a closer look.

Size 7. They don't look like they've even been worn. I'd planned to go over there in my boots, but now that I've got the opportunity… I'm sure it wouldn't bother Aria at all.

It's only when I pull the shoes out that I notice the crumpled photo in the gap between the bottom of the wardrobe and the wall. I carefully pluck it out so that it doesn't tear and have a look.

The guy staring back at me with a wide grin and a beer bottle in his hand is unmistakably that guy Wyatt from Kate's Diner. I don't know the girl next to him. I assume it's Aria. Full-bodied, brown hair tumbles out from beneath her baseball cap and falls to her shoulders in waves. She has freckles, but just on her nose, and her green eyes are shining as she casts Wyatt a sidelong glance.

Suddenly I feel terrible. As if I'd come across Aria's diary and read her most intimate thoughts. I quickly stuff the picture back into the gap and close the wardrobe with the firm intention of never sniffing through her things again.

I slip into my leggings and sneakers, plug my headphones into my phone, and take the hair tie off my wrist to pull my blond hair back into a messy ponytail. Then I pull on my gloves and cap and tiptoe as quietly as possible down the narrow hall, through the door, and down the stairs to the guest area.

The steps creak. It's so quiet that the noise almost feels spooky. Behind one door I catch the unmistakable sound of a loudly snoring guest.

After turning the deadbolt, the front door opens with a soft click, and I step out into the icy morning air.

Although Aspen is one of America's wealthiest cities, right now it couldn't feel any lonelier. The streets are empty. Not even the streetlamps are on; just the pale moonlight casting a gray light onto the snowy ground. In the distance, the tops of the Aspen Highlands tower into the horizon and, for a moment, take my breath away. They're terribly big and bewitching at the same time. Online I read that Aspen is surrounded by four mountains: Snowmass, Buttermilk, Aspen Mountain, and Aspen Highlands.

I don't know if I've ever seen anything more beautiful than this view. Like looking at an image on Google and knowing immediately that it's been retouched with Photoshop because it's so beautiful. It's just that this moment is real. Not Instagram fake. No false perfection. That's why I love nature. It never pretends.

Everything inside me is tingling as I start my playlist and jog off. The icy air cuts my face, but I enjoy it. I enjoy the cold wiping away my thoughts and filling my lungs with energy, allowing the magic inside me to awaken.

I jog without thinking about where my feet are taking me. It's not hard to find your way in Aspen. The city is small, and the houses are arranged in orderly rows, one after the other. On Google Earth, Aspen looks like a *Pac-Man* maze.

The snow crunches beneath my sneakers. My feet are numb with cold, but I keep on running, ever farther, following the melody of winter beating in time with my heart.

At the foot of Buttermilk Mountain there are just a few houses. I slow down. Not because I'm tired, but because of the glittering reflections that jump into my eyes.

At first, I think there have got to be strings of lights in the firs. Every breath turns into a white cloud before me as I move closer to the trees. And then I understand where the lights are coming from.

Beyond this wall of snow-draped firs, there's an ice-covered lake. The moon is reflecting on its surface, causing it to sparkle. Somewhere in the distance, a screech owl is crying. A few seconds later I hear the rustling of its feathers as it sets off into the sky.

I lay my palm against a solid fir trunk and linger a moment to stare at the frozen lake. I'm agog with wonder. Aspen may have some places that are filled with magic. Maybe this city is made for touching every soul in a particular way; I don't know. But for me, it's right here. Aspen's heart. It's right in front of me, so pure and clear, far away from the public, and it reflects my inner world. I feel the magic pulsing within me and connecting with this place, and for the first time I have the feeling that I can look into its eyes.

After all these years. Here I am. And here it is.

For the first time in a long time, I feel alive again. Happy and hopeful.

I can feel life itself.

A sound to my right tears me out of my thoughts. It's coming from the direction of the firs and sounds strange somehow, like a stifled groan. Squinting, I try to recognize something, but the trees are blocking the moonlight. It's too dark.

I tentatively take a step forward while being careful to remain in the shadow of two trees. And that's when I see him.

Knox is leaning against a trunk, his eyes turned toward the sky. Yesterday's take-it-easy vibe is gone, replaced by a distorted face and trembling lower lip.

My God, I think he's crying. Is he? Yeah. Definitely. His whole body is shaking while that strange, stifled groan keeps coming from his mouth.

There's no doubt about it, he's crying. But it's like he doesn't know how it works exactly.

I dig my fingers into the tree trunk. I can't stop looking at him. Yesterday I'd sworn to make a wide arc around him. I thought I'd grasped the core of his being. For me, the situation was clear: Knox was one of those sexist types with a shitty character, a person who was more interested in Instagram likes than any interpersonal relationship in real life.

But what I'm seeing here…this is making a totally different impression on me. Why is he crying? What's wrong? And why on earth does he make such an effort to come off as the badass snowboarder when in reality…

When in reality…he seems pretty lost?

As if paralyzed, I watch his almost silent sobbing. Knox runs both of his hands across his face before lowering his gaze and staring out onto the frozen lake. I swear he looks even more pained. His shoulders are shaking, he's gasping for air, and again that groaning starts up.

For the second time this morning, I feel as if I've invaded someone's private sphere. I shouldn't be seeing this. These feelings aren't meant for my eyes. No matter how Knox treated me yesterday, this doesn't feel right.

Nearly silent, I pad off through the deep snow that has already numbed my feet and bones. I keep looking over my shoulder out of the fear that Knox could notice me, but right now, he doesn't seem to be noticing anything but his overwhelming emotions.

On the way back, I jog faster. My racing thoughts are driving me on, almost causing me to sprint while I'm trying to forget the image of his pain-racked face. I don't want to feel any sympathy for Knox. I'd like to consider him the egoist that I'd pegged him for. But my thoughts keep growing louder, wilder, more transparent. They're confusing me. He confuses me. Above all, because, suddenly, I realize that Knox could be more similar to me than I'm comfortable with.

My legs are burning by the time I finally come to a stop in front of Ruth's. Not from exhaustion so much as the cold. I desperately need a hot shower.

I step into the guesthouse in my borrowed wet Asics. The first early birds are already sitting around the long wooden table in the dining room. Snow falls off my shoes and onto the carpet.

Ruth is standing at the buffet, trading an empty bottle of maple syrup for a new one. She casts a glance over her shoulder when the door clicks in the lock and laughs. "I should call you Elsa."

"Elsa?"

"The Snow Queen," she explains. "Every time I see you, you're frozen. You just need a couple of icicles."

Ruth offers me an apple. I accept it gratefully and take a bite. "I went for a jog."

"I can see that." Her eyes pass over my leggings to her daughter's sneakers. She grins. "Oh, those old things. Aria never wore them. It was her," Ruth makes quotation marks in the air, "'now-I'm-going-to-be-sporty phase.'"

"She doesn't like sports?" I ask in surprise. After swallowing my bit of apple, I add, "In Aspen, you can't get away from sports."

Ruth reaches for the plate with the pancakes, which are gradually coming to an end. "Believe me, Aria was a natural-born talent. She is curious and ambitious, but sports… God forbid." At the memory of her daughter, a smirk crosses her lips before she winks at me and moves off toward the kitchen. I'd love to know what's behind her heavy movements. Osteoporosis maybe? Arthritis?

As for me, I can't get into the shower quick enough to feel the hot water on my body, thawing with every second. I lean against the side of the shower, close my eyes, and heave a deep sigh.

Running into Knox has really gotten to me. For a while, it even drove off my nerves and made me forget that today was my big day.

But now it seems like my nerves have woken back up from their short nap and, within seconds, are ready to resume high operation. It feels like there are ants running back and forth beneath my skin.

I lick the warm water off my upper lip with the tip of my tongue before my gaze wanders down my body to the bruises that are invisible to everyone else.

I carefully run a finger over my left hip to the middle of my thigh. The swelling has gone down quite a bit, but the color has changed. It's a bright green, and the edges are streaked a deep blue.

I screw up my eyes, turn off the water, and don't think about it anymore. Soon, there won't be anything left of the bruises, and I'll never have to see them ever again.

Never. Again.

My body is steaming as I step out of the shower—at last I can feel my toes again—and dry off. I slip into fresh clothes, dry my hair, and gulp when I catch a glimpse of myself in the mirror.

The swelling next to my eye has grown more intense. Knox's words from yesterday echo in my head.

I doubt it... Implying that I can't assert myself. That I wasn't strong enough.

I shake my head to dispel my thoughts and turn away. My eyes stop for a moment on a few makeup tools standing on Aria's bathroom dresser next to the sink.

Normally I don't wear any makeup. As an athlete, it's counterproductive. Your sweat smears your mascara and makes you look like an emo kid. Then the foundation clogs your pores and causes you to break out in pimples.

I make my decision in the blink of an eye. I quickly grab the makeup and distribute the stuff across my face. Better a crater-filled emo kid than getting stared at on my first day of iSkate and everyone forming an opinion of me before they've even gotten to know me.

I've left that part of my life behind. And I have no intention of giving it any space to come back.

I blend in the last little bit across my face and then inspect myself. The early morning sun is coming through the window, causing my blue eyes to shine.

I cling to the side of the sink, trembling. "Do it for yourself," I mumble to myself. "You're strong enough; you can do anything."

Three times I repeat these words until I feel that I have won.

It doesn't matter how weak I feel and how much my past has left traces inside of me; the wolf in my heart will never allow the world to catch a glimpse of the lamb in my soul.

Because I'm strong.

I, Paisley Harris, am a goddamn fighter.

5
The World Knows Me Better

Knox

"Ah, Knox." My father is sitting at the table in front of the panoramic windows, where I can get a glimpse of the sun rising slowly behind the Aspen Highlands. Seeing me come in, he opens his copy of *USA Today* and puts it down between the bowl with the eggs and the pitcher with my protein shake. "Come over here and have a look."

With one hand I pull the cap off my head, with the other I peel myself out of my down jacket. I bend over and look at the paper. Snow falls out of my hair onto the table. "Firefighters Free Man from Chastity Belt." I frown. "With an angle grinder? What kind of…"

"Not that!" He points to the other article. "Here, read this!"

With every line I scan, the furrows in my forehead grow deeper. "Oh," I say.

My father raises his eyebrows so high they almost reach his hairline. A considerable achievement. "*Oh?*" he repeats, flicking the article with a finger. "That's all you've got to say? That's a catastrophe, Knox! Jason Hawk is your biggest rival and pulled off a frontside double-kick 1260° in the first twenty seconds of his ride on the

Revolution Tour! In the first twenty seconds, Knox! Do you know what that means?"

I let myself fall into the chair across from him and pour my protein shake into my glass. "Yeah." The corner of my mouth twitches. "He pulled it off in less time than I need to peel this egg. I could ask him if we could make a new routine out of it." I pretend to be playfully casual, as if blowing my nonexistent bangs out of my face, and lean onto the back of the chair next to me with my elbows. "Hey, Jason. Up for a challenge? You and your snowboard against me and my egg. The winner gets..." I think for a second, then suggestively jiggle my eyebrows twice in a row. "The egg."

"That's not funny, Knox."

No? I think so.

My father's face is grim, his lips pressed into a thin line. He loosens his tie. "Your show on the pipe is today. You've got to top that."

"Dad." I laugh softly while peeling off the last bits of shell and putting my egg on a roll. "It's just a show."

"It's got to do with your attitude," he replies. His eyes become tiny slits. He hasn't touched the roll on his plate. He is staring at me like a wild lion that wants to fill its stomach with a helpless antelope instead. "Every ride is important. If you see the show as no big deal, you'll stay behind at the X Games, too. You need to be more ambitious, son!"

"What I need is coffee. And pronto," I say. Running into that figure skater on the slope yesterday just won't leave me alone. I lay awake in bed half the night, reproaching myself for the way I acted before reproaching myself for thinking about her at all. By the time I finally fell asleep, I was racked by nightmares. Images that I have desperately tried to keep down for years. It was still early when the ever-repeating scream in my head woke me up. Glaring. Bloodcurdling.

Captivating.

My whole body was covered in goose bumps. I felt uneasy.

Panicky. The longer I stayed in bed thinking about the images, the worse my breathing got.

So I went for a walk. And, without thinking about it at all, my legs took me to Silver Lake. The only place that allows my thoughts to grow louder while at the same time quieting them down.

My father ignores my reply. He's long been absorbed in his phone, typing away with a concentrated air. "I wanted to show you this, too." He takes a quick gulp of coffee, without looking away from his phone. Showing me his phone, the brown liquid slips over the side and decorates his roll with a few dark drops.

A quick glance is enough to recognize what he means.

Instagram.

I roll my eyes and reach for the coffeepot.

"Don't roll your eyes, Knox. This is serious."

"Oh, wow. I didn't know that Jason was prone to fucking his underage followers."

"What?" My father pulls his phone back and stares with abnormal longing at Jason's profile before looking back at me. "What are you talking about, Knox?"

Cool as a cucumber I take a bite of my roll and lean back. "Now *that* would be serious, Dad."

The veins in his temples begin to pulse. My father is an investor and real-estate agent. Almost every ski resort in Aspen belongs to him. Normally, nothing upsets him that quickly. But I can declare with pride that I have a natural talent for doing so.

"Over the last few weeks, he gained over fifteen thousand new followers. Almost twice as many as you. You're neglecting your online presence."

"I'm neglecting this coffee."

"Don't be an ass, Knox." Now my father's the one rolling his eyes. "You've got to hang out there more. Let your followers into your day-to-day more. You need the press on your side; your name has to be on everybody's lips. That's the only way you're going to be successful." He locks his phone and tosses it onto the table more forcefully than intended. "I mean, when are you finally going to understand that? If you want to get any further, a few things make the difference. Not just your snowboard. Your last post was two weeks ago."

Behind my temples a pulsating pressure is starting to build. It's not the first time this week that my father has been on my ass with this Instagram crap.

Why is it so important? Why should I allow strangers to take part in when I hit the sack and which series I'm currently binge-watching? Should I invite them into the john, too? If it were up to my father, he'd say yes.

"I haven't had a chance recently," I answer without looking at him and push the last bite of my roll into my mouth. To be honest, I've forgotten my password. I've got to set up a new one, but I'm better off keeping that to myself.

In the silence that follows, I can hear myself chewing. Upstairs a vacuum cleaner goes on and begins to go across the floor with a swishing sound.

My father sighs. I look up to see him shaking his head while wiping his hands on a napkin. "I'm going to see about getting you a content manager," he says, pushing back his chair and standing up.

My heart stops for the blink of an eye before it starts back up in double time. "Hell no!" I stand up and stare at my father, who is looking into the mirror above our sideboard and straightening his tie. "That's bullshit, Dad. I mean, that's my private life."

In the mirror I can see him flaring his nostrils. He continues to fumble with his tie for a few more seconds, then he gives up, cursing, and turns to face me. "Then pay a bit more attention to your private life, Knox! Otherwise someone else will have to." He pauses a moment, then adds, "I'd bet you Jason Hawk has a content manager."

"And I'd bet Jason Hawk has chlamydia. What with all the stories you hear."

My father shrugs. "Who cares?"

"He does, no doubt."

He doesn't laugh. He'd probably prefer I had chlamydia if it'd cause my name to show up more often in the press.

He glances earnestly at his wristwatch. "I've got an appointment. We'll see each other later at the race. Tell Lauren that she should make you the millet bowl with the poached egg. That gave you a whole lot of energy last time."

"Lauren's not there anymore." That's the third time I've told him this week. "I'll eat at the ski hut."

Dad doesn't look happy about it, but he nods. His phone beeps. He casts a glance at the display, curses again, and dives toward the front door. "See you later, son. I'm counting on you."

Yeah, Dad. I know.

The door shuts. Outside I hear the Range Rover's door slam before the engine starts up. A few seconds later, it's already gone. Silence falls over me, interrupted only by the sound of the vacuum cleaner.

Meanwhile, the sun has risen. I wish I could be like it. It doesn't have any thoughts. No worries about the day to come. It simply rises and...appears. New every time. And at the same time ready to infuse every single person with its radiant euphoria.

Like now. It's shining its way through the panoramic windows and making every effort to bathe the entire living area of our ski resort in light. Its rays illuminate my skin as I make my way to my bedroom. The warmth makes my pores tingle and does its best to get through. But it can't get all of me.

I feel a coldness inside that's got nothing to do with winter. A coldness that grows larger every day I give it space to expand. Like an iceberg that uses the increasing frost to freeze the water around it. It turns numb. Motionless and still. The water deprived of the air it needs to breathe.

Like me.

Back in my room, I go to my desk, which gives me an unimpeded view of the snow-covered Rockies.

I love Colorado. And I love my life here in Aspen and snowboarding. I just wish I could set up everything differently. According to how I want things to be.

I run my finger over my MacBook's mousepad and enter my password. Then I lean back in my chair, take a deep breath, and hold it.

I've been doing this for weeks. Just staring at my screen while my thoughts race.

The blue banner with the yellow lettering has officially burned itself into my brain starting from that gray winter day when the first snowflakes began to fall.

I can't think in a different way. Day in, day out. My lips move but make no sound, just silently form the words I'm reading off the website.

Colorado Mountain College.

At the time I applied, I simply didn't count on ever being accepted. My grades in high school were crap. Other than sports, I couldn't point to any particularly impressive activities. I would have loved to be able to say that I'd been a conscientious student, volunteering in nursing homes and dedicating time to fundraisers, but that just wasn't me.

I was Knox.

Knox, the go-getter. Knox, the guy who always knew where the baddest parties were going on. Knox, the guy who knew where to score the best grass and the guy every girl dreamed of getting a goofy note about prom from in her locker. I never went to any dances. Instead, I got blasted and enjoyed our hot tub with considerably older women who were spending their winter vacations in Aspen with their husbands. I was seventeen.

Shit, yeah, I was hopeless. School wasn't for me. I was just happy to have my diploma in my hands, with all its Ds and a couple of Cs. From then on, sports were all that mattered anyway.

That's why I didn't have any real hopes of being accepted to study psychology. The application was a joke. A "give it a go, it won't work out anyway." Had I known I'd be accepted for the upcoming semester, maybe I would've left it alone.

But now I'm sitting here with a secure spot at school in my pocket and no idea what to do.

If it were up to me, I'd change everything. No full-time snowboarding, no annoying groupies, and, most of all, no pointless Instagram. No people with cameras out in front of my house at the crack of dawn just to get a few snaps of me in my boxers and with half-open eyes when I unknowingly open the door.

I'd live a totally normal life. I'd study and give my psychology major all my attention. I'd keep on snowboarding, but without any pressure. Just for fun.

I'd be Knox. Not Knox the snowboard star. Just Knox.

But that would also mean disappointing my father. And not only disappointing. I'd break his heart. Take away his dream, the one that's not mine.

The younger me probably wouldn't have cared one way or the other. But things have changed. In the meanwhile, life happened. And it has been goddamn shitty.

I can't let my dad down. Not after all that's happened. It would destroy him, in full awareness of my actions. And that's something I just cannot do.

"*Fuck!*" More strongly than intended, I slam my MacBook's screen down. I bury my fingers into my hair, my nails scratching my scalp. My chair falls backward when I suddenly stand up, open the bottom drawer of my dresser, and dig through my sweaters until I find what I'm looking for.

I pull out two syringes. One is labeled *androstenedione*, the other *testosterone*.

Doping products.

They help me to improve my hoped-for performance. The one

my father wants, I mean. They give me the endurance, strength, and, above all, the motivation I'm lacking in my heart.

I've been injecting the testosterone every third day for weeks. The androstenedione just on the days I've got a competition. For the quick effect. Short-term, but potent.

I know it's dumb. Snowboarders have to be in the best of health. We've got to have our bodies *completely* under control. Especially when you're a half-pipe snowboarder. But somehow or other, I convinced myself that I needed this stuff. And I can't get these *dumbass* thoughts out of my head anymore.

With a jerk, I pull my shirt over my head, press the remaining air out of the first syringe, and watch a few drops of the transparent liquid drizzle out of the needle. Then I put it on my shoulder, where I know there is nothing but pure muscle below, and shoot. The same thing with the second one.

Only then do I pick my sports bag up off the floor, toss it onto my bed, and begin to pack my things.

Fuck Jason Hawk and his followers. He's not going to win this ride.

6
Ice Is My Heaven

PAISLEY

I HEAR THE SOUND OF BLADES ON ICE ECHOING THROUGH my heart again. Other than that, it's quiet here in the iSkate training center. The smell of disinfectant and the rink enchants me. I've been in a lot of rinks, and they all have the same smell. That smell, it always sets me off on a form of time travel, with all the feelings and experiences I've had out on the ice.

The double-leaf door shuts behind me. Suddenly, I am lost in a vast hall, and to my right and left doors leading who knows where. The sound of my boots echoes off the high walls lined with photos of skaters performing jumps or beaming from the winner's podium. The display cases are full of ribbons and trophies. Running my finger across the plexiglass, my eyes are trained on the largest one, the one that's in the shape of a golden ice skate. I imagine it's mine.

Is it all that unrealistic? Is my gut feeling that I can do more than people say I can true?

My fingers slide off the glass when the sound of panting, followed by that of skates, drifts over to me. I look down the hall. My legs start to move and follow the shallow sound of the skates moving across the ice.

The lights above the stands haven't been turned on yet, just the bright cones of the spotlights. They refract off the fox-red hair of the ice-skater gliding forward with supple movements as she prepares to complete a double axel.

I bite my lower lip watching her rotating body. *She can't get the right height*, I think. *It's not going to work*. And indeed, she finishes the turn on the ice instead of the air. She hits the railing in frustration before skating in backward on both feet to try a loop jump.

"What phase are we in?"

I blink. A girl my age appears next to me, leans her shoulder against the wall of the stands, and twists the stem of a white lollipop around in her mouth. Her eyes are following the skater out on the ice, as if the latter were giving a one-woman show.

"Umm. What do you mean?"

She nods her chin toward the ice. "Harper is my morning entertainment. She always trains by the same standards."

"And those would be?"

My new conversationalist lifts a finger into the air. At the same time, her hair tumbles over the shoulders of her puffy jacket. Her hair is brown, fading into rosé at the tips. Somehow, she reminds me of the Disney princess Moana. Just hipper.

"First phase: Harper attempts a jump she's convinced she can do although that is *definitively*," she emphasizes the word, "not the case. At present, the axel." She looks at me questioningly. I shake my head. "Already over? Okay, a shame. That's always the best part. Second phase: Harper understands she's made a mess of the axel and attempts to feel better by doing a Lutz. Normally, she can't get the right height." Once again, she peeks over at me. I nod and she claps. "Oh, perfect. Now we come to the Rittberger, which, of course, she also thinks she can do. Look. She jumps and…" She snaps her fingers. "Yeeep. *There it is*. She does it again."

"She lands on *both* legs," I note. Frowning, I watch the girl on the ice, how—judging by her expression—she really does seem to be enjoying herself. "Doesn't she know that that results in a deduction of points?"

With a shrug the Moana-girl pushes off from the wall. "Of course. But it's Harper. In her eyes, everything that she thinks is okay is okay. And if you tell her otherwise, well, you're the devil incarnate." She moves on down the hall and waves at me to follow. She tosses the stick of her lollipop into the trash. "I'm Gwen. You must be Paisley, right? My mom told me about you."

That's Gwen?

Pharell Williams's "Happy" goes through my head. I was afraid she might not like me. Or that we wouldn't be on the same wavelength. But maybe I was just panicky, afraid of not getting the start I wanted. But Gwen is nice. Thank God, she's nice.

"Yeah," I reply and follow her into the room that turns out to be our changing room. Gwen tosses her bag onto one of the benches and hangs her jacket on one of the hooks with such a hectic movement that it falls right back down. She doesn't care. She's already digging her skates out of her bag, and it is immediately clear to me that we couldn't be more different from each other.

Gwen is loud. I am quiet. Gwen stands out. I'm the bush next to the hyacinth.

But I like it that way. Kaya was the same. She kept me on my toes. Not infrequently, I had the thought that, without her, I'd have been nothing but a living beanbag hanging around at home, counting the folds overlapping with one another the deeper I sank down.

At home...

"You here?" Fingers snapping before my face. "Anybody home?"

"Oh, yeah, sorry. What did you say?"

"I asked if you know who your trainer is yet. My trainer is my dad, but generally, the real excitement is in seeing who one gets assigned to." Gwen ties her laces and then pulls the ends of her bootcut pants over her skates.

I try not to show how much her words have set my heart racing.

"No idea. We weren't told beforehand which trainers are free." I pull my practice clothes straight and concentrate on the drone of the ventilation above us. Somewhere a faucet is dripping.

"It can't be Saskia," she explains. "She's been away since last week. But I can't think of anyone else who hasn't been taken." Gwen stands up and steps from one skate to the other. She appears to be thinking, then claps her hands again before reaching for mine and pulling me to my feet. I almost lose my balance, as I was just trying to adjust my leg warmers. "It's so exciting! The last three newbies were either a lot younger than me or so conceited that every day I considered running over their feet. Don't look at me like that; I really mean it. You should have seen them."

I don't need that. In the last ten years, I've had enough experience to know the type of girls one encountered most often in the world of figure skating.

"How long have you been with iSkate?" I ask, pulling away from her and bending down to adjust my leg warmers again.

"One year. Before that I was in Breckenridge, under contract. Commuting was hell. Soon I hope iSkate will be paying *me* instead of me paying them, ha ha ha." Gwen cannot stand still. It strikes me that she has to be moving the entire time. At the moment, she's wiggling her legs, as if she had to go to the bathroom in the worst way. "Come on, let's go on in."

I follow her into the hall and see Harper is no longer alone on the ice: two male skaters are holding hands and making parallel steps before the larger of the two lifts his partner into the air.

"That's Aaron and Levi," Gwen explains, a dreamy smile on her face as she opens the door to the ice. "I love them."

"They're good," I say, my eyes trained on the young men's synchronous movements. "How long have they been skating together?"

Gwen presses a skate into the ice and pulls her velvet scrunchie off her wrist to make a quick bun. "Two years, I think. They're a couple. That's why they trust each other so much. Naturally, that has an effect on their skating. Last year they took home a gold twice." She gives me another brief smile, then sets off.

I do the same and within a millisecond it's as if every gray cloud within me has been driven off by sunshine. Gliding across the ice and feeling the cool air on my skin is incomparable. Skating, feeling that magic and not letting it go, causes a sense of euphoria, of unadulterated joy, to well up within me. I would sink into pure darkness if this sport wasn't in my life.

With every step I gain speed, and at some point the other skaters are nothing but blurry bits of color. I change from the forward outside edge to the backward outside edge without changing my leg—a three-turn—before shifting pressure to the inside, springing up from my left leg, turning around my own axis twice, and landing on the back outside edge of my right foot. A double Salchow. Easy. Nothing special. I did it to get myself warmed up, but when I notice the amused look on Harper's face, I feel like I have to prove myself. I ball my hands into fists before opening them back up and running my palms down my training outfit. With the toe-pick, I push off from the ice, past Gwen, who is jumping into a toe loop. I glide around her in a wide arc, bring myself into position, and jump from my left foot. In the air, I spread my legs and bend my upper body horizontally forward. For three seconds I fly like a bird before landing on my right toe-tip and shifting into a pointed spin.

A whisper rushes throughout my entire body as I stand up straight again. It makes me understand that my body wants to jump. Rotate in the air; experience the feeling of freedom, of weightlessness. I start skating backward before shifting my weight onto my left leg and positioning my arms. With a deep breath, I take the chilly air into me and let it fill my lungs as I cut into the ice behind me with my right skate. My bodyweight shifts to my back foot, and my right leg reacts immediately and bounces up. It knows the jump. I could do it in my sleep. I jerk my arms to my upper body, close my eyes, and spin around my own axis in the air. One time. Two times. And a third before the blades of my skates land back on the ice.

I open my eyes and exhale my held breath.

A *triple* Lutz. It belongs to the toe-pick-assisted jumps, like the toe loop and flip, and that's what differentiates it from the Rittberger, Salchow, and axel—all of which belong to the edge jumps. I can count on one hand how many times I pulled off a perfect triple Lutz in the past. My exhilaration bubbles over, and a surprised laugh escapes my lips.

"That was good," I hear a voice say. Blades scrape across the ice as the skater pair comes to a stop next to me. One of the two—Aaron or Levi—gives me a thumbs up. "You're the newbie, right?"

"Yeah." My arrival at iSkate had already made the rounds, it seems. "Paisley."

"Levi," the darkhaired one responded. He is tall, lanky, and reminds me of Harry Potter. He points at his broad-shouldered partner. "That's Aaron. If we had a sword, we'd knight you for what you just pulled off."

I laugh drily. "That was just a Lutz. I'm sure you can do that, too."

"We can," the smaller of the two replies. Aaron. He brushes his red hair off his forehead. His bangs were hiding the large brown birthmark on his temple. With a malicious grin he nods in Harper's direction. "But she can't. And the look on her face just now made my day." He makes a sweeping gesture as if removing a hat from his head and bowing. "Thank you for that."

Levi leans back against the stands and looks up. He wrinkles his brow. "Who is that?"

Aaron and I follow his glance. A woman is sitting on one of the red folding chairs in the first row. She is wearing a fur coat, the collar of which is covered by the strands of her rust-brown bob. She is looking at us with a concentrated expression, her legs crossed, playing with her scarf. Her lips are a thin line.

"No idea," Aaron mumbles. He scrunches his nose, which causes the freckles on his pale skin to dance. "My goodness. It's not even eight and she's making a face like she just came from the funeral home."

Levi nods. He is about to say something when a pair of blades comes to a stop next to us.

Harper. She shifts her weight to her left leg and crosses her arms across her chest. "What's Polina Danilov doing here?"

"Polina Danilov?" Aaron looks askance.

Harper emits an annoyed groan. She rolls her eyes and is about to say something, but I beat her to it.

"In 1988, she was the Olympic winner in ice dance. 1992 single skating and again in 2006. You didn't hear a whole lot about her after that."

Harper shoots me a glance. She looks over me disdainfully. "You're the newbie," she says curtly, then, without awaiting an answer, adds, "Your leg warmers have holes. You should take care of that." She whirls around and rushes off in the opposite direction.

With a tight chest, I watch her go. Her movements are more elegant than mine. Softer.

Levi sighs. "Don't even try to understand Harper. That's just how she is."

"Umm, folks." Aaron points his chin in Polina's direction. "Cruella de Vil has stood up."

"She's moving over the railing," I say.

"And now…she's waving?" Levi squints. "Is that supposed to be a wave?"

"That or she's got a cramp in her hand," I mumble.

"Carpal tunnel syndrome," Aaron agrees. "Terrible thing."

Levi furrows his brow. "Paisley. I think she meant you."

I had the same idea. I just didn't want to say it out loud.

Aaron gives my back a quick two pats. "Go see her. Before she gets mad and takes off to steal some sweet Dalmatian puppies."

I'd laugh if my pulse wasn't 180. Polina Danilov is waving me over.

The Polina Danilov.

I slowly push off from the side and glide over the ice toward her. Gwen swishes past me and wiggles her eyebrows. By the time I'm in front of Polina, I have no idea what I should say. At that moment, even the way my arms hang off me seems weird to me. I decide to put my hands behind my back and wait.

This woman has won Olympic titles! Multiple times! And now she's here, not even three feet away from me, staring right into my eyes. Me! Paisley Harris, the trailer-park roach from Minneapolis. I feel like I could fly.

"Your technique is no good."

Bang! Right back down to earth. My smile dies. "Umm... What?"

"One says 'Excuse me?' So, one more time: your technique is no good. Close your mouth, girl. I'm not a zoo animal."

Oh my God. I cannot believe it. This just cannot be *the* Polina I had posters of as a kid in my room back home.

"I just completed a triple Lutz," I counter. "You can't pull that off without technique."

"I did not say that you had no technique, rather, that it is no good. Listen to me when I tell you something."

I blink. Multiple times in a row.

"Communication and openness are two important prerequisites between trainer and student," she continues. "If you want me to get you to the Olympics, you are going to have to trust me."

Trainer and student? Hold on a second...

"*You're* my trainer?"

"On the condition that you trust my abilities. When I tell you that you are unable to do something just yet, I don't want to hear you respond that that's what you're doing already. I want you to see that and for us to work on your weaknesses so hard until there aren't any left. That's the only way it's going to work, you hear? I demand discipline and ambition. In return, I will belong to you unconditionally and will bring you all the way to the top."

Polina scrutinizes me for a moment before continuing. "You've got fire, girl. What a lot of figure skaters lack is in your blood. You can learn technique, not passion." Her eyes get caught on the swelling on my face. It's like she can see right through Aria's makeup. "It won't be easy. A lot of sweat, a lot of tears. Which is why I want you to answer a single question, right here, right now."

I nod.

"Are you strong enough for this?"

My hands unfold as my fingers seek out a handhold on the side of the rink. *Am* I strong enough? There were times in my life when I could no longer remember what it felt like to be happy. I was broken. Maybe I still am. The truth is, I don't know how much power the past still has over me. Every day it feels like it will grab hold of me again and drown me in its swamp of awful memories. And I know, deep inside, there, where nothing is good anymore, I'm still fighting with that swamp.

But that's the point, isn't it? I'm fighting. Despite its strength I've never given up. And in order to drive it off, I have to create new memories. Better memories. The kind that will warm my heart and allow me to feel happiness. Aspen gives me the feeling that I can find it here. The ice is all I need. It's keeping me alive.

"Yes," I answer at long last and look right into Polina's eyes. "I am strong enough."

7
Breathing in Snowflakes

PAISLEY

DEAR GOD, MY LEGS! WHAT IS THIS? I'M NOTHING BUT pudding. A pudding in the making. Stirred to a nice creamy consistency.

With a groan I toss myself onto my bed, spread out my arms and legs, and decide never to move again. This here will be the rest of my life. Just the bed and me. Forever in intimate togetherness.

Do you, Paisley Harris, take Aria's bed to be your lawfully wedded partner for life? To love and to cherish, in sickness and in health?

I do. God, yes. I do.

My eyelids grow heavy. The dreamcatcher above me begins to lose shape. I feel my blood pulsing through my veins. It's like the mattress is a magnetic field, pulling me to itself.

The training center in Minneapolis was a joke compared to what I had to do today. I was on the ice until noon, and it felt like Polina had something to say about every single one of my moves ("Pull in your leg! It's flapping about like an old rubber hose!"). I did manage to spend my lunch with Gwen, Levi, and Aaron—they are so incredibly nice to me and took me into their circle right away—but I'd hardly gotten my avocado sandwich down when I had to get back to the fitness program. And at its finest.

Now, it's almost six and I can't keep my eyes open anymore. *Tired... So tired... Just a little bit...*

David Bowie's "Starman" is ringing in my ears.

"Mmm." I roll onto my stomach and pull the pillow over my head. "Not now."

But my phone won't give up—it drones on continually. Without opening my eyes, I reach out and run my hand over the nightstand before finding it. I turn my head to the side and sluggishly attempt to make out the name on the display.

It's Gwen. We exchanged numbers during lunch. I press the green icon and put the phone to my ear. "Yeah?"

"Oh. You join the mafia or something?"

"What?"

"Your voice. You sound like Don Corleone."

"Don Corleone?" I pull at a strand of hair that's somehow made its way into my mouth.

"*The Godfather*. Don't tell me you've never seen it."

"Oh, right. Sure." With great effort I heave my leaden torso up to lean back against the headboard. "I am totally fucked."

Gwen chuckles. "Yeah, iSkate is heavy. But you'll get used to it. What are your plans for tonight?"

"Plans?"

"Yeah. Oh, no no no... Shit." In the background I hear something clatter to the floor. Gwen curses. "Mom and her stupid Yankee Candles! Why are they in glasses on top of it all? They're everywhere. A new cloud of scent greets my every step."

"Well, they're nice."

"I guess. Anyway, we were talking about plans. What do you intend to do?"

"Nothing," I reply, without being able to hide the disbelief in my voice. "I feel like I went through bootcamp with Rocky Balboa today. How can you still walk?"

"Like I said, you'll get used to it. I'll pick you up. Be downstairs in ten, yeah?"

"What? Gwen, really, I..."

"See you soon!"

I want to protest, but she's already hung up. For a moment I sit there motionless, staring at my phone. I consider simply sending her a message telling her not to come, but somehow, I just don't manage. We just got to know each other, and I don't want to screw things up.

Exhausted, I crawl to the edge of the bed and shake my limbs. What the hell. If I've already made it this far today, I'll manage this, too.

I don't make the effort to put on makeup again. Instead, I fish my dirty training clothes out of my bag and toss them into the laundry basket that Ruth put in my room. Pulling out my wallet, my fingers graze the folded iSkate contract. My heart skips a beat, just like before when Polina put it in front of me and my eyes got caught on the astronomical sums. That's right. Sums. Plural. Three, to be exact. Membership fees to iSkate, Polina's training fees, and the remaining costs for a choreographer. Before I've proven myself and won championships, I'm on a probationary period and have to pay for everything myself. That's the disadvantage. At some point, they'll be the ones to pay, but I've got a long way to go before that happens.

While signing I thought that, with every stroke of the pen, I was signing my own doom. I really need a job if I don't want to have to sneak out of town, bankrupt, in the dead of night.

"Paisley," Ruth says over the clacking of her knitting needles. She is one of those women whose dimples turn red when they smile. It automatically gives her that tender expression that I otherwise only know from little Christmas elves. "You weren't at dinner. Everything okay?"

"Yeah, absolutely. Sorry, but training..." Instead of finishing, I put on a suggestive expression.

Ruth nods. "Got it. Well, there's still a bit of apple cake on the sideboard. In case you're hungry…"

"We'll get something at the fair," Gwen interrupts, standing up from the sofa and stretching. "Mom's blueberry cheesecake is to die for."

"Fair?" I ask as Gwen puts her fingers around my wrist and tugs.

"Yeah. Today is the half-pipe show, a little foretaste of the X Games. The town fair today is a tradition."

I pull my cap farther down over my ears as we step outside the B&B. "You didn't tell me that."

Gwen shrugs. "Forgot."

As if. She hid it from me, knowing that in my current state I never would have had the strength for something like that. My new friend is pretty clever.

We take Gwen's military-green Jeep to the Aspen Highlands where a considerable crowd is waiting.

"Wow," I say as I get out of the car, closing the door behind me, my eyes directed toward the many stands and the half-pipe behind them. "Were these folks hiding all day long? Where did they come from all of a sudden?"

Gwen laughs. Her boots crunch in the snow as she makes her way around the car to me. "Those are tourists. They want to see the show."

She grabs my arm, which triggers a feeling of well-being in me, and with her other hand points to the different little huts and stands. "Souvenirs and all that. Ridiculously overpriced. Every year I ask myself what kind of person pays twenty dollars for a magnet of a green-haired troll on a snowboard. Totally whack. Oh, back there's where Malila knits her beloved bracelets. She lives near the Colorado River and only comes here for the fairs."

I nod in the direction of a little red hut, behind which a fire is burning underneath a cauldron. "What's that?"

"Mulled wine with rum." Gwen casts me a conspiratorial glance. "It's strong. Wanna drink a mug? I'll invite you."

Thinking it over, I gnaw on my lip. "I don't know."

"You've got to!" Donning the look of a terrier, Gwen tugs my arm. "It's practically your baptism. Every one of Aspen's inhabitants has to be familiar with Dan's punch!"

I've never had much of a taste for alcohol, which has on the one hand to do with my permanently plastered mom and, on the other, training. But I imagine one mug of punch with Gwen will be okay. We're not getting smashed, just toasting to this new phase of my life.

"Well, all right," I say. "A little something to warm us up can't do any harm."

Gwen claps her gloved hands, and we stomp over to the little hut. It's interesting to see the man in the thick winter sweater—Gwen referred to him as Dan—ladle some of the red-wine-and-rum mixture into cute Christmas mugs, lay two slices of orange on top, and then place a sugar cube in a spoon on top before covering them both with rum and setting them on fire. "Don't burn yourselves," he says, grins, and places the mugs in front of us.

"Exotic," I say, my eyes fixed on the dancing flames burning amicably atop both of our mugs.

Gwen runs a finger down the handle. "You're here without your parents, right?"

I acknowledge her question with a curt nod, without looking at her.

Clearly she understands that I don't care to talk about my past, because she changes the topic immediately. "Do you already know what's next? Do you have a job?"

"No." The flame above my mug has gone out, and the sugar dissolved. "Yesterday out on the slopes I applied for a position as an endurance trainer." I glare into my punch. "I could have saved myself the trouble."

Gwen sips from her mug, her eyes looking at me over the rim. "What do you mean?"

I shrug. "Dunno. Because that snowboarder Knox is an ass?"

Her lips open in surprise before she asks, "You met Knox?"

"Yeah." I carefully take a sip and have to keep myself from spitting it right back out. That stuff is burning my throat out. God is that terrible. "You know him?"

"You're asking me if I know Knox?" She gives a bitter laugh but doesn't seem to want to add anything. She points to my mug. "Drink. The second sip's better."

And indeed, she's right. The more I drink, the better the horrible stuff tastes.

"You should see about a job with the Winterbottoms," she says after a little while. "They're looking for a new chalet girl and they pay well. Maybe that'd be something for you."

"A chalet girl?"

"Yeah. The Winterbottoms live in a ski resort close by. In one half of the place are the guests, in the other themselves. You'd take care of the tourists, clean up around the place, that kind of thing."

"I can do that," I reply with the beginnings of giddiness welling up. "Where do they live exactly?"

Gwen takes another gulp from her mug. "I can bring you over there tomorrow after training, if you want."

"I'd be eternally grateful, really."

She grins and points at a french-fry stand next to us. "What you should *really* be grateful for are the thousand-and-one ways you can eat a potato." She starts counting on her fingers. "Mashed, baked, fried, roasted…"

I laugh out loud.

Once we've finished our mugs, we have Malila knot two color-coordinated bracelets around our wrists, and we meander over to the slope to see the next show. My head is smoking from the punch.

It takes a little while for us to make our way past all the people standing next to one another, eying the slope. A snowboarder jolts forward and does a bunch of tricks that make me gasp, as with every jump I'm afraid he's going to crack his head open.

Gwen casts me an amused glance. "Don't worry, nothing's going to happen to him."

"How do you know?"

She nods. "Because Knox doesn't fall. He's a real pro."

"That's Knox?" I ask in surprise, staring wide-eyed at his quick silhouette.

"Yep."

The crowd around us cheers and shouts when he comes to a stop in the middle of the slope before sliding down toward us so that we can see how his speeding board whirls the snow into the air.

"He's good, right?"

Gwen nods. "One of the best. Aspen loves him. But he wasn't always the snowboarder type. In high school, he was the star hockey player. We all thought that, after school, he'd take up his scholarship in Canada."

"Oh." In my head the images from this morning show back up. Knox at the frozen lake, how he was crying without really being able to. His pained expression has burned itself into my mind. "What happened?"

She bites her lower lip. Gwen's brown eyes are watching Knox who is now almost next to us. The butter-yellow reflection of the spotlights lights up her pupils. "No one really knows. After his mom died, it was like he was someone else. The unofficial hypothesis in Aspen is that he just wasn't able to leave his dad alone. And that he wanted to take away some of his pain by switching sports." Her eyes dart briefly to mine. "Back then, his father was a snowboarder, you see. Knox probably wanted to give him something he could focus on. But," Gwen shrugs, "none of us really knows."

I bury my hands into my jacket pockets and look toward him. His board stops before the barrier, and the crowd around us breaks into loud applause. Girls are screeching his name.

Knox slides his protective eyewear over his helmet and gives his audience a wide smile. Then he bends over to undo the bindings from his feet. When he is back upright, his eyes meet mine. Inside I brace myself for the condescending look he shot me yesterday, but it doesn't come.

At the next blink of an eye, he's already turned his back on me.

8
Would Like to Meet You When the Lights Go Off

PAISLEY

ARIA'S BED IS CRYING OUT FOR ME. I CAN HEAR IT ALL THE way out here on Aspen's streets. And my legs are calling back. The way they need each other is almost like a back-and-forth. But when Gwen dropped me off in front of the B&B, I suddenly felt the uncontrollable urge to explore the little town.

A bell begins to toll. It's not a particularly tall bell tower, which is why it fits the center of town like a charm. There are a few ornate cast-iron benches around, painted white. Like the tree trunks and streetlamps, they, too, are wrapped with string lights.

I stuff my hands into my pockets, look up to the top of the bell tower, and slowly take a spin in order to let Aspen's breathtaking scenery work its magic on me. It's just a small town; nevertheless, it's the most beautiful place I've ever been. There's magic in the air.

A lengthy snort interrupts my astonished state. It comes from the other side of the street, not far from Kate's Diner. And when I discover the source of the sound, despite the bitter cold, a warm feeling spreads through my heart.

A brown-spotted Irish Cob with a blond mane is looking over at me. The horse is wearing a brown leather halter and a harness attached to a white carriage. It has two upholstered seats beneath its canopy and the wheels are huge; the ones in back are bigger than the front. It must be historical. I have a slight feeling of having been transported back to the nineteenth century.

I tug on my cap and cross the street. Reaching the horse, I carefully stretch out my hand and allow it to be sniffed. "Well? What's your name then?" I delicately stroke the bridge of its nose down to its soft nostrils. It neighs again before opening its lips and nibbling at my gloves. "That doesn't taste any good. In a second you'll have a mouthful of cotton."

"Oh no!" I suddenly hear someone calling out behind me. "Step back, quick!"

I turn around and as I see the stocky older man hurrying over to me, his bushy eyebrows covering half of his forehead, it becomes clear that he's referring to me. He's wearing a vest over his checkered shirt. When he comes to a stop in front of me, he gasps for breath. His lungs are whistling. "Get away from Sally," he snorts, reaches out, and pushes me two steps back. "She's on a low-carb diet."

"Low-carb?"

The man nods. "I was a little too kind with her food. Now Sally weighs a few pounds too many, and I've got to put her on a diet. But since having reduced her food, she wants to eat anything that doesn't look like a carrot."

I stare at the man. "You mean, Sally wants to eat *me*?"

He nods again. His expression is completely serious. "That's exactly right."

I don't know what I should say. My eyes move from him to the horse—which is just standing there calmly, watching us—and back again. The guy probably doesn't have all his marbles anymore. Or, well, none at all.

"Well, I mean… I'm still here, right? If I was as interesting to your horse as you believe, she would've pounced on me a long time ago."

My odd companion pulls a thoughtful face and strokes his stubble while observing his horse and me intensively. Eventually he nods, as if having come to a decision. "It's got to do with you. You're too skinny. There's not enough there for Sally."

Got it. They're all gone.

"If that's the case, then I can consider myself lucky," I say, reaching my hand back out and letting Sally start nibbling on my glove again.

The man looks at me suspiciously. "Tourists don't come downtown that much. Normally they stick to the slopes and their resorts. Or in the boutiques."

I don't answer right away. My attention has shifted to a group of people walking into Kate's Diner just a few feet away. It primarily consists of loud women, laughing, whose faces mean nothing to me. But I recognize the guys: Wyatt and Knox.

I quickly turn away and concentrate on the old man. "I'm not a tourist."

He appears to consider that for a second. His wild dark brows contract and form one single dark line. But then a knowing look flits across his face and the McDonald's brow separates again. "You must be Paisley. The new resident."

I blink. "How do you know that?"

My question seems to anger him. He puffs up his chest, stretching his tight vest. "I am William Gifford! I know everything that takes place in Aspen!"

"Oh, umm… I didn't know."

"I run the town's social media account," he explains.

"Aspen's got a social media account?" I ask, surprised.

"Of course! But it's got a secret name, so the tourists don't follow us. It's meant for locals only, so that everyone stays up to date. News, breaking news, upcoming fairs and to-do lists…primarily, organizational things. Every two weeks we discuss the most important things in our townhall meeting. Well, just between you and me…the name is @Apsen. I switched the *p* and the *s*, you see." He grins as if incredibly proud of himself. "Shall we go inside? Otherwise I'm afraid I'll get hypothermia."

"Umm." I look around. "Go inside?"

William nods and waves me to come along. "Into my shop. I run the Old-Timer. A store with a vintage movie theater in the back. Naturally, we show popular movies, too, but Wednesdays are retro nights. That's when we only show old movies." We reach the narrow door that I'd never noticed before. "We've got old-school records, too, if music from the old days is your thing."

"Totally," I say as my eyes wander over the window next to the door. Red velvet curtains hanging, and the windowsill is decorated with a few vintage objects. Next to the old tube TV there's a record player on a frog-green velvet cushion of a wooden chair. The upper window frames are decorated with a series of dangling metal cups, some of which have been painted white and adorned with flowers. "You must have all kinds of things to do."

William opens the door. "Find what makes you happy and lose yourself within it. That's my motto. And for me, this town is what makes me happy."

I walk behind him into the shop/movie theater and my eyes grow wide.

Like Ruth's B&B before it, William's store seems to consist of wood and wood only. At first glance, everything seems rustic and thrown together, yet cozy. Not far from the entrance, there's a warm fire going in a tiled fireplace. Two floor lamps with old-fashioned shades flank two sofas. Behind a velvet curtain that's pulled back, I can see the screen where there's a film going that I am unfamiliar with. In front of it a bunch of chairs have been thrown together and there are three sofas; on one of them is sitting a couple.

The place grows even more appealing when I notice the many shelves, buckling under the weight of all the books and records.

Whatever remaining space there is on the wood-paneled walls is taken up by pictures. A lot of them are of various flowery meadows, a few of them with happy-looking women in blousy clothes. Every centimeter of the floor has been covered by oriental rugs of all colors and designs.

"Stop." William stretches his hand out toward me as I move to take another step. He points to my boots, the bottoms of which are covered in clumps of gray snow. "You'll take those off in here."

Indeed, he is already slipping out of his own and places them next to a pair of UGG boots and warm fur-lined winter boots that have to belong to the couple on the couch. I don't really want to pull off my own boots as there are two big holes in my socks—one of them right on my big toe. Nevertheless, I follow William's instructions, slip out of my boots, and then continue my tour. There is an incredible amount of vintage things to discover, the whole place is stuffed to the ceiling. But somehow, it doesn't feel cluttered. On the contrary. It's as if every piece of furniture, every little piece of decoration, was in the right place.

"I love it here," I gasp. My steps take me to a shelf that is filled with records. I look at one after the other, surprised that I recognize a few of the titles. I've always liked the music and movies of the older generations. As soon as I pull a record off the shelf, I hear a voice next to me.

"Simon and Garfunkel. Good choice."

I don't need to turn around to know that it's Knox. Nevertheless, I tilt my head and give him a quick smile. My anger with his behavior on the slope has disappeared. After what happened this morning by the lake, it's as if I know him better. Even though I have no idea who he really is.

"You're a seventies fan?" As discreetly as possible with my left foot I pull the tip of my right sock over the end of my toe in order to hide the big hole.

"I'm a fan of good music. Whatever decade." He leans against the shelf and crosses his arms. He's opened his jacket, underneath it I recognize the iconic Abercrombie & Fitch moose on his winter sweater. "What are you doing here?"

I slide the record back onto the shelf. "Shouldn't I be asking you?" I nod toward the door. "You were just in the diner with your friends."

Knox laughs. "You're stalking me!"

"Not a chance," I reply. "Outside there was a horse that wanted to eat me."

"Oh!" Knox's expression becomes sympathetic. "Is Sally back on a low-carb diet?"

"Yeah. But there's no meat on these bones. That's why I survived."

"What luck." The corner of his mouth twitches. "Normally she's a real beast. Tyrannosaurus rex. Swallows you in one go."

"She really did look pretty scary."

He laughs. "I'm here to save you from William."

I look toward the old man who is standing behind a varnished counter with slender wooden legs, inspecting the popcorn machine. He taps the glass with a finger, before closing an eye and squinting inside, then tapping the glass once more.

"A bit strange, isn't he?"

Knox leans forward. "A bit. In Aspen everyone is smart enough not to disagree with him. He's taken care of the town for what feels like an eternity. He may be a bit kooky, but he simply belongs here." Knox grins as he casts a glance at William, who is now inspecting a piece of popcorn between his index finger and thumb. "I can't imagine Aspen without him."

At that moment, William looks up. His eyes alight on Knox's jacket over the chair. "Hey!" he calls out. William puts the popcorn down on the counter and puts his hands on his hips. "There's no hanging out here, Knox! Whoever isn't shopping has to pay for a ticket to the next film."

Knox heaves a long sigh but looks amused. Eventually he looks at me. "Do we want to stay?"

We?

"Umm." I feel overwhelmed. Not because I don't know whether I want to stay here to watch a movie or not. I'd already made up my mind about that after taking one step in the place. No, what's overwhelmed me is the thought of sitting in a movie theater next to Knox, the star snowboarder. For one and a half hours at least.

"When you say '*umm*' you mean '*yeah*.'" Knox seems strangely content as he strides over to William and buys us two tickets. I follow behind him because I don't want to just stand around looking lost.

"One large popcorn with butter," Knox is saying as I reach his side. Then he looks at me questioningly. "Would you like a cheese sandwich as well?"

"A cheese sandwich?" Not that I'm picky, but…that's not exactly the snack I associate with movie theaters.

William opens a small blue retro fridge behind him and points inside. All the shelves have been carefully filled with sandwiches, one after the other. "I've got the best in town."

My befuddled glance wanders to Knox, who nods in agreement. "Sometimes I come over after training, just to have a few."

I decide not to ask any further. "No, thank you. I don't like cheese."

Knox's eyes almost spring out of his head. "You *don't like cheese?* Who on earth doesn't like cheese?"

With a timid smile I raise my hand. "Me."

"I could take the cheese off for you," William suggests.

And then I'd have…a bread sandwich?

"No, no, it's fine," I say, but give William a thankful smile. "The popcorn's enough."

We make our way to the theater and sit down on one of the sofas. He drapes an array of sandwiches across his lap. I place the bucket of popcorn as a protective wall between us and grip my iced tea.

"Won't your friends wonder where you are?"

"Nah." He devours half a sandwich in just one bite. "It's not abnormal for me to just disappear all of a sudden."

"Ah ha." I decide not to pursue it any further. I've learned enough about Knox to know that he is clearly...not all that easy. "Oh, cool! I love this movie!" I whisper the very next moment, in ecstasy.

Knox smirks, recognizing the credits. "*Signs*? You can't be serious. Isn't this the one where at some point the actors make aluminum helmets to protect themselves from those things out in the corn?"

"They're aliens, not things! And with the aluminum they can protect themselves from their rays."

"I would bet this whole beautiful plate of cheese sandwiches that you ran around with one of those hats after seeing this movie."

I laugh so hard that I almost swallow my popcorn. "I was eight and really superstitious!"

"I knew it."

After that, we're quiet for a long time as we watch the film. Around halfway through, he's finished all his sandwiches, which is why he lets his hand disappear in the popcorn and shovels one handful after the other into his mouth. Back in Minneapolis, I'd seen enough tearjerkers with Kaya to know that, from now on, I shouldn't reach for any popcorn if I don't want our hands to touch accidentally.

Knox's phone vibrates in his pocket, He directs another handful of popcorn to his mouth, wipes his buttery fingers on a napkin, and looks at the display. I see Wyatt's name. Knox doesn't answer and shoots me an apologetic glance. "So, nameless creature with a love for aluminum helmets. I've got to go. Maybe at some point you can tell me how it ends." He grins. "I want to know whether they get devoured despite their helmets."

"Aliens don't devour," I reply.

"True. Just Sally. Right, see you later."

"See you. Thanks for the ticket. And the popcorn. And, umm, the iced tea."

"If you keep on thanking me like that, I'm going to get another halo." Knox stands. "And I really don't deserve that. Believe me."

Oh, Knox. You have no idea *how much* I believe you.

9

Shape Their Minds, Gild Their Hearts

Knox

"Thanks, Dan. Just write it down, will you?"

"As always, Knox," the beefy owner of the ski hut replies. I've known him forever. We went to high school together. He was one year ahead of me, a pimply teenager with braces and arms like french fries. After graduating, he went abroad for a year, and when he came back no one recognized him anymore. His thin body had turned into a machine, and artworks in dark ink marked his torso. A few years ago, he got the idea of opening his bar slash café slash fast-food joint right on the slope. And stumbled upon a goldmine. Business is booming. The tourists love, above all, his wine punch with rum, but I usually come over during a break to get one of his energy teas. Like now. It's his own recipe, and *holy shit* is it strong. Coffee ain't got nothing on it.

"Knox, everything good with the boys?" Sarah, one of the aides, asks as I order my energy tea. She's sitting in a corner of the hut, sipping her coffee while keeping an eye on the kids. Sarah has been working at the Westons for years and has a knack for defusing tricky situations with a smile.

"So far, so good," I reply, but right then…

"Knox!" A kid with a blond Justin Bieber cut bursts in, winds his way through the tables, and runs across the rustic-style floor to me. It's Gideon. He almost knocked a chair into the fireplace as he carelessly pushed it aside. Sarah gets up from her seat and follows him. "What's going on, Gideon?" she asks, her tone calm and steady.

"Trevor stole my snowboard!" Gideon blurts out, his voice shaky.

It's hard for me not to roll my eyes. *Trevor.* That little toad. I can't leave the group alone for two minutes before he starts screwing up. As always, I wonder why I offered to spend time with the boys from the Westons. And, like always, I come to the conclusion that I enjoy it. The Westons is a home for troubled boys, and working with them gives me the chance to apply what I've learned from my readings in psychology and, hopefully, to have a little effect on them.

God, how much I'd love to accept the offer to join the psychology program.

Sarah glances at me, her expression a mix of concern and curiosity. "Do you want me to stay with the others?"

"Yes, please," I say. "I'll deal with this."

After Sarah heads back to the half-pipe where the rest of the boys are practicing, I bend down in front of Gideon, careful not to spill my energy tea. "Why did he steal it from you, Gideon?" Gideon has trouble looking people directly in the eye. It unnerves him, and that's due to his low self-esteem. "No idea," he says, takes a breath, and throws his arms into the air. "I did the jump you showed us. Then Steve hit me with a snowball and…"

"Gideon," I interrupt. "Look at me when you're talking to me, okay?"

His eyes continue to focus on the floor. He purses his lips.

I place my hands on his shoulders. "You got this. We're on the same wavelength, got it? I'm not better than you. We're of equal value, you and I."

Gideon slowly raises his head. It seems as if it costs him, but he finally looks at me.

"Right on," I say. "So, Steve hit you with a snowball. And then?"

"I got out of my bindings, so I could run after him. And that's when Trevor stole my snowboard!"

Before I can respond to Gideon, Paul, the second aide I brought along today, shows up. "What's going on, boys?" he asks calmly, studying Gideon with a careful gaze. Paul is known for his ability to calm the boys quickly, but this time he looks at me, waiting for an explanation.

"Trevor stole Gideon's board," I say curtly.

"Got it," Paul replies. "Knox, you handle Gideon, I'll deal with Trevor."

"Thanks." I think for a moment. "Did you pull off the jump I showed you all? Before undoing your bindings, I mean?"

When Gideon nods, it all becomes clear: Trevor can't take it when others are better than he is. He's got a good heart, but as soon as he gets the feeling that he's not as good as someone else, he turns aggressive. By punching down, he feels superior and, as a result, better. A vicious circle.

I pat Gideon on the shoulder. "Right, let's go. We'll straighten this out."

Gideon's smile widens. "Like real men?"

"Like real men," I confirm, open the door, and step onto the slope. "Which means talking reasonably with one another."

His expression suggests that he had been thinking of something else. Which makes sense, it's all he knows. The thought stings.

Sarah is already back near the half-pipe, keeping an eye on the other boys. I nod in her direction, and she waves me off, silently letting me know she's got things under control.

The boys are hanging around the half-pipe, which I reserved for them for two hours. Two of them are practicing the jump I'd showed them before I went into the ski hut. Three of the others are having a snowball fight, and Trevor is nowhere to be seen.

I sigh. "Stay with the others, Gideon. I'll go find him."

"Trevor!" I call, throwing a glance at Sarah, who's talking to two of the other boys. She gives me a quick nod, as if to say, *I'll hold the fort, go find him.* It's not the first time that Trevor has taken off. In fact, it's his usual. Nevertheless, it burns me up every single time. The kid's just turned thirteen but manages to piss me off more than my biggest competitor, Jason Hawk.

I stomp past the half-pipe and look around. The slope is full of tourists in colorful outfits rushing past on skis or snowboards. From all directions come excited and happy shouts. With Trevor, every time it's like looking for a needle in a haystack.

"Knox," I suddenly hear a voice behind me. Turning around I see the new girl who doesn't want to tell me her name.

She still hasn't put on any ski pants. Like the last time I saw her on the slope, the snow has wet her jeans all the way up above her ankles. Her eyes generate a warm feeling in me that chases off any thoughts of Trevor. For a few seconds at least. She smiles at me, and I have to think of the flowery scent she gave off last night at the movies, how I drank it in the whole time, afraid it might disappear at any moment. The effect she has on me puts me in panic mode.

Pull yourself together, Knox. She's a figure skater and therefore off-limits.

"Hey," I say crisply, turn, and continue my search for the little five-foot-two menace with dark hair.

I hear her take a few steps through the snow toward me. "What are you doing here?" she asks. "Aren't you training?"

"I've got Thursday afternoons free."

Damn, where is the little shit?

"Oh, I see." Her profile creeps into my field of vision. She scratches her cheek. Red stripes on white skin. "We got off early cause our trainers have some kind of meeting or other. I'm meeting Gwen, Levi, and Aaron in the ski hut." She pauses. "Come with me."

I almost laugh out loud. Aside from the fact that Gwen, Levi, and Aaron would definitely not want to share a table with me and engage in small talk, the idea that I would spend my time with a group of iSkate kids is just absurd. The movie last night alone was a mistake. I shouldn't have followed her after seeing her with William. That much went against my principles.

"I've got things to do," I answer gruffly.

"Oh. Okay." I had expected her to be a bit disappointed. But the tone in her voice sounds anything but. She even seems a little relieved. "Are you looking for someone?"

"Yeah. A kid who at this moment is probably setting someone's pants on fire or stealing a bottle of booze from the ski hut."

She laughs. "That's a joke, right?"

"Sadly, no."

"Umm. Okay. Should I maybe…"

"Trevor!" I leave the girl standing and take off after the boy who with his Rumpelstiltskin-like laugh is running away from me. Hard to believe. Does the little jerk think he's going to be quicker than a six-one-and-a-half snowboarder?

I catch hold of the little spawn of Satan by the collar of his jacket. At first, he tries to escape but when he realizes he doesn't stand a chance, he settles down. He turns to face me while hiding a hand behind his back. A second later I see a cigarette hit the ground, which he tries to bury beneath the snow with his boot.

I grind my teeth and let out an annoyed growl. "You really think I'm an idiot, don't you?"

Trevor shrugs and grins. "A bit."

Man oh man, this kid. Growing within me is the burning desire to already have started studying and to know how to deal with him. For the moment, though, my amateur-level knowledge will have to suffice. Trevor wants attention, nothing more. He wants to be seen. Listened to. It's almost a cry for help. *Hello, here I am. Come and give me the feeling that I'm not worthless.*

I sigh. "Listen, Trevor." My voice is calm, although I'm actually ready to scream. In order to be eye-to-eye with him, I bend down a little. It's important to make him feel comfortable. "Let a star snowboarder who's been to a looot of parties and seen a few things tell you something: cigarettes aren't cool. In the same way that drugs aren't cool. Or alcohol. *You're* cool when you've got yourself under control. Believe me, I know what I'm talking about."

Trevor frowns. "You get smashed all the time. We don't hear anything else about you."

"And that's precisely why I know what I'm talking about. Believe me when I tell you that it's *not cool.*"

"Then you're not cool either when you do that kind of stuff." His voice sounds accusatory, and I'm proud of him. He's got to learn to say his opinion and say when he doesn't find something right.

"Anything but," I agree. I could tell him that I don't drink to be cool, but because I'm broken. I could tell him that, one day, he'll be just as broken if he keeps it up. And I could tell him that alcohol and drugs just make everything worse. They numb you off but, afterward, the pain always returns, suddenly, violently, and overwhelmingly.

The only thing I do say is, "Your air-to-fakie before was really badass. Respect."

My plan works. A glow appears in Trevor's dark eyes, and I even recognize the start of a smile. "Really?"

"Hello? Would I lie about an air-to-fakie?" I give him a soft punch on the shoulder. "But you should apologize to Gideon. Stealing someone's board is also something that is definitely uncool."

Trevor seems ashamed. He bites his lower lip, drives the tip of his boot into the snow, and shrugs. "Yeah. You're right." Then he runs off. I watch him go back to the others and talk to Gideon for a moment. The two exchange a few words, without looking at each other, and then go back to doing their own thing.

With a smile on my face I straighten up. At those moments, I'm not just proud of my kids, but proud of myself. And that is goddamn rare.

Suddenly I hear a scream. I whirl around and see one of the older kids, Steve, go after his brother.

"Goddamn…" I take off but stop when I see the figure skater step between them. With a power I never would have expected her to have, she tears Steve off his brother. He moves to hit her, but she keeps him at arm's length.

Everything turned out OK, I think, and at first I am really proud of her until all of a sudden…

She yells at Steve. I can't understand everything, but I don't have to. It's enough for her to raise her voice, because Steve is special. You've always got to speak to him real calmly. No idea what he experienced at home, but he is extremely sensitive to loud voices. Above all, when they're directed toward him.

I know she means well. She just wants to help. She probably just went on instinct, having obviously experienced violence herself in the past. But, damn it, I don't have myself under control. From one moment to the next I feel total rage. This figure skater has no right to butt in. These are my kids! She has no idea how they tick!

Steve's reaction comes quick. He falls onto his back, starts flailing his arms and legs, and yells for all its worth. The tourists are casting us curious looks, and then I am back in motion, running over to him.

She's standing there as if in shock, staring down at the boy. When I reach them, she looks at me with large eyes and helplessly raises her arms into the air. "I don't know what's…"

"Out of the way." I'm a bit too rough pushing her aside, but I'm too angry and worked up to care. I sit down in the snow next to Steve and begin to speak slowly and soothingly to him, just like his caregiver told me. After a while, his yells go quiet, and then his limbs fall into the snow. He's still breathing quickly, but we've made it past the worst part. He slowly gets up, buries his hands in the pockets of his ski pants, and shuffles off. I know that he's got to collect himself, so I let him go. Then he comes back. He's not like Trevor. He doesn't want to provoke anyone. He's just a bit…a bit unstable.

Sarah appears almost out of nowhere. She immediately sits down in the snow next to him and starts speaking to him softly. Meanwhile, I stand back up. It reassures me to see her taking control of the situation, even though it's hard not to intervene a bit more.

My heart is still racing. Only after I've sent the kids back to the half-pipe do I turn to the girl. My jaw is tense. "What the hell was that?"

"I only wanted to help," she answers quickly. Her face reflects a sense of guilt.

"That's what you call helping? Yelling at someone you don't know?"

"He kicked the boy!"

"You don't know anything about these kids!" My voice is louder than I intended, but I'm really pissed off! With a single move she ruined what I've been working on for weeks. I'm boiling, although it's not her fault. She didn't know any better. But, to be honest, it's just the right time to have an excuse to be mad at her. A reason not to have to keep thinking about her sweet laugh or her lovely floral scent. The voice that wants to protect her is too quiet. I don't listen to it and let my temper win out. "Just go, okay?"

She looks as if she's seen a ghost. I even think my behavior has frightened her. Good. Maybe she'll stay away from me now, and I'll manage not to think about her anymore.

The figure skater swallows hard, flares her nostrils, and lifts her chin. What she thinks of me at the moment is crystal clear. In her eyes, I am the worst. A part of me wants her to have a better image of me, the image of a guy who buys her buttered popcorn and laughs with her about aluminum helmets. A part of me wants to apologize for the way I acted, but another part of me, a shattered part, tells me that it's better this way. That, in any event, she is off-limits for me if I don't want to plunge into the abyss.

Because with the abyss comes darkness.

10
Oh, What a Plot Twist You Were

Paisley

"Dad's got the music for my free-skate program already." Gwen stretches down to touch her toes.

Gwen's dad is her trainer. She told me that he used to skate himself before starting to work for iSkate. One of the reasons why one of her childhood dreams was to be accepted to the school. On the one hand, it has its advantages, because they know each other and trust each other one hundred percent. On the other, she said, training's the reason they get in each other's hair a lot. "'Castle on a Cloud' from *Les Misérables*."

"Oh, that's going to be a melancholy program," Levi says, standing in the fitness room behind Aaron who's stretching his back. Aaron has done the splits on the floor and is stretching out his palms in front of him.

"Gwen's programs are always melancholy affairs." Aaron's voice sounds muffled, as, thanks to his stretch, his nose is pressed against the ground. His red bangs streak the floor. "Like Natalie Portman in *Black Swan*, but on the ice."

"Bullshit." Gwen tosses Aaron a scathing glance. "I'm not disturbed."

Her reply is acknowledged with a mocking laugh. Not from Aaron or Levi, but Harper, who is pushing her hands into the wall next to us and has lifted her right leg into the air. "That's news to me."

Gwen snorts before giving Harper a fake smile. "Apropos new, Harper. Pay attention to your fake boobs. Otherwise they'll burst the next time you're lying on the ice after trying another Lutz. It'll be all over the news."

"That did it," Levi murmurs.

I look from Gwen to Harper, who is staring at the wall, her nostrils flared.

"I think 'Castle on a Cloud' is nice," I say in the hopes of taking down the temperature in the room a bit. "The melody is so pleasantly soft."

Gwen doesn't respond. Her mood unnerves me. Has something happened? She closes her eyes and leans her forehead to her shins. Suddenly she shakes her head and straightens back up. "Excuse me."

"Gwen." I am already halfway up and ready to go after her when Levi's fingers softly take hold of my wrist and stop me.

"Don't." His eyes are sympathetic. As if he knows what's going on with Gwen.

Confused, I return his glance. Even Aaron turns his head toward him and frowns.

Harper emits a nervous groan. "What a drama queen."

Now she's really getting on my nerves!

"What's your goddamn problem?" I hiss.

A provocative smile appears on Harper's face. Instead of looking at me, she lifts her leg a little bit higher and touches the wall with the sole of her foot. "I don't have any problem, Paisley." She lowers her leg, turns to me, and shakes it out. "I'm just not afraid of making enemies for being honest."

"Paisley!"

I whirl around. Polina is standing in the doorway to the fitness room staring at me with narrow eyes. "Follow me."

I take a deep breath, shoot Harper one last disparaging glance, and follow my trainer down the hall into the ice rink.

"Where are your skates?" she asks, her head tilted halfway over her shoulder.

"Umm. Still in the stands, I think. Why?"

"I want to practice something with you." Polina nods to the second folding chair in the first row where I'd left my skates after training. "Put them back on."

"But training's over," I reply sheepishly, with the uncomfortable feeling that I'm going to miss Gwen. She wanted to take me to the Winterbottoms'. "Can't we do it tomorrow?"

Polina's look is that of a beast of prey. "Your second day and you want to give up already?"

"What? No! Why would I..."

"I told you it wouldn't be easy. Discipline and ambition, remember?"

"Yeah, but..."

"You agreed. And so you either stick by your word or pack your things and go." Her eyes flit across my face. "Anyone can go the easy route. But none of them makes it to the Olympics."

Gritting my teeth, I cast a glance over my shoulder into the hallway with the changing rooms. I *am* disciplined and ambitious. On any other day I'd have no problem training into the night. But today of all days...I need this job. Otherwise I can say goodbye to iSkate quicker than Polina can impale me with her eagle-like eyes.

There's no trace of Gwen. Is she back with the others?

I bite my lip, give a curt nod, and reach for my skates. The last few years have taken their toll; the leather on the sides is faded and thin, the laces frayed.

But I love them.

"Okay," I say once I'm standing in front of Polina out on the ice. "What do you want to practice?"

"A double axel."

My shoulders sink. "But we practiced that all day long. I can't *do* it. It's impossible."

Polina leans her forearms on the edge of the stands and gives me a hard stare. "You can't do it because your technique is wrong."

"I know. But what is supposed to have changed over the last hour? Only the *exceptionally talented* can pull off a double axel, Polina."

She purses her lips. "You need to trust what I say and not argue. I have an idea."

Sighing, I shift my weight to my left leg. "Good. What should I do?"

"Show it to me again."

What I'd really like to do is throw my arms into the air and tell her there's no point. But the reality is that there is even less of a point contradicting Polina Danilov. So I push off and begin skating backward-outward, just like we'd practiced all day long. With my left foot I move forward, shift pressure to the outer edge, and make a big swing of my arms before I jump. I attempt to focus on my right leg to use its momentum and bring it past the other at an angle. As per usual, I manage the first spin, but the next just doesn't want to come. And so instead of landing in a backward movement, which is usual for the axel, I land forward, stumble, and fall onto my knees.

I wheeze and smack the ice with my palm. "It's just not happening!"

"Tell me what you were thinking about."

"What?"

"What were you thinking about when you jumped?"

I lean back onto my bottom, stretch my legs, and think. "No idea. About the jump, I guess. About having enough momentum in my right leg to pull off another spin plus half to pull off the backward."

Polina laughs. She seems strangely content.

"What?"

"I knew it."

I look at her confusedly. "Right. And how is that supposed to get us any further?"

"In that I now know where the problem is." She pushes off the boards without removing her fingers from the strut and tilts her head. "Listen. We're going to try again, but this time just keep on skating until you're ready. Take as long as you need."

"As long as I need for what?" I ask, getting back up. My knees hurt from the fall.

"Until you can feel the intense swirl of emotions in every centimeter of your body."

"Emotions?"

Polina nods. "Figure skating is passion. You don't pull off the best jumps with your head, but with this." She points to her left breast. "Let your heart work for you, not your body. It knows what to do."

"I'm not sure I understand you entirely…"

"There is too much rage in you, Paisley. Turn it into energy. Into passion."

It feels like my eyes are going to pop out of my head. In seconds my temples are pounding, my heartrate shoots up, and my palms grow damp, which has nothing to do with the ice I was skating on just a few minutes before.

"I…" There's a lump in my throat. "That's… How do you know what…" I can't finish the sentence. Instead, I try to swallow the lump back down. Unsuccessfully.

"My heart is a ghost town, girl." Polina smiles, but it doesn't reach her eyes. "Lost souls recognize one another."

"What… What happened to you?" I whisper.

"Everyone's got their reasons, no?" She looks to the side. She looks toward the scoreboard, but I doubt that she really sees it. "But lost souls give you the task of finding your own." She looks back at me. From one second to the next her former expression returned.

"Use your memories. Bring fire to your movements and let the flame guide you. Try it."

My head is spinning as I push off the boards and skate across the ice. My thoughts are racing, I am thinking about everything, about Polina and what she's struggling with, about Kaya, my mom, and *him*. I grow dizzy, then hot, then cold. Screams, loud, far too loud, just in my head and not really there. But if they're not really there, why do they feel so tangible, so near, so *unbearable*? I'm starting to panic, my head just wants everything to grow quiet, quiet at long last, and calm and secure. But that fear is in me, deep down, far too deep, it's coming back up, high and higher, it's whispering and hissing, becoming clearer the higher it gets. I want to drive it away, I want it to unfold and then leave me alone.

That's when I feel it. Feel its clutches scatter in all directions, feel that it's up to me. The air takes hold of me, lets me become part of it as I spin and allow the memories to come before pushing them away again. Two and a half spins.

I land backward-outward.

Polina smiles. And behind that smile I recognize something that warms my heart and that I believed no trainer would ever show me.

Pride.

Suddenly, I understand why Polina pulled me out of the fitness room. I understand why she had insisted we try the jump now and not tomorrow. What was going on inside of me wasn't meant for anyone else's eyes. She knows that. She, too, is living it.

"Come on, Gwen." For the fourth time I dial her number, but her voicemail picks up. Cursing, I disconnect and look around outside of iSkate. No trace. She wasn't in the changing room, either.

Levi and Aaron walk past. I look at them almost desperately. "Have you all seen Gwen? She wanted to take me with her."

"No idea," Levi says and presses the key to his car. Not far from us the lights of a silver Mercedes blink on. "I think she took off. Her Jeep's not here."

"She's not answering her phone."

Aaron shoots me an apologetic look. "We'd take you, but we've only got a two-seater."

"Don't worry." I wave it off. "See you tomorrow."

The two raise their hands in goodbye before getting into their car and driving off. I wonder what to do now. Last night, Ruth gave me Mr. Winterbottom's number. We talked and agreed that I'd come by around six-thirty for an interview. Now it's ten past, and I have no idea how I'm supposed to get to Aspen Highlands that quickly.

A white Range Rover pulls into the parking lot. At first my heart skips a beat thinking it could be Gwen with another car, but then I recognize who's driving.

It's Knox. Wyatt is sitting next to him in the passenger seat, leaning all the way back with his boots on the windowsill. I roll my eyes and pretend to type into my phone to look busy.

What are they doing here?

Behind me a door opens up and Harper strolls past. She is wearing her sports bag like a little designer purse, its strap in her elbow. The Range Rover stops right in front of us, the back door opens, and a girl with long black hair waves Harper over. "Move your cute ass, Davenport. Kate's burgers are waiting for us."

Harper swings herself into the car. Before she closes the door, she leans over to Knox and…kisses him. As he doesn't turn toward her properly, she just catches the corner of his mouth, but it is definitely a kiss.

I slowly put my phone back down. I don't even realize that I am unabashedly staring into the car. Harper reaches out to pull the door shut. Noticing my stare, she narrows her eyes. "Don't gawk."

She slams the door and Knox turns the steering wheel. His eyes meet mine. I almost expect a mocking grin to appear while he makes a comment about me that I cannot hear. But I'm wrong. A second later all I have in front of my eyes is its taillights as it turns the corner.

My chest tightens, and I feel a light pain in my stomach without really knowing why. Okay, apparently Harper and Knox have something going on, but what do I care? Especially after the way he behaved yesterday.

Or?

I catch myself shifting my weight from one leg to the other, thinking about that movie night at the Old-Timer. The Knox I was with there seemed to be a different person than the one I ran into yesterday. He bought me buttered popcorn and even made me laugh. I haven't been doing much of that for a while.

Suddenly, I'm really angry. Angry at Gwen for leaving me hanging, angry at Knox for hurting me. And for getting involved with that dummy by the name of Harper. But maybe I'm angry at myself, too, for caring what he does and with whom. I shouldn't have watched that movie with him.

I look back at my phone and call Mr. Winterbottom.

He picks up after the second ring. "Jack Winterbottom."

"Yes, hello…this is Paisley," I say. "There's a problem. My, umm, ride has disappeared, and I need to take the bus."

"Gotcha. Which bus are you taking?"

"Umm…" I look around. No bus stop far and wide.

On the other end of the phone Mr. Winterbottom gives a friendly laugh. "Where are you right now?"

"At iSkate."

There's a brief pause. "Good, you can catch the Highland Express. Going out of the parking lot, turn left. You'll come to a yellow sign. That's where it stops. Just tell the driver you want to go to the Winterbottoms'."

"Oh, okay. Thanks a lot!"

"See you soon."

I follow his directions and indeed I'm in luck: The Highland

Express shows up just a few minutes later at the yellow sign. During the ride, I have to keep forcing myself to keep my eyes open and not nod off. Knowing my luck, I'd wake up somewhere in the Rockies, staring right into the eyes of a malnourished bear.

"This is where the Winterbottoms live," the gum-chewing driver says. It can only be directed toward me, as there is no one else on the bus. The doors open and I step out into the snow. A couple in snowsuits are making their way down the driveway to the wide front door, and I remember what Gwen told me, that this resort is divided into the area for the guests and the private one of the Winterbottoms'.

And so I've got to go to the other door. My assumption is confirmed by a hefty brass plate upon which *Winterbottom* has been written in elegant letters. I take off my cap, undo my messy training bun, and shake my hair out. I stifle my nervousness, take a deep breath, and ring. I hear steps approaching the door, and as it swings inward, I find myself before a well-built man, who is quite attractive for his age. His light-colored hair is streaked with gray and his toothpasty grin gives Brad Pitt a run for his money.

He stretches out his hand. "Hello, Paisley, I'm Jack. Come on in."

I'm met by a blast of warm air as soon as I step inside. Between the wooden beams I take note of the perfectly matching furniture, which, judging by its extravagant look, no doubt comes from an interior designer. Naturally, there's a fire going.

"Have a seat. Would you like something to drink? I've just made some coffee."

"Coffee would be great," I say while attempting to put on a confident smile.

Jack nods, disappears into the kitchen, and comes back shortly with two steaming cups. He puts them on the coffee table in front of the couch and sits down across from me. "So, Paisley. Tell me about yourself. You're new in Aspen, you were saying?"

"Yeah." I clear my throat and grip my cup. "I'm originally from

Minneapolis. Last summer I applied to iSkate and was accepted." A tentative smile crosses my lips. "Yeah, well, and now here I am."

"Nice, really nice. I'm happy for you. Aspen is a great town."

I nod. "It's got a charm I've never encountered anywhere else."

Jack nods in agreement and takes a sip of his coffee. A phone begins to beep in his pocket. "Excuse me a moment," he says, places his cup on the saucer, and types something before turning back to me. "Do you have any experience as a chalet girl?"

"Not directly," I admit. "But I worked at a hotel for a few years while going to school."

Mr. Winterbottom nods. He looks at his phone again, and I start to feel the beginnings of panic. If he doesn't find me interesting, he certainly won't be giving me any job. "Nice," he mutters, without looking at me. I can see that he's messaging someone.

Right now? This is my interview, and he can't even concentrate on me for five minutes? I lose my courage. Nothing's going to come of this. Ever.

I swallow. I restlessly move about my velvet-covered chair. "I can cook, too. Well, no one's ever complained, in any event. I'm an athlete, so naturally I cook really healthy things, and…"

"Paisley, excuse me, please," Jack interrupts. He lets out an impatient sigh and continues to type into his phone. "I've got to go. When can you start?"

"I… What?"

Finally Jack looks back up from his phone. "Tomorrow? That would be the best. If you need someone to bring your things over, let me know."

"My things?"

His phone rings. Jack rolls his eyes, takes the call, and puts the phone to his ear. "Give me ten minutes, okay? I'm on the road." He hangs back up. It's like I've been hit on the head. I have no idea what's going on. Do I have the job or not?

"Your room should be ready by then. Come on over tomorrow

with your things, and we'll go through the schedule together. Basically, all of my chalet girls receive the same salary. Seven hundred fifty dollars, every week. Is that acceptable?"

"Umm..."

Seven hundred fifty dollars...*a week*?! Where do I sign?

"How much in rent do you want for the room?"

Jack blinks. For a moment he looks confused, before he stands up, laughs, and waves my question away. I don't understand what he means. Does he think I'm joking?

"I've got to go." Yeah, unreal. He took my question to be a joke. "Come on over tomorrow, at your convenience, and..."

The door opens. I turn my head—and for a fraction of a second my heart stops. Really. It simply stops. Whether it'll start back up, I don't really know.

Well, apparently it does, because I'm sitting here. Whereas, to tell the truth, I'd rather sink into the ground and become part of the waxed parquet.

"Ah, Knox." Mr. Winterbottom points from me to Knox and then back. "How good that you're here. This is our new chalet girl, Paisley. Paisley, this is my son. Knox."

This has got to be a bad joke. This could never happen in real life. I'm dreaming. For sure.

The door closes. Knox stares at me.

I stare back.

Then he tilts his head. "Paisley, huh?"

Oh, my Lord. *This* isn't going to go well at all.

11
And Suddenly She Was My Baymax

Knox

"Be so good as to show her everything, would you?" My father doesn't look up from his phone. I'm not surprised. This weekend there's going to be a big celebration here with important sponsors, and he's been involved in last-minute preparations for days. Actually, our former chalet girl Lauren would have been in charge had she not...well...taken off. Because of me.

He types one more message with a frown, then turns back to Paisley. She is sitting straight as a board on our couch, unmoving. "So, Paisley. It's good to have you with us." He goes to the front door. "If you need anything, just ask. Knox will help you out."

Ah. Will I?

Paisley seems to be thinking the same thing, because her fine features don't manage to hide the look of disbelief in her eyes. In fact, rather than getting started with us, she seems like she'd rather just quit on the spot. No idea why that amuses me.

The front door closes, and an oppressive silence falls over us, interrupted only by the crackling wood of the fire. Paisley's bright cheeks turn pink. Her fingers are gripping her sports bag that's next to her on the couch, and she's staring at her coffee cup.

I go to the fridge and get myself a soda. "You sure you want the job?"

"You sure you want to keep on being an ass?" she counters cuttingly. Got it, she's pissed. Which, after my behavior on the slope, doesn't surprise me. Once I've closed the refrigerator door and turned back to face her, she's moved her eyes to mine. She looks combative, which doesn't really fit with her delicate features. "Well, in any event, I'm going to be living here and can sneak over to your room at any time to plant a kiss on your face."

I grin. "Freak." The soda can hisses when I open it. I take a few noisy sips, then point to her with the can. "Right, Paisley. Let's establish the ground rules."

She rolls her eyes. "Now I'm curious."

"First: My room is off-limits. I don't want to see you there. My private space is your boundary. Got it?"

Paisley shrugs. "Sure."

I hop up onto the kitchen island and take another sip. "Two: To the best of our abilities, we're going to stay out of each other's way."

"We're going to be living in the same house," she responds. "How is that going to work out?"

"That's not what I mean." It's starting to get too hot for me next to the fire in my hoodie, so I pull it over my head and put it down next to me on the granite. Paisley's eyes stop for a second on my arms before she pretends to stare at my shirt. Once again, I've got to keep myself from grinning. "Of course, we'll see each other. It's unavoidable. But you'll do your stuff, and I'll do mine. Okay?"

"I didn't have anything else in mind," she says. For a moment she grits her teeth before a sudden snort escapes. "Why do you think I even want this job? Certainly not to stick to your butt and adore you. Maybe that's what you're used to, but that's not going to work with me. I've got priorities. And to be honest, I don't give a shit about you, Knox. Seven hundred fifty dollars a week is what interests me. Not you."

Her angry look eats away at me. If it weren't for the fireplace, I'd swear the crackling was coming from her eyes.

"Then we're all set." I nimbly hop off the island and down the rest of my soda. Actually, Paisley was right. I'm not used to women not being interested in me. And it's a damn strange feeling that triggers something in me. "Come on, let me show you around."

Only now does she let go of the strap to her bag and take off her white down jacket, which is so puffy I've got to think of Baymax, the Disney character. Her hair is sticking to her neck.

"We've got a sauna. For your next sweat cure, you don't need to sit next to the fire in your jacket."

She casts me a poisonous glance. "Just show me the house."

With a grin that comes from who knows where I point to the ceiling. "There are three floors. Down here, we've got the living room, kitchen, two bathrooms, and the sauna. Outside is the pool." Paisley follows me as I point through the panoramic window onto our vast terrace with the heated pool and then walk on down the hall next to the stairs. I point to a somewhat smaller door. "Utility room. Here you'll find the washing machine, dryer, and everything you need to clean. Disinfectants and all that, too."

Paisley opens the door and takes a short look around before closing it again. "It's incredible that you even know this room exists."

I lean against the doorframe. "There are definitely more... *incredible* things about me, you know?"

For a moment she looks as if she's considering her response, but then she simply turns and points to the stairs. "What's on the second floor?"

"The bedrooms." I push myself off the doorframe and wave her to come along. Once we're upstairs, I point to the first door. "That's mine. The three next to it are guestrooms. Then there's my father's bedroom."

Her eyes linger on the last varnished wood door before falling onto a photo standing on our roughhewn sideboard. It's a picture of my mom, hugging me from behind. I was still small. Seven at the most.

"Is that...?"

"From up here on the mezzanine you can see everything," I say quickly before she can say what I don't want to hear. I turn abruptly and point downstairs. "Over there, the tourist area is laid out exactly the same. Which is practical when keeping an eye on everything while folks are eating."

Paisley runs a hand along the wooden balustrade, her eyes trained on the chandelier and nods. "Good." She turns and nods at the three empty rooms. "I get one of the guestrooms?"

I shake my head and point to the stairs at the other end of the gallery. "You get the attic room. It's got a large bathroom and a little kitchen niche. That way you'll have more privacy."

She casts me a curious glance. "Why didn't you take over that area yourself?"

Once again my chest tightens. Earlier the attic room was indeed mine. My bed stood directly by the window that is inserted into the sloping wall, with the stunning view of the Rockies. Mom and I used to watch the sun go down when she brought me to bed, I don't know how many times. After her death, I couldn't stand the view anymore.

"Too big," I lie. "I'm hardly ever at home and don't need it."

I turn away from the stairs and look at Paisley. She seems to be lost in thought while leaning over the balustrade and letting her glance wander through the foyer. When she turns her head to look through the panorama window into the outdoor area, which is lit up by recessed lights, the butter-yellow glow of the chandelier falls onto the left side of her face. Only now do I see the swelling again, which is clearly visible to the side and below her eye. Without thinking, I reach out and carefully caress the redness with my fingertips.

Paisley immediately gasps and bats my hand away. She flinches away from me so violently, that I'm almost afraid she'll tumble over the railing.

"What happened?" I ask quietly, without really thinking she'll answer.

And I'm right. Paisley moves away and rushes silently past me to the stairs.

I follow her. "Paisley, wait. Sorry... We don't have to... Hey, where are you going?"

Dumb question. Of course, I understand that she wants to take off as she slips back into her Baymax costume and zips it up to her chin. And I shouldn't care, right? But it bothers me. No idea why. Paisley's presence is somehow...pleasant.

And that's not what I want at all. I've got principles: No figure skaters. The thing with Harper was a one-off mistake due to too much booze and too little self-control.

But I'm not drunk now. I am as clear as the mountain air and slopes and nevertheless feel that slight stab when I see Paisley snapping shut her bag, her nostrils flared.

"I'll be here tomorrow after training," she says between her teeth, in order to keep a neutral tone. "I won't make it sooner."

"Okay. Should I, ummm, I mean... Who's going to bring your stuff over?"

Her neck flushes. "There's not a lot. I'll manage on my own."

"Okay." My glance drifts to the window. In the meanwhile, it's grown dark. "How will you get back?"

She shrugs. "On the bus?"

"On the bus?" I laugh. "Paisley, you're in Aspen Highlands. You're more likely to run into a bear than a bus."

"Then I'll call a taxi." She pulls her phone out of her bag, types, and then pauses. "What's your address?"

"I'll drive you."

She hesitates. "What about your '*You do your thing; I'll do mine.*'"

I am already on my way to the little wooden stand by the front door to take my keys out of the drawer. My snowboarder charm jingles. "Starts tomorrow."

Paisley shifts her weight from one leg to another and sucks in her lower lip.

I tilt my head and let out a deep sigh. "What are you waiting for?"

"I'm weighing the situation."

"Ah. And?"

"Whether running into the bear would really be worse than having you drive me."

"We can test it if you want. At the next bear, I'll let you out." I toss my keys from one hand to the other and grin. "Or, nah. Maybe not. My dad would kill me if his new chalet girl was unable to make me a millet bowl after ending up in some black bear's stomach."

"Funny." She puts her bag on her shoulder and sighs. "Fine. Let's go."

"You could also get a snowboard, naturally," I joke, open the door, and we go outside. The recessed lighting is emitting warm light and illuminating the dancing snow. It's ridiculously cold. "If you stick to the slope, you'll be downtown in no time."

Paisley gets snow in her eye. She blinks several times before wiping her lashes with her fists. "If I knew how to snowboard, I probably would."

"You don't know how to snowboard?" I stop and repeat in disbelief. "You move to Aspen, and you *honestly* don't know how to snowboard?"

Paisley knits her brow. "You're acting as if that was some kind of deadly sin."

"No but…it's just so unusual. What about skiing?"

She shrugs and walks over to my Range Rover. "I can ice skate. That's enough."

"At some point I'll teach you," I say. "Snowboarding is cool."

Paisley opens the passenger's side door and sits down. "Maybe I'll teach myself." Her side-glance seems amused. "You know…the '*my thing, your thing*' deal."

"Good, do that." I turn on the heated seats, start the motor, and back out of the driveway. "And I'll secretly film you."

"Oh, how nice! A stalker."

"Oh, how nice! Bribery material."

She laughs. "For what?"

"Who knows. At some point it will no doubt come in handy."

"For sure."

I grin. "So, besides Simon and Garfunkel, what kind of music do you like?"

"Hmm, let me think…" She pushes the tip of her tongue between her lips thoughtfully. I can't stop staring. Paisley turns her glance away from the road and looks at me. "I really like old-school stuff, you know, like The Jackson 5. And Wham! Oh, and Katrina and the Waves did some good stuff."

"'Walking on Sunshine.'"

"*Wohooo*," she adds. And laughs. "You?"

I point to the glove compartment. "Open it up."

Once the CD is in her hands, she lets out a surprised laugh.

"*Best of Disney*? Are you messing with me?"

I laugh. "What do you mean? Disney is cool."

"Sure," she counters, opens the case, and puts in the CD. *Aladdin*'s "A Whole New World" starts. "But I wouldn't have pegged you for a Disney guy."

"No? What kind of guy would you have pegged me for?"

"No idea." She grins. "Gangsta rap?"

Now I'm the one who has to laugh. "*Gangsta rap?* Oh, Okay. Got it. You caught me with my baggy jeans, bandana, and fake gold chains."

"Don't forget your huge dollar-sign rings!"

"Who's the stalker now?"

Paisley has to lean her head against the headrest, she's laughing so hard. The sweet tone fills the entire car. My body reacts with a warm feeling in my belly.

Once she's calmed down, she lifts the case into the air with an amused expression. "No, but really. Who still listens to CDs? Don't you have Spotify?" She nods in the direction of the radio. "Aux?"

"I do. But I like CDs." We leave the mountain range and I turn right, toward downtown. "You can count on them. I mean, in fifty years, you won't be able to find a song you had on some playlist or other. But with a CD you can say, 'Hold on a sec, that song was on the *Best of…*'"

Paisley looks at me for a moment before giving a faint smile, which is impossible to interpret. "I wouldn't have imagined you to be like that at all."

I cast her a brief glance. "Already the second time you've said so. Maybe you shouldn't judge people before you know them."

She looks like she's been hit on the head. Her lips part as if she wants to say something, but then close again. Before she can try again, I change the subject.

"Where exactly should I let you out?"

Paisley's glance moves from me back out onto the road. As if she hadn't been aware of our having left the mountain range at all.

"Up there," she says eventually. "At Ruth's."

I stop in front of the bed and breakfast where, not too long ago, I used to stop by almost every day. Back when Aria and Wyatt were still together. Before my best friend cheated on her at a heavy après-ski party. The idiot.

The click of the seatbelt tears me out of my thoughts. "Great, thanks," Paisley mumbles, puts the CD case back in the glove compartment, and tucks the blond strands of her hair behind her somewhat protruding ears. "Then see you tomorrow."

"Yeah. See you tomorrow."

She gets out and hurries around the car. I can't stop thinking of Baymax seeing her trudge across the street in her big white down jacket.

Fuck. Why can't I stop grinning? I pinch the bridge of my nose, shake my head, and turn around more quickly than I should, considering the weather. Snow whirls up, and tracks decorate the street in the rearview mirror.

Paisley is a figure skater. I've been staying away from those girls for years. They call to mind bleak thoughts that follow me into my dreams and won't let me sleep. They make me hear screams that I'd rather forget. They turn me back into a broken little boy who wants nothing but to hide in a corner for hours and to dissolve.

I take a deep breath. Whatever part of me decided to feel drawn to Paisley…enough. The demons in me shouldn't be given any room. And I'm giving them room every second I grant Paisley.

From now on I'm going to be more careful.

12
Coffee O'clock

PAISLEY

The red leather creaks as I plop down. Kate peeps over her shoulder at me while pouring coffee into the blue-dotted mug of a stocky man with a mustache and a lumberjack's shirt. From the jukebox come the raw sounds of James Arthur's heartache.

"Paisley!" she calls out with a warm smile. With her free hand she tucks a loose strand of hair behind her ear and walks over. "How nice to see you. Coffee?"

"Absolutely," I nod, and blow into my hands to wake up my still-numb fingers. "Are you sure that we're in Aspen and not somewhere in…I don't know, Siberia?"

Kate laughs. Her flower-covered apron swells as she spins around to grab a colorful mug from behind the counter. "You need thicker gloves," she says and offers a meaningful glance at the thin woolen ones I bought last year at a ninety-nine-cent store. Back then, they were red, but now the material is so faded that they could pass for pale pink at best. "With those things on, I give you one week before you show up here without any hands."

"I bet you're right…" With a thankful smile I take the now full coffee cup. My nerve endings immediately begin to tingle as I'm filled with warmth. After taking a sip, a pleasant sigh crosses my lips. "I was hoping to run into Gwen," I say. In the meantime, Kate has begun to arrange donuts and muffins in the display case. "Since training yesterday, I haven't been able to get in touch with her." I lift my phone up and frown. "Her phone's off."

For a moment Kate glances at the ceiling before turning back to her muffins. Suddenly her jaw looks tense, her lips a narrow line. "I don't know if she'll be coming down," she says. She pauses a moment then sighs, closes the display case, and smooths out the lines on her forehead with her thumb and index finger. "Gwen is…"

She doesn't manage to complete her sentence. Gwen rushes through the back door. "Morning!" Her thick, wavy hair flies through the air, and the right side of her wide-cut woolen sweater almost slips off her shoulders as she reaches for a muffin. She kisses her mother on the cheek, then sees me. "Paisley, hey!" Gwen beams. Her gloomy mood from yesterday has obviously disappeared. She sits down across from me cheerfully, takes a bite of muffin, and washes it down with a gulp of my coffee. "How cool that you're here! Should we go over to the rink together?"

"Everything okay?"

"Of course," she smacks. "Why?"

"Your phone," I say and point at my own. "I've been trying to reach you since yesterday. I thought…" Hesitating, I lower my eyes onto my cup and run my finger over a deep notch in the ceramic. "You were going to drive me over to the Winterbottoms'."

"Oh, *shit*." Gwen was moving to take another bite. Instead, she pauses and opens her eyes wide. A few dark crumbs fall from her mouth onto the table. She puts the muffin to the side and looks at me apologetically. "Shit, Paisley, I totally forgot! God, what a mess. Can I make it up to you somehow?"

"It's all good," I answer and wave my hand, happy to know she just had a bad day. "I was just surprised. But now that we're on the subject…" I allow my glance to wander over my left and right shoulders, then bend down and whisper, "You could've told me that *Knox* was a *Winterbottom*."

"I didn't?" She sounds surprised, which doesn't quite fit the mischievous grin on her face. Without further ado, she grabs her muffin, takes another bite, and shrugs. "I must've forgotten."

"Of course."

"How'd it go? Do you have the job?"

"Yeah, but…"

Gwen stops eating midmouthful. "What?"

"There's a catch."

"You slept with him." Her jaw drops, giving me a rather unappetizing glimpse of the mushy muffin inside her mouth. "No way. How was it?" She puts her elbows onto the round table and bends forward. "How was he? Did he pull the washing-machine number? They say he pulls that one with all the chalet…"

"Stop!" I interrupt her and am about to stick my fingers in my ears and start humming a tune to get the images out of my head. "We…ugh. God, no." Think of something else. Quickly. "There's nothing going on. Nada. And there's not going to be, ever. Okay?"

Gwen shrugs. "Whatever you say. Where's the catch?"

"I'm going to be living there," I say and make a face. "Not with the rest of the tourists, but with *him*!"

My new friend blinks. Then once more. "I don't understand the problem."

"For real?"

"Yeah. I mean, you're going to be living at Knox's. Now, the guy's a walking problem for sure, but, holy guacamole, you've got a free ticket to see him without his shirt on all the time!" Her eyes become dreamy. "Or without his underwear."

Okay. Unwanted film in my head.

"Why should I? I mean, it's not like his house is a swingers club."

"Oh, my dear, sweet, clueless friend. If you only knew." Gwen lifts my coffee cup out of my hand and takes the last gulp. "Knox throws the heaviest parties."

"Super," I mumble. We're both quiet for a moment then I add, "Were you ever there?"

She raises her eyes and hesitates. She runs her tongue absentmindedly over her lower lip while her little nose curls. "Yeah," she says finally. "Back in the day. But that's all in the past."

Kate rushes past our table and fills up my coffee. "Gwendolyn, dear. The coffee beans are empty. I asked you yesterday to bring some more."

Gwen makes a face. "Whoops."

"Super." Her mother sighs and places the coffeepot back on the counter. "I'll go over to Woody's and get some. In the meantime, you're in charge."

Gwen raises her hand and salutes. "Yes, ma'am."

Kate just shakes her head, hangs her apron on the hook by the back door, and disappears outside.

While Gwen takes a look around the diner to see that all the tables are taken care of, I bend toward her, "Why are his parties a thing of the past for you? Did something happen?"

Gwen frowns and casts her glance at a table with two women who are so made-up, it's as if they were just coming from a party or had it in mind to tear someone apart at seven-thirty in the morning. "It's not that things *happen* at Knox's parties, Paisley, it's that full-blown catastrophes come together." She looks at me. "Nuclear catastrophes."

"Now you're exaggerating." Actually, her words shouldn't make me so curious. What Knox gets up to in his life should be of no interest to me. But I have to admit that my curiosity is gaining the upper hand.

"You'll see for yourself soon enough," she replies, her eyes drifting over my shoulder to the large display case. "Speak of the devil," she mumbles. Her brown eyes go dark. "Don't turn around."

Naturally, I turn around immediately to see Knox walking into the diner. With Wyatt right behind him, who however is having a bit of a hard time getting his hockey bag through the door. Knox's brown hair is disheveled, as if he had difficulty getting it together. Our eyes meet and I don't know what I expected after last night. Maybe a smile. Maybe just a simple, "Hey."

What I didn't expect was him to immediately turn away from me and…ignore me. As if I didn't exist. As if looking at me was worth less than looking at a thick cockroach.

A roach…

Voices make their way into my head. Voices that I have tried to drive out for years.

"I'm not going to play with her. That's Paisley, the trailer roach."

"Look out! Get away from her! Mom says that they've all got lice over there."

"Why do your pants always have holes?"

"Well, it's obvious. Her mother is one of those junkies who hang around the old drive-in getting high. As if she had money for clothes!"

"Why are you staring at Alex Woodley? He would never like you. You're a trailer roach!"

Trailer roach, trailer roach, trailer roach…

"Paisley?"

I look up. "Yeah?"

"Everything okay?"

"Yeah, let's go." Getting up more quickly than I'd intended, I bang my thigh against the table and my coffee…

Oh, dear, my coffee!

It falls right off the table. Right when Knox walks past. And the brown liquid lands right on his jeans. Or rather…his crotch. The mug shatters on the floor.

Gwen just stands there, halfway up from the booth, staring wide-eyed and open-mouthed at the floor. And Knox, he… He doesn't react. No idea if it has to do with his *I-am-the-*

hottest-snowboarder-in-the-world-and-every-chick-likes-me schtick, but he doesn't even let an angry snort escape. Instead, he raises his head, real slowly, and…grins. A grin that digs deep dimples into his cheeks and makes my legs weak. For a second my brain short-circuits, and I am incapable of doing anything but stare. It's a good two seconds until I'm able to get myself back on the ground of facts.

What am I doing? Presenting myself to him like a piece of vulnerable fresh meat whose heart is beating into her throat, just like all the other women every day out on the slopes? Giving him the feeling that I'm just another challenge he can take with his snowboard before forgetting her once more?

No way. The mere fact that Knox Winterbottom makes me nervous doesn't mean, not by a long shot, that I'm afraid of falling for him.

The thought of my weak past-self sends a shiver down my spine that threatens to take me over. I'm doing well here in Aspen. I'm not going to risk that. Not for an adrenaline-driven, narcissistic snowboard star who thinks he can get any woman into his bed with his *oh-my-God-look-at-my-perfect-face smile*.

At the thought, a wave of rage shudders through my body and at long last—at long last!—I manage to react.

I glare at him. "Not my fault if you're in the way."

His grin grows wider. Apparently, my rage amuses him. When I become aware of that, I'm up for dumping a second cup of coffee over him.

Wyatt, who until now has watched the proceedings in silence, just gives an appreciative whistle. "The little one's got a temper, Knox. I like it."

Knox doesn't reply. Instead his amused expression slowly begins to change. He turns and reaches for a napkin from one of the holders on the counter before…oh my God. Really.

Rubbing his crotch!

My sense of control is definitely getting shaken. It's hard for me to keep my angry expression up. It doesn't matter how angry he makes me… I can't lie about the fact that Knox is attractive. Normal men only look this good when they're photoshopped.

I mean, Knox lives in Aspen! A winter wonderland. Most of the time he's surrounded by snow. His skin must be pale. Like Wyatt's. Like all the others in town. But no, naturally, his genes got together beforehand and decided unanimously to make an exception. And now, here he is, standing in front of me with his perfect, bronze tan—*goddamn it*—rubbing his crotch with a napkin!

Something begins to make my face tingle. It takes me a moment to realize that I'm biting the inside of my cheek. My nerves are prickling and protesting, and when a slight feeling of numbness sets in, I am brought back down to earth.

This is Knox. Knox Winterbottom. He may be an attractive snowboarder, but definitely no sparkling vampire.

Calm down, Paisley.

I clear my throat. "Don't you know we're in a public diner. That there," I say, pointing to his hand that's still rubbing his pants, "could be considered exhibitionist."

When he looks at me, I see surprise flash in his eyes. A small part of me crows because I have the feeling that not a whole lot can throw him off track. I'm probably the first woman to talk to him that way since his voice broke. Vaguely I take in the glances of the women at the neighboring table who are staring at Knox as if they were ready to jump him right here and now. On the counter. The tables. The floor. Everywhere. Here in front of everyone.

But that doesn't interest me. I don't care about the throngs of women in Aspen, trying to win him over—even if only for one night. Or an hour.

Even if I was interested in him, it wouldn't matter. After what I left behind, I wouldn't let him get near me under any circumstances.

"Just to summarize," Knox says, tilting his head. "You spill your whole coffee on me and then portray me as an exhibitionist? You know, for me, things are clear. You're actually concerned with something completely different."

"Of course," I respond, talking myself into a rage, hardly aware of how closely Wyatt and Gwen are following our conversation. "Knox, the superstar. Knox, the know-it-all. Knox, who thinks he can turn every statement around until it suits him." I waggle my wrist as if he were just an annoying fly. "So, go on and tell me."

I see something crazy flash in his eyes that makes my body tingle far too strongly to ignore. Knox puts the napkin down on the counter and takes a step toward me

By the time he speaks, his voice has taken on a darker tone. "The next time you want me to take off my clothes…just ask."

Next to me, I hear Gwen take a sharp breath. Wyatt grins and keeps on running his hands through his dark hair, and me… I simply stand there staring at Knox. Everything in me is boiling. And the thought that from now on I'm going to be living with this dude under one roof is almost enough to make me explode. "I'm going to have to disappoint you," I say coolly. My eyes dart to the fleck on his pants. "I'm not into playing little games in public."

Knox opens his mouth to reply, but Wyatt interrupts him with an amused grunt. "Let it go, Knox. You're just scaring the little one off." His glance flits over to the neighboring table before, with a low voice, he continues, "On top of it, those women are staring at you like they're waiting for you to do a striptease at any second."

Knox follows his gaze and, seeing the two groupies whose eyes are almost sticking together with every blink from all their makeup, falls silent. A strange silence overcomes all of us.

Apparently, Wyatt feels the same way. Suddenly he says to me, "There's a party tonight at Knox's. Come on by."

It's as if he's dumped a whole bucket of ice over me. Of all the times to throw a party, Knox has decided to throw one *tonight*? On my first day of work? He can't be serious. He truly can*not* be serious!

I look back over at Knox, who deliberately avoids my glance and decides to mess around with the cookie tin on the counter. "She'll be there anyway," he says to Wyatt. "Paisley's our new chalet girl."

For a moment, Wyatt looks like he's lost the power of speech. Then he laughs out loud, seemingly unable to get his head around it. Only after a few seconds does he give Knox a few soft hits to the shoulder, causing his snowboarding bag to slide down a bit. "Sorry, man. But…you trying to set a record or something? The last one made it two months. This one here hasn't even started and *you're already coming after her like this?*" Wyatt shakes his head, still laughing. "Crazy, man. Really crazy."

And right then, Kate walks in. With a harried look on her face she lifts the coffee beans into the air and rushes past us, having no idea what kind of situation she's just burst into. Putting the bags behind the counter and standing back up, her glance falls onto the broken cup on the floor and then onto Knox's pants. She sighs before looking at Gwen and putting her hands on her hips. "So, what have you done now?"

"It's all good," Knox says, walking forward. He looks at me briefly. "My new chalet girl just wanted to show us how *nimble* she can be."

The way he speaks about me, as if I wasn't even there, freezes the blood in my veins. I feel like I've been degraded into a meaningless object that Knox Winterbottom possesses. As if he had complete power over me. As if *someone, anyone*, still had power over me.

Without replying, I crouch down and gather up the pieces. It's humiliating because I know Knox is looking down on me. But it was my mistake, and it would be a lack of respect to expect Kate to clean this up. Without looking up, I stand up and dump the shards in the trash. I grab my jacket, toss my training bag over my shoulder, and leave the diner, my cheeks aflame.

Gwen follows me. I can hear her steps in the snow. "Okay," she says, panting softly as she catches up to me, "either you lied to me and something is *definitely* going on between you and Knox or…

you've got to go to the can. I've never seen someone take off that quickly."

"I've got to go to the can?" I repeat as we turn the corner and Gwen drags me over to her Jeep.

"Yeah, the can."

I look at her without understanding.

She rolls her eyes and opens the trunk. "Go to the toilet?"

"Oh, my God. No!" Disgusted, I make a face, throw my things into the back, and go to the passenger side. "Neither of the two. Knox…or the other. Let's just go to the rink, okay?"

"Fine. But," she nods in the direction of the diner while opening the door of the Jeep and sinking behind the wheel, "we've got to talk about what just happened there. Otherwise, it's going to go real bad."

I close the door and look at her. "What do you mean?"

Gwen casts me a sympathetic glance, switches on her turn signal, and reverses. "Let's just hope I'm wrong. Knox is hot. But he is… I don't know. Like forbidden fruit. He's not good for people. Not healthy."

"That's clear," I say. "It doesn't interest me. I mean," I point my finger back over my shoulder, "did you not catch any of that back there?"

Gwen purses her lips. "Of course, Paisley. I'm just wondering if we didn't observe two totally different situations."

I think about her words for a long time. So long that I am unable to say anything until we reach iSkate. The whole time I have to wonder what I see in Knox. What he triggers in me.

The problem is that I feel two things: affection and distance. Knox could be the lighthouse in the night or the storm over the roaring waves. I'm afraid of trusting the light, of getting closer to it, of feeling safe only, right at the edge of hope, to be torn down into the depths.

13
Sound of Silence

PAISLEY

TRAINING WAS HARD. FOR SOME REASON I CANNOT fathom that Polina seems to think I am ready for a triple axel.

The triple axel! I can just about pull off the simple one with perfect form now. I can land the double, too, but on really unsure legs and not without some balance issues. So how on earth am I supposed to pull off the triple? That's why today's training wasn't exactly all that great, and my mood could certainly be better.

"You coming along to the diner?" Gwen asks.

Levi is holding open the iSkate door for me, and the icy wind immediately cools my shower-warm cheeks.

"I'd be happy to," Aaron says. He runs a hand across his stomach. "I could eat a bear. Levi?"

"Wherever you go, I will follow." The glances the two share are heartwarming.

I look at my watch. "I've got about an hour, then I've got to start cooking dinner for the tourists."

"Oh, right, today's your first day at the resort!" Gwen gives an excited squeak. We walk over to her Jeep, and she raises her hand toward Aaron and Levi, who are already standing by their own car.

"Yep." My instep hurts from all the unsuccessful jumps. I lean over and undo my laces as Gwen starts the engine. "And I would happily stay here all night practicing the triple axel rather than helping out at Knox's party later."

"Ughhh." She drives out of the parking lot and shoots me a glowing look from the corner of her eye. "You excited?"

"No. Why should I be?"

Gwen ignores my question. "Listen. There's just one thing that should absolutely set off the alarm bells for you. And that's when Knox walks around shirtless. Cause it means that either he is on the hunt for a new piece or his new piece is already past. Both suboptimal."

"Why?"

"Well...in the former case, you could be his quarry, which, at first sight, might sound good. But seeing as that Knox is known for his short-term stories, that wouldn't end well. The latter case wouldn't be all that much better because it would clearly hurt you to learn that he had something going on with someone else."

"What?" I let an unbelieving laugh escape. "That wouldn't hurt me in the least."

"'Sorry to my unknown lover,'" Gwen sings, quoting Halsey. "'Sorry I could be so blind.'"

I roll my eyes. "'Babe, I'm gonna leave you,'" I sing, grinning. "'Oh, baby, you know, I've really got to leave you.'"

"Led Zeppelin!" Gwen's eyes widen. "I can't believe it. You're a fan? I didn't think that anyone other than me knew who they were anymore!"

"Guilty as charged."

"I like you," she says. "I'm gonna hold on to you."

Walking into the diner I stop in my tracks.

"Oh," Gwen mumbles, following my glance. Of course, Knox,

Wyatt, and the many long-legged women in crop tops that would cause me to catch frostbite within a second are impossible to overlook. They are sitting at one of the backmost booths; one of the I-feel-like-it's-summer girls lolls about on Knox's lap like an Egyptian cat. "I totally forgot that they might be here." My friend looks at me apologetically. "The boys often get warmed up by eating here before a party."

Knox's eyes bore into me as if he wanted to take an X-ray. I feel extremely uncomfortable under his gaze and quickly turn to Kate. She is hurrying about behind the counter, gives us a quick, stressed-out smile, and disappears into the kitchen.

"Levi and Aaron are back there." Gwen grabs my hand and pulls me along. I make sure to walk on her left side in order to ignore Knox better. But as we come by their booth, it's as if neither Gwen nor I even existed. One of the girls gives a shrill laugh in response to something Wyatt has said. Knox says, "Dude. With our history teacher? You're nuts."

"Thanks for keeping a place," I say to Levi and Aaron, sitting down across from them. Unfortunately, right in Knox's line of sight, who looks up at me briefly from his burger before putting his arm around his red-haired companion. I'd really like to ask Levi if we couldn't switch places, but that would mean that the situation is too much for me. And I do *not* care to admit that at all.

"Of course," Aaron replies. He takes a sip of his ginger ale. "This place is hopping."

Gwen grunts, almost spitting out the lemonade she pilfered from Levi's glass. "Aaron. No one says 'this place is hopping' anymore."

Kate comes over to our table, a trayful of glasses in hand. "Okay, looks like I've got a special Coke here that William *supposedly* didn't order." She looks over to the counter where William is sitting and rolls her eyes. "And an iced tea from I don't know who." Gwen's mother pouts. "Take pity on me."

I laugh. "Give me the Coke. I could use some caffeine."

Gwen narrows her eyes, leans back, and crosses her arms. "Dear lady, I don't know," she says. She begins tapping her arm with a finger as if in thought. "What should I think about your work? Am I, a paying customer, not worth a thing?"

"You're worth this iced tea, my child." She puts it down in front of her daughter and winks. "It's great that from now on you intend to pay. I'll remember that."

"Oh, my God, what a joker my mom is! May I have a nibble of you?" Gwen makes a move to grab her, but Kate avoids her hand, the tray wobbling, laughing all the while.

There's an awful tightness in my chest, and I can't stop the memories of my mother from coming. I wish she'd been a little more like Kate. A little more normal. Sometimes we goofed around, but that was rare. Mostly when she'd had a few well-paying clients and her excitement over her next shot had put her in a good mood.

Kate looks at the clock. "If you want to eat something, it better be now. In twenty minutes, we've got two reservations."

I order a wrap, the others order cheeseburgers, and after they arrive, we talk about our free skating and what kind of outfits we'd love to have. I even manage to block out Knox's presence, until Wyatt sits halfway up from his booth and looks over at us.

"Hey, chalet girl," he calls out. He's clearly drunk. "Am I gonna get your number?"

I can feel myself turning red.

"Just ignore him," Gwen says. "He's a total idiot."

And that's exactly what I do. Wyatt whistles once more like an immature teen and then falls back into the booth next to his date. I can't understand why she doesn't pick up her little designer bag and go. In reality, it doesn't seem to bother her at all. She nestles into Wyatt's shoulder even deeper than before. Incredible.

I secretly look over at Knox. I don't want to, but I cannot stop myself. Which I immediately regret, for, right at that moment the girl on his lap is whispering something in his ear with a dirty smile on her face. Knox emits a coarse laugh, turns to her, and runs his lips across her temples.

I'm jealous.

The unexpected realization hits me all at once and with full force, but I can't deny the ice-cold stab of pain I feel move through my body. At this moment there is nothing I could wish for more than undoing the night at the movies. It complicated everything.

Confused, I bend back down over my wrap as a pickle falls out of Gwen's mouth and she emits a surprised sound. "Take a look at this," she says, laying her phone down on the table and pointing to an article in *Ice Today*. I'd uninstalled the app when I turned my back on Minneapolis. "Ivan Petrov is presenting his new skater. He aims to take her to the Olympics."

The ground beneath my feet begins to give way. A kind of tinnitus blocks out all the conversations going on around me. I no longer catch what Levi and Aaron are saying.

Ivan Petrov.

I feel sick. The name alone makes me dizzy and brings up images I'd rather not see. All of a sudden it's like the pain never stopped. I can feel it throughout my entire body.

"Who?" It's more of a gasp than a word but, all the same, getting it to cross my lips is incredibly tough. I spit it out.

Levi runs a hand across his beard and bends over the table in order to read the article better.

"Kaya Ericson. Hmm. Don't know her."

It's like I'm frozen.

Kaya. *My* Kaya.

She was my best friend for over a decade, but apparently my disappearing act doesn't bother her. The only thing that seems to matter to her is her success.

"I know her," Gwen mutters. "A few years ago she got first place at Skate America. Figure skating."

She did indeed. I remember the championships. It was rainy, and I cried and cried because I couldn't compete. Because of him. He had been preparing for that day for a long time, had invested all of his strength into my performance only to break me and to rejoice in my pain. It was the worst form of psychological terror: at first building up my hopes to the skies only to then destroy them at the deepest level. I think that's the year everything started. The hell on earth that crept into my life. Quietly and dimly, on black claws. Ready to dig into my insides and tear me apart.

"Ivan Petrov…" Levi murmurs before sticking the last bite of hamburger into his mouth and reflecting. "I haven't heard anything about him in ages. And he used to be a real media whore."

"Truth." Aaron nods while rubbing the freckles on the bridge of his nose. "Back in the day he used to always get first place. Back when he used to skate. When I was a kid, I remember cheering him on whenever the championships were on TV."

Gwen tilts her head. "I didn't know he was a trainer now."

Well, I did.

I'm ice cold, and I've only heard his name. I cannot manage to look at Gwen's phone. I know why Ivan's creeping back into the media. With Kaya of all people. He has no interest in making his new figure skater famous, but…

It's got to do with me. He *wanted* me to see this article. Even now, with over one thousand miles between us, he won't give up. He simply won't give up wanting to humiliate me—wherever I am. There is nothing I'd want more than to tell him it won't work. That he lost. But that's not the case. With nothing but a single act, he's managed to tear back open the wound that had begun to heal so well over the last number of days. Ruthless and cold. A monster beneath his human mask.

I'm overcome by panic. What if he finds me? What if people find out I'm training at iSkate? It's just a matter of time before that goes public. At the latest, with the first competition… Ivan, he…he could wrest my new life away from me again with one clever chess move. And he knows it.

The first notes of a melody dance through the diner and pull me out of my state of shock. I blink and slowly things come back into focus. Levi appears and then Aaron's profile begins to take on shape as he wipes ketchup and a lonely roast onion from his boyfriend's mouth. Gwen is busy putting her phone away again.

The tune is coming from the jukebox, a song I know all too well. I know the lyrics by heart. Simon and Garfunkel's "The Sound of Silence."

My heart is pounding in my throat. I turn toward the jukebox and see Knox going back to his table. His eyes dig into mine. I am incapable of looking away, so it's up to Knox to break eye contact first. He sits back down next to the woman who had whispered in his ear and yet: I can't be angry at him anymore. Maybe he doesn't know, but the simple thing of playing a song by my favorite band pulls me out of the darkness. I don't know how long that darkness would've lasted otherwise.

14

Not Just the Chalet Girl to Me

Knox

My shoes leave deep prints in the fresh powdered snow as I make my way to the half-pipe on the slope behind our house, snowboard over my shoulder. Within minutes the sky is royal blue, the pink streaks that had followed the sunset gone. At this time of year, the darkness chases off the day so quickly; it's like there's some kind of light switch.

I shouldn't be here. Not at this time of day when the slope is spookily empty. And especially after having downed countless shots with Wyatt and the girl his sister Camila brought along to the party. I have no idea where my own date is. I should probably go look for her, but...

I can't help myself. I love the quiet that envelops me out on the slope at night. The cool air takes me in, as if greeting an old friend, and carries me along in a whisper, all the way up the mountainside. On top, I need to clear my head. I thought I could wipe Paisley's face from my thoughts by getting hammered. Instead, it just got worse with every drink, her blue eyes more brilliant in my imagination with every shot.

Outside it's no better. The color of the sky in its purity makes me think of her, which is driving me crazy, and Paisley... Whatever she is, she definitely isn't pure. The way she acts, the wall she's built around herself, and then the wounds on her face tell me that she's probably just as broken as I am. Maybe even more. And that's why I've got to stop thinking about her. I've got enough of my own shit to carry around. I can't afford to lose my head over a girl. I want to hold no complications. Sex when I want it, no obligations and unnecessary headaches. One night, and the next day everything's over. That's always worked out well. Sure, there were a few tourists who were persistent and kept on bothering me. But after their departures and a few desperate Instagram messages, all that passed, too. Which is why it's even more important to get Paisley out of my head once and for all.

I stop in front of the half-pipe. It's both dumb and risky to get on your board drunk, but, truth be told, I don't give a shit. I just want to get my head straight. And so I drop my board onto the ground, step into the bindings, and take a few easy jumps to warm up. Following two simple 720°s, I can feel my pulse starting to increase. My body wants more. More adrenaline, more risk, more height. After landing another spin and going down the half-pipe with an air-to-fakie, I get ready to take another jump. Although I'm definitely not sober, I've got the half-pipe clearly in front of me. Landing difficult jumps always gives me a kick that fills me with ecstasy and makes me forget everything else.

And that's how it is now. My body is tense, in the perfect position while I focus on the end of the half-pipe and jump at exactly the right moment to pull off a McTwist. The air cuts into my face as I go into the 540°, and for a bit I don't perceive anything but the twist, the feeling of being free, of lightness, and joy. My board lands perfectly back on the pipe, and I drift off to the side and come to a stop. I don't even gasp. I'm used to even more demanding jumps in training, but the McTwist fills me with satisfaction every time. It was the first jump my dad ever taught me. The first jump that my mom...

I interrupt the thought before pain can set in and bend down to undo my bindings. My breath is heavy as I strip the board off my feet and let myself fall backward, my eyes on the sky. The first stars are beginning to sparkle, one brighter than the other. Little white clouds form in the air with every exhale. Although the party is in full swing down the slope, I can't hear the music up here. It is absolutely quiet. Aside from my breath, there is no sound at all.

I mostly take advantage of this time of night up here when I want to think. Or need some quiet. For a second, I think about Wyatt; he lives every party as if a single night without loud noise and a lot of people around would be impossible. Since Aria's been gone, as far as Wyatt is concerned, silence means nothing but emptiness and loneliness. But for me, it isn't empty. It's full of answers. To understand yourself, you just need to know how to listen.

Looking into the stars, my thoughts wander back to Paisley. How big her eyes grew when she spilled the coffee over my pants and made a great effort to let me know how she felt. Deep in thought, I pull off my gloves and let the snow trickle through my fingers, without once turning away from the stars.

Today was Paisley's first day at the resort. My father put her in the tourist area, which is why our paths didn't cross, and shortly before she got off, I came up here. No idea how this all is going to work over the next few weeks. Avoiding her is going to be tough. Especially because I don't really know if I want to. My head is yelling at me to ignore her in order to protect myself. *No figure skaters, Knox. No figure skaters.* But my heart is doing its best to tell me otherwise. There is that strange warmth I feel when I think about her features. How she lifts her pointy chin every time she wants to assert herself.

I breathe out and push myself back up. There's no point being out here any longer. Sooner or later, Wyatt and the others are going to wonder where the hell I've been, and I'll have to be able to give them an answer why I went out on the half-pipe alone, in the dark.

The closer I get to the resort, the louder the music grows. There are so many people behind the windows, and I don't know half of them. Most of them are tourists. I run my hand through my hair, wiping out the snow. If Dad knew that I went out without my helmet, he'd kill me.

Wyatt is sitting in the whirlpool with the girl his sister dragged along. The sunken lights highlight his heated cheeks. His arms are stretched out behind his head, and he's running one of his hands through the brunette's hair. I'd bet my snowboard that he gets her into bed. Wyatt was always extroverted and into parties, but ever since the thing between him and Aria went down the tubes, he's been an outright sex addict. No idea if that's his way of trying to forget her. We don't talk about our feelings.

I decide to make my way around the house and go through the garage in order to avoid any unnecessary attention. Getting out of my snowboard clothing and pulling off my boots, I pray that Paisley is already in her room and that for the rest of the night I won't have to be aware of her. I curse myself for not having talked Dad out of hiring her. No idea what is going on with me. It's that warmth in my stomach driving my actions again; my head is on stand-by apparently.

I hear shouting coming from the living room. It sounds like people cheering someone on. Closing the door behind me I consider how much more I can drink to forget Paisley and yet still be halfway passable at training tomorrow. Then I discover the reason for all the uproar: Camila is up on our pool table doing a striptease. The guys, more than half of whom no doubt have ladies back at home, are giving her dollar bills. She takes them, smiling seductively.

Suddenly, I hear a voice next to me. "Actually, I couldn't care less..."

Seeing it's Paisley, I flinch. Good thing right at this moment the bass goes all the way up in the song that's playing, and she can read my response as somehow related.

Watching Camila slink out of her jean skirt, Paisley's expression is both disgusted and sympathetic. "But shouldn't someone stop her? There's no way she realizes what she's doing anymore."

Paisley is carrying a tray of empty glasses and something undefinable in her hands. I think it's a pile of paper towels full of…vomit? Oh, God, yeah. She is actually carrying around someone else's vomit. Her blond bun looks disheveled, and strands have come loose to hang limply in her face. There are dark shadows beneath her eyes.

"Camila knows perfectly well what she's doing," I reply, my eyes focused on Wyatt's little sister.

"Ah." Paisley wrinkles her nose. "So why is she doing this?"

I shrug. "No idea. For the attention? The money?"

"The money? She lives in Aspen. I'm sure her folks have mounds of cash."

"Wyatt and Camila don't have any parents anymore," I say without thinking and could kick myself. That kind of information doesn't have anything to do with Paisley.

Her eyes grow wide as they move from Camila out through the panoramic windows where Wyatt is getting out of the hot tub. "What happened?" she asks softly.

I lean back against the sideboard. For a moment, I hesitate to tell her, but then decide to do it anyway, she could learn about it from Gwen if she wanted to.

"On a hike out on Snowmass Mountain, their dad was hit by an avalanche. Their mom died a few years ago from cervical cancer."

"God." Out of the corner of my eye, I can see the hairs on Paisley's arm standing up. "That's horrible." She looks at me. "Where do the two of them live?"

I don't answer right away. I watch Camila play with her bra straps to coax more bucks out of the tourists. The guys look like hungry hyenas with a juicy antelope in front of them, ready to pounce before too long. Wyatt slides open one of the panoramic windows, a towel wrapped around his waist, the girl doesn't leave his side. He casts a brief glance at his sister, before turning away again with a neutral expression and reaching for an abandoned whiskey glass. He gave up telling Camila what to do years ago.

"In their parents' house," I say before deciding to change the subject. I nod at the tray in her hands. "Coffee not enough for you?"

Paisley looks confused. She looks from Camila to her tray and frowns. "What do you mean?"

I grin. "You planning to pelt me with vomit-soaked paper towels?"

Now that Paisley appears to understand, her jaw tightens. She glares at me. "I just want to keep my job. That's it."

"Pretty nasty stuff," I mutter.

Paisley snorts. "It's your fault. If you wouldn't throw these parties…"

"My life would be pretty boring."

"No," she hisses. "Then there'd be the slightest chance that we could get along while under the same roof."

I put on an indifferent face. "Who says that I want to get along with you while under the same roof?"

She briefly gasps for air. And I have to admit that I feel that annoying stab, just like the last time I hurt her. But if I can't get her out of my thoughts, maybe my assholishness will keep her away.

Paisley gets a hold of herself more quickly than I expected. She flares her nostrils and turns away in order to fill up her tray with more glasses. "You're rotten, Knox. You hide off in that world of yours where you're the snowboard king and everyone just kisses your feet. And you throw one party after the other and get smashed." She shakes her head. "The way you act, people might think you don't give a shit about anything. You don't give a shit about the people around you." She looks past me and then at the glass that I am in the process of filling halfway up with vodka. "You don't give a shit about yourself." Her eyes turn into slits. "What kind of game are you playing, wasting time to block out reality? The fact is, Knox, that you're not going to get anywhere this way. In sports or in life. But keep on doing it. Go on getting drunk every night and growling at people who haven't done anything to you. I think it's a winning plan."

It's not the ice in my glass that causes me to shudder and my insides to go cold. Her words hit home without me wanting them to… Paisley has hit the nail on the head. It's like she took a mirror and reflected my inner life back to me. No one has ever taken me apart by being that open to my face. I doubt that anyone beyond Wyatt and her have ever even noticed.

And that's precisely what scares me. I don't want someone to be able to see behind my facade. I don't want how broken I am on the inside to become obvious. Everyone just needs to keep on thinking I'm living my take-it-easy life. Knox, the snowboarder. Knox, the famous guy from Aspen. Knox, who doesn't have any concerns, doesn't have any problems.

I live in the public eye. And so any tiny thing the press can pounce on is immediately made public. The idea that my past and somewhat fragile psyche could be a topic on everybody's lips makes me cramp up. I feel nauseous.

Wyatt comes into my field of vision. He's still got a towel draped around his waist and a drunken film over his eyes.

He lets out an unbelievable laugh and points at Paisley, who is balancing the tray in one hand while using the other to wipe a spot off the table. "She's actually here."

"Yeah," I reply, the tone in my voice darker than I'd intended, but, according to Paisley, I don't have myself under control. "I told you, she's our new chalet girl."

"Yeah, but…" Wyatt hiccups. The girl next to him chuckles, as if it was cute. I have no idea how Wyatt manages to make himself understood to all the women in his drunken state. "I thought you changed your mind and were firing her."

Paisley stops. She stretches her shoulders and puts the rag down on the tray, then turns to Wyatt. I can see panic in her eyes. "Fire me? Because of…because of the coffee?"

"No." Wyatt makes a gesture like he's throwing something away. "Because you're at iSkate. Knox doesn't hire figure skaters."

For a second my heart stops. I feel hot and cold and can hear my blood pounding in my ears.

Paisley looks from him to me and back. "Why not?"

"Wyatt, shut it."

He meets my glance and immediately seems to grow clearer. At the very least he seems to understand what he's just said, for he looks sorry. "Oh, man," he says and rubs his forehead before turning to the girl next to him. "Let's go upstairs, huh? I want to get rid of this towel."

The girl giggles again and nods. She digs her nails into his arm, Wyatt shoots me another apologetic glance, and the two disappear up the steps. Feeling Paisley looking at me, for a while I simply watch them go. When I can no longer ignore it, I put the untouched vodka glass back down on the sideboard and wipe my damp hands off on my pants.

"I'm hitting the sack," I say, without looking at her. All the same, I can sense her incredulous glance.

"For real? What about all the people?"

"Leave them alone. They'll take off on their own."

"You probably don't believe that yourself." Paisley's eyes dart around taking in every guest. "It doesn't look like any of them are going anywhere anytime soon. They'll probably sleep here on the floor, as drunk as they are."

The corner of my mouth twitches in amusement as I watch her glare at all the guests, half-speechless, half-raging. "Then let your temper go and toss them all out." With a grin I give her a thumbs up. "I believe in you."

"But…"

She doesn't get any further, as I've already turned and am making my way up the steps. And although I can't see her physically anymore, her face burns in my mind. Those slightly protruding ears, those great big eyes, her little rosebud-like mouth. In truth, I'd love to turn around to get just one more look.

But I don't.

15
We're Broken, Aren't We?

PAISLEY

For what feels like the hundredth time, I wipe the mop across that point of the floor with the spot. I don't know how—and I don't want to know how—it got there. It's sticky and colored a black-green. It looks really toxic.

"Morning."

I blow my hair out of my face, hold my breath, and look up. Knox comes down the stairs…wearing boxers. Really *short* boxers. I can see how his lateral muscle cords merge into his lower parts and disappear beneath the white waistband marked *Calvin Klein*. With every step, the muscles of his washboard stomach give me a considerable show. Everything in me begins to tingle. Despite what a prick he was being last night, I can't stop my body from reacting to him. How could it not? Knox looks like a Hollywood star on the cover of *GQ*.

When I realize that I'm staring, I quickly look away and go back to the spot on the ground, only to recognize that it's finally disappeared. "Morning," I reply. I lean the mop against the wall and walk into the open kitchen to make him breakfast. I hate that I'm responsible for that, too. It's humiliating to have to serve him despite his arrogant attitude. But the benefits of the job outweigh it. Mr.

Winterbottom pays me more than I could have dreamed, and I don't have to look for an apartment.

Instead of sitting down at the table, Knox slides onto one of the stools, rubs his eyes, and plants his elbows on the granite of the island. "Sleep well?"

For a while, I stare into the full refrigerator, wondering what to make him. Then I decide the effort isn't worth it. "You mean, after needing two hours to get all the party animals out, and after waking up three hours later so I could get everything straight before your dad came home?" I shrug, close the fridge, and open one cupboard after another until I come across a box of Cheerios stuffed into a back corner. Together with a bowl, spoon, and jug of milk, I shove everything across the island and feign a smile. "Yeah, Knox. Thanks a lot. I slept really, really well for those three hours."

Knox blinks. His eyes are still crusted with sleep. His eyes wander from me to the cereal before the right side of his mouth begins to twitch. "Cheerios, wow. I haven't seen those since I was in high school. Have to have hit the expiration date a few years ago." He grabs the box and looks around. "No way. They're good until next week!" He stares in disbelief at the date for a second before grinning and shaking his head. "Dad, you old fox..."

I roll my eyes, turn, and take a package of eggs out of the fridge. Then I put a pan on the stove, throw some oil inside, and steal the jug of milk out of Knox's hands in order to prepare some scrambled eggs.

Knox follows my movements. "Am I right in assuming that the scrambled eggs aren't for me?"

"A second ago you were happy to have your Cheerios," I reply, without looking at him, and pour the eggs into the pan. It hisses. "How could I ruin that for you?"

Knox snorts and tips his cereal into his bowl. Reaching across the island for the milk his hand brushes my underarm and I feel like I've been hit by lightning. I hold my breath.

Why is my body reacting to him like this?

Knox pauses in the middle of his movement. Halfway over the island he looks up at me, his lips spread lightly, a surprised look in his eyes. "Sorry." Then he grabs the milk, pours it over his Cheerios, and shovels one spoonful after another into his mouth. At the rate he's going, I seriously ask myself how long it'll take before he chokes and I have to perform the Heimlich maneuver. I can already see the headlines: "Snowboarder Knox Winterbottom overdoses on Cheerios. Chalet girl fails to revive him."

I clear my throat, take a plate out of the cupboard, and put my scrambled eggs on it. "Why are you even awake? It's shortly before six."

"Jogging," he replies between mouthfuls, a drop of milk trickling out of his mouth and dripping onto his chest. Suddenly the scrambled eggs taste surprisingly dry as I watch the trickle make its way down his muscles to land on the floor. Knox casts a glance over his shoulder. "Is Wyatt still here?"

"No." The memory of his pal and the brunette make me groan. I put a forkful of scrambled eggs into my mouth. "They were the last ones to go. They spent a good thirty minutes drowning out my knocks and entreaties for them to leave with unambiguously...*suggestive* sounds."

Knox guffaws. In the process, managing to distribute some milk and a few Cheerios onto the granite. Unfortunately, some of it hits my plate, which I angrily push to the side.

"Suggestive?" he repeats, without caring that he's just spit on my breakfast. "Who uses the word *suggestive*?"

I ignore him and stand up instead, pushing a cup beneath the automatic coffee machine and then leaning back against the sideboard with a latte macchiato. I contemplatively stir the foam. "What did Wyatt mean when he said you didn't hire figure skaters?"

Knox's face darkens. He stops stuffing himself with Cheerios and pokes the milk with his spoon instead. "Nothing."

"Nothing? You're telling me he just happens to think so?"

"Yeah."

I sigh. "You don't want to tell me. Got it. That's fine with me, but just say so."

"I don't have to tell you anything." His tone is cutting, and his eyes grow small, but then he lets out a sigh and his tense features smooth out. "Sorry. I shouldn't speak to you like this."

His words surprise me. Just to do something, I down the rest of my macchiato. I keep my eyes on what's left of the foam as I twirl the glass in my fingers. Eventually, I look at him. "Then why are you?"

Knox is uncomfortable. It's obvious. His wide body slides back and forth on the small stool. He keeps drowning one single Cheerio in milk with his spoon. "No idea." He pauses before continuing. "Maybe to protect myself."

His words remain hovering between us, creating an imaginary energy field. The tension is almost tangible.

"From what?" My voice has grown quieter, too. Softer. "I'm not going to do anything to you."

Knox looks up. His eyes suddenly look endlessly tired. "You know what, Paisley… Inside every person you know there's a person you don't." He pushes his spoon to the side and stands up. "Excuse me."

I watch him go up the stairs and disappear into his room. A part of me wants to go after him. A part of me—and this doesn't make me happy at all—wants to take his face in my hands and caress his cheeks until that sad look leaves his eyes. And then another part of me says I should just get Knox out of my head.

I came to Aspen to start a new life and to concentrate on myself. I have a great goal, and I'll only meet it if I'm focused. My intention to leave Minneapolis and find myself anew as a powerful woman in the Rockies is what gave me the strength to escape Ivan. It took me years.

And now? I'm standing in the kitchen of a star snowboarder,

allowing myself to feel more for him than I should. I shouldn't care about Knox one way or the other. I'm here to get to the Olympics. This job is a means to an end. The fact that I'm under one roof with Knox cannot distract me.

I never want to be bound to someone ever again, because, in the end, it will destroy me.

Once again.

16
My Mind Is a Battlefield

PAISLEY

That latte macchiato from two hours ago definitely didn't have a positive effect. If I could have one wish at the moment, it'd be a caffeine drip. In my mind's eye, I see myself out on the ice, one hand out for balance, the other pulling an infusion stand behind me. Last night's bass is still ringing in my ears.

With fumbling fingers, I bind my hair into a bun, grab my skates, and leave the changing room. Training hasn't begun yet, so I take the stairs up to the iSkate lounge. Most of the time, it's full of mothers watching their young ice-skating daughters. Minneapolis wasn't any different; all day long they'd drink coffee, gossip about the girls' outfits, and purse their lips whenever their own daughter didn't land a jump. When I was younger, I always wished my mom would be one of them, watching and waiting for me at the end of the day. Maybe even treating me to a burger at Wendy's afterward before going home. But she never did. Instead, she let total strangers pay her to give them hand jobs. Or more.

The server behind the counter smiles understandingly when with heavy eyes I ask for a strong coffee. She hands me a large mug. I thank her, turn, and look around the lounge. I see Aaron, Levi, and Gwen at one of the back tables.

"You can't bring that, Gwen," I hear Aaron saying as I approach the table. He runs a hand through his red hair, pushing it out of his face before it simply falls down again.

Levi nods. "Your dad would have your head."

"Only if I don't pull it off," Gwen replies. Fidgeting in her chair, her hands clasping a cup, she gives the impression of an excited child waiting on Santa to bring the gifts. I notice that she's dyed her hair. Instead of the formerly rosé color, from her shoulders down her brown mane now is a daring silver.

"If you don't pull what off?" I ask, pulling up a chair. Gwen squeals, throws her arms around my shoulders, and hugs me.

That's when it happens. My heart begins to race, my hands begin to sweat, and my chest constricts. Her embrace triggers panic; the pressure and proximity catapult me back to Minneapolis. Suddenly, they are no longer Gwen's arms, but *his*. No longer Gwen's floral perfume, but *his* sharp aftershave. Not Gwen's soft skin, no, but his scratchy stubble. My head is spinning, an unending whirlwind raging and killing all the colorful flowers that over the last number of days have found the strength to grow. And yet, every feeling of pain is an experience, too, and every one of them makes a nest for itself inside me. They never really disappear. Sometimes any little old thing can bring them back to life.

The panic came up quick, overpoweringly and unexpectedly. I feel like I'm back there again. Back in that house. And it hurts. It really fucking hurts.

"Gwen," I hear Aaron say. In my head it sounds far away and dull somehow, as if I was underwater. "Let go of her!"

Almost immediately, I sense her pull her arms away. I feel free, the fetters around my chest disappear. I gasp for air and, luckily, the dots in front of my eyes soon disappear and my heartrate goes back to normal.

Gwen, Aaron, and Levi are staring at me. They all have the same concerned look on their faces.

"Everything all right?" Aaron asks, his forehead wrinkled. "You're paler than Harper was when Polina told her that her Lutz was a catastrophe."

"All good," I murmur. My hands are trembling slightly as I wipe them off on my pants. "It's just my circulation. Knox…didn't let me sleep all that much."

Gwen's eyes widen and Levi's dark eyebrows shoot into his forehead.

When I realize what they must be thinking, I let out a sigh. "People. Do you all only connect Knox with sex?"

"Yeah," Gwen and Levi answer in unison.

Aaron looks from me to Levi and back before shrugging and adding, "I shall hold my tongue, but the other two are right. Everything you hear about Knox has to do with sex, parties, and scandals."

"Then take the second category there. Yesterday was my first day of work and he threw a *Project X* party with total strangers."

"His parties are *always* full of total strangers," Gwen says. "Nothing strange there."

Levi nods. "John McEnroe showed up once, but no one noticed but me."

"Who's John McEnroe?"

Gwen rolls her eyes and waves a bored hand through the air. "Just some tennis player that no one's ever heard of. So, what went down at the party?"

I lean back in my chair and take a big drink of my coffee. "Wyatt's sister did a striptease on the pool table."

"She often does that," Aaron says.

Levi nods in agreement.

"And Wyatt was getting it on with a woman in the hot tub to such a degree I thought they were going to have sex right there and then. Really. It was cringe."

Strangely, my friends do not respond and exchange sheepish looks instead.

"What?"

"Well…" Aaron scratches his stubble. "We avoid the topic of Wyatt to the best of our ability."

"Okay." They've aroused my interest. "Why?"

Levi and Aaron immediately look over at Gwen, but don't say a word. When I look over at her as well, she throws her hands into the air and sighs.

"Well, you'll hear about it sooner or later. So. Between Wyatt and me…there was something going on."

"And?" I insist, not yet understanding why that would make the topic taboo.

Gwen bites her lower lip and casts a brief glance over her shoulder before continuing. "Back at that point… I wasn't totally myself. In any event, I know that Wyatt wasn't exactly disinclined. That's why I thought the whole thing between him and Aria must've been over. But, well…"

My mouth drops open. "Oh, my God. You mean it wasn't?"

Gwen presses her lips, stares into her coffee, and shakes her head.

"But afterward it was," Levi says drily. Aaron expands, "We don't really know what happened. Shortly after, Aria dumped him and went off to Brown, when she'd originally had Aspen University in mind."

"There were a lot of people at the party," Gwen mumbles. She looks remorseful. "I wouldn't be surprised if someone started a rumor about us. But…no idea. I don't know anything for sure. Afterward, I stayed away from him."

"God." I look down onto the ice too stunned to say anything. Once I've collected myself to some degree, I shake my head. "What kind of asshole is that guy? Knox is a real lamb in contrast."

Gwen groans. "Don't say that. The two are like peanut butter and jelly. A real Dream Team."

Aaron leans forward. His dark eyes focus on a point behind me, before he nods toward the stairs. I turn around to see Harper coming into the lounge in a purple outfit. She's let out her bun, and her red hair hugs her waist with every step. "You heard about her and Knox?"

I sit up expectantly. My movement annoys me, but I can't help it. My curiosity is simply too much. "No. What?"

Gwen beats him to the punch. "Apparently there was something there. According to Harper, they were together, but I don't have any idea if I should believe that. Knox usually stays far away from iSkate girls."

"Wyatt said the same thing yesterday," I say, without letting Harper out of my sight. Her eyes look swollen and red. Has she been crying? Maybe even because of Knox? "But when I asked Knox about it, he clammed up." I glance back to the others. "What's the deal?"

"No idea," Levi answers, and both Gwen and Aaron shrug, their expressions blank.

"No one knows why," Gwen says. "Somehow it's just always been that way."

"Okay. Weird." I sigh, finish off my coffee, and put the cup back on the table. "Enough about Knox. Why is your dad going to take your head off, Gwen?"

My friend rolls her eyes, pulls a hair tie off her wrist, and makes a bun. "Levi and Aaron are overdoing it."

"If anything, we're *under*doing it," Levi says, making Aaron nod thoughtfully before adding, "Gwen wants to add a triple Lutz to her program at Skate America, but her dad has only planned for a double." Skate America is the next international Grand Prix of the season and what we're currently training for.

"Why do you want to do that?"

"Because the double Lutz is worth less than the triple and will never get a chance to win," Gwen replies. Her voice drips with disappointment, and I can understand her. It probably wouldn't be any different for me, instead, I'm worried about not living up to Polina's demands. She's worked a combination of a triple axel and a triple toe loop into my program, and, at the moment, I really have doubts about getting it together flawlessly for Skate America.

"And now you want to change your program behind your trainer's back." I pause. "I don't think that's a good idea, Gwen. Talk it over with him again."

"There's no point," she answers. Her body language is stiff, as if she'd made up her mind a long time ago. She lifts her chin, pushes back her chair, and stands up. "Training's about to start."

Aaron, Levi, and I look at one another as she hurries off.

"That's Gwen," Levi mumbles. "Once she's got something in her head, no one's going to stop her."

"More stubborn than a bull seeing red," Aaron sighs.

We all stand up to make our way to the rink. But watching Gwen, how concentrated she is practicing the triple Lutz and seeing her wobble as soon as her skates hit the ice, I realize it's not a simple case of being stubborn. I haven't known her long, but her ups and downs and behavior patterns that I've noticed 'til now make me think she, too, is fighting some kind of battle in her head. One I don't know a thing about. But I know how difficult it is for her to pretend that everything's okay. As if she were nothing but the energetic bouncy ball that everyone takes her for.

Because the most difficult thing is killing the monster inside without damaging yourself in the process.

17
Still Searching for You in Every Sunrise

Knox

"THAT WAS CRAP, KNOX." MY TRAINER'S FACE IS HARD, his lips a thin line. Cameron Pierce is one of the best coaches in snowboarding, and with his gray eyes, dark hair, and tanned skin, he's most likely the most sought-after bachelor in the world of sports. For years he won the X Games and took home the gold a bunch of times from the Olympics. As far as training is concerned, he is strict and critical, but normally pretty happy with my performance. Not today.

He comes stomping over to me through the snow as I'm getting out of my bindings following that miserable ride. "How hungover are you, man? That was your worst performance in weeks! You want to show up at the X Games with that crap and disgrace yourself in front of the whole world?"

I can feel the sweat running down my neck and disappearing in the collar of my ski jacket. Frustrated, I shove my goggles over my helmet and pull my board after me. It's one of the most expensive boards on the market, sponsored by Rockstar Energy, and yet I don't give a shit if I bang it up. "Sorry. Heavy party yesterday."

That's a lie. I hardly know a thing about the party because

Paisley was there. It's got a lot more to do with her going back to Wyatt's frigging comment this morning. I could still kick his ass for that one. But, sadly, I know him too well. If he hadn't been so fucked up, he never would have mentioned it.

Cameron snorts and digs his snow boot into the ground, which means he's really pissed. "*Heavy party? Knox*, goddamn it, do you take your success seriously at all?"

Truthfully? No. Success interests my dad, not me. If it were up to me, I'd throw away all this fame to study psychology and only ride this board here when I wanted to. But, at this point, it hasn't been up to me for a long time. This here is Dad's dream. And after Mom died, it's the only dream he still has.

I sigh, stick my board into the snow, and squint against the sun in order to be able to look into Cameron's face. "Sorry, Cam. You know what I can do. This won't happen again."

He shakes his head. "I don't care how many parties you throw or how drunk you get, Knox. What I am interested in is what you do on your board. And what you just did was a goddamn catastrophe. That's enough for today. Just make sure you bring what I'm used to seeing from you tomorrow."

"Got it."

Cam puffs up his cheeks, shakes his head again, then lets the air back out. "I know what kind of day today is, Knox. You haven't lost anything yet. Go and let the pain happen. You're strong. You know who you are." He smiles. "Sometimes these kinds of days even allow you to forget things a bit."

My breath is shaky. There's a lump in my throat that's growing bigger and making it tough to breathe. I hadn't realized Cam knew what today meant.

I nod. "Thanks."

Cameron puts his hand on my shoulder and pulls me into a brief but strong embrace before turning around and walking off the slope. For a while, I stand there motionless, breathing the cold air into my lungs, the smell of the snow. I look toward the sun rising over the tallest range and close my eyes. The warm rays grace my cheeks, give me a feeling of security and comfort. Only when they've melted the lump in my throat do I turn and make my way to the gondolas. The whole way there I feel fuzzy, can hardly get my thoughts together, I keep seeing alternating images of my mother and Paisley. I try to shake them off a few times, but it doesn't work.

Paisley is so similar to my mother. Her fiery personality, the blond hair and blue eyes, the iron will, and, above all, ambition as far as skating is concerned. I hate the fact that I associate her with Mom, because that makes me think about her constantly, and that hurts, goddamn it. A stinging sensation right in my heart, one that leaves me with a fierce craving.

The gondola jerks to a stop and the doors open. Lost in my thoughts, I get out and walk a bit. I am so caught up inside myself that I don't even notice Harper coming toward me. I only become aware of her when she's right in front of me, placing her hands on my hips and snuggling into me.

Her showing up doesn't exactly make me feel any better. The opposite, in fact. Every time I remember that I opened myself up to a figure skater—even if just for one night—I hear her again. The screams.

I try to get loose and take a step back, but Harper is holding on tight. Only once I pry her hands off my hips do I succeed in freeing myself from her climbing-plant-like grip.

"Hey." Harper is beaming, she tucks her red hair behind an ear and bats her fake eyelashes so showily, I'm afraid they'll fall off. "Nice to see you. I…umm…called you."

"Yeeeah…" In fact, she didn't just call me; she subjected me to a total onslaught of calls. I know I should have told her that what happened between us was a one-time thing. No big deal. But to be honest, I was hoping she'd understand when I didn't respond.

I put on an apologetic smile and scratch my neck. "Harper…

between the two of us... I'm sorry. Really. But it's not going to turn into anything."

Ouch. I can see how badly my words have stung her. Her face looks like I've slapped her. "You used me," she says. I can tell how hard it is for her to put on a cool tone in order to look like she's got herself under control. "For sex."

"No, look..." I pause because, essentially, she's right. Even if I don't want to see myself as that kind of guy, I have to admit that that's exactly what I did. And it wasn't even important to me. I could have done without the sex. But I was bombed, and she was there, and then... Well, one thing led to another. In the meantime, I don't even know how the night played out. I only know that we got together, but how it was? No idea. My God, I'm a real shit.

"Yeah. I did. I'm sorry, Harper."

The skin around her eyes turns red. It's clear that she's trying really hard to make sure I don't see her cry. She turns away for a moment and looks in the other direction, most likely to get herself together before looking at me again. She swallows. "And I thought I saw something in you. I really thought you were more than what women say about you. Clearly, I was wrong. But let me make one thing clear, Knox." She takes a step forward. Her voice has grown dark. "I'm going to go now. You for me are history. But not because you won and because you hurt me. No. Because your stupid ass isn't worth a single second more of my time."

In one last graceful gesture, she raises her chin, turns, and stomps off. I watch her go. It's not true, I *do* care about her feelings. We used to be a little crew. Aria, Wyatt, Gwen, Harper, and I. We spent half our lives together before all that shit between Aria and Wyatt went down. I know that Harper's got power. Somewhere beneath her hard shell, there's a soft core. But unfortunately, I am just as sure that I'm not the man who's supposed to discover it. The one it's meant for. Maybe she wanted me to be but... Shit, I'm an asshole. Totally broken. I can't even be in the presence of an ice-skater without getting this claustrophobic feeling that's ready to take me off to where everything's dark. Where the screams are the loudest. Where naked fear overcomes me, makes my hair stand on end, and makes me feel like I'm a little kid again. Helpless and panicky in a moment of my life that broke me.

My feet are moving without me being aware of where they're taking me. I put my board, helmet, and sunglasses into the trunk of my car, then I walk off downtown. My limbs feel numb as I shuffle through the snowy streets and come to a cast-iron door. Two stone ravens flank the fence, their watchful eyes trained on the horizon. My heart is beating into my throat as I put a hand on the ornate handle and step into the cemetery.

Every time I feel the frozen ground beneath my feet here, I get the feeling that countless lost souls are drifting around me and whispering in my ear that I shouldn't be here, that I don't belong here. I've never liked cemeteries. They freak me out. Still, I walk on, step by step, making my way through the snowy lanes where one headstone follows another. In the distance an owl cries.

Suddenly I stop. Cold air fills my lungs as I gasp for breath. Even after so many years, it's really hard for me to come here. It's painful. Every time it's like my heart is being torn into tiny pieces, pieces I'll never be able to reassemble.

My sight is blurry with tears as I go onto my knees and stretch out my hand to wipe the dancing snow off the gravestone. It's hard to swallow when my mother's name becomes visible. Eliza Winterbottom. I pause a second at the *z*, whose lower line has become slightly faded. "I miss you, Mom." My voice is trembling. I'm ashamed I didn't even bring flowers. "I miss you so much."

Nothing but silence. I'd love an answer. An answer I know will never come. I slowly sink onto the ground. "She's like you, Mom," I whisper. "She's like you, and that makes me nuts. Every time I expect to feel bad in her presence, that…that I'll hear the screams, but…I never do. I want to stay away from her but it's so hard." I gasp for breath. Tears are running down my cheeks. I wipe my gloves across my face and shake my head. Snow trickles from my hair. For a long time, I'm quiet, my eyes trained on my mother's name.

"Already another year. December sixteenth. Ten years today," I mumble at some point, so quietly that I can hardly understand myself. "Another year, and I still feel guilty. I'm so sorry, Mom. I am so sorry that you had to die because of me."

18
Can't Get You Out My Mind

Knox

ALL THE WAY THROUGH THE CEMETERY, I FELT LIKE I'D taken leave of myself. I feel lonely and abandoned in this town, the town I loved so much until it decided to welcome death.

My hands buried into my coat pockets, I leave the cemetery behind and take the street to the right, heading downtown. One of William's carriages is coming toward me, on the horse one of the girls that helps him out at the stables. Smiling, she lifts a hand to me in greeting as she zips past with tourists in the back.

At the bell tower I stop. Spirit Susan, Aspen's spiritually touched dance teacher, is in a penguin outfit, just like the group of kids behind her. Seeing me, she shoots a smile and nods in the direction of Vaughn, our local street musician. He nods, strums his guitar, and begins to sing "Little Drummer Boy." I join the group of glittering-eyed onlookers who have gathered to watch the show. Spirit Susan is a talented dancer, her movements are elegant, like liquid silk, weightless, while the kids give it their best. Vaughn gives the first *pa rum pum pum pum pum*, the kids turn their heads in time, right, left, right, left, while a little boy with a long open beak framing his entire face gets caught on the tips of the penguin queen's tiara. Attempting to bat off his beak with her underarm, he starts crying and the whole formation falls apart. Only Spirit Susan is in her element, her lids heavy, the movements full of passion, as if this little square was her Broadway. It's all so absurd, I can't help laughing until someone elbows me in the ribs. I look to my side and see our old Patricia—the baker from the little pastry shop. Her watery blue eyes tunnel into mine, then she nods her wrinkly chin to the right. Following her eyes I discover Wyatt's sister Camila. She's standing at the edge of the square, arms wrapped around herself, watching the show.

"It's a shame she doesn't dance anymore," Patricia says. "She was so good."

"Yeah," I answer, without taking my eyes off Camila. "She was."

A few of Patricia's thin hairs fall onto her forehead, as she shakes her head sighing. "It's just terrible what all the Lopez kids have been going through ever since their mother Inès left us." Her sunken lips form a thin line. "You as well." She casts me a brief sidelong glance. "Cut the crap, Knox. Don't give up. Life is too precious."

Once again I feel a weight on my chest. I absentmindedly run my hand across it, as if I could make it disappear. I look from Camila to Spirit Susan and her penguins, who have brought themselves back under control and are now dancing in time.

"Maybe it will get easier at some point," I say quietly.

Patricia nods. "It will, my son." She reaches out a delicate, papery hand and caresses my head. She used to do that when I was younger, and for some reason the gesture gets rid of the pressure and makes me feel warm. "It will when you let it."

Dad is sitting at the table when I get home. He's digging through a pile of papers and only looks up when I enter. His eyes are red. For him in particular this is a tough day.

His forehead is deeply lined. "I didn't hear your car at all."

"It's still at the foot of Aspen Highlands. I was in the mood to walk."

My father's eyes rest on me for a moment too long. "I understand." I point to his papers. "Can I help with anything?"

He sighs, gathers the papers together, and puts them into a single pile. "No, it's fine. But you could do something else for me."

"Sure. What's up?"

"It's about Paisley."

My stomach goes into knots. I was just getting out of my snow gear when I stop. "What's going on with her?"

Dad's glance darts to the left, and I know that he's not looking at our fireplace but is beyond the wall with the tourists. "You know how important the event is tomorrow night. Your most important sponsors are going to be here, Knox, and I want everything to go off perfectly."

I slip out of my snowboard pants real slowly and hang my jacket up. Melted snow drips onto the ground. "And what's that got to do with me?"

"Paisley's new here," he says, putting his elbows onto the table and tenting his fingers. His smartwatch lights up with a message. He ignores it. "I realize that I cannot expect her to understand the rules of the upper class from one moment to the next. But you can help her, at least with the basics. Show her the different kinds of champagne we have, how to pour them properly, and what all she needs to pay attention to during dinner. Oh, and take her to a boutique. She needs a dress." His mouth twists in sympathy. "I noticed that she showed up with a single jute bag. The poor girl."

With a jute bag? Jesus. What the fuck happened to her?

"Dad," I answer slowly. "I don't know if I'm the right guy…"

At that very moment the front door opens, and Paisley comes walking in. Her hair looks disheveled, and there's a big brown spot on her shirt. It looks like a baby puked on her or something. Her annoyed expression confirms my suspicion.

"Paisley, good to see you. Are you finished upstairs?"

She nods. With a tired smile she nods at the spot on her shirt. "My nerves are too."

Dad laughs. "I bet. You're doing a great job. We're really happy to have you with us. That's why Knox just said he'd be happy to take you under his wing tomorrow. He'll help you out with a few things, and you all can go look for a nice dress for you. Okay?"

"Ummm…" Paisley looks over to me. Her eyes grow wide and the displeasure in them mirrors exactly what I'm feeling.

"Great." Dad gives her a big smile, looks at his smartwatch, and pulls his phone out of his pocket to send a message. Without looking up, he walks past us, gives me a pat on the back, and then takes a call. He casts me one more glance over his shoulder. "Thanks, son. Don't wait for me to eat. I'm going to be late tonight; I've still got a number of things to do." With that, he disappears through the door.

Paisley and I look at each other, but neither of us says a word.

Eventually, I let out a sigh. "Give me ten minutes. I've got to shower." My eyes fly to the spot on her chest. "You should, too."

Paisley makes a face like she would rather be spit on by a hundred newborns than spend any time with me. But she knows that she doesn't have a choice if she doesn't want to lose her job. And I know that I don't have any choice because, damn it, I simply cannot tear myself away from this girl.

19

Beauty in the Broken

PAISLEY

MY BODY GETS CARRIED AWAY BY TWO EMOTIONS: TINGLING joy and a heart racing with uncertainty. I shower longer than necessary and take even more time drying my hair. But the more time I take, the more nervous I get. So I put the hair dryer to the side, shake out my hair, and take a deep breath before going back to the living room.

Knox is lying on the couch playing with his phone. Hearing my steps, he looks up. "Weird."

"What's weird?"

"I was *positive* you'd been swallowed up by the drain."

"Ha, ha," I say, sitting down at the other end of the couch and digging my toes beneath a cushion. "Do we wanna get started?"

"Yeah. I just need your help for a sec." Knox sits up and hops over to me. He gives me his phone. "How does he do these polls?"

He's referring to the snowboarder Jason Hawk, his face and wide smile staring back at me from the whole flood of images of his Instagram posts.

"He's terrible," I say.

"Right?" Knox scrolls through the photos before stopping on a particularly terrible one showing Jason with a trophy and flashing that smile. I can see his molars. "His mouth is huge. Like Cheshire Cat in *Alice in Wonderland*."

I nod. "What kind of poll are you talking about?"

"Wait." Knox clicks on Jason's profile image and his story covers the phone. In the background, I see him midjump, in the foreground the poll button. The question: Who thinks I'm going to stomp @knox-winterbottom into the ground at the X Games?

Possible replies: Me and You know it!

"Oh, wow. What an ass face."

Knox grunts. "I don't really give a shit. But my dad just called and naturally is of the opinion that we can't let something like this stand. Now I have to write something, and I have no idea how it works."

"Seriously? You're a star snowboarder, you've got…" I hit the back button and look at his own profile, "seven hundred thousand followers, and you don't know how to do a poll?"

He pouts. "Help me."

I laugh. "Okay. Take a photo from your own gallery or just take a new one. Wait a sec." Our faces appear on the display as I switch camera positions. I change the angle so that only half of my face is visible next to his and scowl. The moment I push the button, Knox looks at me and laughs. It's…a cute photo. Even if I hardly recognize myself. "Right, and now…"

"Wait." Knox reaches for my hand before I cover the photo with a sticker. My heart plummets three floors down. He clears his throat, takes his phone, and turns it away from me. Then he gives it back.

"What did you do?"

He ignores my question. "So, how does this poll thing work?"

"Here, look. You see? These are stickers. You click on them and find one you like."

"Okay, cool." Once again he takes his phone back, clicks on the poll, and types: Who takes their big mouth too far? Answers: Jason Hawk and The Cheshire Cat.

Men.

We spend the trip downtown in silence, an embarrassing one that I try to break here and there with questions about tomorrow night's event. It turns out that there are going to be a few of his sponsors, so, all in all, some fairly big fish. Knox asks me whether I know what I would like to serve already. When I reply that, in fact, I have no idea, he recommends a pot roast. "Those guys love that stuff. Especially Big Po."

"Big Po?" Whenever I think of sponsors, I get the image of serious men in serious suits. Big Po sounds more like some big highschool football player. "Do I really need a dress when the guests have names like Big Po?"

Knox laughs. "That's not really his name."

Nooo, really?

"His real name is Dr. Edward Hansing."

"Which would naturally lead one to think Big Po, I mean, of course."

"He's an insider." He stops on a side street by the bell tower. William is right in the middle of having a lively discussion with a street musician. "*Po* stands for *potato*, actually."

"Do I need to know what Dr. Edward Hansing and potatoes have in common?"

Knox grins. "I don't think so."

We get out, and Knox moves around his car to me. In the glow of the iron streetlamps, I see the snow whirl around him, a single flake landing on his cheek. He wipes it away and smiles. I catch myself wanting to reach out and caress his dimples. The thought frightens me.

"We've got to motor a bit," Knox says with a glance at the big clock on the bell tower. "The shops are closing."

"But that's just *nuts*, William," we hear the musician saying as we walk past. "You can't mean that at all seriously."

"It's in the municipal code," William responds severely. "It has been in the municipal code for years, and for years street musicians have respected it."

"But I am the *only* street musician in Aspen."

William shakes his head in exasperation. Then he notices us. "Knox, how nice. Could you please tell Vaughn that he needs to respect the municipal code?"

"What's up?"

A deep sigh breaks from the musician as he leans against his guitar case with his underarm. "I was singing Christmas songs. William, however, is of the view that that is only allowed from the twentieth of December onward. Any sooner," he made quotation marks in the air, "*and the municipal code forbids it*."

"Oh, Will," Knox says. "Really? Right now?"

William seems enraged. "The ordinance…"

"It's not even official." Knox rubs his temples and shuts his eyes. "We've been having this conversation forever. It is simply a piece of writing that you've drawn up."

"And the inhabitants of this town are thankful to me for it!"

I doubt that. And the way Knox smiles at William's words leads me to believe I'm right. He looks at the street musician apologetically. "Keep on playing your Christmas tunes, Vaughn. It's the middle of December. It's totally fine."

William looks like he's about to explode. It takes all I've got to keep a neutral expression. The way this little thing has totally unnerved him is just too funny.

He points at Knox then at Vaughn. "We're going to have a word about this at the next city council meeting."

Knox rolls his eyes. "Whatever, Will."

We move on, and for the second time since arriving in Aspen, I am introduced to the exquisite side of this little town.

"This is where, above all, the tourists go shopping," Knox says.

I look at the elegant clothing in the shop windows and am amazed as one designer outfit after another catches my eye. "There's no way we can buy anything here," I say. "It's all far too expensive!"

He shrugs and waves me to follow him across the street. "Look at it as your work uniform."

I follow him to a store with *Valentino* written above the entrance. "Sure. My work uniform for over a thousand dollars?"

"Will it make you feel any better to know that Dad can take it off his taxes?"

"A little."

"Good. Then let's go."

We step inside and it's like I'm no longer in Aspen. Everything looks so different! No rustic wooden floor, no fire going in a fireplace. It's as if the town had two sides. And I have to admit that I prefer the magical winter wonderland with its cute little cafés, comfortable restaurants, and small decorated streets where everyone knows each other.

Seeing as we don't have much time left, I need to find a dress here, but I have my doubts after trying on the first one. The saleswoman has me try on various cuts and colors she thinks match my eyes, but I'm not enthused about any of them. Not because they aren't nice, but because they simply aren't me. The version of me in one of these expensive things…just isn't me.

I come out of the fitting room with two more dresses, shaking my head. The saleswoman purses her lips but doesn't say anything when taking them back and hurrying off.

With a sigh, Knox gets up from the velvet-covered stool. "It's just for one evening, okay? Afterward, you can burn the thing for all I care."

"I know. It's just…" I lean my head against the fitting room wall. "No idea. It's just weird."

"I get it." His voice sounds sincere. I think he truly understands me. "But give it a shot, can you? You can pretend it's not real. A role play, just for one evening."

I smile faintly. "Well, okay."

The saleswoman returns. A strand of hair has come loose from her ponytail. She looks hopeless as she holds up another dress. "This is the last one in your size."

With a thankful smile I take it and disappear into the fitting room. It's a black dress that goes to just above my knees, the fabric is decorated with pearls and sequined fringes. I like the V cut, it shows off my collarbone, and, interestingly enough, that's the part of me I like the most. Through the chiffon shift, my body will be covered at all the right places and, I've got to admit, I like the dress. With a somewhat unsure smile, I come back out.

Knox looks up from his paper. I can see him swallow. His glance wanders from my face across my body, and his lips part for a fraction of a second before he catches himself. "Okay," he says slowly, rubbing his thighs. "I was just about to say something, but, ummm, sorry... You look *so beautiful* that I forgot."

My smile grows wider. "I'll take it."

For a while we walk through the streets of Aspen in silence. I am happy that Knox is carrying the black Valentino bag that has my new dress. Somehow, I would have felt uncomfortable with it, and I think Knox knows it.

Having left the area of the expensive shops behind us, next to Abercrombie & Fitch I see two women pointing at us and squeaking. Or rather, at Knox. I elbow him in the side to draw his attention to his fans but by then they're already falling all over him. They keep on grabbing him everywhere, all the while repeating how he looks even better *"in real life."*

"I saw you at the show," one young woman wearing a red parka and a pink scarf announces.

Her friend wearing teal blue from head to toe agrees enthusiastically. "You were fantastic. And your attitude... really sexy."

His *attitude*? That makes me laugh—I've seen so much more of his attitude than these women ever will.

I cast Knox a sidelong glance. His smile looks tense, but I don't think the women notice.

Then I get an idea. "We should get going, Knox," I say. "You know, Jason's party…"

"Jason *Hawk?*" the woman in red and pink squeals while from her friend comes an awestruck "Oh, my God."

Knox shoots me a genuine *you serious?* look. I smile and shrug.

"We didn't want to bother you," one of them says. "It's just that seeing you was really rad. Wow."

They both look starstruck as Knox says a polite but firm goodbye, and I am relieved once we're finally past them.

Knox exhales. "As if I would ever go to one of that idiot's parties. You're incredible, Paisley."

"I know."

His phone buzzes. He looks at the display and rolls his eyes before taking the call. "What's up? Ah ha. Yeah, beforehand." He pauses a moment, then, "No! Which magazine? Fine, Jennet, then tell the *Mirror* they won't get any statement." Knox presses his lips together. "I don't care that there's room for speculation. You're my spokesperson and you tell them in no uncertain terms that I am not going to make any statement about that. Yeah, right. Yeah. See you."

"Everything okay?"

"Yeah. The story earlier, the one with our picture…the press wants to know who you are."

"Oh." I look at him. "Please don't tell them."

His eyes grow wide. "Of course not. My private life has nothing to do with anyone else."

"Isn't it tough, being in the public eye all the time?"

Knox nods. "That's why I often need peace and quiet. Like now."

"Oh," I say again. I sound like an idiot. "Should I leave you alone?"

He shakes his head. "You've misunderstood. I mean, being with you right now is…really nice."

I begin to tingle. "Thanks."

Knox nods toward a narrow path leading to Buttermilk Mountain. "Come on. I want to show you something."

He leads me to a barn that is off the beaten track between the town and the mountains. It's dark out here, so Knox turns on the light on his phone as he lifts up the door's heavy iron bar.

"Why isn't it locked?" I ask.

Knox laughs. "No one in Aspen steals horses, Paisley."

The smell of hay and dung fills my nose as we step into the stable. I can't believe my eyes. "That's Sally!" I point at the spotted Irish Cob in the back box before turning to Knox. "Are these the carriage horses?"

He closes the door. Dust whirls up from the floor.

The light from his phone only lights up half of his face, the other remains in shadow. "Yeah. They belong to William."

"I love horses," I whisper. The wood beneath my feet creaks as I walk up to a Haflinger rubbing its head along the beam of its box. I softly run my fingers through its mane. "They are so pure."

I hear a rustling. Turning around, I see that Knox has laid down in the big pile of hay by the door. The Valentino bag next to him just doesn't fit.

"I'm tired," Knox mumbles in a voice that's both sleepy and throaty. I get goose bumps.

"Me too. And cold."

In the light of his phone I can see his eyelids growing heavy. He pats his hand at a place in the hay next to him. "Then come on over here. The hay's warm."

I hesitate. "You still have to show me all the different kinds of champagne and how to pour them properly."

"We'll do it tomorrow. Come here."

I continue to hesitate, but now I don't have any more excuses. I slowly make my way over to the pile of hay, as though it were a ticking time bomb.

Knox grins. "I don't bite. If you want, I can separate our two piles."

"It's fine." The hay rustles when I lie down next to him. It's warmer here.

"Wow," he mutters. "Now you look like Baymax playing a tin soldier."

I turn my head. "What?"

"Nothing."

I don't know how long we lie there, but at some point Knox's breathing becomes heavier. For a while, I listen to him and the breath of the horses until my eyes can no longer stay open either.

My last thought before falling asleep is that I haven't felt as comfortable as I do now in weeks.

20
Forever Be My Almost

PAISLEY

I AM WOKEN BY THE SCRAPING OF HOOVES. AT FIRST I don't know where I am, but when I realize it, I close my eyes even harder. In a childlike way I convince myself that, if I don't see it, it doesn't exist.

The hay is poking my cheek. Wanting to turn on my side, I am suddenly blocked by a heavy weight by my hip.

Oh, God. This isn't real, is it?

I open one eye, just a sec, real slow, and when I see what I assumed, I shut it again as quick as I can. My heart is beating faster than these horses can gallop. Knox has put his arm around me! I am positive it wasn't intentional. It probably just happened. But what should I do? Push it away? Leave it there? Maybe I can roll on my side before he realizes it and take off.

Before I can decide one way or the other, I hear the heavy iron bar being moved upward and…voices. I hear voices.

For one excruciating second I go through all the various possibilities in my head. Without much success, as the only way we could disappear from this stable with no back door is by disintegrating.

"Knox," I hiss. "Knox, wake up!"

Too late. The door swings open and…a whole throng of people surge inside. At least a dozen, led by William and Ruth.

"Please stay calm," William says to the group. He is standing with his back to us, but the tourists have already discovered Knox and me. They are staring. Some of them open-mouthed. "There is one horse for everyone and…"

He doesn't get any further as he is interrupted by a girl's shrill cry. "Knox Winterbottom!" She reaches out her hand and points at Knox, whose eyes flash open in panic. "Oh, my God, it's him! It's really him!"

"Who's the girl?" someone asks.

"Oh, God. He's got a *girlfriend*?"

"No way," says the first. "People would know about that!"

Ruth and William turn around to look at us. Everyone is staring as if we were exotic zoo animals that they had never been able to look at up close. Not knowing what to do, I dig my fingers into the hay. Knox's arm is still around my hip. I wish he'd pull it away, but apparently he's fallen into a kind of shock. His normally tanned face is as white as chalk.

And then it happens. Several women pull out their phones at the same time and turn them toward us. They are taking photos of us and, suddenly, I can't breathe. This is a nightmare.

Finally, Knox comes to. He pulls his arm away, jumps up, and stands in front of me. "Stop that shit! Put your phones away. We're not animals, damn it!"

Ruth seems completely confused. She looks from me to him to the tourists before jumping to Knox's side, waving her hands, and calling out "Enough!" In the meantime, from William all anyone can hear is, "You're frightening the horses, the horses!"

But the tourists are not to be stopped. They're going crazy. I don't know what shocks me more: the insane situation or their absolutely insane behavior.

Ruth tries to calm the women down, but as the first few begin to fall over Knox, grabbing him wherever they can as if having to check that he was real, it becomes clear that we have to get out of here. Right away. *God, they're nuts!*

I struggle up out of the hay and grab the Valentino bag just as Knox manages to free himself from their tentacles. We run for the door. It's only when we're just about outside that I realize the women want to run after us, but Ruth and William block the way. I've got to thank them later on.

Knox and I run the snowy path back into town. As I'm considering whether to call a taxi or whether we should try to catch a bus, a black Volvo pulls up and Wyatt sticks out his head. "You want to tell me why you all look like you're on the run?"

I hear Knox let out a sigh of relief. "Thank God." He pulls open the passenger side door and swings inside next to Wyatt. When I don't move, he looks at me. "If you've got stolen diamonds in that bag of yours, you'd better jump in. Unless you want to get caught, that is." He looks over my shoulder and his eyes grow wide. "Oh, man, they're coming! Paisley, get in, quick!"

The panic in his voice sounds so real that I spin around, my heart pounding. But of course there's no one there.

Wyatt breaks into laughter. "Your face! You should have seen your face!"

I glare at him, but hurry into the car. Those women were truly insane. They could show up here at any second and start running after the car; I wouldn't put it past them.

Wyatt is still laughing as he drives off. "Man, are you all lucky that I'm on my way to the game. What did you all do?"

"Nothing." Knox rubs his neck and closes his eyes. "Some fans totally lost it back there in the barn. That was sick, man. I've never experienced anything like that before."

"Oh, shit." Wyatt looks back at me in the rearview mirror. "You okay?"

Wow, that's...nice of him.

"All good. I mean, I don't know…they took photos."

"Photos? For real? Right now?"

Knox looks at him. "Dude, those were red fans. No shit."

"Red fans?" I ask.

Wyatt turns on his signal and leaves town in the direction of Aspen Highlands. "Green fans are sweet. Shy and reserved, hardly get a word out. Yellow fans are a bit pushier, they want autographs and don't let you go. It's harder to get rid of them. But red fans are crazy. For them, you're the best pair of shoes at a going-out-of-business sale."

Knox turns around to look at me. "Don't worry, I'll take care of the photos. The tourists were with Ruth, which means that they're staying at her B&B. Jennet will get in touch with them."

"Your spokesperson?"

He nods.

I pray to all the gods I can think of that Jennet can take care of everything. If the fact that I'm in Aspen goes public… I swallow. That can't happen. Not at all. My career would be over before it even got started.

Wyatt lets us out in front of the resort and drives off. Knox is already on the phone with his spokesperson. "Yeah. Yeah, Jennet, I'm aware of that. My God, you think I did that intentionally? Is my name Jason *fucking* Hawk, or what?" He opens the front door and attempts to take off his boots with his other hand before simply kicking them off. They land next to the sideboard. "I don't care. I fell asleep, that's what. Shit, Jennet. What the *Independent* will pay for the story doesn't interest me. Make sure these photos disappear!" Then he hangs up. He falls onto the couch and runs a hand over his face. I sit down next to him, pull up my legs, and rest my chin on my knees.

Knox's eyes look really tired when he looks at me. I can see little bits of hay in between his hair. "I'm sorry that you have to go through all this."

"It's worse for you," I say quietly. "They *touched* you."

He sighs. "Yeah. They do that often." Seeing my look, he laughs softly. "Not what you're thinking right now."

"You don't know what I'm thinking."

"True." Knox turns to observe me. "But I'd really like to know."

I embrace my legs and bury my fingers between my calves. "Why?"

"You're so different," he says after a moment's hesitation. "I think you're always looking forward, no matter who's running behind you. And I think that you're a real mess, Paisley."

He's moved closer. I just sit there, my eyes wide. My head is telling me to interrupt the crackling tension between us, but I can't.

"If I'm such a mess, why do you want to know what I'm thinking?"

"Because there's a fire in your eyes that's showing me a history. But I think it's one that you will never share."

The light from the chandelier is glowing in his eyes, and he laughs gently. His gaze is deep. As if he would understand a lot of things. As if he would understand *me*. And the way he's looking at me... As if I was something precious, as rare as the beginning of a rainbow. Not Paisley the trailer roach. Not Paisley with the crackhead mom. But Paisley from Aspen. Paisley the ice-skater.

"I think you're hiding," I whisper. "I think somewhere behind your smile there is something that's tearing you apart. People think they know you. But they don't have any idea."

Knox swallows. "That's the beautiful thing, right? No one has any goddamn idea."

"I don't know if that's really a beautiful thing, Knox."

"Well, I know that *you're* beautiful, Paisley."

His words rouse all the nerve endings in my body. I feel electrified, the air around me explosive. It's like a competition; the tense seconds on the ice before the music starts and the program begins. Just that this time, it's scarier cause I don't know what will happen next. There is no carefully curated run-of-events to hold onto. No steps to execute with precision and security.

There is only Knox and me. Knox, who keeps on moving closer. Knox, who smells like hay and vetiver. Knox, who I feel drawn to at this moment like no one else.

But there is something else that comes between us. Real quietly, crawling, ugly. Way too dark for it to be good. It tugs at my memories. Reminds me what happens when you begin to trust. When you begin to fall for the trap of the illusion of safety.

At the beginning, it's always good. But at the end, all that's left is pain.

His face is really close. I notice a small birthmark next to his full lips. The green of his eyes is shot through with even brighter, glowing spots. I observe every centimeter of his face, I can hardly pull away. I want this moment. I want it so bad.

Knox is waiting, he's giving me time. He's leaving it up to me. And it would be so easy to choose him right now. Just the slightest tilt of my head, a tiny movement, and our lips would touch.

But I can't. Fear wins out.

"The champagne," I whisper. "You wanted to show me the champagne."

Two blinks pass before the moment is over. Slowly Knox leans back. He rubs his neck again and briefly looks over my shoulder through the window. The bright snow is reflected in his eyes.

Then he nods. "True."

Never has the word sounded so false.

21
I'd Be Yours, If You Asked

KNOX

IN THIRD GRADE I HAD A CRUSH ON THIS GIRL, OPHELIA, and she was a grade ahead of me. Ophelia was *the* it girl in line at the cafeteria. The boys acted like idiots around her, like eight-year-old boys do when they're head over heels. And I was one of them. And so to show Ophelia how much I liked her, during break, I kicked the football against her head. Clever plan. I thought I was the shit. Absolutely on fire. Ophelia didn't think it was so cool. She fell into the mud with her white dress and had to get picked up by her mother. She didn't show back up at school for the next two weeks—it turns out that my declaration of love caused her to have a slight concussion.

I can remember the tightness I felt in my chest when Ophelia came back and looked at me like I was the plague incarnate. I didn't feel well. Something in me felt strange, and I could feel an odd pressure in my chest. I thought I was sick. So I went to my mom and told her what was going on. She laughed. I can still hear how clear her laughter was. "Knox," she said. "You're not sick. You're in love."

That was horrible. I didn't want that, so I started to howl.

My dad had a logical explanation. "Bronchitis. That's what bronchitis feels like."

Yep. Crystal clear. I hung around in bed for a week, played with my Game Boy, and now and again produced some made-up coughs I convinced myself were real while ignoring my mom's knowing grin whenever she came in to bring me tea.

And now it's back, that terrible bronchitis. Following Paisley's rejection, it crept up quietly to claw its way into my chest and expand. It's getting worse from minute to minute and I'm getting more and more pissed off. Above all, because I let Paisley borrow my car to go buy groceries. Why? I never—and I mean *never*—let anyone borrow my Range Rover! And now I'm sitting here on a stone-hard seat on my way to Breckenridge and freezing my ass off while, instead of warm air, some undefinable stink is being blown through the bus. I have no idea the last time I took the bus. I really cannot remember, but the pain I feel in my tailbone as we take a detour through the bumpy mountains makes it abundantly clear that I haven't missed a thing.

The bus stops in front of the Highline Railroad Park in Breckenridge. The doors slide open, and two kids with their grandparents and a heavy man who took up two seats and spent the whole ride breathing heavily in a whistle get off before I do.

The ice arena is just a few minutes away from the park. Back when I still played hockey, Wyatt and I were here a lot. After that, however, I totally ignored it. I should have come to see him play more often; today I was overcome with a guilty conscience. Wyatt is always there when I need him. He comes to every one of my competitions, he's at every show. At this point, his game is over thanks to how slow the bus is and that frustrates me.

I stuff my hands into my pockets and dig my face into my scarf in order to protect it from the cold. The wind blows the fresh powder toward me, a few delicate flakes find their way into my eyes. I blink them away before opening the door.

The entrance area is overflowing with people talking. Probably about the game, which has to have been over for at least thirty minutes. I automatically sink my head while making my way through the crowd and heading for the players area. It can only be opened from inside, so I send Wyatt a message.

Not even a minute later the door swings open and my man is standing there in in jogging pants and a T-shirt holding a beer. His hair is still wet from the shower. He smells of that *Alaska* deodorant of his. "I would be happy to see you here if I wasn't seriously worried."

"Why?" I slip past him into the players area where it's not exactly any calmer and hang up my coat and scarf. A woman with dark hair and long—I mean, really *really* long—legs catches my eyes and winks. I'd like to keep eye contact and shoot her my famous smile that, without saying a word, gives away just what it is I'd like to do with her right now.

But Wyatt interrupts by placing a beer in my hand and letting a relaxed burp drift into my face. "Because the last time you were at one of my games was to tell me that Aria had taken off."

His words sidetrack me from looking past him to the darkhaired beauty. Instead, I raise my eyebrows in surprise. Normally, Wyatt doesn't speak about Aria at all. He doesn't mention her. Ever.

"Boredom," I reply, and shrug with a look of feigned indifference while taking a sip of my beer.

"Ah." His tone tells me that he doesn't believe me. He leans against the bar table in front of us and lets his eyes wander over the crowd, before adding in a seemingly indifferent tone, "What's Paisley up to?"

"How should I know?"

"Man, chill." Wyatt grins. "Whatever your problem is, you'd better deal with it. This weird Knox is really fucking stressful."

I grit my teeth. "When are you getting out of here?"

Wyatt puts his bottle to his lips and takes a long drink. Then he wipes his mouth with the back of his hand and shrugs. "No idea. Later on there's a party at a dude from the other team's house. Maybe I'll let myself get hammered and forget how shitty life can be sometimes."

"And you're telling me *I'm* the one who needs to deal with his problems?" As Wyatt just looks at me grimly in response, I add, "You can't go."

My boy gives a grunting laugh. "Right, totally forgot that you're my custodian. Next time, I'll submit a request."

I roll my eyes. "You've got to give me a ride back to Aspen."

Wyatt, who was just about to put his bottle back to his lips, stops and frowns. "Why?"

I avoid his glance and look instead back at the woman who looks over at me immediately. I run a hand through my hair and grin. "I came on the bus."

Wyatt stares at me. Apparently, he's at a loss for words, as it takes a long time before he has anything to say. "You came here on the bus?" he repeats, his voice full of disbelief.

"Yeah."

"Why?"

The woman pushes back her hair and turns her back to me so slowly that I can see her ass move in her skintight jeans. My crotch begins to throb. I like the feeling, it distracts me from this damn "bronchitis."

"Paisley's got my car."

Wyatt chokes on his beer. He coughs and tries to catch his breath. Once he's gotten it back, he says, "*She's got your Range Rover?*"

"Did you catch a puck to the head or something? Why are you repeating everything I say?"

He ignores my comment. "Did you let her?"

"No, she stole it. Of course I lent it to her."

For a while Wyatt just stares at me. Then he says, "Shit, Knox. Now I know what's wrong with you. You like this new chalet girl."

"Shut it."

Wyatt laughs in disbelief and shakes his head. "Your ride. Incredible."

"Are you going to give me a lift later or not?"

"Of course."

"Good." I polish off my beer in one go, put the empty bottle on the table, and start to move past Wyatt.

"What are you up to?"

"I'm going to get myself what I need."

I hear Wyatt clicking his tongue as I move toward the brunette beauty. Her full lips break into a wide smile. She shoos off her friend with one hand and leans forward onto the bar table so that her breasts are squeezed upward, giving me an even deeper look into her cleavage.

"You better warn me if I've got to count on your friend joining us any second."

She giggles. "No friend. Just me."

"Not someone's girl?" I lean onto the table toward her. "You got a name?"

"Amanda."

She doesn't ask what my name is. Of course she doesn't. She knows who I am. "Nice, Amanda-without-a-friend. What did a beautiful girl like you lose in here?"

Before answering, she wets her lips. *Fuck*, is she hot. Just what I need. Just what I've been missing. I am positive that if I follow my desires, this insufferable feeling that I feel when Paisley is around will disappear.

"My father dragged me here," she says. "And it's *terribly* boring."

I nod in the direction of the changing rooms. "Shall we change that?"

Her eyes follow mine before she looks back at me. Her sexy glance makes my blood start to boil while transporting it to deeper realms. "I hope you're good."

I give a rough laugh. "You have no idea."

"Then change that." She turns and moves toward the cabins without looking back to see if I'm following. A self-righteous smile steals across my face. This is exactly how it's all supposed to go. Quick and without any obligations. A coming and going. No long-term bronchitis settling into my lungs and weighing me down.

I've hardly stepped inside the cabin when I feel her full lips on mine. And at that moment it starts. The pressure in my chest becomes immeasurable. My heart begins to hammer uncontrollably and wildly; no pleasant throbbing but something that makes my hands tingle and panic start to spread. Images of Paisley appear before my inner eye. Suddenly this all feels wrong. This here—her powerful perfume, her warm breath mixing with my own, her hands working at the buttons of my jeans—all this makes me feel something that I don't like at all. Something inside me wants to defend itself. I have to fight back the feeling of pushing her hands away and simply walking off.

Pull yourself together, Knox. This is what you want. You need this. You've done something like this a hundred times. And you've always enjoyed it.

Amanda pulls away. Her breath becomes shallow as she goes onto her knees in her high heels and my waistband brushes my knees. I lean my head against the wall of the cabin and close my eyes, try to concentrate on the here and now, on the fact that I want this.

But, fuck, it's not working! I can feel her lips closing around that part of my body that just a minute ago wanted this so bad, but now…

…it reacts. But in the opposite way to what I need.

"Are you serious?"

I open my eyes, ball my hand in her long mane and touch myself with the other. "It'll be fine in a second. I just have to… Hold on a sec…"

Amanda stares in disbelief at my penis, which simply doesn't want to stand up. Regardless of how quickly I move my hand up and down while staring at her breasts, it doesn't move an inch.

With a disappointed snort she shakes her head. "And to think you were so cocky about *this*."

This has got to be the biggest humiliation of my life. And naturally, as far as I'm concerned, it's all Paisley's fault. I am so fucking angry at her right now that I might even fire her later. But then there is that other feeling that goes against it. And suddenly I feel as if I don't know myself any longer.

"*Fuck!*" I smash my hand against the locker next to me before leaning my head back against the wall. "Oh, fuck off, will you?"

It's not her fault. Truly. But right now I feel humiliated and dirty, embarrassed and degraded and powerless, powerless in a way I haven't felt in ages.

The resounding slap comes two seconds later. I take it. I deserve it. I press my lips together and try to fight the feeling of being small and defenseless.

Unsuccessfully.

Heels over tile. The door slams. Quiet comes down, takes me in, tries to comfort me, but I don't know if I actually want to be comforted, to be honest, I have no idea what it is I *want at all*. It's as though the quiet wanted to send me a silent whisper, the answer on its lips, word after word, but I can't hear it. I could, but I don't want to. And that's the thing, right? The reason I can't help myself. Why no one can help me. Because I'm not interested. Because on the day, on that fucking day that I learned death was real, that it laughs in your face while it poisons your heart, on that day I felt so *goddamn much* that, afterward, I started not to feel anything at all. And I was okay with that. It was better for me that way.

But ever since Paisley—ever since this girl with the protruding ears and the soft smile, whose dark past I want to kiss away until the sun can shine in her and bring her to shine—I want to feel again. To *live* again.

And that fucking terrifies me because it's been a really long time since I've known how that even goes.

22
Sad Birds Still Sing

Knox

I'm drunk. And off my ass tripping. After that thing with Amanda, nothing mattered, and I went to the party with Wyatt. I must have looked pretty bad because it wasn't too long before some creepy dude with half his face tattooed offered me some Molly. Actually, after Paisley's announcement from the last party, I swore I'd leave this shit alone, but I felt so bad that I just couldn't do anything else. Strangely, I had to think of Trevor, who I was just recently telling how shitty drugs were. I'm a terrible example.

Wyatt hasn't taken anything, but he's been drinking. I hate that he always drives afterward anyway. And I hate that I get in, but, unfortunately, I'm too fucked up to make any long-sighted decisions. Sooner or later, he's going to have an accident. I tell him over and over, but he doesn't seem to care. It's the dumbest thing he could possibly do. And me going along with it is, too. I plan on giving him a lecture as soon as I'm straight, but I doubt it'll have any effect.

It's been hours since the party ended. No idea how many. Five? Eight? In any event, it's dark by the time Wyatt reaches our driveway. There's light inside, and I can see shadows in the living room. The sponsor evening isn't over yet. For a moment, I simply stare at the window and make a face.

Wyatt seems to be reading my thoughts because he erupts into laughter. "Your father's going to murder you."

"Take my head off. Abuse me. Curse me. Ship me off to the military."

My buddy leans his head against the window and runs a hand over his dark stubble with a drunk smile. After a few seconds, his smile collapses and his glance drifts over to the recessed floor lighting in front of the door. The light illuminates the left half of his face, while the right remains dark. "I'm tired, Knox."

"Then sleep."

"No, you don't understand."

"I think I do." I look at him. "My head seems to have this particular talent for finding the darkness and driving myself crazy."

Wyatt stretches his fingers and runs them over the steering wheel absentmindedly. "I can't sleep. I'm afraid of my dreams."

"Yeah," I say quietly. "Me too."

"Do you think it'll ever stop?"

"No idea. Maybe someday. Maybe never. Maybe we'll nosedive, and the nosedive is what we call flying. Who knows."

Wyatt looks at me. "I don't think I want to nosedive."

"I want to fly." My eyes dart to a blackbird that's leaving fresh tracks in the snow. Then it flies off. My eyes follow it until it is nothing but a distant, small point, swallowed up by the dark. "Like a bird."

"Yeah," Wyatt says. "They always sing. Even when they're in pain. Did you know that? Even sad birds still sing."

I am quiet for a moment. Then a soft laugh escapes, one that couldn't be more joyless. "Shit, we're messed up."

"Nothing new, right?"

"I'm going in."

"Yeah. And, Knox…" He looks at me. "Stop blaming Paisley for everything. It's not her fault that you're so broken."

"No," I say. "It's not." Then I get out and tramp through the heavy snow toward the front door.

I'm having some trouble with the key. I only manage to get it in the lock on the third try. The ecstasy is slowly wearing off, but the keyhole still seems to be moving back and forth a bit.

Stepping inside, I am greeted by the sound of silverware. Then all of a sudden it stops.

"Sorry," I mumble without looking up, while trying to undo the laces of my boots. Attempting to step out of them, I stumble a few steps forward. I almost fall over but manage to save myself at the last minute with the sideboard. Unfortunately, this causes the vase Aunt Harriet gave us last Christmas to hit the ground. "Oops," I say slowly and heavily. Somehow everything is dippy. My finger lands on a shard, which I start to observe with interest. It's just white, but suddenly it seems like it's some kind of museum piece or other. I push it back and forth, back and forth. I like the sound. It's scratchy and makes me giggle.

"Knox." My father clears his throat. "Get up."

I stand up, but somehow it doesn't feel right. My body is telling me that it wants to lie on the ground, stare at the ceiling, and look at the lights of the chandelier morph into various shapes.

Fuck. I'm not just drunk, I am absolutely off my ass. I push the shards to the side with my foot, when a hand touches my arm. Small, delicate, and totally different from mine. I like it more than the glass shard.

"Stop," I hear a soft voice say next to my ear. "You're just cutting yourself. I'll do it."

I blink, but all I recognize is a blond mop of hair. "Paisley?"

She tilts her head to the side and smiles, while sweeping the rest of the vase into the dustpan. I don't think I've ever seen a nicer smile.

"Maybe you should come into the kitchen with me for a sec to collect yourself?"

All I hear is 'come into the kitchen with me,' and think it's a fantastic idea. With narrowed eyes, I glance over at the table to locate my father. But everything still looks fuzzy and, what with all the people in white shirts, I quickly start to feel overwhelmed. So I turn and follow Paisley into the kitchen. Low voices drift over to us from the table, but I can't understand what they're saying thanks to the wall that's halfway dividing us.

Paisley tips the rest of the vase into the trash can. Then she slides me a plate of roast, potatoes, and a wonderfully smelling sauce, along with a glass of water, over the island. "Here. This should help you get your head together a bit."

I take the plate and wolf the food down in not exactly the most elegant way. "Oh, my God. This is nuts." One potato just will not fit into my mouth and falls back onto the plate.

Paisley is looking at my food orgy with a half-amused, half-pissed off air. "Would you like to tell me why you showed up way too late and way too drunk?"

"Naw."

Paisley begins preparing to take the roast away.

"Don't even think about it!" I turn to the side and laugh, which I probably shouldn't have, as all I succeed in doing is spitting a kind of brown rain.

"Ugh." Her nose twitches and she makes a face. "You're a pig."

I swallow noisily and take a big swig of water. "How bad was it?"

"Well, it looked like you were spewing diarrhea out of your…"

"Not that!" I'm getting dizzy and I have to hold onto the island until I can stand up completely straight again. "With the sponsors, I mean."

"Oh. Pretty good actually. Things were a bit tense because, well…they're here for you. And you weren't here. Kind of like being at a birthday party and the birthday boy doesn't show."

"Yeaaaah." I consider what I should say, but, truthfully, I have no interest in talking about sponsors at all. Paisley takes the carafe and fills my glass back up. I notice fine white lines on her hand. I narrow my eyes into slits because, at first, I think they must be the result of my alcohol-soaked imagination. But as my sight becomes sharper, they don't disappear. I impulsively reach out and grab her hand before she can pull away.

She seems surprised. "Knox, what…"

"Your hand." I turn it over, and back, and over and back, to confirm that I am really seeing what I am seeing and not suffering from hallucinations. "It's full of scars."

Only now does she seem to grasp what I mean, and attempts to pull away but I don't let her. Somehow I've got the feeling that, if I hold onto her, I can heal her. "What happened?"

Paisley looks at me for a moment with an expression that is impossible to define before saying, "Sometimes there are people who act like monsters. And sometimes there are monsters that act like people." She gives me a sad smile, then gently pulls her hand away. "The man who did this to me was pretty good at both." She meets my stunned glance and shrugs. "You'll forget by tomorrow anyway…"

"Definitely not." Sadly, at that very moment my words seem a bit less than believable, as I lose my balance for a split second, but I really mean it. To make that clear to her, I push my plate to the side, put my hands on her shoulders and turn her toward me. "Paisley. At this very moment, I would kill that person, is that clear?"

Her smile is weak. "Don't say such things."

"But I am *raging*."

"Me too. But it doesn't help anything. Come on, your guests are waiting."

"I don't give a shit about my guests."

"But I do." With a concentrated look, she pours champagne into a flute. "I need this job, you forget already?" She's walking ahead of me and only now do I realize she's wearing heels. They clack across the tiles, and I feel compelled to put out a hand to support her, she seems to be moving forward so unsurely, like a newborn fawn. She is concentrating on her tray. And at that moment, watching how concentrated she is and how she's pushed her tongue between her lips while her little nose is twitching, I am overcome by a prickling feeling. As if the Molly was making a comeback. The drunk numbness in my body is replaced by a warm tickling, and suddenly I feel the crazy desire to rip the tray out of Paisley's hand and press it to myself. To take the flowery smell of her hair into myself and to feel the sequins of her Valentino dress against my skin.

Her glance takes my breath away. She is beautiful in a way that only unassuming girls can be: at first you don't notice them because they are hiding behind their hair or their books or whatever nerdy thing they're up to, but as soon as you get the chance to *really* look at them, it's almost impossible to stop. A wide grin creeps across my face—and disappears as soon as we reach the table. In the blink of an eye, I stop staring at our chalet girl like a psycho. An ice-cold shudder flows through my veins and puts me into a state of shock. Right in front of me, in the middle of the table next to a man with black, gel-spiked hair, is Amanda, the girl from the ice rink. She gives a little cough, and the light breaks across something gold on her left ring finger. She's *married*!

Her look doesn't even begin to reflect my surprise. Of course not. She knew who I was. Everyone knows who I am. And she *knew* that just a few hours later she'd be sitting in this house.

I'm here with my father, I remember her saying. Her father…that must the guy I don't know. Dad had told me that a new potential sponsor would be coming. *A big fish*, he'd said, from Red Bull, and was excited about it for weeks.

What a load of shit.

Her dark eyes drive into me, and I think my bewilderment gives her satisfaction. This woman is a monster. A real monster. Okay, I was an ass to her. A true ass. That wasn't cool. But who's going to beat someone up for not getting it up? How ill is that? As if it wasn't clear enough how humiliating that is for a guy.

"Nice to see you, Knox." My father exaggeratedly pulls out a chair and makes it abundantly clear that I am supposed to sit down and play the perfect son a.k.a. star snowboarder a.k.a. sponsor's darling. "Training, I take it?"

"Umm." I blink at him and can hear the words rattling in his head and know he would prefer to yell in my face that I just need to nod my head and play along. But this is all too overwhelming. How fucked can my karma be that Amanda of all people is sitting at our dining room table and staring at me as if I was the annoying mouse that finally got caught in the trap?

My eyes dart to Paisley, who is standing at the head of the table and nods at me discreetly. So I do the same. "Yeah. That's right. Training was, umm, hardcore. Cameron wanted to try out this new jump, and, yeah. That's the deal." I sound like a fifth grader who snuck off during recess and is now giving their teacher some lame-ass excuse. My slight slur isn't all that helpful either. "Sorry."

Right as I'm about to sit down, a spiky-haired man offers me his hand. His long fingers are as thick as the rest of him. "Joe Dubois. I am so happy to be able to meet you, Knox. I mean, can I call you Knox? Or would you prefer Mr. Winterbottom?"

"Umm." My vocabulary seems to have stopped at this particular word from the moment I walked into the living room. "Knox is great, absolutely." My eyes flit to Amanda as I shake his hand. She is playing around with her spoon in the cream of her dessert, pretending not to notice anything.

"Wonderful." He sits back down and rubs his hands. It pains me to see him beaming at his daughter, hoping to share his joy with her. If he knew what she was up for just a few hours ago, he wouldn't be grinning so dumbly. His long fingers take a raspberry from his parfait, and he points his spoon at me. "You were world-class at the show. A true spectacle."

"Thanks."

My father seems to notice that my conversational skills don't appear to be surpassing the one-word mark; he clears his throat and puts on a smile. It's his artificial business smile, the one looking down from every single real-estate billboard.

"Knox, he's traveled all the way from New York to meet you."

I am trying hard to focus on Amanda's father and to block her out in the process, but she is sitting right next to him, so I don't manage. Above all, because I'm still kind of shitfaced and my head is trying to fuse his suit with her face. "It's really great to meet you, John."

"Joe," my father corrects me. I shoot him a glance and notice that red blotches are creeping up his neck.

"Oh. Sorry. Joe, I mean."

The corners of Paisley's mouth twitch suspiciously, but she hides it skillfully by putting a flute of champagne down in front of Big Po.

"Well, Knox, your track record is really impressive," Joe says. His head is weird. Rectangular somehow. And his chin wobbles with every movement he makes. "When did you switch to snowboarding?"

"Seven years ago," I reply and take the tall parfait glass that Paisley has just brought me from the kitchen. I guess she doesn't think I'm in any danger of giving anyone a shower from my mouth, now that I can somewhat hold a conversation.

Joe Dubois shoves a big spoonful of vanilla ice cream into his mouth. I am waiting for him to get brain freeze and to make a face, but it doesn't happen. Instead, he just keeps on munching away. "A considerable achievement. Your goal is the Olympics, I assume?"

I almost laughed. *My goal?* No, that would probably be sitting on a folding chair in a lecture hall at Colorado Mountain College, listening to an ancient professor talking about differential psychology.

"Exactly," my father jumps in when he notices me taking too long. He seems relaxed and for the most part at ease, but I know—I *know*—that inside he's boiling. "And I think that the Olympic Games in two years are a realistic goal for Knox."

"Yep." The bitter undertone in my voice is impossible to hide.

The Olympic Games…a realistic goal for Knox… I could say that that's all a load of crap, but what my real opinion is isn't worth shit at this table. All that counts is my snowboarding. Okay, that's not totally right. That I'm *good* at snowboarding. Nothing else. "The Olympics." I press my lips together. I am starting to get furious, and every time I get furious, I start to sweat. A nice side effect of the anabolic steroids I'm shooting every day.

Suddenly I feel the desire to stick my finger into the parfait, my drunk brain telling me it'll cool me down. So I do—even two fingers—and lick them off. Then a second time. After the third, I grow cocky and begin to scoop a lot onto my fingers when Paisley's hand appears in front of me and snaps the glass up and away from me. Subtly, with a neutral smile on her face, as if she was just cleaning up some silverware. Her poker face doesn't accomplish much though, because everyone at the table is staring at me as if I wasn't totally right in the head. Even Mr. Spiky Hair. My biggest fan. *Oops.*

The sponsor next to Big Po clears his throat. I don't know him well, but he was one of the first my dad could win over for me. He works for DOPE. I always forget his name. Thomas…Jensen? Jerkins? No idea, but he looks like Yoda, and I celebrate that. "You feeling okay, Knox?"

"Awesome." I reach across the table and take a strawberry from a bowl. "In high spirits."

"Oh, I doubt that *highly.*" Amanda flashes a sugary sweet smile that couldn't be more diabolical. Oh, God, I hate her. I have never actually hated anyone, not even Jason Hawk, but I hate this girl. Her eyes dart to Paisley. She snaps her fingers and points to her empty champagne glass. "Fill me up."

"Don't speak to her that way," I say.

Next to me, my father grinds his teeth and makes it clear that *I should keep my mouth shut,* but, please, I'm Knox Winterbottom. I never keep my mouth shut.

Amanda blinks preciously. "How am I not to speak to her?"

"As if you were better than her. You're not."

Joe Dubois's spoon skewers his parfait and comes to a rest next to his glass a little too powerfully for it to be by mistake. I look over at him and he flares his nostrils. "With all respect, Knox. The girl is your chalet girl. It's *her job* to serve us."

"She's not here to…"

"Knox," Paisley says, while taking Amanda's glass. "Settle down. It's okay."

What I'd really like to do is jump up and yell why, no, it isn't okay, not at all, because she is everything, simply everything, whereas Amanda is arrogant and underhanded and—as it suddenly becomes clear—just like everyone else I've gotten with over the last number of years. The idea of just going on like that now that I know Paisley is…impossible. The thought alone makes my stomach growl. Okay, it might be the booze, too, but I don't think so.

"Yeah, Knox," Big Po hisses in my ear so that only I can hear him. His bald patch has grown considerably bigger since the last time I saw him—exponentially in relation to his belly. All the same, just one more spoonful of parfait, and I'd bet the middle button of his shirt will throw in the towel. "What's wrong with you, man? I love you, buddy, but you're screwing this up right here. And big time."

He only loves me because we're related. Not really, but kind of. Big Po is the cousin of the brother of my uncle by marriage on my mom's side. Or something like that. He works for Rockstar Energy.

"I could give a shit," I mumble and start to tilt back in my chair. "It's all the same to me."

For a second, my father looks like he's about to explode. His poker face slides as he reaches out and pulls the wooden chair back onto the ground with a thud. "Pull. Yourself. Together," he sputters between gritted teeth.

I just can't anymore. The evening is annoying. *Amanda* is annoying. I am considering simply getting up and going to bed when the clacking of heels announce Paisley's return and I decide to stay.

"So," Paisley says and places the champagne in front of Amanda. "Here you are." Her voice sounds sweet. Like sugar. Or honey. Or brown sugar-cinnamon Pop-Tarts.

Brown sugar-cinnamon Pop-Tarts? Oh, man. Now things are taking off. I'm becoming one of those tools who compares people with sweets. For a second I wonder what kind I'd be. Something unspectacular, something that overestimates its effect on others. A cough drop or something.

Amanda doesn't thank her. She sips from her flute and makes such a face that it's impossible for anyone else at the table to miss.

Mr. Spiky Hair turns to his daughter in concern. "Everything okay?"

I roll my eyes. Unfortunately, Joe notices, but I don't care.

"No." She blinks her eyes so forcefully, it's as if she'd drunk the water of canned mushrooms. "I wasn't drinking Dom Perignon, but Ruinart Rosé."

Amanda wouldn't be any kind of candy. She'd be a jar of mustard.

"Oh." Paisley's face turns red. "I'm sorry. Let me take care of that."

Maybe it's because of the booze in my system, maybe it's because of too much testosterone. In any event, I'm about to totally lose my shit when I notice how uncomfortable Paisley is. I am so angry at Amanda that I would gladly pour her Dom Perignon over her far-too-short dress.

"Don't worry about it, Paisley. Stay here." I give Amanda an icy stare. "Drinking Dom Perignon won't kill her."

The atmosphere around the table is horrible. There is a heavy silence, not a trace of cheerfulness. You can see that Joe Dubois is close to losing his cool. Big Po reaches for his linen napkin to wipe sweat off his forehead. Yoda is staring holes into the air and now and again plucks imaginary bits of fuzz off his suit pants. My father is chalk white, and Paisley is uneasily shifting her weight from one leg to the other.

"I'll drink whatever I want," Amanda hisses. "And whatever I want, I get."

I raise an eyebrow. "Apparently not."

She gives a high-pitched laugh. "Oh, sweetheart, are you talking about me or you?"

Before I can respond, her father clears his throat. He loosens his bow tie and sits up straight. "Enough childishness." He looks at me. "What's the problem, Knox? The girl will get a new glass of champagne, and that's that."

"She's got a name. It's Paisley. And not *the girl*."

"Knox," Paisley says, narrowing her eyes. "It's no problem at all. I'll bring her the Ruinart and—Oh my God! Shit! I am so sorry, I…"

At first I can't believe what I'm seeing. And then I can and laugh out loud while all the others emit a collective gasp: Paisley has knocked over the glass and spilled the Dom Perignon all over Amanda's white dress. She just sits there, open-mouthed, wide-eyed, while Paisley vehemently rubs the wet fabric with a napkin. In itself a good approach, it's just that—*what a shame*—just a second ago Mr. Spiky Hair used it to wipe a smashed raspberry off the table. And now, said smashed raspberry is all over Amanda's dress. *Oops.*

I am still laughing, and everyone is looking at me like I just announced that I was quitting my sports career to become William's stable boy. But it stops abruptly when Amanda springs up and pushes Paisley away. Paisley is so unsteady on her heels, though, that she loses her balance, stumbles, and bangs against the table.

"Stop touching me!"

Paisley collects herself more quickly than I expected. She folds the napkin and gives Amanda a poisonous stare. "I only wanted to help. But with someone like you, any help would be too late."

Yep. Ladies and gentleman, may I present to you, Paisley *gorgeous* Harris.

Amanda gasps. "What do you think you're *doing*?"

"I do *whatever I want*," Paisley repeats Amanda's words. I am so proud of her, I can hardly express myself in words. At this point, I'm in the mood to lean back and say something cool like *"that's my girl!"* until I realize that, actually, she's not my girl at all—and all of a sudden I notice my bronchitis again.

To my right, my father buries his head in his hands, to my left Big Po lets out a breath of air, causing his button to shoot off and land on the floor. I knew it.

"You're nothing but a silly chalet girl," Amanda says. She sounds like a poisonous snake, but her words don't have all that much power, what with the giant raspberry stain on her chest. Her delicate features are distorted into an ugly grimace while she looks condescendingly at Paisley—my beautiful Paisley. "You haven't earned that dress. You're not one of the women Valentino is made for, *sweetheart*."

A sharp sting pierces my heart, which is suddenly pounding against my chest so hard, it's as if it wanted to break it. A millisecond later it becomes clear to me that it doesn't have to do with what she said, but with Paisley. Her face collapses, and a hurt expression causes her eyes to shimmer. I can't help but think of what my father said when he asked me to buy her a dress: "*I noticed that she showed up with a single jute bag. The poor girl.*"

She must have been *so* happy about that dress. Before dinner she probably looked at herself in the mirror and felt beautiful for the first time in a long time, I mean, who knows what kind of shit she's left behind. And now that moment's been ruined, that happy feeling simply destroyed by a woman who has no idea what her dirty words can make such a fragile person feel.

God, I hate it when people think they're better than others. I hate it when they talk without thinking. No one can ever really know how and to what degree someone is suffering. We can be standing next to someone who's wearing a huge smile while inside they're completely wiped out, and no one has any goddamn idea. I'm the best example.

The fact that Amanda didn't think about her words for even a single second puts me into a kind of aggressive frenzy. I jump up, but my father gets in the way. Fiery rage is burning in his eyes, but he's got himself under control better than I do. Always has. He knows I'm about to create another scandal for the press; he looks at me and almost imperceptibly shakes his head. Then he looks at Amanda and Joe and says, "You all should be going now."

Joe looks at a complete loss for words. After a moment of silence, he snorts loudly, pushes back his chair, and hisses, "I came all this way for *this*? What an ungrateful bunch. There's an epilog to all this, Jack."

My dad narrows his eyes. "That would turn out poorly for only one of us. And we both know who that would be, Joe."

They engage in a silent duel of looks until Joe snorts again and with a wave of his hand lets his daughter know it's time to follow him.

But even once the door's closed, the mood doesn't improve at all. It is so quiet, you can hear every breath.

Big-Po-Without-a-Button ahems. "Well, maybe it's time for me to..." With his thumb and a strange twitch of his face—as if he couldn't decide between an apologetic smile and a resigned gesture—he points toward the door, while standing up. "Thanks for the invitation, Jack." Yoda, too, takes advantage of the favorable moment to escape. Within a few seconds, we're all alone. Just Dad, Paisley, and me.

"Wow," I say into the silence. "That went quick. It's like Billie Eilish was giving a concert out front."

My father flares his nostrils and doesn't engage my attempt to lighten things up. The vein at his temple is pulsing at an uncontrollable rate. Not a good sign. Shortly thereafter, he shoots me a glance that seems to suggest he's honestly considering packing me up and leaving me behind in the cage of a ravenous black bear.

"Again and again and again." My father, his eyes closed, is rubbing his nose up and down with his index finger. "Every day I told you how important this meeting was, Knox. Not only in terms of increasing your sponsor money, but for me. There was supposed to be business talk, too. Possible investment plans discussed. But, like always," he slams his palm down on the table, "you don't give a shit!"

I don't know what to say. On the one hand, I want to disagree and ask him whether he understood what was going on there, on the other I think he's right. If there hadn't been anything between Amanda and me, the evening would've gone pretty differently.

"I... I'm going to clean up." Paisley turns to my father. "I am very sorry that the evening went downhill because of me, Mr. Winterbottom."

Dad gives her a mild smile, rubs the furrows in his forehead flat, and shakes his head. He looks tired. "It's not your fault, Paisley." I can hear between the lines. *It's mine.* The glance my dad gives me confirms my suspicion.

"Dad," I begin.

But my father lifts his hand. "Don't, Knox. I've had enough." He dabs at his mouth with the napkin, tosses it onto his plate, and gets up. "I'm going to bed. Excuse me."

His footsteps fade away. In the dim light, I see Paisley swallow. She bends over the table and begins to gather everything onto her tray.

"Paisley," I say slowly. "I'm sorry about what Amanda said to you. It's not true. I mean, the thing about the dress. It's made for you."

She smiles. "It's all good, Knox."

"No, it's not." I stand up and wobble a bit after having sat for so long. Then, wanting her to look at me, I take the tray out of her hand and put it back on the table. "I don't want you to believe what she said because you—*in every conceivable way*—are absolutely beautiful."

Paisley grins. "Impressive."

"What's impressive?"

"That a word like 'conceivable' even occurs to you in your state."

"I'm not that drunk. That'd be worrying."

She laughs. "Oh, man, Knox. Go to bed."

"Your ears are beautiful."

"You're not all there."

"True. I have never seen such beautiful ears. I like how they stick out. Somehow, that seems ethereal…or…uhm…aesthetic."

Paisley blinks. "Okay. What can I do to make you go to bed?"

"Bring me to bed."

"Exactly." She rolls her eyes. "And I almost found you charming."

"How could you have?"

She sighs. "Right, I'll bring you to bed. But I'm not staying."

"God forbid! What kind of *indecent* ideas are going through your head, Paisley?"

"My goodness, are you stressful." She pushes my shoulder and nods toward the stairs. "Get going."

Paisley does indeed follow and is still there when we reach my room. She crosses her arms over her chest as if uncomfortable with being here and looks around curiously. "Pretty respectable."

"Always this undertone of surprise." I slip out of my clothes until I'm just in my boxers, but Paisley pointedly looks in the other direction and acts as if she's interested in the signed puck on my dresser. She only turns back around once I'm under the sheets.

"Great. Can I leave you alone now?"

"Yeah," I murmur and notice how sleep is already tugging at my eyes. "Paisley?"

She's almost out the door. "Yeah?"

"I really do think your ears are beautiful."

My eyes are already closed but I can hear the smile in her voice.

"Maybe you are actually charming."

Yeah. Maybe.

23

Turn the Pain into Power

PAISLEY

KNOX'S EYES BORE INTO MINE. WELL, NOT REALLY KNOX, but a twelve-inch image of him on the front page of *USA Today*. The photo shows him on the slopes, snapping himself into his snowboard, but the look on his face suggests he'd rather attack the person behind the camera. Written in thick red letters above it is the headline:

Knox Winterbottom Loses Sponsors—Because of Her!

Levi is nibbling at his fingernails and keeps on shooting me hesitant glances out of the corners of his eyes. "At least they don't mention your name," he says for the fourth time in the last two minutes.

Aaron nods. "For people, it's just another scandal à la Knox. They'll have forgotten it by tomorrow."

I doubt that. For what feels like the hundredth time this morning, I read the article through, stopping at the same place as each and every other time. "I simply don't get it," I say, pointing to the sentence: "'No one knows who she is. But the girlfriend of my cousin's best friend caught them just a few nights before in a stable in Aspen.

It's said to have been a *very heated* affair.'" I angrily throw the paper onto the table in the iSkate lounge. "A *very heated affair*? We were sleeping!"

Aaron wants to say something but is interrupted by Gwen walking in. Her face is very red, and her hair is disheveled. "Hey, people." The covers of her training tights shuffle behind her as she waddles her way toward us on her heels. She looks like a duck. "I went jogging for two hours and have *the* worst blisters! You wouldn't believe it. No idea how I'm supposed to make it through training if I…" She stops when her glance falls on the paper. "Oh. You've read it already."

"Yeah," I say bitterly. "And it's nonsense. We fell asleep in the stall, nothing else."

Gwen plumps down onto the chair next to Levi and begins making circles in the air with her feet. "Sure. But what about what Amanda Dubois is saying?"

Amanda Dubois. The sound of her name alone makes my blood boil. It was only after the dinner that I learned her father was a big shot at Red Bull and that his daughter regularly did fashion shoots for famous designers. Admittedly, Dubois did a clever job of getting the ball rolling without going into the nitty-gritty. When a reporter asked him if he had anything to say about a great Red Bull event, he said that, sadly, that evening he'd been at a catastrophic sponsors' dinner at Knox Winterbottom's. He didn't care to give further details, but, naturally, the press immediately went to find his daughter. And she couldn't wait to spill her guts.

"Knox is a terrible person," she said. "Arrogant and unfriendly. He attacked me verbally when I attempted to start a polite conversation with his girlfriend, and totally lost his cool. It is hard for me to say this publicly, but I was truly afraid of him. It wouldn't have taken much for him to have gone after me. Thankfully my father was there." When the reporter asked whether she really thought Knox Winterbottom would hit a woman she said, "Oh, yeah, definitely."

After that, the headlines came flooding in. Every paper had

some kind of story, one more ridiculous than the other. No idea how Knox is taking it all. It's been three days since the whole affair, and I've hardly caught a glimpse of him since. Naturally, his father reacted immediately and engaged Jennet to beat all the advertising drums and have Knox release one statement after another. It's all degenerated into a mudslinging match. As far as I know, the only sponsors he has left are Big Po and some other guy.

"Amanda's full of it," I say, responding to Gwen's question. "Really, the woman's nuts. There is nothing to her words at all."

"So he didn't insult her?" Levi asks, sipping his isotonic drink.

"Not really. He just didn't want her to order me around."

Gwen looks confused. "So he didn't verbally attack her?"

I think for a moment. "No. It was obvious that the two couldn't stand each other. It was pretty mutual, you know? An exchange of words. At times him, at times her." I am overcome by the insane need to defend Knox. "And she's lying. He wasn't going to hit her, Knox isn't a woman beater. Never."

The thought makes my nerves start to tingle in an uncomfortable way. A voice in my head keeps whispering words that make my heartbeat increase. *You were gullible before. And where did it get you? Are you sure you want to make the same mistake again? Aren't you afraid? You should be. You really should be.*

Aaron shakes his head. "Enough about Knox, people. It's getting to a point where I can't even stand to hear his name." He looks at me and lifts the right corner of his mouth. "Don't worry, Paisley. No one knows you. The whole thing doesn't have anything to do with you."

I nod, but his words don't calm me down. Again and again, my thoughts whirl around what consequences there would be if I ended up in the public eye. My future at iSkate would be history. For no one outside of me and Ivan Petrov know that I'm not even supposed to be here. If he finds out where I am, it's all over.

Gwen swings her feet over the balustrade and sighs. Although she's been jogging, she seems restless. She is fidgety, she keeps drumming her fingers against her thighs and wriggling around. It looks like her body is about to start vibrating. I frown, but right when I'm about to say something, she pulls back her head and looks out onto the ice. "We should get down there. Polina's staring at us."

I risk a quick glance and see my trainer across from us in the stands. "Indeed."

Levi makes a face. "Heavens. Sometimes she's really creepy, isn't she?"

Aaron laughs. "Sometimes? All of my worst dreams have her in them, chasing me across the ice."

"We're the Avengers, and she's Thanos," Gwen mumbles, tosses her head back, and attempts a scary laugh that, to me, ends up sounding more like Gargamel from *The Smurfs*.

"And even if she was…" I stand up, toss Knox's face into the trash, and down my coffee in one go, "she's taking me to the Olympics. As far as I'm concerned, she could be the spawn of Pennywise and I wouldn't care."

Gwen shivers after me. For a moment, she gets caught on one of the table legs, but holds on to me and gets free. "You've got a terrible imagination, Paisley."

Levi and Aaron laugh, and for one lighthearted moment I even manage a laugh myself. I feel happy and free.

"Tension!" Polina's voice echoes across the ice and in my ears as I stretch out my leg and jump. I press my arms close to my body and manage two and a half twists before gravity pulls me back down to the ice and screws up my triple axel—once again. My legs buckle, and for a millisecond I wobble like a five-year-old trying to find their balance on their ice skates for the first time.

I smack my palms against my thighs in frustration and look at Polina. Her lips are a thin line, as always, her face shows no emotion.

In the meantime, I've come to believe that the last time I pulled off this jump was due to pure chance.

"How many times was that now?"

"Twenty-seven. And only four of those were a two-and-a-half turn."

"Okay. One more time."

Polina nods sharply as if she wouldn't have accepted anything else, although regular training has been over for an hour already, and, aside from the two of us, no one else is out on the ice. I wipe the sweat off my forehead and take out a hairpin in order to tuck a few loose strands of hair back into my bun. Skate America is getting closer every day, and last week Polina said that she was thinking of only allowing me to do the double axel. Needless to say, as a result, my ambition shot up even higher. A double axel means fewer points—not what I'm after. I want to be the best. I want to make it through the roof, to become the next Polina Danilov and show everyone what a hungry, roach girl from Minneapolis was able to achieve.

"I got this," I say to myself, little clouds of frost forming before my mouth. "I got this, if it's the last thing I do." Even if I hit the ground a hundred more times, ripping open my knees. I'm not giving up. Cause this thing here, this dance on the ice, carried by the melody of my passion, this here is what I was born for. My feet are bound to the ice and when I jump, my heart grows wings. Every. Single. Time.

"Pay attention to your movement when you come up," Polina says. "You've got to have the tension under control. Then you'll automatically be smoother in your finish."

I nod, take a start, and stretch out my arms. I stretch my toes in my skates, to the degree I can, while raising my foot and get ready to take my next jump.

"Keep your eyes closed until you jump!" Polina's words bring me back to reality and interrupt my jump.

My eyes wide I whirl around. "*What?*"

"You're not feeling it," she says, her hands clasped around the railing. "Because you're desperately focused on the jump. Don't skate with your head, Paisley. Skate with this." She taps the left part of her chest, and I think I even notice the suggestion of a tiny smile. "Jump only when you feel the emotions within you, let them overwhelm you. You have the technique. Don't think about it. Simply jump and *feel* it."

I take a deep breath, ignore my growing heart rate, and close my eyes. Everything inside me screams for me to open them again as I take one step after the other in long strides. But I keep them closed, try to turn off my thoughts, and increase my speed. At some point, I'm no longer thinking, I just feel the cold, cutting air on my skin. My body knows how much time there is before I run into the railing. It knows this rink. It knows the ice. I fly over the ice and open my eyes the second I jump off on an impulse without thinking about it beforehand.

The wings of my heart spread out and carry me. I count one, two, three twists before I land firmly and under control. My tension has champion potential. At least right now it does.

I let out a surprised gasp and open my eyes. Out of sheer euphoria a mad laugh escapes me. "I did it!" My skates carry me directly over to Polina. Coming to a stop, a trace of ice whirls in the air. "Oh, my God! Did you see that? That was crazy!"

"It was a start."

"*A start?*" My body must be overproducing serotonin and dopamine, there's no other way to explain grabbing Polina's shoulders and pushing. "That was world-class!"

My trainer attempts to keep a neutral expression but can't keep from raising the corners of her mouth. She nods. "You're going to go far, Paisley." Now a smile actually appears on her usually so hardened features. "The Olympics are closer than you think."

And at that moment, it becomes clear to me what makes a true coach. It is someone who pushes you to try something over and over though you don't want to in order to become what you *really want to be* one day. Sure, training doesn't necessarily bring glory, but without training there isn't any at all. Polina knows that. And every day she makes sure that I don't forget it.

24
Chocolate Lips

Paisley

After training, I always feel so high that I decide to walk instead of taking the Highland Express. The quiet is pleasant, broken only by the creak of the snow that follows my every step. It's snowing pretty heavily, and after a little while my jeans are damp. At some point, the warm lights from downtown chase off the path's darkness. One of William's carriages rattles past, the horse snorting happily and the glitter-eyed tourists gawking at Aspen's houses in their Christmas finest. Walking past the diner, I see Kate taking an order. She looks up from her pad, and waves to me through the window. I smile and wave back before walking on.

In the meantime the snow has become a downright blizzard and it's tough to see. Only now and then a light from the streetlights shows me the way. When it gets so bad that I can't even put one foot in front of the other, I randomly reach for the doorknob of the store next to me and push myself inside.

"Oh, Paisley! Thank God." Snow whirls through the open door and collects on the thick Persian carpet. It takes all I've got to push it closed, and then I see William. He comes out from behind his popcorn machine—only now do I realize I've ended up in the

Old-Timer—raising his arms as if my appearance were some kind of blessing. "Can you take over for a moment? I've got to bring the horses to the stable. The storm is expected to get stronger."

"Of course." I don't make an effort to ask him how the popcorn machine works or how much tickets cost. No one's going to be showing up in this kind of weather.

"Wonderful. You're my savior." He places his hands on my shoulders for a second, and squeezes. "As a thank you, I'll reserve a seat for you in the first row at the next city council meeting."

"Umm. Okay."

"Grab yourself a cheese sandwich."

"I don't like cheese."

"Oh, right. Well, then… Just wait. I'll be quick."

I smile. "No worries. At the moment, I can't really get anywhere anyway."

William gives me a thankful smile, then slips off. My fingers numb, I pull off my shoes and take a deep breath. I love the smell of the Old-Timer, burning logs and old furniture. It makes me feel at ease.

I blow on my hands and rub them together while walking across the soft carpet and stop in front of the shelf with the records. I flip through the albums, one after the other, before deciding on David Bowie. I put the record on and curl up in one of the wide leather chairs in front of the fireplace. I pull up my legs to get my jeans to dry and enjoy the feeling of warmth driving the cold out of my limbs.

For a while I just stare into the fire and watch the flames eat through the wood. Suddenly the door opens with a ring and The Old-Timer is filled with the cutting sound of the storm.

"Shit, is it cold!"

I whirl around in my chair and lean my head over the backrest. "Knox? What are *you* doing here?"

Knox looks just as surprised as me. He stops midway through taking off his shoes and blinks. "Paisley?"

"William asked me to take over for a sec," I explain.

"Ah." He begins moving again and slips out of his shoes. "Well, then I've got to keep you company. Truth be told, I really just wanted to pick up a few sandwiches after training but now not even ten horses could pull me away."

"Well now..." I take a deep breath. "We can only hope the storm stops soon."

Knox laughs out loud before coming over to me and falling into the chair next to mine. The leather creaks as if it were letting out air. "It's obvious that you're not from here."

I frown. "How so?"

"Well, a snowstorm in Aspen doesn't just *stop soon*. We can be happy if we manage to get out of here before tomorrow morning."

"Before tomorrow morning?" I squeak. "Impossible. I've got to take care of your tourists!" The idea of spending another night next to Knox Winterbottom chokes my breath. That won't do. No way. It would just throw me deeper into the mess of feelings I'm already in.

"They'll be just fine without you for a while." Knox casts a glance over his shoulder to the left and right before getting up and then coming back with a whole tray full of cheese sandwiches.

"You're disgusting."

He takes a bite. "And you're abnormal," he counters, munching away. "Everyone likes cheese."

I wrinkle my nose and refocus on the fireplace.

From the corner of my eye I can see Knox looking at me. "We haven't talked since...that evening."

"True."

"So... I mean... Are you okay?"

"Of course."

He lets out a pent-up breath. "Okay. Good."

I finally turn back to face him. "And you?"

Knox shrugs. "I've never cared what the press has to write about me."

That surprises me. "You don't care what the world thinks about you?"

"No."

"Why not?"

"Why should it think about me at all?" He stuffs the last bit of sandwich into his mouth. "As long as I don't forget who I am, everyone can think what they want."

I pick at a loose thread sticking out of the chair. "Are you ever afraid of forgetting?"

Knox takes his time to respond. Eventually he says, "More often than you think."

"Me, too," I say quietly, without knowing why.

Knox looks at me for a moment, then places the tray to the side and slouches down farther into the chair. "Strange."

"What's strange?"

"I'm living with you in the same house, but have the feeling I don't know you at all."

"That makes two of us."

Knox tilts his head and looks at me thoughtfully. "Well, all right. We're going to play a little game. A truth for a truth, okay?"

I hesitate. I don't really want to do this, but my absent will collides with my curiosity to learn more about Knox. "Okay. You start."

He looks at the ceiling and begins bobbing his foot. "My dad is always disappointed with me, and I don't know how to change that without disappointing myself."

Oh. Wow. That's honest.

"I'm sorry."

"You don't have to be. Your turn."

"Right. Umm. I love this place."

Knox laughs. I wish he'd do it again. "That doesn't count."

"Well, fine. I'm afraid of not being good enough."

"For what?"

"For... I don't know. The ice? Life? Everything?"

"Oh. I hear you." He looks to the fire and loses himself before looking back at me. "I'm sure that you don't need to be."

"Yeah. Maybe. Your turn."

He takes another sandwich. "I'm a star snowboarder, though I don't want to be. You."

"*What?*"

"No questions. Just answers. Your turn."

Umm. Okay. At first I want to object and tell him that we need to talk about that, but then I let it go because I like the idea. Just being able to say things that are weighing me down without having to go into more detail sounds so *freeing*. Just saying them, not having to carry them around with me any longer. Suddenly the whole situation strikes me as something out of a parallel world where we can both be open without having to go back to everything again later. Just the here and now, sealed off from our lives outside. The thought is exciting, so I stand up and consider ways of making it more comfortable for us. Bowie's song "Heroes" is fading out as I lift the needle off the record and look around the store.

Knox wrinkles his brow. His hair falls across the leather as he turns to watch me. "What's your plan?"

"To turn on a movie. Well, when I find them, that is."

"They're over there." He gets up and leads me to a shelf full of boxes. They are labeled with years. "What decade are you in the mood for?"

"Hmm. The eighties?"

His eyes scan the shelf before he pulls out a box and opens the top. The rolls of film are packed in Tupperware containers and ordered alphabetically.

"*The Breakfast Club!*"

"I knew it!" Knox laughs. "Seriously, seeing the title I thought, *This is what she wants to see, I'm positive*, and then you said it."

"Maybe you know me a bit already." I take the film out and go to the projector. "Can you tell me how this thing works?" I come back to the sofa from the record player and sit down.

He laughs again, takes the film out of my hand, and puts it on. The credits begin to roll across the screen. and Knox says, "I'll be right back." Knox disappears behind a door. I have no idea where it leads. I take the opportunity to scratch the back of my thigh like a crazy woman, as, while drying out, my jeans have begun to chafe. Then I curl back up on the sofa under a blanket.

Knox comes back and remains standing next to me for a bit. He holds a cup of hot chocolate under my nose. "Here."

I sit up. "Oh, my God. Where'd you get this?"

"From the kitchen." He sits down on the couch, too, but grabs his own blanket. "I didn't poison it. I swear. Drink away."

I close my eyes and breathe in the sweet aroma before taking a sip. "This is the best hot chocolate I've ever had."

"Don't change the subject. You're up, Snow Queen."

My stomach begins to tingle. I blame the hot chocolate. "Okay. No one knows that I've moved to Aspen. You."

He sips his hot chocolate. "I was accepted at Colorado Mountain College to study psychology but am not going to go. You."

I choke. The drink goes down my throat and I cough a few times. *Knox* is interested in *psychology*? Can someone please pinch me? That's hot. Really fucking hot.

"Is there a joker in this game?" I adopt a mischievous grin. "I'd like to play it and ask a question."

"Nope, sadly not. Your turn, Paisley."

I look at the movie. "My mother is a crack whore, and the youth welfare office took me away from her when she attempted to sell me for two backpacks full of drugs. You."

Knox jerks up. His hot chocolate sloshes over the side of the cup and lands on the blanket in a big brown spot. For a second he doesn't know what to do with his cup, then puts it down on the carpet and looks at me. "Wait. *What?*"

"No questions. Just answers," I repeat. In the meantime, I regret having told him this, but it was like I was intoxicated somehow. I really wanted to just throw this truth away from me, I thought I'd feel better. But I feel even worse.

Knox doesn't move a centimeter, but deep lines form across his forehead, and he looks at me with an expression I don't know how to interpret. "Paisley…"

"Your rules," I say. "No answers."

He pulls in his lower lip, then thoughtfully runs his tongue across his lips. "Then I'm a spoilsport, but… My God, Paisley. I'd be a serious asshole if I didn't respond. We can't simply sweep past this one."

"Sure we can." I'm holding onto my hot chocolate like a life preserver. "We can." My voice is trembling, and I can feel my eyelids prickling. So I lower my head and pretend to inspect the reindeer on my cup more closely. But then I feel a finger on my chin, and let Knox gently lift it back up. I'm sure he sees the tears in my eyes that I'm trying to keep down. Of course he does.

"I don't know anyone—and I mean *anyone*—who impresses me as much as you do, Paisley."

His words awaken the strong desire in me to live, to put my hands to his face and pull him toward me. After what I just told him, this should be the last thing coming into my head, but I can't stop it. And I'm sick and tired of going against my own feelings. I'm so sick and tired of this constant fear of being hurt. I want to be happy. Simply happy.

Before I can think about how to get closer to him, however, Knox runs a hand through his hair and turns to look at the floor. He looks like he's thinking about something. Or wrestling with himself. "Fuck it." He takes the cup out of my hand and puts it down on the ground without looking. Then he gives me a look as if his life depended on this very moment. "I've got to do this, Paisley."

And then Knox kisses me.

25
You and Me Are Wild Magic

PAISLEY

VETIVER.

That's the first thing that crosses my mind when his lips meet mine. Knox smells of vetiver, and, God, I *love* this smell. So much so that I dig my hands into his hair and pull him closer. My heart is pounding. I am sure that Knox can hear every single beat.

As he delicately runs his fingers down my throat he makes a rough sound, like a lion's purr. I shudder. The center of my body begins to tingle and then contracts. I have never wanted anyone this bad.

I feel dazed. Absent. Intoxicated. His lips are soft and electrifying. Silk and storms.

The sounds of the music and the crackling of the fire are nothing but background now. Transparent. Not here and not there, as Knox's caresses are taking me in completely. A powerful line I am clinging to as he holds me.

My fingers stroke his scalp. I can feel his fine hair tickling my skin. I can't get enough, I can't get enough, I can't get enough. Knox can feel how badly I want him, I am sure of it; he keeps making that noise, you can barely hear it, barely catch it, it's almost a whisper, but so intense that something inside me explodes.

God, I'm so hot, he's so hot, and it's got nothing to do with the fire and our warm bodies. I am dizzy and suddenly I wonder if this is all okay. But it has to be, it simply has to be, because the thought of stopping everything causes a black hole to appear within me.

"Paisley…" Knox whispers in between two caresses, and the way he says it makes it sound like something saintly. Like something delicate he is holding in his hands, carefully and thoughtfully, so that it won't break. I have never felt the sound of my name like this before. I never knew you *could* feel your name, but now I know you can. It's rare, I know that much immediately, I *feel* that much immediately, and when that feeling comes, for a moment there is nothing more beautiful. I briefly hold my breath, enjoy the soft tingling beneath my skin—who knows when I'll feel *this* again? *If* I'll ever feel it again?

Knox's hands burn my cheeks and yet I want him to leave them there forever. The way he's kissing me, as if he needed it, as if he was thirsty, the way he's turning me on, his breath quick and flat between every touch of our lips, it's like he's dying of hunger. As if he had to take everything he could from this moment out of the fear of never being able to experience it ever again.

I know this because it's the same for me. The *exact* same. The idea that this moment and this kiss on the scuffed, sinking couch—the most valuable couch in the world for me right now—could be it, the only one, is unacceptable.

And that makes me terribly afraid. I shouldn't want this. Knox isn't someone I've known for a long time. That I know *well*. I don't even know what I think about him. Whether I feel anything for him. And if I do, well, then that's even worse, because, as I said, I *don't even know him.*

His fingers wander up and down my shoulders, my arms, before making their way to my waist and digging in. A bit too powerfully, just a bit, but it tells me that he's holding back so as not to go too far. Here and now, on this wonderful couch, although he wants to. I *know* he wants to. I catch myself imagining what would happen if I let it. When I was the one letting him know with my jittery fingers that I wanted *more, more, more.*

Our kisses are heated, too uncoordinated, too quick to be perfect, though it's perfect anyway, the two of us, he and I, me and him, alone at this moment.

I run my fingers through his hair and wander deeper, touching his neck, as he continues to hold me, and I try not to think about how the moment's growing more intense. I run a finger across his face as he bends over me, his forehead against mine.

It would be thrilling. Mesmerizing and hot, captivating and fraught with tension, every movement, every breath, every touch. And I'd want it. Absolutely. *Absolutely.*

And this is the thought that suddenly causes me to choke up, because I notice how much my self-control is crumbling. That's the problem. It shouldn't be crumbling. Never. I am here to leave my past behind me and to concentrate on my career. If I open myself up to a snowboarder who is known for having a different woman in his bed every night, things in Aspen won't be off to a good start. Not the one I want.

All of a sudden everything has changed. Instead of joy I'm panicking. I feel constrained, as if I might suffocate in too small a space, one where the walls are closing in and my heart with its jumps is telling me something's not right.

Before Knox can kiss me again, I turn my head and stretch my palms out until they touch his chest.

His lips graze the corners of my mouth, then he moves away from me so quickly, it's like I was poison ivy. For a little while, we just look at each other. A moment ago you couldn't have fit a leaf between us, now the sudden distance seems like the edge of a cliff.

It's impossible to overcome. Impossible to ignore.

I look at Knox. Analyze him carefully. Not because I really want to, but because I have *no other choice.* Knox is hot. In a way you don't think is even possible. Now and then, you see pictures of these kinds of people on Pinterest or Instagram, and you pause for a second, two, three, four, five. You wonder why you never run into these kinds of people in real life until you realize that everything—*everything*—has been manipulated. From their perfect brows to their full lips down to their symmetrical features. Having realized that, you usually feel better. It's just Photoshop. It's not real.

Well, false. Here's the proof, right in front of me, close enough to touch and yet so far.

Red lips, chapped from our heavy kisses. Big green eyes. More than green, with that bright spot in the irises. No idea how it's even possible. Maybe it's an anomaly. I resolve to think about anomalies from now on. If I added a *-philia* to it, it'd even become a technical term. *Anomalyaphilia*. It probably exists already.

And then of course—how couldn't it be—there's that perfect birthmark right under his left eye. It's *only* a birthmark, but at the same time it's the *ne plus ultra*. I can't get enough of it. Whenever I think of Knox, that little brown spot is the first thing I see. It's nuts. I mean, it's *a spot*, really, I've observed it a few times already, but my head keeps insisting on its being something beautiful.

Birthmarkaphilia.

My hand breaches the distance between us and slowly moves across it; it's just too beautiful for this world.

Okay, not *really*, but that's what I imagine. My nerves are electrified because they want my thoughts to become reality. I think Knox can see what I'm thinking. His lips open, and I hear him release a trembling breath.

"I could be," he murmurs.

Could be what? What's he talking about? I should ask him, that would be the logical thing to do, but I can't manage to make a sound. I try, really, but something's blocking me. Every time I try to raise my voice, nothing comes out, and I feel like my attempts make me look like I am somehow gagging.

"I could be," he repeats.

"Could be what?" Finally.

"Ready."

What on earth is he talking about? No idea, but his birthmark is blinding me, even if, in reality, it can't, but I've already established that there's something weird about that thing. I look at my hands, they're far too dry, and begin to massage them. Then I scratch the scar on my thumbnail, wondering whether I am getting enough vitamins, doing anything to avoid thinking about what Knox could be ready for. I don't want to know because I'm *dying* to know, and that makes sense, actually. It means that I am already too invested. I can't deny it. It doesn't matter how much I try to fight it. It doesn't matter how much I concentrate on other things, the voice in my head is too present. Too loud. It's yelling that I want him. God, yes, I *want* Knox Winterbottom, and if he doesn't tell me what he's ready for, I'll die.

I'd love to yell at him. But while he was caressing me, my mind made it clear that I simply can't. I ran away from something in order to start over and not to swan dive into the next catastrophe. It took all my willpower to stop things from continuing, and now Knox is talking weird shit and making it impossible for me to break away. He's cast a spell over me, again, and has given the electrifying tension between us space to persist. But it's got to give. It simply has to.

I'm too curious. I have no other choice. "Ready for what?"

"To change for you." He runs his tongue across his lips. "No more parties. No more women. If you want."

If I want. All it takes is three words to turn everything upside down again. Knox is a mistake in my plan. An unexpected valley on my hike. Far too beautiful to ignore. Far too beautiful not to see.

But I can't. *I simply can't.* I've been here before. It was just as beautiful. With bright lights that dragged me in only to show me that, inside, all was swamp instead of brooks, darkness instead of light. It didn't want to let me leave. It wanted to destroy me. To pull me down until I couldn't breathe and suffocated from the pain. And yet, it had looked so pure.

But beauty deceives. If you aren't careful, it'll take you behind the light to show you its real face.

And it's a horrific one. I saw it. For far too long and far too frequently to allow myself to risk opening up again to something that is *all too beautiful, too beautiful, too beautiful.*

"Knox…" I squirm. My body resists what I want to say. His eyes are hanging on my lips. "That's not a good idea."

Instead of being hurt, he seems amused. "You were the one preaching to me about giving up the parties and scandals. Now I want to change and that's not a good idea?"

"You should. For you. But not for me."

"Why?"

I run a finger over a hole in the couch. "The two of us don't function well."

"The two of us function wonderfully."

I look up. "How do you know that?"

"How do you know that we *don't?*"

"Stop turning my words around."

He laughs. "What do you mean? Because you'd have to admit that you don't actually have any reasons not to want this?"

"I *have* my reasons." I pause in order to look at his face, which at this moment is at least as hard to read as *Anna Karenina*. "I'm keeping them to myself."

"I don't believe you." His glance is urgent, so urgent that I struggle to keep looking into his eyes. Instead, I turn back to my thumbnail, whose white spots *definitely* suggest a vitamin deficiency. Maybe stress, too. I risk a quick glance back at him. My heart is racing. Stress. Definitely stress and Knox and stress and *Knox, Knox, Knox.*

"It's not as if I tell everyone my reasons for my decisions."

"That's not what I mean. I'm not dumb, Paisley. I *know* you want me as much as I want you. But I accept your decision." He raises his hands and stands up.

Suddenly I panic. Even more than when we were kissing. "Where are you going?"

He laughs, looks around the store, and bows his head. He looks so alluring that I feel the need to pull him back onto the couch and to change my assertion. I want to tell him that I want him and that he shouldn't accept my decision. *Please, please, please.*

But I don't. Of course I don't.

"If you want me to freeze to death in no time, I'll go. Otherwise, I can simply move to another couch, and we can spend the next few hours pretending that nothing ever happened between us." He shrugs. "Believe me, I've got a talent for that."

Oh, I believe you. I believe that immediately.

As I don't answer, Knox begins to hum while moving through the room to a shelf with books. I recognize the melody. It's Disney's *Frozen*.

"'Let It Go?' How melodramatic, Knox."

He takes a book off the shelf, the edges of which are already slightly creased. His eyes dash across the blurb. "Hmm. I prefer 'pathetic.'"

"Same thing."

"You think?"

"I know."

Knox tucks the book under his arm, disappears from my field of vision, and reappears a moment later with a bag of popcorn. He sinks onto the couch, opens the book, and tosses a handful of popcorn into his mouth.

"You'd be surprised at how many things turn out to be different than you think."

I don't respond. And neither does Knox. He leans back onto his couch—his, not mine—leafs through his book, and eats his popcorn. Every time his chewing breaks the quiet, I look at him, I don't know why. Maybe I just want his attention. For sure. That tracks.

But Knox doesn't notice. And if he does, he's uninterested. His chewing grows louder. Every now and then he laughs, it must be a good book, and I catch myself wanting to ask him if he could read me the passage out loud. If he could laugh again because I like the feeling it gives me. I like him. I like his laugh.

I don't. Instead I attempt to ignore him.

I decide my plan is to stay awake and to wait for Knox to fall asleep so I can watch him. It sounds crazy, feels that way, too, but I want to do it. I want to watch his chest slowly rise and fall, a small angel-like smile on his lips, and to imagine being able to kiss them whenever I wanted. To imagine they were for me alone. Strange to think that that is exactly what I want and that that is exactly what I could have had just a little while ago, but stopped.

I'm angry.

I'm pissed off, and I mean really pissed off.

With myself. As if glued to the couch I glower over at Knox. There's no mirror around or I'd glower at myself. I ball my hands into fists and drive my nails into my palms until it hurts.

Apologize. Talk with him. You didn't mean it. Tell him.

It doesn't work. I can't get my mouth open although I cannot lie: I *really* want Knox. There are a variety of reasons why.

He listens to Disney songs in his car.

He puts Simon and Garfunkel on the jukebox as if he simply *knew* me.

He says my ears are ethereal when he means aesthetic.

He finds me beautiful *in every conceivable* way.

I have shattered into a thousand pieces, some far too small, far too broken and fractured to be glued back together to make a whole. But Knox can do it. Put me back together. Close to him, I have the feeling that his very glance could put me back together. As if it would save me. As if he would say, "Come on, Paisley, truth for a truth," and all of a sudden, I could tell him everything. Everything I have left behind—everything I like to pretend is in the past, although it isn't at all.

It's clear to me that there's just no way. To tell him everything. Knox would not put me back together. He would do something or other, something dumb, and break me more than I am already.

It'd be better to make the great effort to push Knox away, to keep him out of my life so that he never gets the chance to hurt me. But it already hurts. No, the fact that I want him, that I really want him, but can't allow it is *tearing* me apart. I am torturing myself. Freely. Masochistic, right?

I cannot manage to stay awake. I'm the first to fall asleep.

By the time I wake up, Knox is gone.

26
The Smell of Snow

PAISLEY

GWEN DOESN'T HAVE A BED. INSTEAD, SHE'S GOT A RABBIT named Bing Crosby. I know that because there's a sign on his cage saying: *Hell yeah, call me Bing Crosby.*

She sleeps on a thick down blanket, a pillow that looks like it belongs on a garden chair, and a red yoga mat. Levi and Aaron are squeezed next to each other on the blanket, their legs tucked in, and I look over to Gwen questioningly.

She shrugs. "It's better for your back."

"After training, you seriously manage to sleep *on the floor?*"

"It's a matter of getting used to it." She closes the door behind her, freeing up a view of an oversized poster of a guy whose palms are shooting blue lightning bolts.

"Who's that?"

Gwen looks at me as if I've personally offended her.

"Seriously?" Levi says. His face is so skeptical I count four furrows. "You don't know who that is?"

"Umm. No?"

"It's Magnus Bane," Aaron says, as if that explained everything.

I'm still confused. Am I supposed to know who that is? "Is he a K-pop superstar or something?"

Gwen snorts. "He's the High Warlock of Brooklyn!"

I blink.

"*Shadowhunters?*"

I shake my head.

Levi buries his head in his hands, Aaron groans.

"Cultural philistine," Gwen says, grinning. "I'll let you borrow the books, if you want." Then she points at a lilac-colored piece of material covering her entire desk. "Here, I've been working on this the last couple of days." She presses a lever on her sewing machine so that the needle moves upward and pulls the fabric out from underneath. It's a dress. For her program. Gwen's face is glowing with pride as she holds it out under my nose. "Nice, right?"

More than that. The straps lead in an elegant herringbone pattern into a perfect neckline that only just covers the cleavage and frames the completely open back.

"My God, Gwen! You sewed this yourself?" I take a few steps forward and run my fingers over the ruffles. "It must've taken you ages for the sequins!"

"Show her the bow," Aaron says, and Gwen turns the dress over. At the lower back the herringbone pattern shifts and becomes a delicate bow.

"This isn't a dress for a program; this is a party dress for Kate Middleton."

Gwen laughs and punches my shoulder. "Kate Middleton's eyes are brown. That would never match."

"Your eyes are brown, too."

"Yeah, it's not for me." She pushes the dress against my chest and jumps up and down twice. "Do it, try it on!"

"You made this *for me?*" I can hardly breathe. Really. The last time I received a gift was in kindergarten. Josephine Hangster didn't like her Tater Tots and nudged them onto my plate. "Gwen, this is… too nice. I can't…"

"You can. Mine's been ready for weeks already, and if you don't wear it it'll just rot away in my closet."

"On top of it, we can't let you go out on the ice in your training dress tonight," Levi says. He says the word "training dress" with a rumpled nose, as if it had to do with the lice that Josephine Hangster found on my head after giving me her tots. I close my eyes a moment to collect myself, suddenly everything's just a bit too much for me. Although it's just a dress, it means the world to me.

"Thank you, Gwen. Really, thank you."

She shrugs as if it were nothing. As if it were normal. Maybe it is now. *Normal.* The idea that my life could simply be normal triggers a tingling feeling in my body; "normal" is the most beautiful word you can use. It wasn't clear to me how much I had missed, how much I *needed* to have friends. From the moment I took off, I've been a castle with thick walls. Secure. But lonely. Levi, Aaron, and Gwen pulled me out. It's nice out here. Frightening sometimes, but beautiful.

I pull the dress on, twirl around in a circle. Levi whistles and Aaron says, "Shit, Paisley. If I wasn't gay, I'd eat you up."

Gwen falls onto her desk chair. She's wearing thick Frodo socks, really, his face is everywhere, and pushes off the ground with them to spin in circles. Then she says, "If you ate her up, Aaron, you'd have a big problem."

He runs a finger down the freckles on his arm. "Why?"

"Because Knox is into her," Levi and Gwen say in unison. They look at each other, the corner of Levi's mouth curls in amusement and Gwen laughs in her way, which always sounds a little bit like a pig's grunt.

"Can we please not talk about Knox?" Pulling my wool sweater over my head, my voice comes out muffled. A week from now it's Christmas Eve, and today Aspen's Christmas party is taking place at

Silver Lake. Those of us from iSkate are showing a selection from the programs we'll perform at Skate America. It's a tradition.

"Why not?" Gwen takes a step toward me in her Frodo socks. "I thought you two got along?"

I mutter something incomprehensible and hope that the issue is now closed, but of course it isn't.

Gwen covers her mouth with her hand and makes a weird movement, which causes a chair caster to bang into her rabbit cage and makes her wobble dangerously for a second. Bing Crosby flattens his ears and crawls into his little house.

"You slept with him!" she shrieks.

"God, no! Why do you always think that?"

"It's Knox, Paisley." Levi wipes his dark bangs off his forehead, slides across the floor to the cage, and tries to lure Bing Crosby out of his house with odd squeaks. I think it's more disturbing to the little guy than Gwen's attack with the chair. Levi gives up and looks back at me. "*I* even find him hot, and I think ninety-nine percent of female tourists come here in the hopes of running into him."

"And hauling him off."

"I'm not one of the ninety-nine percent of tourists. Hey, can I use this to mend my legwarmers?" I grab a ball of gray wool out of Gwen's basket and lift it into the air. Gwen nods, hands me a needle, and says, "Something happened between you two. And I want to know what."

I rummage around in my bag for my legwarmers and begin to sew. "What makes you think so?" I say, putting on an indifferent tone.

"For days you've avoided any discussion when his name pops up."

That I can't deny. So I don't say anything and choose to ignore her instead. Gwen starts throwing Skittles at my head. I manage to avoid most of them, but one hits my ear and, being small, manages to find its way in.

"Great," I hiss while trying to fish it back out. Levi and Aaron double up laughing. I think Bing Crosby may very well become my new best friend. "We kissed."

"You're not serious!" At the word *serious* Gwen slams both of her palms on the arms of the chair. She scoots forward a bit, her eyes wide, hoping to learn everything. Her expression reminds me of Kaa, the snake in *The Jungle Book*. "Tell me everything!"

I prick myself with the needle and curse. "There's nothing to tell. He made me hot chocolate, and we hung out. Then there was the kiss, and when I noticed that it was all a bit strange, I stopped things."

My finger on my lips, I get up to grab a tissue from Gwen's desk. She watches every move I make with Argus eyes and when I turn to go back to my seat, she blocks my way with one of her Frodo socks. "Are. You. *Nuts?*"

"What?"

"That's not how Knox Winterbottom comes on to women! Women come on to *him*, he sleeps with them, and that's that. But he made you a hot chocolate, Paisley, a *hot chocolate*! Do you realize what that means?"

"Umm. I've got the feeling that you want me to give you some deep answer or something, but, well…it's just hot chocolate…"

"It's love!" she cries, jumping up out of her chair and throwing her arms into the air. "Holy Mary, Mother of God, Knox has *feelings* for you!"

"Okay, Gwen, you're crazy. Your rabbit is afraid of you. Do you see that? Bing Crosby is distraught."

"Knox has feelings for you, and you pushed him away." Gwen grabs a huge jawbreaker off her desk that, judging by its appearance, she's been working on for a while and begins to suck it. "But we'll get it straightened out."

"You're going to have to brush your teeth afterward, Gwen, that thing is pure sugar."

"He's going to be there, too."

"Who?"

"Knox."

"What about him?"

"He's going to be there," she repeats, licks her jawbreaker, and raises her eyebrows at me. "At the party."

I moan. "Guys, can you *please* get Gwen under control?"

"Naw." Levi doesn't even look up as he ties his skates. "No chance."

Aaron shrugs, a bemused smile on his face. "Tried and failed many times. Dear, you're at her mercy."

"Paisley!" Gwen grabs my shoulders and shakes me, causing her jawbreaker shift in her hand and stick to my skin. "Listen. You pushed him away, which means he'll come back. One hundred percent. And that's why you really need to consider what's going on between the two of you!"

I want to say something, but Gwen puts her hand across my mouth to stop me. "There *is* something there. Before you lose your job for having your heart broken and he fucks you over, or he has *his* heart broken because you're stringing him along and going to drop him, you really need to think things over."

What's going on between the two of us. That's it exactly. We're not a *we*. We're not a *he and I*. It's just something that's *going on.* Ever since the first night, the two of us have acted as if nothing happened. Somehow it's okay. It's just like that between Knox and me. Somehow okay. It's not what I'd really like, but I need it to be this way.

The music is loud. We can already hear it as we're leaving downtown and taking the snow-covered path to Buttermilk Mountain. Additional lanterns—probably from William—have been set up, their gas lights almost swallowed by the deep snow. My attempt to avoid thinking about Knox has failed. A nerve-racking tingle is running through my fingertips and making my heart beat faster. Not because I'm going to see him. I do that every day at the resort. But because he will see me on the ice. On Silver Lake. That's where I saw him crying. Where I got to know the *real* Knox. I wonder why that is. Why he makes such an effort to keep people from seeing what's really going on inside of him. Maybe for the same reasons as me. Maybe he's scared. Maybe he wants to forget.

"Earth to Paisley." Gwen is waving her pink-dotted glove in front of my face. "You still with us?"

Looking up I have to blink twice to make out the backdrop. I almost stumble over one of the gas lights or my own foot, I don't know which, but I've got to grab Levi's arm.

He laughs. "Everything all right?"

I nod as my eyes wander, trying to take in every centimeter of this winter wonderland. "I think this is the most beautiful place I've ever been."

The fir trees around Silver Lake have been decorated with Christmas balls and colored lights, causing the laughing faces of the many people to glow in the most varied colors. I catch a glimpse of Polina beneath a snow-draped pine, her hands around a pewter cup and a fox-colored fur hat on her head. I really hope it's fake. She's talking with Gwen's father. Seeing me, she nods, and I nod back. Polina and I like each other, and we show that through nodding, because we both live in the same ghost town, and that's what you do. You nod.

Gwen tugs at the pom-pom on her hat. The glow of the colored lights makes the golden thread in the fabric shimmer. "There's Mom. Let's grab something to eat before Harper stabs us with her eyes. I can't stand that on an empty stomach."

Harper is sitting on a bare log, tying her skates. Her Bordeaux-colored cashmere coat reaches all the way to her knees. Underneath she seems to be wearing her program outfit because she's already pulling her boot covers over her skates and adjusting her legwarmers. Her hair falls in red waves to both sides of her face, and I see her sit up, shake it out, and tie it up into a bun, all the while her glance is wandering over to a group of people beyond the pines, at the foot of Buttermilk Mountain. I have no idea why they're all standing there until a guy on a snowboard does a double twist over their heads and a collective "oooh" and "ahhh" escapes the women.

Knox. Of course.

"If you keep on staring at him like that, Gwen will lie awake all night." Aaron doesn't look at me as he speaks, but his amused expression speaks volumes. "She won't let poor Bing Crosby sleep with all the plans she'll be making while waiting for him to give his two cents."

"He's a rabbit."

"Yeah. Rabbits have ideas. That's why he's always hanging out in his house."

"He's hanging out in his house because his owner is a freak."

Gwen whirls around. "Who's a freak?"

"You." Aaron smirks. "But we love you anyway."

"You'd better. Or else I'll get Mom to take more money from you." She narrows her eyes and points to Kate, who is running around behind her stand and handing out sandwiches. Actually, it's not a stand, but folding tables decorated with tinsel and white felt to represent snow. Michael Bublé's "It's Beginning to Look a Lot Like Christmas" drifts over the square. I don't think I've ever seen nicer folding tables.

"We worship you, Gwendolyn," Levi says, taking her face in his hands and covering her cold-flushed cheeks with kisses. She fends him off with a laugh and slips under his arms.

Kate pours a ladle of hot punch into a tin mug and hands it to me. "Your first Christmas party in Aspen, Paisley. Don't let the reindeer frighten you."

I take a gulp, burn my throat, cough, for a moment think I'm going to die, then everything's okay again. "Reindeer?"

"Not real ones," Gwen says after taking a bite of her sandwich and delighting me with a view of it in her mouth. She points to one of the brightly flashing plastic animals missing half its face. A few feet past it, there is one with its stomach missing. I can see the cables that are lighting it up. The deer are horrible.

"They're William's. He got them from his father, who got them from his father, who got them from *his* third cousin's great-grandmother."

"They look like Halloween decorations."

Levi nods. "Beautiful, right?"

"Very."

Aaron points at Silver Lake with his sandwich. "Harper's warming up. She's up next. Do we want to watch her flutz?"

"Oh, do we ever." Gwen grabs hold of me and Aaron, who quickly shoves the last bite of sandwich into his mouth in order to take Levi's hand with his other and leads us toward the ice.

I watch Harper. She seems concentrated, her jaw tight as she puts one step in front of the other and glides gracefully over the ice. In one smooth movement, she turns around and continues skating backward. Her concentration wavers as her eyes dart over the crowd.

She's looking for someone, I think. It doesn't take long for the colored lights to reveal the disappointed shimmer in her eyes that makes it clear it's in vain.

Maybe her parents. Maybe Knox. I don't know, but I feel sorry for her. But when her program begins and she not only fails to land her Lutz but the Rittberger, too, I feel really bad for her. Harper can be terrible. But I don't think that's everything. I think she's more than that. She makes an immense effort to keep everyone at bay, from looking inside her walls.

Maybe she'll begin to pull them down someday. I have no interest in walls. I can't climb.

The moment her music ends, and she slumps down like a dying swan, I can't see anything. Everything is bright, everything is blinding. Harper looks like she's burning up' and all I can think is, *what is happening?*

"Too bright, William!" It's Ruth's voice, definitely Ruth's voice. "Turn down the damn spotlights!"

Then it stops and I can see the real Harper-swan on the ice, not the burning one.

Life is beautiful.

But Gwen is continuing to squeal so unmercifully in my ear.

She grabs my arm and jumps up and down at my side, shouting something about "fate," her breath smelling of sandwiches and jawbreakers, and then I see Levi conspiring with her, patting her on the back again and again as if the two of them had won something.

My eyes drift over to Aaron because his sympathetically contorted mouth gives me hope that he'll tell me what's going on.

He shrugs and points his thumbs to the silhouettes at the top of Buttermilk Mountain. "You've been chosen," he calls.

"What?"

"By the tandem oracle."

It is so loud that I can hardly understand him. So I try to read his lips but what reaches me is "tan-demo-racle," and I don't really know if I'm all that interested in any kind of demonstration.

I want to tell him as much, but then I see the great big black spotlight, in whose sphere of light I'm standing, which was the reason for my temporary blindness. Suddenly everyone starts yelling things like, "Tandem oracle!" "It's on the tandem oracle!"

What in the hell is the tandem oracle?

The people push me across the square with them, past the tinsel folding tables, past the monster reindeer, until I find myself in front of some red-and-white barricade tape, behind which there's Knox standing in front of a gondola.

Next to him a snowboard. A...tandem snowboard.

Now it's clear what the tandem oracle's all about. I put two and two together. I've been chosen. The happy chosen one who gets to stand on this thin board with the snowboard star and take a death-defying ride down Buttermilk Mountain.

I think my diaphragm is starting to cramp, but before I can listen to my body more closely, William and Wyatt are putting pads on every part of me they can think of and pressing a helmet into my hand. I stumble over Knox's snowboard and stagger toward him, and he grabs me with an arm.

He doesn't look at me. He hasn't since we were in the store together. He's holding onto me but looking at my boots.

I'm standing right in front of you, I think. *Lift your head and look at me.*

He doesn't. Instead, he opens the gondola, waits until I'm sitting on the bench and then gives a signal to have it start up. He gets in and sits right next to me, two inches away at most. I can smell him; he smells of snow and vetiver and *Knox*. The fairy lights shine in and envelop him in color, orange on his ear, green on his neck. I don't want to touch him, even though my fingertips tingle and crave it.

The gondola begins to move. Knox doesn't look at me. He keeps on looking at the floor—right where all the unstated words are.

27
The Ice Is Burning

KNOX

THIS ORACLE—ONE OF WILLIAM'S *GREAT IDEAS*, naturally—could've chosen anyone. Truly anyone.

Now I'm sitting here with Paisley, crammed into a tiny nutshell attached to a cable, and I have no idea what to say. Or if I should say anything at all.

I don't like her sitting so close to me and her breath fogging up the window. It forces me to think about her, and I don't want to think about her. Because if I do, I'll start imagining her breath wetting my skin instead of the windowpane, her lips gently brushing my ear...

"Do you want to act as if I don't exist from now on or something?"

She asks this amusedly, with a soft laugh in her voice, but she doesn't really find it funny, and neither do I. I don't want to pretend that she doesn't exist, but I don't want to look at her either, I don't want my heart to suddenly make unnatural movements, I want to pull her close to me, even though hugs have never been my thing. I don't want something if she doesn't.

I finally look up. Ouch. I wasn't prepared for her hurt expression. It makes me choke up. Her eyes are big and full of hope, two little pieces of heaven set in her face.

I look away again. "Don't be goofy."

She flares her nostrils. "You're *ignoring* me, Knox. You've been ignoring me for days."

I try to move away from her a bit, but it's impossible. I lean back with a sigh and run a finger over the corrugated ankle strap of my board. "You're my chalet girl. Nothing more. And that's how I'm treating you." I turn to face her.

Paisley looks like I've smacked her. "I'm your chalet girl and *nothing more?*"

"You didn't want to be anything else," I remind her. "It was your decision."

For a moment, it looks like she's wrestling with herself. Her cheeks turn pink and blotched, and the sensitive part of her neck tells me her pulse is racing. I love when that happens. A frighteningly large part of me wants to put my lips on that very spot and enjoy feeling the hairs on the back of her neck stand up.

"This isn't all that easy," Paisley says. She seems to have put her nervousness aside, because now she straightens up, but the dignified posture is somewhat ruined by the pads *all* over her body. They're the ones you usually wear to play rugby—on your knees, shins, thighs, arms… There's even a larger one across her upper body. At the last city council meeting, William insisted that we get these things.

"You wander through life, and everything just falls into your hands. I mean, Knox, the superstar. Knox, the millionaire's son. Knox, the stud. You get what you want because everything has always been easy for you." She takes a deep breath, puffs out her chest, her face real small in her armor. "But it wasn't the case for all of us, you know? It's not *easy* for everyone. Some people have things they need to work through, Knox, for some people things are *really dirty*."

"You have no idea how I'm doing, Paisley." Her words hit home. They cover my heart like a dark veil that tightens with every breath. "You have *no idea* what I've got to work through."

Paisley turns white. A bit gray and opaque, like the sky on

particularly snowy days. She is looking at me as if she knows something, but there's no way. Her eyes make me even angrier, I've got to catch my breath before continuing. "You pigeonhole people, you know that? Could be that you have a *horrible* fucking past, Paisley. Could be that you're broken, totally done. But that does *not* give you the right to judge others as if you know them, though you clearly do not."

"Knox…"

"No, you wait. I'm sick of the two of us circling each other like two lions before a fight. I'm sick of constantly being worried about you, wondering whether you're okay, only to have you hit me over the head. You don't want me, fine, no big deal, but stop going on and on about how I'm just treating you like a chalet girl."

At that moment the gondola reaches the middle station. Before Paisley can say anything, I slide the door open and step outside. The fresh air smells like new snow and black night. I breathe it in deep, enjoying the burning cold in my nostrils. Up here, it's dead quiet.

Out of the corner of my eye, I see Paisley having trouble getting out of the gondola with all her pads on. I could help her, a part of me even wants to, but it doesn't matter because the very next second she lands knee-deep in the snow and trudges over to me.

I could *eat her alive*. First and foremost, of course, I'm pissed off and hurt. But God, the way she's doddering across the slope in her thick armor… I have to look up at the sky and take another deep breath to get the twitching of the corner of my mouth under control.

"Knox, listen…" Paisley wheezes upon reaching me. I can see her chest rising and falling while she looks at me as if she wants to say something really meaningful. Two strands of hair are hanging over her face. Her fingernails brush her cheek as she tucks them back under her cap, leaving two red streaks. "I, umm, don't know how to snowboard."

Yep. Real meaningful.

Just one big step and I'm standing right in front of her. Paisley has to look up at me, but she's not looking into my eyes. Instead, she's staring at my snowboard jacket, at the huge X that separates the letters D-O-P-E. The brand that sponsors me. If they only knew how *well* that jacket described my current life…

It takes a while for Paisley to let out her held breath. When I put my index finger to her chin and force her to look me in the eyes, she shudders. I grin, real short, uncontrollably, an angel's smile, then run the tip of my finger along her face, stopping right under the sensitive spot right beneath her ear, there, where her cap ends. It feels like I'm painting her, and I like it. I like it so much. My finger wanders farther, caresses the delicate bridge of her nose and explores the curve of her lower lip. She opens her mouth a crack, licks her lips with the tip of her tongue and, *oh fuck*, my little guy down there begins to throb. I can feel her breath on my face. It would be so *easy* to kiss her. So *easy* to just overcome the last inch and let her breath become mine.

Paisley fogs my mind. I know myself and at the same time don't anymore. I don't know who I am at all. Suddenly she is everything that defines me, and that fact supersedes any rational thought as to why I shouldn't be holding her chin right now, why I shouldn't have my hands around her face, my fingertips beneath her cap, between her cold lips, in her warm hair.

Paisley looks at me. I think she sees it all. I don't think she sees a thing. But maybe more than I do, because, right now, I have no idea who or what I am. I only know that Paisley is here, right in front of me, a hundred miles away. Something isn't right with her. No, something isn't right with both of us, but I want us to find out together what that is. I want us to find out together and then decide what we want to be. Broken together, lonely together, or simply Paisley and Knox.

I swallow. My throat feels raw. We are so close that my lips are touching the corner of her mouth when I talk. "I won't kiss you," I mumble. It's cold, but Paisley's skin is on fire. "Not today, Paisley."

When I take a step backward, I can see all the tension leave her body. Her shoulders sink. She's standing there ruffled up in her body armor in the middle of the slope beneath the pitch-black sky, looking at me like I've abandoned her.

"Why not?"

The words are hardly more than a whisper, but they hover above us for what seems like forever, before fading at the peak of Buttermilk Mountain.

The corner of my mouth twitches again, but this time I'm unable to keep it down, and I break into a grin. I look to the ground, push a bit of snow to the side with the tip of my boot, then look back up. "You're a cassowary bird, that's why."

"I'm a...what?"

"A cassowary."

"A cassowary," she repeats, as if she wanted to see how the word tasted. "What's that?"

"Look it up."

She just stands there, confused, looking at me, but doesn't say a thing. My snowboard makes a dull sound as I let it drop onto the ground, ending our moment. If we even had one. I think so. With Paisley and I, this is how things are. We collect moments. Moments, but nothing more.

"I don't know how to snowboard, Knox," she repeats, her eyes on the board before shifting to the slope. She swallows.

"Doesn't matter. I'm good enough for both of us. My discipline is really the half-pipe, but I can make it down a mountain, too. Easy peasy."

Her mouth is agape. "You are *so* full of yourself."

I kneel down to open the bindings and wave to her to get on. "Nothing wrong with being full of yourself when you know how to do something."

Her breath comes in bursts. She looks down the slope again, kneads her hands, exhales trembling. "I don't know. I don't think I can do this. What if I break something? Or throw a concussion into the mix? I wouldn't be able to skate anymore, I wouldn't know who I was, and…"

"Hey." Her hand is in mine; without noticing, I must've grabbed it. Her delicate fingers jerk for a second, as though she wanted to pull them away, but she doesn't. I should take her hand more often, now that I know I can. "You're riding with me. I can count the number of falls I've had on one hand. On top of it, this here's the first slope. It's not a long way down. Just a few minutes. *Trust me.*"

Two words, so much meaning. As I'm saying them, I realize how dumb they are. Her eyes are telling me that she's going through 285 reasons why she shouldn't trust me. No doubt she's making a list of all my scandals. Man was that *dumb*, telling her to trust me when I don't even trust myself. *Seriously dumb.*

But she nods. For some unfathomable reason she nods, puts on her helmet, and sticks her feet into the tandem board's bindings. I snap her in, check everything over two and three times before stepping into my own.

"Listen, you've got to play along a bit, okay?" When her eyes widen in panic, I continue. "Don't worry. I'll do most of the work. You weigh as much as a fly, I won't have to compensate much. But make sure you stay like you are right now." I grab her shoulders lightly to check her balance. "Yeah, and keep your balance a bit with your arms. No, wait, let me show you." I lift her arms into the right position, check her stance. "Perfect. You'll see how you have to move, but it won't be much. I've got it. Don't squirm too much, okay?"

"Okay." She swallows half the word so that it sounds like *Nkay.*

My soft laughter gets lost on the slope. "Ready?"

"No."

"Good. That's the best moment."

I lower her goggles over her eyes before putting on my own, then give a push forward.

Paisley shrieks. Until she's got to gasp for air, then she starts shrieking again. But then she starts to laugh, and, really, it's the most beautiful thing I've ever heard. I didn't know that something like that was possible, but my heart reacts and makes me warm all over. Paisley coughs, she's laughing so hard. I don't want her to ever stop.

The last time I felt this happy on my board was when I wasn't yet a pro. When I just did it for myself, here and there, when I felt like it. Ever since, I've had all this pressure to be perfect, to not make any mistakes, every course has felt endless. I'm a half-pipe snowboarder, so I rarely give any fans a ride, but when I do, even that causes me stress. It never lasts longer than a few minutes, but they stretch out and feel like hours while I convince myself that I've got to be quicker, more precise, more elegant. It's not fun. It hasn't been fun in a really long time; it's just pure pressure, the pure fear of failing. Of being a disappointment.

Right now, though, I can't disappoint anyone. Right now it's just for us, Paisley and me, and we're laughing. We're laughing like we weren't broken, like we were simply happy, and, right now, maybe we even are.

Everyone is cheering when we arrive at the foot of Buttermilk. It's the first time we've ever offered this tandem ride for guests at the Christmas party. Dad had brought it up at the city council meeting because Jennet thought we should do something in the meanwhile for me publicity-wise. William was all over it immediately. No wonder. He agrees to anything that's good for Aspen's image. Whether or not I was interested wasn't of interest to anyone, and I was pissed, I mean really fucking *pissed*, but, at the moment, I'm loving it.

While I'm getting out of my bindings, Paisley is taking off her helmet. Her cheeks are red, and her eyes are glowing with excitement. "I didn't die!" she calls out. "I made my way down a steep mountainside on a thin board and didn't die!"

"We've got to make sure of that first," William says, who suddenly appears next to us in this full-body down snowsuit and raises his hand into the air. I don't know how he can move in that thing. It looks so *uncomfortable*. "How many fingers am I holding up?"

"Three," Paisley says.

"Wrong! Four."

"No." Paisley frowns. "Three."

"You sure?"

"Yeah."

"Okay. Three. You're good."

William begins freeing her from her armor, and Paisley peers over his shoulder toward Silver Lake. Levi and Aaron are gliding with parallel moves across the ice and turning before Aaron puts his arms under Levi's underarms, leans back, and lifts his partner into the air while making a spin. The crowd breaks into applause. Some people are whistling.

They're good but, I can't watch them for too long. It hurts. That sound. Skates on ice. It hurts.

"I'm coming up," Paisley says. She looks at me expectantly. "You going to watch?"

You going to watch?

She asks as if it was nothing. She asks as if it was something I could simply *do*. Watch.

William's eyes dart toward me as he's undoing her kneepads. His mouth twists in sympathy. He doesn't quite know what's wrong with me, but he knows that I gave up ice hockey. Everyone in Aspen knows that I avoid the ice. Everyone except Paisley.

"I, umm..." Actually, I just want to tell her I can't. What with these tandem rides and all, I'd have a good excuse. But standing there with her slight smile and open expression, as if she'd be happy about it, as if she'd be *really* happy about me watching her just confuses me completely. "Yeah. Yeah, of course I'll watch."

Did I just say that? Did that come out of *my* mouth? Judging by the way she's beaming, I did.

"Okay. Cool."

Yeah. Cool.

Paisley slips under the barricade tape and immediately runs into Gwen who grabs her and brings her over to Silver Lake.

I watch her go with a sinking feeling in my stomach. I put my hand on my neck and briefly look into the sky before turning to William. "Can we hold off on the tandem rides for a sec?"

He's still holding all of Paisley's pads in his arms. Usually, William would start to bitch and moan and give me a song and dance about how all the times are set so that so-and-so-many people can get a ride but this time he doesn't. This time he just nods.

"Thanks."

I turn around and slip under the tape myself. Standing back up, I meet Ruth's glance.

"My dear boy," she says, her voice full of sympathy.

That's how I feel. Like a boy. Like being twelve again, distraught and afraid. But I go on, step by step, on past the folding tables. My heart feels like it's pounding out of my chest.

I stop next to one of the blinking pines. "White Christmas" stops playing over the speakers, and Paisley comes onto the ice. I hear steps behind me, very clearly, as everything is quiet, and Wyatt creeps into view.

He doesn't look at me. He's looking at Paisley. But he asks, "All good?"

It's a *you-don't-have-to-do-this* all good. A *don't-torture-yourself-man* all good.

"All good."

Wyatt can hear what I say next. Though I'm just talking to him in my head—*Can you stay here next to me until it's over?*—he can hear it. He nods and stays put.

That's how things are between us. We stay put.

Ed Sheeran starts up. "I See Fire."

Paisley begins to move. Just a second ago she was stiff as a rod on our snowboard, now she's dancing on the ice, gracefully, elegantly, as if she'd never done anything else. She doesn't just skate across the ice. No, she *hypnotizes* everyone who's watching. Everything about her, every step, every facial expression, the smooth movements of her arms, is art. The way she throws her head back, strokes her cheeks with her hands. She looks like she's suffering, like she's screaming. She radiates so much feeling, so many emotions, that my whole body breaks out in goose bumps.

The bridge begins, and Paisley outdoes everything else. She jumps, does a double, a triple, and lands flawlessly. Then she moves into a dance, brushes the ice with her palms, turns, falls to the ground, and covers her eyes with her hands to match the lyrics. She rears up, falls to all fours, digs her hand into her hair and pulls, really pulls, smacks the ice. For one moment, I think she feels, she really feels everything she's showing. It's all so *real*, goddamn, is it real.

At the end of the song, I lose myself. I lose my heart, I lose everything I spent all these years erecting around myself. Every bit of protection. Every ounce of control. It doesn't matter, nothing matters, because *she's* there, and she is everything.

I lose myself. And fall in love.

I forget why I even wanted to stay away from her, why I had priorities.

But then I hear them. The screams. Suddenly, without my being able control them.

They're loud. They're in my head, but loud. It's like they were right next to me. And then Paisley just disappears. Everyone disappears. I'm alone at Silver Lake, alone with my mom while she's *screaming, screaming, screaming,* in truth, she had only screamed once, and real loud, but in my head it's thousands of times, over and over.

The ice turns red. It turns red and I remember what I've been running from.

28

Cinderella Story

PAISLEY

I GOOGLED "CASSOWARY." IT'S A BIRD WITH A RED-BLUE neck and golden eyes. They're beautiful, but shy, and if someone comes too close, the birds kill them.

I get it. I get it and can even understand the reference, but I don't like it. I'm a cassowary, and I don't like it.

Knox watched my program. I know it because my eyes have developed a Knox radar and in between jumps I was able to locate him.

He watched me the whole time, but looked as if I wanted to cause him pain, as if I was a cassowary and would hit him with my wings. As the last sounds faded and, puffing, I assumed my final position, Knox was gone. The tandem oracle had started back up, so he had to be back on the slope. But something tells me that's not why he left.

After my program, I didn't have the chance to talk to him. I had to leave the fair earlier than everyone else in order to clean the tourist section of the resort, put out new towels, and get the fire going in the fireplace before everyone came back. I have to wait until ten to serve tea, fill up the buffet in the lounge with salad, baked Camembert and lingonberries, and then wait until every single one of them is full and happily goes to bed, so I can then clean everything up and set the breakfast table for tomorrow morning.

My limbs are heavy as lead when I finally make it back to the hallway of the Winterbottoms' resort. I consider taking a bath, maybe even with a muscle relaxant. I'm dreading tomorrow and the sound of my alarm, far too early, so I can go for a jog before heading off to training. I already know that I'll be tossing and turning and pressing the pillow to my head to make the annoying beep stop, so that I can fall back asleep to the gentle trickle of snow on the window. But it won't stop, and I won't go back to sleep. I will get up, as I do every morning, far too tired. I will have a cup of coffee, *think about Knox*, jog through the snow, *think about Knox*, get breakfast ready for the tourists, *think about Knox*, and eventually head off to iSkate with Gwen.

But first things first. I need sleep. Deep, refreshing, peaceful sleep.

I reach the front door, enter the code, yawn, pull the door open and…

Stop dead in my tracks.

He can't be for real. This cannot be *for real*.

My mind doesn't want to accept what my eyes are seeing as they dart across the room and see all the dancing, groping, drunk people. A few hours ago, I thought something in Knox had changed. I thought he'd become deeper somehow, more *mature*.

But this here…this isn't just some après-ski thing. This is a full-blown *Project X* party.

They've set up a zip line. A *zip line*! I have no idea how that's even possible, but the thing is stretched across the entire living room and out through the sliding glass door. They've fastened it to a tree and, here inside, to the balustrade. People are huddled up on the stairs waiting their turn to be so world-weary as to take their chance of climbing over the railing, hopping onto the swing, zipping outside, jumping off at least ten or fifteen feet above the ground, and landing in a screaming pile of limbs in the pool.

The house looks like it's going to burst, there are so many people. Strobes are lighting up people's sweaty faces, accentuating the half-naked women's smeared makeup. Mascara around their mouths, lipstick on their cheeks.

People are everywhere—in the heated pool, in the hot tub—*everywhere*, like ants on an ice cream cone. Some song or other by Drake is coming out of the speakers, and women are *rubbing their asses* against dudes' junk like this was some kind of competition.

I slam the door, but no one pays any attention. No one hears me. Of course, they don't. This is an orgy, and everyone is writing their own film.

The women eye me suspiciously as I venture into the lion's den. They scrutinize my body, wrapped in an oversized woolen sweater that I have to roll up the sleeves of, my skinny jeans, colorful knit socks from Ruth, and slippers. I can hear their thoughts—so obvious, so loud—as if they were being shouted right into my face. Seeing as that I'm not half naked like they are, I'm an alien body. Someone who doesn't belong because I didn't follow the dress code. They look at my wool sweater like it's the strongest male repellent in the world.

I push myself past a particularly sweaty group of women who are all wearing bikinis as if it wasn't winter in Aspen but the Hamptons in summer. One of them stumbles while making room for me and spills the contents of her red cup across my arm. Judging by the smell, it's got to be whiskey. I wriggle my nose.

"Oops," she mumbles, followed by a burp. "Accident." Which comes out like *cinent*.

I look at her face and suddenly recognize who it is. Camila. Wyatt's sister. Who at the last party let strangers stuff money into every orifice of her body. Camila, who is *clearly* completely off her ass. She can hardly stand. One of her friends has to hold her up, and her head is wobbling strangely back and forth.

"Camila," I say, reaching out my hand and grabbing her waist to keep her from falling over. "Where's your brother?"

"My brother," she repeats. Her eyelids flicker. "Everywhere and nowhere."

I look at the poor girl and see in her perfect, symmetrical face framed by chocolate-colored waves of beach-look curls how *shitty* things must be for her.

"Okay, come with me. Come on."

I pry her loose from her blond friend and lead her through the huge living room, which, if it were a sport, would definitely bring me a gold for my country. For Camila can hardly walk. She stumbles right and left, is hanging off my arm like a sack of potatoes, and looks like she's going to topple over at any moment.

Wyatt is leaning against the kitchen counter, pushing his tongue into the mouth of one of the hundreds of bikini gals as if he wanted to melt into her. I lay my free hand on his shoulder and pull him away from his lady friend so that he can see me.

"Yo," he says. His eyes are blurry. "What's it going, Paisley?"

"Your sister," I hiss and have difficulty keeping Camila standing up straight. "Whatever other shit you've got to take care of, Wyatt, *take care of her first.*"

He looks at Camila and blinks a few times as if only becoming aware of her now. Then he lets go of the woman next to him as if he'd burned himself on her skin and is next to Camila in a second.

"Mila," he says quietly, taking her face in both hands. There is so much affection in his glance, so much *love and care,* that for a moment I feel a stab in my chest: I wish someone would look at me that way. Just once. "Mila, look at me."

She tries, I can see her really trying, but at the last second she turns her head and vomits into the sink. I grab hold of her hair reflexively. Back in Minneapolis, when I was small and helpless and another person, I had to do this often. For my mother. I was a world champion hair-holder, holding her thin, brittle hair while she threw up into our disgusting trailer toilet following one of her alcohol-drug-whatever binges. Camila's retching sounds remind me of that, and those memories are even worse than that toilet was.

Repulsive. *Repulsive.*

"Jake!"

A tall dude sticks his head out from the refrigerator, a bottle of water in his hand.

"You're sober, right?"

Jake nods. "Why?"

"Can you drive my sister and me to the hospital?"

Jake's glance wanders to Camila, whose body is surging up again. I can hear her whimpering.

"Everything's fine," I whisper, while moving my hand in calming circles on her back. "Everything's going to be okay."

"Of course," Jake says, coming to our side and handing Camila the water. "Here. Drink this on the way to the car, okay?"

Camila is chalk white, there is vomit on her cheeks, and a single strand of hair has gotten caught there. Her fingers trembling, she takes the bottle while Wyatt puts his muscular arms around her and nods to me. Tense jaw, stony expression.

I watch the three make their way to the door. Camila can hardly walk without slumping, so Wyatt puts his other hand under her knees and lifts her up to carry her.

An annoyed snort tears my gaze away from the front door. Wyatt's bikini-clad friend is plucking at the skimpy band of her bikini bottom and looking at me like she'd strangle me with it. "You like him?"

"What?"

"I asked whether you like him." She picks a red cup off the counter, looks inside for a moment, then gulps it down. *How stupid*, I think, *drinking out of someone else's cup. How stupid.* "Wyatt."

I stare at her. "Why in the world are you *asking* me something like that?"

She clicks her tongue, tosses her blond hair over her shoulder, and gives an affected laugh. "Why else would you have interrupted us? *Intentionally?*"

I blink. She can't be serious. "I have no idea if you had anything but *Wyatt's dick* in mind over the last few minutes, but his sister was just…"

"Oh, Camila." She waves her cup as if I was about to tell her something she's known forever. "She's always like that."

I'm filled with rage. I can feel my blood beginning to boil. "Oh, I see, and because someone's like that all the time, naturally it's just fine to leave them to themselves? Even when they *quite clearly* need some help?"

Her fingers twitch. I wouldn't have noticed if she wasn't clutching the cup, which is becoming slightly dented. "It's Camila," she repeats as if there simply wasn't any response. "She does that every time."

"For God's sake." I take the cup out of her hand before she can have another drink and dump it in the sink. "You ever wonder why? Did it ever occur to you that she feels *far too much* and so takes any opportunity to not feel at all?"

The girl stares into the sink where I just tossed her drink. And doesn't say a word.

I snort, push myself away from the kitchen counter, and walk past her without another word. It makes me sick to see how people close their eyes to reality. The world isn't just beautiful and full of colorful flowers. There are bushes and poisonous plants, too. The sun doesn't just rise; it also sets. Every day it's new, and it makes sure that darkness falls. Life can be ugly, so ugly, and if we do nothing about it, if we look away as soon as the beauty fades, then the days get darker and darker. And we will have failed. Failed all along the line.

I discover Knox in the pool. He's floating on his back, his eyes on the roof. It looks like the world has stopped turning for him. As if he didn't notice anything going on around him. Everyone seems to be making out with everyone else, right next to him some guy tumbles off that stupid zip line into the water.

A woman is pouring beer over her chest and letting two guys lick it off, which is super nasty and makes me think of all the tongue bacteria, and that later on this girl will go to sleep drooling with Streptococcus mutans all over her body, but there's Knox floating there, like it's nothing at all. He's just there, like a waterlily or a tanned corpse with an *incredibly ripped* body. I want to yell at him until I'm hoarse, I want to pound my fists against his chest until my knuckles hurt and ask him if he *really* brought all these people over. I do all of this in my mind, I can see it right before me, crystal clear, but in reality...

Well, in reality, I just stand there in my slippers and colored knit socks, staring at him and thinking that he's both December and July. Which makes sense, because his skin is snow-white but warm, it really is, every time I touch him. He's December and July. *How beautiful he is*, I think.

How *beautiful*.

Okay, I've got to stop. I've got to stay focused or in less than a minute I'm going to jump off this zip line myself and let my skin be smeared with Knox's *Streptococcus mutans*. And that wouldn't be a good idea, we all know that—bacteria is bad.

I push myself through the half-naked bodies and gasp for air as I slide the huge glass door open and step outside. It is damn cold. God. Maybe I should hop into the heated pool myself to fend off the frostbite I'm sure to get.

"Knox," I say, reaching the side of the pool. My teeth are chattering. Around us there is nothing but total snow chaos; even the silhouettes of the Aspen Highlands are difficult to make out. He doesn't seem to hear me though; no wonder, he's off in his own world, so I crouch down next to him and splash water in his face. "Knox!"

He jerks up. I've disturbed his corpse position, but it's no big deal because he's gone completely underwater, sparing me from having to see disturbingly lovely upper body. Okay, maybe it is a big deal. Just a little bit.

"Get out."

"Why?" he asks, scratching his birthmark. God, that birthmark! A drop of water drips over his face and pearls upon his lip.

"Because I want to talk to you, and if I spend one more second on this frozen ground, I'm going to freeze to death."

"Then get in."

"I'm not dressed appropriately. I'm wearing clothing, you see."

"Take them off."

"Yeah, right." My fingertips are growing numb, holding them against the ground as I am. "As if I'd jump in in my underwear."

"I don't understand the problem."

He says it so nonchalantly, so typically *Knox-like*, but it's not Knox. Not really. He's not himself. His smile looks weird, as if raising the corners of his mouth was difficult, and somehow he seems… I don't know, as if looking at me was a kind of torture.

"Get out, Knox."

"And if I don't?"

"Then I'll tell your dad about the candy stash I recently discovered in the linen cabinet."

I don't wait for him to respond. I get up, without having seen his reaction, and march back into the living room. The music is so loud that the bass is making my slippers vibrate. By the time I reach the fireplace, my feet have been stepped on twice, some kind of sticky substance has been spilled on my arm, and I have been elbowed by three different people. I have to take a deep breath, close my eyes, and slowly count to ten so as not to lose it.

When I open my eyes back up, I lose it anyway. Knox is in front of me, a step away at the most, drying himself off with a towel. He's wearing blue-and-white-striped Gucci trunks, and for the first time,

I'm aware of his knobby knees. They look like two uneven scoops of ice cream.

"What's up, Paisley?" Knox shakes his head like a wet dog. He's sweet and his hair is scruffy, not blond and not brown. Something in between. He flicks his towel against my arm and laughs. A bit soft, a bit raw, a bit too lovely.

"What's up with *you*?" I cross my arms and lift my chin. The fire is defrosting my fingers and making them itch. "What's this shit all about, Knox?"

He tosses his towel over his shoulders and pulls on it like it was a rubber band. "No idea what you're talking about."

"Seriously?" A group of women walks past—"Hey, Knox"—one of them runs her hand down his back while the other two cast me mean glances. Knox gives them his famous *I'm-going-to-eat-you-for-breakfast-babe* smile and, in return, their looks make it clear that they'd love to tear off his Gucci shorts immediately.

As Knox makes no effort to interrupt the *let's-have-sex* looks, I roll my eyes and snap my fingers in front of his face. He turns to look at me and sighs annoyedly.

I wasn't aware that such small things like sighs carried such weight. Now I know it, for the sound makes me break out in goose bumps even though I'm standing next to the fireplace. It stings, so much so that I put a hand on my chest and swallow a gasp.

Knox is annoyed. By me. *I* am annoying him. Of course, I am. I'm his chalet girl, after all. His chalet girl who's getting in the way of his fun. A buzzkill. I've always been one of those. I can hear the voices in my head whispering. *Paisley, don't be such a party pooper. Let Mommy have her drink and go back to bed.*

I didn't have a bed. Our trailer only had one, and that belonged to Mom and her lovers. Sometimes, on good days, I was allowed to sleep with her. Otherwise, my "bed" was the little corner bench behind the little table. It wasn't terrible, really. I liked it. I could lift up the cushions because they'd come loose from the rivets, and when Mom and dude number four, eight, twenty-six, one-hundred-twelve were too loud, I could count the wood grain. The bench was my good friend. I carved my initials into the wood with a rusty breadknife. It belonged to me, and I was proud because, back then, beyond it, nothing belonged to me. I didn't even belong to myself. If I had, Mom wouldn't have tried pawning me off to the junkie with the dead cat in our front "yard," which grew worse day after day.

Now Knox is snapping his fingers in front of *my* face. "Hello?"

"What?" My tone is bitter because I don't see Knox right now, but my mom, and I hate her, I hate her profoundly for calling me a party pooper, for letting me down, and, quite simply, for *not loving me* even though I loved her immensely. Immensely. "What do you want, Knox?"

"Me? You're the one who called me over, threatening to blackmail me with telling my dad about my candy."

True. I did. But I forgot. I even forgot the party going on around us the moment Mom came to mind. But suddenly it all comes back: Knox. The music. All the people. The half-naked women. *The zip line.* And I'm pissed off, so pissed off at Knox for having thrown the party although I'm tired, although we were on the snowboard together, and I thought that we had shared a moment—a moment where he looked at me and touched me and made me *tremble*. I thought he had changed, for me, and other women were of no interest. But then I come over here and see that I was wrong, so wrong, and that it's because of me. He wanted things this way. Knox wanted me. *I could be ready.* He said that, just a few days ago, but now he's anything but ready, and all because of me. Because I didn't want it. That's what's making me so angry. *I* am making myself so angry.

"It's eleven o'clock, Knox!" I wave my hands around without knowing why. I think it probably looks stupid, but I keep doing it because it feels good. "Eleven o'clock! Do you know what that means?"

"Umm." Knox picks at the tag of his towel and tries to keep

himself from breaking into a grin. "No idea? Is this a new version of Cinderella or something, where, instead of midnight she's got to leave at eleven, or else she'll break out in warts or…"

"Knox!" He called me Cinderella. *Cinderella.* My eyes are burning with tears although I don't want them to be. It simply happens.

Only now does what he said seem to become clear to him. His amused grin disappears as if the moist gleam in my eyes had come from his. "Shit, Paisley. Sorry. I didn't mean it that way. Really, I wasn't thinking. It wasn't referring to you, I swear, it wasn't."

It takes all I've got to swallow the lump in my throat and hold back my tears. I don't want to cry, not now. I know that I will as soon as I'm under the shower upstairs and then once I'm in bed I know I'll make my pillow wet and my voice hoarse, but not right now.

"It means that I've been on my feet for more than eighteen hours. I went jogging, then I worked, then I had to train. Do you have any idea how hard training at iSkate is, Knox? *Do you?*"

His face contorts like I've given him a smack, but his pain doesn't interest me, for a change. I am far too angry.

"After that, I couldn't relax but had to get on the snowboard with you and go down the damn slope and then get back on the ice *one more time* de*spite* my trembling, exhausted legs, de*spite* my weak limbs and aching muscles. And then I get here but not to finally—*finally!*—fall into bed, but to take care of all the tourists, and to clean—yes, Knox, like *Cinderella*, you're right. You can be proud of yourself there. I'm fucking done, I just wanted to sleep, but then I get over here and find myself in the middle of one of your wrecking parties or orgies or whatever the hell it is and am now trying not to say anything, cause it's your party. You all set up a zip line, Knox, *a goddamn zip line!*"

I'm out of breath, I spoke so quick. Knox is plucking at the hem of his trunks. He's at least six-two, and he's got a hard chest, a bit like Jacob Black in the second part of *Twilight*. He's someone you just want to devour, but right now he looks like a beaten little boy.

Knox opens his mouth to say something, but I'm in such a rage I don't let him. "I don't get it, Knox." I push the arms of my wool sweater up and down, up and down. The fire is hot. "Your father is paying me to take care of the tourist area and your resort, *you included*, but I'm not here to be your nanny and to clean up after your parties so that Daddy doesn't find out. I'm not doing it anymore. You've got training early in the morning, Knox, just like me. Maybe you don't care about snowboarding anymore, but then you should be a man and say something. Say that you don't want to do it instead of half-assedly going through the motions and disappointing all the people who believe in you. And, on top of it all, making my life more difficult, although I am doing *everything* to try and straighten it out. So, I don't give a shit if you want to keep on partying. I don't give a shit if your dad comes home tomorrow and sees everything. I'm not taking care of it. I'm going to bed because I'm tired and, yeah, I have to take care of myself because it's eleven, and I'm Cinderella, and this is my own, brand-new story!"

Knox just stands there staring at me, he doesn't say a single word, and I don't let him. I turn around and push through the dancing crowd and the terribly long line for the zip line and walk up the stairs. In front of my room, I stop. There's a piece of lined paper on the door, it looks like it's been stuck there with carpet glue. The scrawled words read: *Anyone who steps foot in here is going to end up a naked mole rat out on the slope of the Highlands—Knox.*

I smile. I smile even though I am so angry. I convince myself that I'm smiling because of the carpet glue, seeing as that, in this house, there aren't any carpets, but I know that's nonsense.

I'm smiling because Knox has this strange talent of making my belly tingle with joy only seconds after making me just about insane.

I'd like to say that my move to Aspen changed everything, but that's just not true. Aspen didn't change me. Knox and me, it's one of those things.

We met, and everything changed.

29
The Boy Who Healed My Heart

PAISLEY

THE SILENCE WAKES ME UP.

Normally I'm a mummy in its sarcophagus: I only fall asleep when it is completely dark and still. But at the Winterbottoms', still is a foreign concept. Either Knox is having one of his parties or he's having people over, Wyatt and assorted groupies, for example. And on those rare days when he's alone, he keeps his TV running all day long in the room underneath mine. Not a soft, pleasant tone of some kind of documentary, say, but some action film or other, full of lots of shooting and all. Most of the nights I've been here at the resort I've cursed Knox and longed for days when I can fall asleep without earplugs and curses on my lips.

Now, it is quiet. But instead of enjoying it, my heart is starting to hammer against my chest, and I tear my eyes open. It is *alarmingly* quiet. Suddenly I'm afraid that something's happened. Maybe there was a break-in, and now Knox is chained to a chair while a guy in a black hoodie is holding a gun to his head, demanding millions.

Okay. Stop.

You have definitely *seen too many of Knox's action films, Paisley Harris.*

I dig through my various pillows and stick an arm out from under the beaver-fur blanket to grab my phone. It's 5:20 a.m. I love the early morning hours when the rest of the world is asleep, and it feels like I am the only person in the world. When everything feels a bit unreal, a bit like a dream, a bit hazy, a bit surreal, magical somehow, as if all my cares and concerns didn't exist, as if I was all alone. Just me and the world.

Getting up, my hair falls into my face like a tattered bird's nest. I yawn, rub my eyes, pull the heavy curtains back a bit, and enjoy the panoramic view of the Aspen Highlands at night. It's snowing, of course, and like every other time, the view takes my breath away. I want to pull the curtains shut again and toss myself into my pillow-dream-come-true, but something flashes in the corner of my eye.

It's the moonlight reflecting on one of the sunken iron lights by the pool. And in the pool, I see Knox. All alone. None of the other guests are around anymore, and all the beer cans and cups and stuff are gone. The outside area is…clean. This confuses me more than the sight of Knox in the pool.

Pulling my thick socks back over my feet, I slide into my slippers and go downstairs. Here, too, everything is clean. Even the garbage bags have been changed. The zip line is gone. I examine the area beneath the balustrade where it had been mounted and can only find the holes with effort. They've been filled in and painted over with some kind of brown paint so well that I doubt Mr. Winterbottom will ever notice.

I can tell Knox hears me slide open the glass door and walk toward him by the way he tenses up his shoulders, but he doesn't turn. He's leaning against the side of the pool, his back to me, elbows on the icy ground, looking off toward the Highlands. It's not as cold as before, as Knox has lit the big fire bowl on the terrace. Flames are licking the cold air and chasing it off. Crackling. I crouch down next to him and look off to the mountains as well. In the distance an owl is hooting.

"You cleaned up."

He doesn't say anything. This makes me feel insecure. Knox isn't usually the kind of guy to stay quiet. Most of the time he says too much. But never nothing at all. I think this frightens me. The idea that I could lose him, although he was never really mine. And my body immediately reacts by panicking. It's fascinating. My mind isn't asked whether it agrees as my hands pull my baggy AC/DC hoodie over my head and my woolen Christmas pajama bottoms with *ho-ho-ho* on them down. The clothes land in a pile beside the pool. He turns and looks at me.

My underwear and bra don't match. There are women who can manage that. Matching underwear and bras. I'm not one of them. My panties have purple dots. The elastic is coming away from the cotton to reveal a slice of my hip bone. My bra is black. The underwire is sticking out of the fabric and poking me in the side. I always wear a bra, even at night, because I'm afraid of someone coming and touching me. Because of Ivan. But I don't want to think about Ivan. I won't let him dictate my life. Not anymore.

Knox is staring at my hip bones. The gap between the elastic and the cotton is embarrassing, but the panic of losing Knox is greater. And so I'll give him everything. I will give him all of me, though I'm not all that sure how much is left.

My feet are naked, my toenails unpainted. I get hot when Knox's eyes finally leave my hips and wander across my stomach, linger on my simple cotton bra as if it were made of the nicest fabric. He licks his lips, inconspicuously, unchecked, but my abdomen reacts with a violent pull. His eyes reach mine and I see it, I see it real clearly.

Knox *wants* me. Not my body. *Me.*

I slide into the water. It's warm. Almost hot, but maybe that's just my blood boiling.

I sidle next to him. My thighs touch his. We don't look at each other. We're both staring forward. But our hearts are beating together in time. They are racing, as if they wanted to break out.

Eventually, I look at him. *You're allowed to*, I tell myself. I'm allowed to because I know that Knox wants me. It's time for me to stop moving and to turn toward him instead of always walking away. It is time for me to let go, so I can finally start over.

"Hello, Snow Queen." Knox's eyes are glowing. The bright points in the green combine with the black light of the recessed lights. He looks at me hungrily. As if he had been fasting for weeks, just for this moment, just for me.

I like it.

My nerves are tingling, I want to touch him. It feels like having a plate full of french fries in front of me. I can taste the salt on my lips. I can smell the fat. I want them, but I can't because my life isn't made for fries.

I've always stuck to that. To the rules. But I don't want to anymore. I want my fries.

I want Knox.

Water pearls from my hand as I raise it and touch his face. He's burning. His lips open and he lets out a soft sound. Something like *hruhh*, meaningless, in other words. Just for me. For me, this *hruhh* is everything.

My body is pulsating. With the outside of my hand I caress the outline of his face, past his ear, past his birthmark until stopping where his pulse wants to nestle up against me.

"Is this okay?" My voice is fluid, very soft. It lands on the quiet surface of the water and is carried away, but Knox smiles. Real faintly, and a little cloudy somehow.

"Yes."

His Adam's apple bounces. With fluttering lids his eyes wander to my collarbone. He caresses the tender bones as if wanting to explore them, and then along my jaw. For a second, he stops at the point below my ear, and I know why. He can see the faint, semicircle-shaped scar, a white half-moon on my skin. I break out in goose bumps.

"Here," he says, before moving on to my nose and drawing the direction of the sky. "Here, too."

My cheek grows wet as Knox moves the knuckle of his index finger across it: my skin tingles, electrified and charged, as his little finger runs along the shape of my ear. He stops at my earlobe, rubs it between thumb and index finger. "And this here."

"Tell me," I whisper. "Tell me what you mean."

"These are the places I lost myself and found you." His glance is careful. Slow. His eyes like a spring leaf, like the spot beneath the morning dew. Water is dripping off his hair onto my arm. I don't even feel it. "I can't get past these places when I look at you."

My fingers leave his throat and wander upward. Stop at his birthmark. Touch it.

"Here," I say.

Knox's fingers slide away from my ear. They dig into my hips, just a bit above the loose elastic band. His thumbs are on my hipbones. He strokes them, takes me as I am, with my tattered cotton panties and broken heart. We look at each other, we both see it, this longing, this *hunger*, and then he kisses me.

His caresses feel right. They feel sure. As if I could let myself fall and he would catch me. He will always catch me, no matter how deep the earth below me breaks. That's what his kisses say. And I can feel it.

Seconds pass. Minutes. Time goes by but neither of us interrupts what we have. I think of a jar of jam. I think about capturing this moment and being able to keep it forever. The feeling of his warm lips on mine. The warm water on our skin. The cold air in our faces. The crackling of the fire. The silent snow falling from the sky. This hot, irrepressible, and unconditional longing.

This here. Jam-jar moments. My moments, and I take them, hold them, they belong to me. I hold Knox, because he belongs to me, too. His lips. His birthmark. His caresses, soft as silk, wild as fire.

Knox and I are a storm. We are storms and flashes of lightning; we are thunder and rain. We are perfect chaos; we've lost control, each of us in our own way, but together we make sense. He the violent heat, I the long-evaporated water—ultimately, we had to come together. Ultimately, nature wanted it this way. Water and heat have to touch in order to explode.

Knox and I have exploded. We touched each other and exploded.

My hand makes its way through his wet hair, makes its way over and over through every individual strand before my fingernails move to scratch his back and come to rest on his wide shoulders. Knox growls against my lips and, with a single movement, spins me around so that my back is now against the side of the pool. His chest is pressing against mine, his hips against mine, his thighs. I lay my hands on his back, can feel the taut muscles, wrap my legs around his body out of the fear that he could slip away if I don't.

All around us is water. Heat. Cold. But when Knox lays his forehead against mine in order to catch his breath and makes that sound again—that *hruhh*—I don't notice any of it any longer.

Swollen lips. Lowered eyelids. Blotchy neck. That's Knox.

Racing heart. Pulsating desire. Captivating, *authentic* feelings. That's me.

I kiss him; his kisses are everything. They are the light in my darkness. They are the line that pulls me to him in my isolation. They are quiet and peace where previously there was only a hate-filled hissing, where previously there were memories that did not want to let me go.

I don't want to stop kissing him. I am hooked on how he makes me feel.

But then I do. I stop. I back away from him, lower my head and gasp, while looking at his blurry hands, there, on my hips beneath the water. I stop because I'm afraid of Knox wanting to go away again. I want to, I really want to, but I can't. Not yet.

But Knox doesn't go any further. He doesn't say a word. He just exhales heavily, just like me. And then I feel his cheek against mine. His wet lashes brushing my temples. His heart beating against my chest. It's quick.

"I could do it," he says.

My lips pucker against his skin when I smile. All of a sudden, we're not in the pool anymore. We're in the movie theater. The moment repeats.

"What could you do?"

"Be ready." His breath brushes my ear and suddenly there's a hot pulsing between my legs.

When I speak, my voice is husky and out of breath. "For what?"

His lips leave a warm and damp trace across my cheeks that get lost at the corners of my mouth. Knox looks at me, hardly an inch of space between us. "To change myself for you." The end of his nose brushes mine. I feel his breath on my skin. "If you want."

A gust of icy snow blows through the air. I can see it. I am sure.

"I do," I say. "Be prepared, Knox."

He smiles against my lips.

Kisses chase kisses and nothing has ever felt so right.

30

There Is Beauty in Surviving

KNOX

WE PUSHED THE LOUNGE CHAIRS TOGETHER AND COVered them with pillows and blankets. Tucked in nice and warm, each of us with a hot chocolate in hand, we're roasting marshmallows from the linen cabinet over the fire.

The sky is dark. Silent snowfall. Protected by the awning we're waiting for the sunrise because I told her that the moment the sun begins to rise behind the Aspen Highlands and the sky looks like it's been painted in pastels is something that feels a little bit like magic.

We don't have a lot of time, because we both have to go to training, but I notice how Paisley is trying to stretch the moment out. She's holding her cup with both hands and blows into it multiple times before taking a sip. She puts it to the side and has to bend down over the edge of the sofa to keep her marshmallow over the fire. It slowly turns golden brown. She holds it to her lips and breathes it in. I watch it. I watch every one of her tiny movements.

She looks at me. Laughs. "What's up?" *Whashup?*

"Nothing." The caramelized sugar sticks to the corner of her mouth. I reach out my hand and run my thumb across it. "I want things to work out between us."

"Yeah," she says. Swallows the marshmallow and puts the stick to the side. "Me too."

"But I don't have any idea how that works."

"How what works?"

I observe my own marshmallow, but do nothing. I held it directly into the flames, and now it's just a sticky black mass dripping onto the wood. I put my own stick to the side. "Doing it right."

Paisley observes my tar-like mass of marshmallow. The flames reflect in the glassy haze of her eyes. She licks her lips, and I want to kiss her again.

Again and again and again.

"There's no right or wrong between us. We'll make mistakes, but we're allowed. We *should*. For this to function doesn't mean everything has to run smoothly. It just needs to be *real*, Knox."

I know that that's what I want to be. For her. It might be tough though, because I haven't been that for a long time. *Real.* But I'm certain that I can be if I'm with Paisley. When I'm with her, I want to be myself. I have the feeling that she hates me the moment I pretend, the moment I'm no longer *Knox*, but loves discovering me, loves when I show more of myself. When I allow her to get a deeper look. Like a ragged, brittle map that you have to unroll carefully, piece by piece and not too quickly or otherwise everything will fall apart and then all is lost.

"Both of us," I say and tug at the tattered drawstrings of her hoodie. "Both of us have to be real."

Paisley turns away to watch a lonely piece of chocolate floating in her cup.

"The rules of the game have changed, huh?"

I pull the blanket straight, so it covers Paisley's naked skin where she's rolled up her hoodie. "Rules of the game?"

She looks at me. God. Those *ears*. What's the deal?

"A truth for a truth. Only answers, no questions, remember?"

I nod.

"If we want to be real, we should be allowed to ask questions. We should be honest with each other."

My pulse increases. I make circles on the white fabric of the pillows and know that she's right. I know it, but that word causes me to panic.

Honesty.

"Okay."

She turns to face me. The cover rustles. "If you had one wish, what would it be?"

I take a breath. I smell fire. Smell ice. Paisley looks at me attentively, seems to notice every detail. I readjust the pillow behind my head and look through the white fog to the snowy mountains, because I can't bring myself to look at her while saying what I want to say. What I *have to* say if I finally want to make peace with the monsters underneath my bed.

"I wish my mom had never died."

I wait for Paisley to ask the question of questions. The question that has been dogging me all these years and destroyed me. That calls the moment into my head over and over.

How did she die?

Paisley doesn't ask. She doesn't do it. She simply turns onto her back, glances past me toward the sky, and says, "If your mom was here, she'd tell you to stop."

"Stop what?"

"Dying before you die."

My limbs turn cold. Cold and then numb. My whole body breaks out into goose bumps even though I'm underneath a blanket next to the fire and have my hand wrapped around a cup of hot chocolate. Paisley has put her fingers around my heart and squeezed. She's grabbed hold of the black cloud that took possession of my soul and dangled it in front of my nose so that I stop running away from it. Although you can't grab hold of a cloud, she managed. *She grabbed it.*

"How do you do that?" The words float above us. Dissipate.

"How do I do *what*?"

"See what no one has ever seen."

"Knox." Slowly, I can almost count the milliseconds, the corners of her mouth stretch out. It's a sad smile—and the most beautiful I have ever seen. "You so clearly hide your feelings that I can't *but* see them. You're a first-quarter moon. A little radiant, a little luminous, but the greater part of your heart is pitch black." She puts her hot chocolate to the side and begins to draw imaginary lines from mole to mole on my arm. "Sometimes I wonder how much you'd shine if you'd just let the full moon appear."

I say, "You don't let it appear either."

She opens her mouth. Her pupils grow large, small, large. I see pain. "No," she says. "No, I don't."

I take her hand in mine. The hand with the scars. Trace the fine white lines. I think of her honesty when I ask, "What happened?"

Paisley looks at her hand. I think she sees a lot more than I do. I think she sees memories she doesn't want to think about. She exhales her fear in one breath, and it disappears in a white cloud in the vastness of the Aspen Highlands.

"I didn't have any money," she says. "I never had any money. But I wanted to ice skate. It was the only thing that gave me a sense of support. In all the years, I'd have lost myself, I'd have given up so many times, if the ice hadn't been there to catch me. After high school I could have started to work and gone to community college, but I didn't want to. I had a goal: the Olympics. And then, at some point, to start a kind of boarding school for sports. At four, I bought my first pair of skates at a flea market. I've skated ever since. I could never imagine *not* doing it. And when, after high school, I was accepted by a really good club in Minneapolis, I was ready to do everything to make the most of my chance." Her lips are trembling. I lay my arm across her delicate shoulders, kiss her, and taste tears. I kiss her again and again and again, until they're dry. Paisley continues. "We trained from early until late. I didn't have any time for a job, and there was no one there to support me. I lived in the home. And then..." She stops. Takes a deep breath. "Then my trainer was there. Ivan. He was everything I thought I needed: charismatic. Good looking. Talented. Well-to-do. *Caring.*" She almost spits the last word, as if she wanted to throw it away and let it go forever. "And in love with me. I gave us a chance. I really thought he was made for me. But then...Ivan got strange. He'd *lose his mind* when I spoke to any other men from the club. Whenever I went out with my friend Kaya, he'd stalk us. One time I talked to a homeless guy, and he beat the guy up, Knox, he really *beat the shit* out of him. And after that... After that, he started to beat me."

Her hand is still in mine when I reflexively make a fist. As soon as I notice, I relax again and run my other hand across it, as my limbs have grown numb. I feel sick. I want to say something, anything, but I'm afraid I'll have to vomit. He hit her. He *beat* this delicate, precious being.

"That was the beginning," she says. "After that I wanted to end things, but he blackmailed me. He... He said that if I left him, he wouldn't pay for my training anymore and would make sure I'd get kicked out of the club. And I... I was so *dumb*, Knox. I stayed with him out of fear of losing the biggest love of my life."

"The ice," I say.

"The ice." She nods. I wipe the hair out of her face. Her skin is ice cold, so I pull her beneath my blanket and press her body to mine. Paisley places her hand on my chest, crumples the fabric of my hoodie in her fist. "I stayed, and that's when things got really sick. *He* became really sick. Ivan did everything he could to build me up at training. Before every competition, he rehearsed the best programs with me, gave me the greatest hopes only to destroy me every time, before every run. He built my hopes up, as high as they could go, just to make it that much more painful when he smashed them to pieces with a sledgehammer."

"What do you mean?" The air surrounding me is crisp, but it hardly reaches my lungs.

"He got *hot* seeing me in pain, Knox. Once, before the regional championships, he locked me in the basement and made it look like I'd done it myself. Another time, two nights before the Grand Prix, he was drunk. Totally smashed. I told him he should lie down, and he…" She lets go of the fabric in her fist and raises her hand. The scars glitter in the light of the fire. "…he hit me over and over again. With the bottle. I was unable to compete. Once again."

"Come here, babe." I put my hand to the back of her head and pull her to me. I press her so tightly, it's like I wanted to merge with her so that she would take away the pain I'm feeling right now. As if she hadn't been the one hit, but me. For a while, we just lie there like that, sadness in every breath, sadness in our hearts.

Then she says, "That wasn't the worst though. Not the reason I left."

"Tell me," I whisper. "Tell me everything."

Her breath trembles at the slope of my neck. I don't think she wants to say it, and at the same time I can tell she wants to at all costs. She finally wants to be rid of it, to tear down a wall that should have disappeared a long time ago.

I know a thing or two about those kinds of walls. They're ugly. They should be forbidden.

"Last year, right before Skate America, I… I was ready. I intended to do everything right, not to make him mad, to finally make it. To participate. I did everything he liked. It made me sick, *he* made me sick, but I did it anyway. Everything went well. We were in the car, on the way to the championships, and I thought I'd finally managed. Then he stopped in the trailer park. I knew that something was about to happen when he asked me to get out of the car. I knew it, but I did it anyway. The cheap green fence made that sound when the wind blew against it. I can hear it as if it was yesterday. That sound tore at my guts, and I knew that the best thing for me to do would be to stay put. To not go inside, into the trailer park. But Ivan pulled me. My sneakers stumbled past the junkies I still remembered from my childhood. And then there we were in front of my old house. Our trailer. Just the same as ever. Just three hubcaps. *Fuck the system* over the door. In pink spray paint. A can of Bud Light on the plastic table in the front yard. He said, *Go inside*. I didn't want to, but he pushed me. *Go inside, Paisley. Go inside.*"

"Did you?"

She nods. Her temples rub against my hoodie.

"And?"

"My mom was lying on the bed. A picture of me between her fingers. Bruises in the crook of her arm. Track marks. Her eyes were open. She was dead. Ivan knew it. He was in contact with her, drove out there every now and then. Brought her money after I'd begged him. She was my mother, you know? Despite everything I always wanted her to be okay. Ivan, he… He knew that she was dead, and he *wanted* me to see it."

"God." My voice breaks. "Paisley, my God."

My head is empty. I'm cold, but I want to be warm. I want to warm her heart and kill these demons, want to protect her, make her feel safe. I want to be strong, but right now I feel like the weakest deer in the woods. When it comes to her, I'm weak. When it comes to her, I'm vulnerable. And, *fuck*, her pain is my pain. Her pain hurts me so much, shit, I can hardly breathe.

"Paisley…"

"It's okay," she says. "It's okay. I'm here now. Aspen is healing me. Aspen… *You are Aspen*, Knox. And I need you. I've resisted this for far too long."

I bury my nose in her hair and breathe the fresh apple smell in deep.

Paisley traces the Abercrombie deer on my hoodie and asks, "What was she like? Your mom?"

I had expected the question to tear me apart. Just like every memory of my mother tears me apart. But it didn't. Instead, I feel a kind of happiness thinking about Mom's bright laugh and the way she'd always toss her light wavy hair over her shoulders just before she came to me with some crazy idea or another. Eating hamburgers late at night. Tickle attacks against my sleeping dad. Cotton candy before a hockey match. Drawing lipstick reindeer on the windows.

"She was like you," I say. "Competitive. Strong. She knew what she wanted. Quick-witted. Grounded. She could always make me laugh, no matter how bad I felt. And she was..." My voice dries up midsentence. I have to try a second time, but this time it works. "She was a figure skater at iSkate."

"I'm sure I would have liked her."

I kiss Paisley's temple. "You would have. And she'd have loved you."

"That's why you couldn't stand me," she murmurs. "I reminded you of her."

The whole time I've thought how ill it is that Paisley reminds me of my mom and that I felt attracted to her all the same. But now that Paisley says it out loud, it doesn't sound so sick. It sounds sad. And understandable.

"Yeah," I say. "Among other things." I take a deep breath. And then I say something that has been weighing me down for years but that no one outside of Dad, Wyatt, and me know. "She died out on the ice. On Silver Lake. It all happened so quick. She wanted to practice a jump, slipped, and landed on her head. There was blood everywhere. I wanted to help her but didn't know how. I took off my jacket and tried to stop the bleeding because I thought she would open her eyes, would say something, something like she always did, you know, something like: *Knox, did you polish off my peanut butter?* She'd do it, with her crooked grin, I was so sure of it. But she didn't say a word. Didn't say a single word. The last thing I heard from her was a cry. Then she was dead. I was twelve."

Paisley stiffens. I can hear her catch her breath before slowly letting it back out. Her hand wanders across my chest and up to my face. She runs her fingertips along the edge of my jaw. "That's why you stopped playing hockey," she whispers. "The memories are torture."

"The memories. Her cry. What I felt at that moment...it's never gone away. It's been with me for eleven years."

"Knox..." Her voice breaks. Her fingernails dig into my skin. It burns a little, but it feels good. Especially as, at the moment, I feel numb, and it reminds me that I can still feel. "Don't let that happen. Don't let the worst memories of your mom become the only ones. I am positive she wouldn't have wanted that. I am positive she would tell you to remember the beautiful moments. The peanut-butter moments. The happy moments. All those laughing-so-hard-my-stomach-hurts moments. Full of love. I didn't know her, but I know you, and you have her heart, so I think that's what she would have wanted. To see you happy, not suffering."

I exhale in one go, as I am afraid of having to cry. My chin has already started with that suspicious tremble, and when that happens, it's not long before I fall. And I don't think Paisley would be able to catch me, because, typically, I don't fall that slowly. It's quick and deep. I don't want it to happen, but then it does because I'm just too weak not to when we're talking about Mom.

The tears come quick. Raging waves, not soft and not loud. My heart finds the sound pleasant. It snuggles into the melody of my grief and begins to come together, a little bit more every time I give space to my feelings. And at the moment, with even greater impact, because Paisley is here, and Paisley is more.

She lets me cry. She holds me and I can tell from her irregular breaths that she's crying, too.

The sun rises. The white sky turns a pink pastel. Holding onto each other. Crying next to each other. Crying silently.

Mute tears. The loudest pain.

31
Maybe, Maybe, What a Word

PAISLEY

KNOX STOPS HIS RANGE ROVER IN FRONT OF iSKATE. I can see by his glance that the place causes him pain. I am proud of him for trying to face his demons. It will be tough, but I think he's doing exactly the right thing. Small steps. Big results.

Harper sees us. Her UGGs leave traces behind in the snow and her Bordeaux-colored cashmere coat blazes. Her eyes flash in our direction, stop on the car, then move upward to stare at us. They narrow into slits, but she doesn't look angry, just hurt. *Broken.* Then she goes inside.

"What's with her?" I ask.

"Hakuna Matata" is playing on the car stereo. Knox looks to the door of iSkate where Harper has just disappeared. His mouth is agape. "Before meeting you, I was an asshole."

Harper has never been nice to me. But never really vicious either. She's always been honest. Sometimes it hurts, but honesty isn't vicious. We just think it is because we don't want to hear those things, and when we do, we feel pain.

"Do you regret it?"

"I regret having hurt so many women," Knox says. He runs a

hand across his gray Calvin Klein jogging pants, then begins fumbling with the heater. "I shouldn't have given any of them false hope."

I nod. "They'll forgive you. At some point they'll find someone, and then they'll forgive you."

"You think?"

"Of course."

"Come here, Baymax."

"Why do you call me that?"

He laughs. Soft and somewhat hoarse. There's nowhere for the sound to go in the space of the car, so it keeps resounding. "Because you're my Baymax. You with your puffy white jacket."

His fingers take hold of my collar. He pulls me to him, over the gearshift, and a second later I feel his lips on mine. It's contagious. We both smile, we kiss, Pumba is singing about having no worries and at this moment, this very second, I believe this little warthog, believe his words, believe that Knox is my *Hakuna Matata*.

Knox moves away from me, rubs his nose over the corners of my mouth. "Get going. Show 'em how it's done, Snow Queen."

"Will we see each other later?"

"We live together."

I run a finger over his birthmark. "I mean, dating-wise."

"Say that again."

"Dating-wise."

His smile grows bigger. "One more time."

"Dating-wise."

"Crazy."

"What?"

Knox leans his head back against the seat and shoves his fingertips into the band of his jogging pants. An absent-minded gesture that makes me react so strongly, I have to keep from gasping.

"It's really true what people say about butterflies in the stomach. They exist. And the tiniest little things the right person does can get them going. Like you, when you say *dating-wise*. It's nuts."

I lock my fingers with his, which, at the moment, are still in his pants, and run my thumb across his skin. "So, we'll see each other later? *Dating-wise?*"

"Of course. You're my girlfriend."

I have to smile like a teenager in love for the first time.

"Say that again."

"Girlfriend."

"Again."

He grins. "*Girlfriend.*"

"These butterflies," I say. "They're so manic."

Knox tugs at my earlobe and laughs. And all of a sudden, I'm thankful for my *ethereal* ears because he likes them.

"Later," he says.

"Yeah. Later."

I slide out of the car, my bag over my shoulder, and don't think I've ever felt this happy. Suddenly everything seems brighter. Suddenly everything seems *more real*. Maybe this is the way life's supposed to be. The way everyone should *experience* life. Full of joy and ease.

In the changing room, I run into Gwen. She looks up as I enter and frowns. "What's with your face?"

"What should be up with it?" I plop down onto the bench next to her and undo my boots. Snow falls to the ground.

"It's doing this weird thing." Gwen waves her hands around as if trying to push air in my direction. "It's glowing from the inside out."

I undo the buttons of my jeans and pull my hoodie over my head. It smells of Knox. I press it to my nose for a second because I want to hold onto the scent a little longer before putting it in my locker and pulling on my skating dress.

"No idea. The party at Buttermilk Mountain yesterday was nice. I rode a snowboard for the first time ever."

I'd like to tell her the real reasons for feeling the way I do, but Harper is sitting behind us and listening in while tying her skates. I don't want to hurt her.

Gwen pulls her legwarmers straight and casts me a doubtful glance. "When you were leaving, you were totally over it and were bitching about having to take care of the tourists."

"Yeah, but I managed to sleep and I'm good."

"Well, well." She stands up and steps from one foot to the other, just like always. "After training you want to go to the warm-up for the X Games? It's fun, there's always something going on and the beer's good. Levi and Aaron are going, too."

"Of course." I don't tell her that I'd hoped she'd ask me so that I could watch Knox snowboard. I pull on my boot covers and put my hair into a bun. "What's with your Lutz?"

"What do you mean?"

"Yesterday you landed a double. Didn't you want to do a triple?"

Gwen waves it off while holding open the door to the rink for me. Harper is right behind us. "Yeah. But not until Skate America. If I'd done it yesterday, Dad would've freaked."

"If he could see you pull it off, maybe not. Maybe he would've let you incorporate it into your program."

Gwen rolls her eyes. "Maybe, maybe. Such an awful word. Not a *yes* and not a *no*. Who can do anything with that? I don't like ambiguity, so I do things my way."

"*Your way* won't work," Harper hisses as she pushes past us out onto the ice. "It never does, Gwen."

"Not like your wobbly Rittberger yesterday," Gwen fires back with a bittersweet smile.

Harper glares at her but doesn't say anything. I watch her glide across the ice, elegant and graceful. She is beautiful, like a model, and I wonder what it is about me that Knox likes when he didn't want someone like her.

"She's gone," Gwen says. "Out with it."

"What?"

We set off backward, parallel, not looking at each other, but I know Gwen's rolling her eyes. It's as if I could hear it.

"What happened last night? All of a sudden Gargamel's gone and you're walking around like the happiest little thing."

"Paisley!" Polina's voice cuts across the ice and takes in the whole rink. "Tension!"

I imagine being pulled into the air by an imaginary little man, chin up, chest out, farther and farther until Polina gives me her slight nod.

"Well done, Watson," I say, get ready to perform a double Lutz, jump and land clean with my blades on the ice. Gwen follows my example. Then I say, "Something has come up between...Knox and me."

Gwen squeals and it feels like everyone in the rink casts us a glance. Polina doesn't look particularly impressed, but, then again, she never does, so I don't give it a second thought and quickly perform an axel to make her happy.

Gwen and I turn and skate on, when Levi and Aaron come toward us, skating backward so that they can look at us. Aaron is wearing a new outfit. It's pale green and goes wonderfully with his red hair. Before either of them can say anything Gwen repeats, "Something has *come up* between Knox and Paisley!"

Levi mimics Gwen's squeak and Aaron asks, "What exactly has come up?"

"Something real?" Levi asks.

"What wouldn't be real?" I ask. The cold wind cuts my face.

Gwen spins backward, forward, backward, forward. Watching her makes me a feel a little dizzy, but Gwen does it regularly. She needs all the movement because she's got too much energy.

"Well, if he got you on your back and now you're reading too much into it like every other girl before you, then you go back to the resort and he ghosts you."

"Or if he got you on your back and now you're reading too much into it like every other girl before you, then you go back to the resort and he gets you on your back *again* before ghosting you," Levi says.

"Has he ever done that?" Aaron asks. He truly sounds interested, as if it had to do with planning his program and not Knox's sex life. "I mean, laid someone twice?"

"Good question," Gwen says. "I've never heard of things ever lasting more than one night."

"Then Paisley would be the first," Aaron says. "And maybe that means that something *real* indeed did come up."

"There it is again, that word," Gwen says. "*Maybe, maybe.*"

"People." I stretch out my leg, go deeper and deeper, pull it in and spin, which turns everything around me into a swirl of color before I stand back up and continue skating with clean movements. "He didn't *lay* me. And anyway, that sounds *so* demeaning. Why are you even using that term?"

"It's Knox," Gwen and Levi say in unison, while Aaron shrugs as if there wasn't anything he could do to counter their words. "He does that kind of thing," he adds.

Gwen, Levi, and Aaron look at me as if I had told them I was giving up figure skating and leaving Aspen.

"Oooooookay," Levi says. "That doesn't fit."

"What doesn't fit?" I'm a bit out of breath after executing a Biellmann—grabbing my free blade and pulling the heel of my boot behind and above the level of my head.

"Knox and the word *real*," Gwen says. "But keep on talking, bestie, keep on talking. I'm curious."

Those butterflies again. Gwen just called me her *best friend*. I can feel my head begin to whirl a little. It could have to do with my spin, but I think my body today is overproducing serotonin, and it's not used to it. Not at all.

"He said that I was his girlfriend."

Gwen stumbles, Levi screws up his Lutz, and Aaron runs into

the side of the rink. Harper skates past and considers the three with a frown. I have to bite my lower lip in order not to laugh. "People, I said that I was his girlfriend, not that Skate America was canceled."

"That's even heavier," Gwen says. "That thing about being his girlfriend."

Levi nods. "Knox and the word *girlfriend*? That's miles beyond Skate America."

"If William knew, he'd fire off a tweet," Aaron says.

"Woe betide you if you tell him!" I threaten. "If you do that, I'll burn his monster reindeer and blame it all on you."

"He'll find out anyway," Gwen says. She lands a double axel surprisingly well and flails her arms. "I mean, *Knox has a girlfriend!* That's going to get out quicker than a stink bomb going off in front of a fan in a windowless room."

Levi nods. "You'd best give us an autograph already, Paisley. You're a *celebrity* now."

"Which paper is going to bring it out first, do you think?"

"*Ice Today*," Gwen says right as Aaron shouts out, "*USA Today*."

Gwen shakes her head and almost loses her balance. "When it's got to do with their little star, *Ice Today* will never let anyone else drop the *girlfriend* bomb."

"It won't go public at all," I say, louder than intended. Polina casts me a severe glance and I attempt to collect myself, but my heart is racing more quickly than the spin I make to keep my face hidden from my trainer. When I come back up, I say more quietly, "I don't want it to go public. So, not a word to anyone, okay?"

"But, Paisley," Gwen says. She exchanges a look with Levi and Aaron, who are both wearing the same expression.

Levi's voice is careful when he speaks. "Knox Winterbottom having a girlfriend is virtually impossible *not* to go public."

I don't want to hear it, but I know he's right. The thing is, I don't want to admit it because that would mean having to face reality, and reality is ugly, and, right now, things are just too damn nice to be ugly.

"Simply promise me you won't say anything to anyone. *Please.*"

"Promise," they all say simultaneously, but it sounds sympathetic somehow, like *poor-thing-it's-going-to-get-out-anyway.* I hear it, I know it, but pretend I don't. I pretend to be dumb, so that things remain beautiful. Maybe it'll work.

Maybe, maybe. That word.

32
You Hold Me Without Holding Me

PAISLEY

THE X GAMES ARE TAKING PLACE IN THE SKI AREA ON Buttermilk Mountain. There are still two weeks to go, but preparations are already going full steam ahead. I've never really been interested in snowboarding, but I'm familiar with the X Games. Everyone is. They're on ESPN and ABC and are something like the Super Bowl of winter sports. It's a little like a huge festival in the snowy mountains, with a big stage, live music, and various competition areas.

"The pipes for the big air and slopestyle course are already there," Gwen says as we make our way past the barriers of the music area with its huge X Games banners.

"The superpipe is still going to take a bit," Levi says. He runs a hand across his dark stubble, here and there coloring them white with snow. He's right. By the superpipe there are two big excavators, digging into the snow with their buckets.

"Where is everyone?" I look around but it's empty and dark. I thought everyone would be celebrating preparations already.

"At the Inn in Aspen," Aaron says. He points into the distance, and I really do make out a few warm lights. Little glowworms hovering over the snow. That's what it looks like. Floating glow-worms. "That's where the party's going on. Right next to the freestyle pipe."

We cross the parking lot. The closer we get to the Inn at Aspen, the more the quiet disappears. Music drifts over along with the sound of conversations of drunk, laughing people. I take out my phone and text Knox.

Where are you?

He responds almost immediately: Athlete Lounge with Cameron and the others.

Cameron?

My trainer.

Ah, right.

And you?

I look up. We're standing in front of the Inn. There's a kind of fountain surrounding a large fire. The glow of the flames is reflected in the building's warm glass walls. It looks decadent and cozy at the same time. Luxurious in that subtle, *Aspen-like* way.

At the Inn.

I'll be over there soon. He adds two heart emojis, and I smile at my display.

Is Jason Hawk there too? I ask.

Yeah. A spooky GIF of the Cheshire Cat appears right after. I laugh out loud. Gwen, Levi, and Aaron look at me questioningly. I wave them off but follow behind them while continuing to stare at my phone. How so?

I want to meet him, I write. I'm such a huuuge fan.

Knox replies: .

I answer: You just sent me a period.

I came across the button while pushing him down the pipe.

I bite my lower lip. But, but, I write. ☹

He's lying on the ground, Paisley. He's not moving.

But, but.

It is what it is.

He sends me a GIF of a dancing pig in a gold sequin dress. While I'm looking for a suitable GIF to answer with, Gwen grabs my phone out of my hand.

"Enough," she says. "We're at *the* party of the year, and you are *not* going to spend it with your head bent over your phone."

We're almost at the door, which is flanked by two men in dark suits. I wink.

"You said that this was real informal, Gwen."

"I did not." She digs about in her handbag and pulls out a pair of heels. They are so high—I swear, in just two minutes I'd have two broken bones.

"You said there'd be good beer. That *implies* something informal."

"Otherwise you wouldn't have come," Aaron says while pushing me to the side in order to make room for a group of women moving toward the entrance.

"And now I'm coming with you?"

"Yeah," Gwen says.

"No."

Levi sighs. "You can't say no. You're already in front of the door."

I purse my lips and have a quick look at myself. Winter boots flecked with white because they're old and I never had enough money to get them winter-proofed, black skinny jeans, and my down jacket, beneath which I'm wearing my baggy wool sweater.

"They'll never let me in. Oh my God, Gwen, *what is that?*"

Gwen starts and stumbles in her heels. "What?"

She's opened her coat to reveal a black minidress, which exposes most of her cleavage. I give it a tug. "This!"

"Umm. A dress?"

My glance wanders to Levi and Aaron, who are also taking off their coats to reveal elegant suits. "And you all! My God! You look like royalty or something, and here I am like a stable girl!"

"I've got a dress for you," Gwen says. "We'll fix you up in the bathroom."

"Why didn't you all just warn me beforehand?"

"Because you *wouldn't have come*," Levi repeats.

"Come on, Paisley. They're playing really awesome songs already, and we're missing all of them." Aaron grabs me by my coat and attempts to pull me along, but I stay put. Next to the fire.

"They'll never let me in," I repeat.

Gwen snaps her hand mirror shut, tosses her lip gloss into her handbag, and puts both her hands on my shoulders. She smells of raspberries. I like raspberries. "Listen. We're on the guest list. Everyone from iSkate is on the guest list. They *have* to let you in. We'll get you ready in the bathroom, you'll turn Knox's head, maybe tonight he'll give you the washing-machine number I told you about, I'll meet some hot athlete or other, Levi and Aaron can do their weird samba-thing out on the dance floor, and everyone's happy. Right? Right. Come on."

I pull off my cap in order to look halfway presentable but when we make it to the two guys in black, I see my reflection in the glass and get a brief *oh-my-Lord-am-I-ugly* attack. I look like I've put my fingers into a socket.

"We're on the guest list," Gwen says and gives them our names. One of the men checks us off the list while the other watches me going in.

"My cap causes static electricity," I say and shrug my shoulders apologetically.

"You're good," the other one says, making room. I shoot the staring dude one of my most winning smiles, with my white-flecked boots, with my rat's nest of hair, and feel big, bigger than him. He's at least six-five. Doesn't matter. I'm bigger.

The music is good. They're playing Kygo. The Weeknd. Drake. It's hot, people are heating one another up at the same time, the windows are for the most part fogged. It smells of damp armpits, alcohol, and expensive perfume. The bass is making the floor vibrate and cuts waves through the dancing mass and laughing faces.

"Bathroom!" Gwen shouts into my ear. I nod, we give Levi and Aaron a sign, and disappear past the bar and down the hall to the bathroom doors. Gwen turns around, pushes the door open with her back, and points at me with her index finger. "It'll all be good. I'm telling you, it'll all be good."

I see my boots against marble. It's far too chic to be a bathroom. My shoes seem dirty. They're me. The floor is Aspen. But then I think that maybe there's a reason for the marble. At parties, bathrooms are the places that make history. This is where secrets are whispered. The place where plans to kiss someone out on the dance floor and, who knows, maybe seal your fate are hatched, then a trip to the Himalayas, a wedding, bike tours with kid trailers. Smudged lipstick mouths telling the truth while the booze makes your nerves tingle. Of course the floor is made of marble. Of course it is.

"Well now." Gwen pulls a breeze of fabric out of her big bag and holds it up. It's got a rose-colored top with elbow-length sleeves and an airy skirt that just about reaches the knees. "It's a gift. Mom bought it for me for some Christmas party at iSkate, but I hate pink. The color makes me all moon-faced."

"You're always giving me clothes," I say while pulling my sweater over my head. "Say it."

Gwen hands me a pair of nylon tights. "What can I say?"

"*Bibbidi-Bobbidi-Boo.*"

"Not today, Cinderella. I've got to conserve energy. For emergencies."

I slip out of my boots, thick socks, and jeans, stuff everything into Gwen's bag and pull out a pair of ballet flats. "What kind of emergency?"

"We'll see when we get there. Turn around."

Gwen takes off my hair tie and shakes out my hair. She twists the strands, puts the top hair into a loose bun, and leaves the others loose. Then she takes mascara and nude lipstick out of her bag and turns to my face.

"God," she says. "I'd kill to have your lips."

"Thanks."

"Shhh. You'll smear everything."

"Sorry."

"Paisley! Okay, good, good, I'm done."

I look into the mirror and see someone else. The girl across from me has pink cheeks. Cheeks full of life. Big, shining eyes that look like they'd never seen anything but joy. Lips that speak of love. Without a sound. I don't see myself, but I see what I could be if I stopped being Paisley with all those shadows in her eyes. Man, oh, man, how lovely I'd be. How *beautiful*.

Gwen's standing next to me. Her mirror-self is smiling. Her real self is, too.

"Do you think that things between Knox and me can work?"

Gwen turns around, leans her hips against the sink, and pushes a strand of hair behind her ear. Her pendant earrings clink softly. "Do you remember when we were at the diner, and he came in with Wyatt?"

"When I spilled my coffee on his pants?"

"Exactly."

I nod.

"That was the day I knew Knox had found what had been missing."

"What do you mean?"

Gwen smiles. "He came in trying so hard not to look at you, as if you were his sun, and, in so doing, revealed that, for him, you'd been precisely that the whole time, whether he was looking at you or not."

My heart grows faint. So light, it wants to fly away. "I didn't notice that at all."

"Of course not. You don't notice *a thing* when Knox is close by, my dear."

I bite my lower lip.

"Stop doing that. You're smearing your lipstick. Now, let's go."

We go back to Levi and Aaron. They're waiting for us at a bar table with four beer glasses on it. Gwen grabs one and downs half of it. The foam sticks to her upper lip. She licks it off. That's Gwen. She drinks milk out of the carton. She burps after eating a fatty meal. She parks in the spots reserved for trainers at iSkate. She laughs, she lives, she's sassy and wild and abnormal. I love her.

"What did we miss?" she asks.

Levi points to a guy sitting on a stool with his head hanging down. He doesn't look all that comfortable.

"You see him? He sat himself down cross-legged on the dance floor and busted out in some breakdancing moves. In so doing, he caught that woman there in the red dress in the knee. She fell over and took her friend with her, who landed on homeboy's face with her ass."

"No way," I say.

"For real. I took a video. Here." Aaron holds his phone out under my nose. I look at the whole thing, frowning, before asking, "How can you record so quickly?"

"I just wanted to turn it into an Instastory."

"And Jason Hawk hooked up with Francine George," Levi adds. "The skier. On the dance floor. At first, he danced up to her, totally creepy, wait, like this." He rubs his bottom against Aaron's hips, up and down his leg, Aaron says, "Oh yeah, baby, clean my shoes, that's how I like it," and we double up in laughter. Levi wobbles back upright. "Then he slobbered all over her, like this." He sticks out his tongue and pretends to lick Aaron's face, but Aaron moves away laughing. Clever.

"Come on," Levi says, but we can hardly understand him thanks to his slabbering tongue. It sounds like *humm-ahn*. "Don't be like that."

I can't stop laughing, I even spill my beer until I suddenly realize what Levi's actually said. My laughter dies. "Jason Hawk is here?" I look around. If he's not still at the Athlete Lounge, then Knox might already be here at the Inn.

Gwen groans. "You've already got a snowboarder. Leave one for me."

"I don't want a thing from Jason Hawk."

"Yes, she does." Hands on my shoulders. Big hands. Warm. Warmer than the sticky air. They stroke the lace. I lean back my head and see Knox's lips from below. Curved and lovely. A bit sad, but not right now, right now they're simply lovely. He looks into my eyes and the corners of his mouth twitch when he says, "She's got a thing for him."

"Yeah, well, Knox," Gwen downs the rest of her beer. "Then you've been dealt a bad hand."

He raises an eyebrow. "I never get a bad hand." Then he pulls me into his arms, bends down, and kisses me. No doubt smearing my lipstick. But whatever, because: Knox, oh-my-God-Knox, what are you doing?

The kiss lasts all of two heartbeats. *BOOM. BOOM.* Just two, but it feels like two hundred, I have to gasp for air when I turn my head to interrupt it. I look left then right, right then left. Did anyone see us? No. I don't think so. But then I see it. Knox's expression. Like a beaten dog. Levi and Aaron are staring into their glasses, but Gwen casts me a *you-see-that's-what-you-get* look. She's right. Knox doesn't know that I want to keep our situation a secret. He doesn't know that my future at iSkate will be over if the fact that I am here becomes public knowledge. And I am not ready to share the reason why with anyone but myself at this moment. I'm not ready yet. I'm too afraid. The pure desire to live, you might say.

"Knox," I say, running my fingernail along the inscription—*treat yourself*—on the beer glass. "Can we go somewhere else?"

I can see that he thinks I want to end things between us and that just about tears me up more than his beaten-dog look. I rub my lace-trimmed sleeves, wait until he nods, and then I follow him outside. I don't have my jacket, Levi gave it to the coat check, and it's really goddamn cold. Knox leads me over to the fire pit. People are staring at him. Staring at *us*.

"So," he says, sitting down on the bench next to the fire and putting his arms behind him on the backrest. His legs spread a bit. Not manspreading but spread in that way guys often do. My glance lands in his crotch and it's almost too much. My body responds to him. "What's up?"

He's Knox, but at the same time he's not. It doesn't sound like him. His voice has taken on the *it's-all-the-same-to-me* tone it always had when we were getting to know each other and that, in the meantime, I've learned is a defense mechanism. Some guy or other walks past—"What's up, Winterbottom? Rad big air at training today, man!" and they give each other a high five. Knox laughs, and it occurs to me that he just may be the best actor in the world.

I sigh, sit down next to him, and run my hand across the fabric covering my thighs. "I'm not ready for us to go public, Knox."

He looks at me for a long time before opening his mouth then closing it again. Eventually he says, "Okay."

I blink. "Don't you want to know why?"

He shrugs. "You've got your reasons. And if you want to tell me, you will. I accept that." He leans back, runs a hand through his hair, and grins. "Even if I take the fact that you find me embarrassing personally."

"That's not true."

"Just kidding. Who on earth could find me embarrassing?"

"You are *so* narcissistic."

"I prefer self-assured."

I have to grin. "It's amazing that you even know a word like *prefer*."

"You always say that."

"What?"

"It's *amazing* that you even know that word. It's *amazing* that you're not dumb. It's *amazing* that you can even speak." He laughs, stands up, and moves in front of me. He bends down toward me, his arms to the left and right of my face, his hands on the back of the wooden bench. His face is close. He nods and grins lightly. "Is it really so incredible that I'm handsome *and* smart *and* athletic?"

"Careful, or else you'll really become embarrassing."

His lips graze mine, a gossamer-thin touch and over so quickly that I want to capture the moment and not let it go, but I have to, because I'm panicking that someone is watching us. I discreetly cast a glance around, but no one is looking.

"We both know that's not true." Then he stands back up. "Should we go in?"

"Okay."

We walk in side by side. His finger stroking the back of my hand. Inadvertently, I think, but everything within me is tingling. Knox looks at me.

"What's up?"

He sighs. "I'm mourning my shattered dream."

"What do you mean?"

He pulls open the door. The doormen don't say a word as we pass. The big one doesn't even cast my hair a quick glance.

Knox twists his mouth. "Falling all over you in front of Jason Hawk."

"I don't think Jason would notice at all." I nod toward Knox's competitor, who is lingering over the face of a woman out on the dance floor. He looks like he's ready to eat her. "My God, his mouth is *so* big."

Knox nods. "He's a carnivorous plant."

I watch him for a second, but then notice Gwen, Levi, and Aaron not too far away.

I look at Knox questioningly. "Wanna go dance?"

"I don't know how."

"Doesn't matter. You can just bob around if you want."

"Is that even a word?"

"Bob around? Yeah."

"Okay. Well, then no. I can't *bob around* either."

"You cool with me going alone then?"

Knox looks at me as if I'd asked him if I could have sex with Jason Hawk out on the dance floor. "Why on earth *wouldn't* that be okay?"

I shrug, bite my lower lip, look away, and watch all the dancing people. They're laughing. It all looks so joyful, so real that all I can think is: *How is laughing like that even* possible *on a winter evening like this one in this world that never hesitates to show you how* ugly *it can be?* Because it's good at that. Really. And when you forget, it's right there to remind you. Over and over.

Like now.

Next to me Knox lets out a breath. "I still want to kill that guy, you know that?"

Yeah, I know. My fingers are holding his hand, pressing it lightly. I smile at him, then hurry over to the others out on the dance floor. Gwen throws her arms into the air when she sees me.

Levi and Aaron are actually dancing samba, they twirl about the others as if the room belonged to them, as if they thought they were alone on the ice. I often feel the same way when I dance. My movements are similar, fluid. I want to let go and to perform my program, just let myself go and dare to do so, and I think: *It's too bad that you're not so* hardcore, *Paisley.* Too bad.

All of a sudden I understand why everyone is laughing here, it's impossible *not* to laugh. This dance floor exists inside a bubble, a big, pulsing red bubble of serotonin, dopamine, and endorphins, and when you enter, it takes you into its circle of happiness, pumps you full of these messenger substances and doesn't let you drift off. *I like this bubble.*

Gwen takes my hand, and we spin around, I don't know how

many times but at least the whole BTS song and half of the one by Jason Derulo because I'm dizzy, sweaty, and make a sign to Gwen that I'm going to get us some drinks.

The bar is sticky but cool when I rest my forearms against it. I order a beer for Gwen and some kind of prosecco-strawberry-lime drink with a straw for me. It's out of paper, the straw, and seeing that I can't help but think: *this party is the absolute* shit.

Suddenly a mass of red hair appears next to me, exuding a glamorous, eccentric perfume. Orchids and honey. Very feminine. Very extravagant. Very *Harper*.

"Hi," I say, sip from my straw, and cast her a smile that she doesn't return. Instead she raises her hand, snaps her fingers, and then rolls her eyes when the bartender takes someone else's order first. She ignores me completely. Although it's *incredibly* loud, I can hear the silence between us. It bothers me but I refuse to be the one to break it. Not after she ignored me completely. I'm too tired for her walls today.

I grab Gwen's beer and my strawberry drink and am just about to go to the others when Harper says, "He's going to toss you to the side, you know that, right?"

For a second I consider being the one to ignore *her*, but then I'd be like her, and I don't want that. I stay put. Drops of water pearl off the beer bottle into my palm. Cool. It feels good.

"Harper," I say, slowly and softly, "he hurt you, huh?" When she doesn't respond and just stares into her glass, I add, "'Someday someone will see your shine, will recognize how you hold the whole universe in your hands although you haven't done anything but look into the sky. But until then, you need to stop giving your heart to someone who thinks you're just a *maybe*."

Only now does she look at me. In her eyes there's something like fury, even rage, but, looking more closely, I recognize sadness. That's not good; I know that expression from my own eyes and know how *terrible* she must be feeling.

Harper covers it up. Of course she does. I would, too. She snarls, "You think that Knox wants you, and I won't judge you for that. He's got a talent for making people feel like they mean everything to him. But can I tell you something? Knox cannot feel. He puts on an act for you, takes you right to the edge, all the while holding your hand and showing you how beautiful the water is from up above, how beautifully the sun dances across the surface. He does that, and you laugh, he laughs right along, and everything feels right." The bartender shows up with her beer. She takes a sip, her face is hard, a solid mask. There's a pop as she pulls the bottle away from her lips and puts it down. "You both laugh, Paisley, and then he pushes you over the cliff. That's what loving Knox feels like. Too deep a fall into black water. A fall that's impossible to survive."

Oh, shit, Knox, shit, what did you do to this girl?

I look at her, openly, no mask, so she can see who I am, so she can see that she's not alone, but she doesn't go along. She remains hard.

"Knox is going to take you down," she says.

I smile. "He's going to hold me, Harper. He's going to hold me while I work on loving myself."

Her lids flutter. It gives the impression of distress, as if she desperately wanted it to be untrue, even though she already realizes that I'm right. "How can you be so sure?"

"You can feel when something is right."

Harper looks at me, and I think she's just about to let her mask fall and say something, but I'll never find out because at that very moment, Knox walks up and she falls off the edge of the cliff, incapable of holding herself. I hope one day she'll manage.

Knox looks at me, with his birthmark and his blue-checked Ralph Lauren shirt and says, "You want to take off?"

I press Harper's hand for a second—it's cold, slender, lonely. Then I walk off with Knox, who's holding onto me without holding me.

33
What a Man

Knox

Paisley is trembling even though she changed back into her Baymax outfit. I turn up the heat and turn on the seat warmers, too.

She lets out a sigh of pleasure and snuggles into the leather as it warms up. "I can't feel my feet," she says as I start the motor and turn onto the road leading away from Buttermilk Mountain. She stretches out her legs in the footwell and moves her boots back and forth. "I'm telling you, it's meningitis."

"I'm not aware of any sources naming cold as the cause for any kind of meningitis," I say, adjusting the heater to make sure it's blowing out onto her feet, and cast Paisley a sidelong glance. She seems surprised, and I've got to laugh. "Come on, tell me."

"What should I say?"

I turn the wheel and drive left, downtown. The road markings are no longer visible, and the traffic lights are hidden by the heavy snowfall. The falling flakes turn red, then green, and I drive on.

"It's *amazing* that you even know what meningitis is, Knox." I mimic her voice, a bit over-the-top, a bit too much surprise in my voice, to get her to laugh. It works, and the sound warms me more than the heated seats ever could. Then the sound fades until all we can hear are our soft breaths and the heater.

Paisley is picking at the cuticle of her ring finger. "Can I ask you something?"

"Of course. I'll give you all the answers you want. Where should I start? Baby spiders are known as spiderlings. Banging your head against the wall burns one hundred fifty calories. Hmm, what else? In some countries a woman can get divorced if her husband doesn't serve her coffee."

"Can you stay serious for a single second? You always have to—wait, what? For real? When *her husband doesn't serve her coffee?*"

"I find that totally legitimate."

"That go for cappuccino, too?"

"No. Just straight coffee."

"How unfair. What if I don't like straight coffee?"

"You're American."

"But if I was in that country, could I get rid of my husband if he didn't serve me cappuccino?"

"No."

"That's bullshit."

"Well, think of the effort. There's a difference between simply lifting up a coffeepot and pouring and making a coffee, steaming some milk, and pouring."

"I am sure that there are fully automatic machines there, too."

"Shhh. You're spoiling the theory."

"Knox?"

"Yeah?"

"Can you be serious for a sec?"

"Only as an exception, Snow Queen."

"You said that you applied for the psychology program and were accepted."

Shit. I would've preferred sticking to theories about coffee. Two heartbeats pass before I nod. "Correct."

Paisley looks at me. "And you said you didn't want to be a star snowboarder."

That dumb game. A truth for a truth. Who even came up with the idea? Oh, right. That'd be me.

I sigh. "Also true."

"So, your goals are pretty clear. You're just not pursuing them. Would you like to tell me why you feel trapped?"

"What, you a hobby psychologist now?"

Paisley flinches, and, naturally, I realize that I'm an absolute idiot. I bite the inside of my cheek and put my hand on her upper thigh. "Sorry. It's just...the subject's not all that easy for me."

"It's okay if you don't want to talk about it, Knox. Really. But don't be mean."

"Yeah. I'm sorry." I repeat, running my fingers across her jeans and gathering up all my strength to climb over my walls. They're taller than they look from down below, but I've always been athletic. "When I was younger, I played hockey with Wyatt. I was really good, seriously. In middle school my teachers thought, if I kept it up, I'd easily get a scholarship. That was my dream. I loved hockey."

"But then your mom died," Paisley says. Her voice is soft, but her words bury into my guts and echo through my head. I hate those words. I *hate* them.

I nod. "After her death I wanted to spend every second out on the ice because that was always the one thing that made me forget everything. But pulling on my skates a few days after the funeral and making my way out onto the ice, I thought I would die. It was absolute *hell*, Paisley. I heard Mom, but not how I'd wanted to hear her, but that sound, the breaking of her skull bone and her scream, over and over her scream. I broke down and vomited. Wyatt was there, and he helped me, picked me up off the ice and all, after that I managed more or less okay, but I couldn't go out on the ice anymore."

Paisley swallows. She places her delicate fingers over mine.

Our trembling hands find each other and quiet down, as if all they needed was each other.

"Ever since, you've been a snowboarder."

I stop beneath a tall pine tree next to a big pile of snow. "Snowboarding had always been Dad's dream. He wanted to get out there himself as a kid, but, when things got serious, my grandparents were against it. 'Do something *sensible*,' they said. That's why I started snowboarding after Mom died. Well, that and for something to replace hockey. It was fun. And it made me happy seeing Dad coming out of his cocoon more and more. He said, 'Knox, you're so talented, live it up.' It made me so proud. And he had that shine in his eye that he usually only had when he saw Mom, and I just knew I couldn't say no. I simply couldn't. And so I said, '*Sure, Dad, let's do that,*' and from there on it was a steep climb."

Paisley is looking out the window at the mound of snow. There's a cardinal hopping about, leaving delicate traces of its feet. When she speaks, the window fogs up.

"I understand that. But, you know, I think that if you live a life that is any less than the one you'd actually like to be leading, your mom's screams will never go away."

My mouth goes dry. "What do you mean?"

The cardinal takes off, a red shimmer in between the white snowflakes. "I think the screams are following you because you aren't moving forward. This isn't your life, Knox. It's one you chose to make your father happy, so that he could go on living. You accepted standing still in order to make him happy. That's altruistic of you, but I think it's high time for you to choose yourself. I think it's time for you to leave that moment at Silver Lake behind and to move on."

She turns her head to look at me, with the sea in her eyes, the sky, and that great, all-embracing *hopefulness* she makes me feel but that she shouldn't. Paisley's right. Of course she's right. But I can't tell her that, if I did, I'd have to be able to give her a reason why I won't change, and I can't even explain that to myself. It simply doesn't work. Dad is counting on me, my sponsors are counting on me, the whole world of sports is counting on me. I wonder what Paisley would say if I told her about the steroids. If she knew that the reason I shoot anabolic steroids daily has to do with how *badly* I want to make Dad's dream come true, how *badly* I want to make him happy, how *badly* I don't want to think about Mom. I couldn't quit all that easily, even if I wanted to.

Paisley opens the glove box and pulls out *The Best of Disney*. Her eyes scan the song titles on the back, then she slides the CD in, clicks forward, forward, forward, on past track six, before stopping at eight. Then she clicks the case shut and leans back. She looks at me and smiles. Waits.

I'm waiting, too, but I know what song's about to come on. I know this list by heart, but right now everything feels different because this moment is giving the song a different meaning.

Phil Collins's voice fills the car and my heart.

I'm listening to the song with my eyes shut because this is one of those moments that's just too much, full of too many emotions.

His voice fades. I turn off the motor, touch Paisley's chin, and kiss her. Warm lips. An electrifying tingle. The smell of snow along with something else, no idea what exactly, maybe love, maybe longing. Maybe something in between.

I pull away, run my finger over her ears, then push the button that opens the trunk. Cold air blasts inside like a relentless current that wants to carry me away.

"Come on."

"What are you planning to do?"

I grin. "Something *date-like*."

34
Everything I Ever Hoped For

PAISLEY

IT'S DARK. THE FIR TREES AROUND US ARE GLOOMY. They sway gently in the middle of the whirling flakes, their every movement melancholic.

Knox is holding my hand. Our steps crunch in the snow. At some point, we reach a cabin. I put my hand onto wood and hear iron sliding upward into a hinge. Knox opens the door, and as I follow him inside and the smell of hay and horses reaches my nose, I realize where we are.

"William's barn," I say.

I stay put in the pitch dark for a bit while Knox curses several times as he bumps into various things. But then I hear the click of a lighter and am able to make out the silhouettes of buckets, pitchforks, and saddle racks, and a few seconds later Knox gives me one of his widest grins in the glow of an old-fashioned lamp. The flames cast a shadow over his face, an interplay of dark, bright, black, red, shadows, light. The candle strips Knox down to the skin. Emotionally vulnerable. It says: *Here he is, take a good look, I am showing you who he is, do you like it?*

And how. And how.

"What are we *doing* here?" I ask.

Knox lights a second lantern and hands it to me. "We're going to ride."

"Ride?"

"You need me to explain? Well, okay. You sit on the back of a moving horse that carries you along in the process. Ooor you sit on a man's lap—mine, for example—and start to move while…"

"Finish and I'm going to hold food in front of Sally's nose without giving it to her so that she'll back out of her stall while you're standing there."

Knox laughs. The lantern scratches the floor as he puts it down and kisses the crown of my head. "I'd love to be romantic and saddle a horse for you, but, sadly, I am terribly incompetent in such matters. William gave me a hand." He points toward two of the horses that are already saddled and tacked up. "You get the Andalusian."

"I don't know how to ride."

There's a mischievous glint in his eyes. "Oh, how much I'd *love* to say something just now."

"Shut it."

Knox rumples his nose a few times to keep from laughing until he's got himself under control again. "It's a cinch. You just sit on top, and they move. As long as you can hold the reins and keep in the saddle, all's good. They're constantly carrying squealing tourists around on their backs. They're used to it."

"Okay." My eyes scurry through the stable and stop on the dappled Irish Cob. The mare has buried her face in the feeding trough and is snorting. She sounds angry. "But I'm taking Sally."

Knox follows my glance while opening the box of a fox-red Andalusian. The horse rubs its head against Knox's shoulder and then its nostrils across his face. No doubt it's not his first time here.

Knox pats the horse's neck, while looking at me with raised eyebrows. "No way. I can't be responsible for that. I've got to ride her."

"Why?"

"She's on low-carb."

I pout. "But, but…"

Knox holds my glance for a few seconds, then curses. "Those damn lips of yours. Fine, take Sally. But if William gets wind of it, it was your idea."

I grin and get a carrot out of a bucket for her. Her large dark eyes glow with a look of annoyance as she turns her head to the side and ignores the vegetable. With a sigh I toss the carrot back into the bucket. "William wouldn't say anything."

"I'm begging you." The Andalusian gives a lazy snort while Knox comes up to me to help with Sally. "You're going to be the subject of the next town hall with the screening of a film called *Why No One Is Allowed to Touch Sally When She Isn't Getting Any Carbohydrates. A Film by William.*"

We lead the animals outside, each of us with a horse in one hand, a lantern in the other.

"Do you need a hand getting into the saddle?"

I shake my head. "I land triple axels and spins out on the ice, my entire weight on a one-and-a-half-millimeter-wide blade. I think I can manage getting my foot into a stirrup."

I don't. Knox has to help me get a leg up to swing onto her wide back. Eventually, I manage. It's high, and I want to come back down. My stomach is a bit weird. I wish I'd secretly fed her some feed.

Knox hands me a helmet that's been outfitted with a headlamp. He's wearing one, too, and that makes me feel better because, to be honest, I feel a bit like a miner.

He smoothly swings up onto his Andalusian, as if he didn't do anything else, and shows me how I can direct my horse with my knees. Then we set off.

It's wonderful. Aspen by night during a snowfall, between us only the sound of horses' hooves in the snow, the occasional snort, and the metallic rubbing of the bit as the horses slide it between their teeth.

We circle Silver Lake. Ice floes drift toward one another on the dark water and drift apart again. Reaching the mountains, the horses pant as they climb uphill and speed up when they go downhill again.

At some point Knox says, "YouandI without any spaces."

Sally steps over a snowy root, I look at Knox and ask, "Without any spaces?"

He nods. "Nothing comes between us anymore."

I smile. I smile and am in love.

It's the middle of the night by the time we reach the Winterbottoms' resort. In spite of the heated seats, the cold is eating at my limbs. Our horse ride was one of the most beautiful moments of my life, but, honestly, I almost froze to death. No idea if any life will ever seep back into my feet.

Knox opens the door, and we're back in a sea of golden rays. The panoramic windows have been decorated with string lights, the banisters of the wooden stairs have also been hung with garlands of fir, and the walls have been hung with wreaths covered in little candy canes, gifts, and reindeers.

"When did all this happen?" I ask. "Did the little Christmas elves show up while we were out?"

Knox puts his keys into the wooden bowl on the sideboard and looks around. "Dad has a decorating firm come over to decorate the house. We used to do it all together—Mom, Dad, and me—but after her death all he's ever said is that he has no time, patience, or talent for any of it."

I slip out of my boots and slide across the warm wooden floor to the fireplace in my wool socks. It's not a classic fireplace, but one built into the wall, and above it towers a varnished wooden beam with two rustic consoles as support. Three ivory-colored bows decorate the cornice as well as an elongated fir tree and four advent candles. Tomorrow is Christmas Eve. But what really catches my eye are the long, white knit stockings with pom-poms at their ends dangling between the bows. There are three of them.

Three.

And they each have a name.

Knox.

Jack.

And Paisley. *Paisley.*

I run my fingers over the firm, curved lines of the yarn and feel like I'm dreaming.

"Knox," I say, without looking up from the socks. I wave him over. "Knox, look at this."

He comes out of the bathroom with a half-eaten Twinkie in his hand. "Hm?"

"Come here. Have a look at this."

His footsteps make a hollow sound as he crosses the large living room. On the way toward me he stuffs the rest of the Twinkie into his mouth and tosses the wrapper into the umbrella stand. Over the last few weeks I'd been wondering which of the two Winterbottoms used the thing as a trash can, but somehow it was obvious.

"What's up?"

"My name's there, too." I point to the sock as if it were some kind of relic. "There. Paisley."

Knox looks at me. "Yeah. And?"

"Why?"

"Umm. Because you live here?"

"I've never had a Christmas stocking."

Knox frowns as if in pain. The touch of his hand between my shoulder blades warms my heart and drives the cold of sadness out of me. He pulls me to his chest, kisses my head, and says, "And now you have one, babe. Get used to it."

It's dumb, and I don't want to, but I start to cry. Strange how it's always the little things that make the cup run over. I've just carried so much.

Blows. Mental abuse. A shitty childhood. Shattered dreams. Abandoned friendships. And now, here I am, and it's this white stocking with my name on it that brings it all back. I howl like a dog, drench Knox's expensive shirt, and smear it full of snot. Sometimes it's just like that. And right now is a good moment to do it, here in Knox's arms, in my new life, filled with joy and gratefulness. Now I can just let everything out, let everything go. It's all good. *It's all good.* Go away, rotten thoughts. Go away, and don't you dare come back.

The whole time Knox just runs his hand through my hair. Then he puts his hands on my shoulders, pushes me away from his chest, looks at me, and wipes the tears off of my face. I sniffle like a little kid to stop the snot from continuing to flow. My eyes feel swollen.

"You'll get one next year, too," he says, taps me on the nose, and smiles. "And the year after that. And the year after that one, too. Forever. Because you belong to me now. No one *will ever* mistreat you again, you hear? That's a thing of the past."

"Can you stay with me tonight?"

"Of course," he says, kissing my nose. "Of course."

But then his glance wanders up the stairs and I know he is imagining my room. He swallows.

I take his hand and make small circles over the outside of his middle knuckle. "We don't have to go to my room."

Knox looks at me. His lips spread. "How do you know…"

I caress the close-cropped hair by his right ear. The minimal stubble prickles. "You carved your name into the wall by the bed. *K-n-O-x.* Crooked and bent but legible."

He smiles faintly. "I was six, I think."

"Does the reason you don't want to step foot in there anymore have to do with your mom?"

He swallows again. His eyes drift toward the ceiling, as if he could look directly into the room, as if he could jump into a time long since past when his heart was so much lighter.

"She used to read a goodnight story to me every night in that room once the sun had disappeared behind the Aspen Highlands. She always said: 'Tomorrow morning, once the sun has returned to greet the new day, I'll be there to kiss you awake and to remind you how much you are loved.'"

"She's never stopped," I whisper. "She still does, every time the sun rises. Just remember that with a smile on your face. She's there, Knox, and she doesn't want to see you fall."

Knox nods. The little golden lights on their strings dapple his face, the corner of his mouth, above his eye, next to his ear. He looks sad but not hopeless anymore. It's a melancholic sadness, and that's better, I think. I don't think he'll ever completely lose that expression, but he doesn't have to. Because then Knox wouldn't be Knox. It's a piece of him—that love for his mother who is no longer here—and denying that would be insincere. Knox isn't insincere. He's real, and he is sad. Just like me. He and I, we're broken, but we're slowly putting ourselves back together again. We will function again, but the cracks will remain visible. That's a good thing. It reminds us that we're strong every time we forget it.

We go upstairs to his room. Everything in this resort is upscale, from the lamps to the designer furniture to the silverware—but Knox's bedspread is dark blue, with spaceships and planets on it. It's got to go back to when he was a kid.

He sits down and seems completely overwhelmed. "To be honest, I have no idea what I'm supposed to do." He crosses his feet and begins to rub his toes, right, left, right, left. "There has never been a woman who I was serious with in my room."

At the word *serious,* everything in me starts to tingle. I sit down next to him cross-legged and bob my knees.

"You don't always need to know what to do. Sometimes it's nice just to experience new things. Don't you think?"

Knox pulls a leg up onto the bed. I admire the spaceship beneath his knee because I, too, want to touch him, and then I just do. I start with his knuckles, raw from the cold, move up his arm, the fine little hairs under my fingertips. At my touch, they stand up, and for two, three, four seconds Knox stops breathing.

"Paisley." His voice is soft, gravelly, mixed with an undertone of something I have never heard from him before. My fingers stop at the cuff of his rolled-up shirt, wander to his elbows because I am certain that no woman has ever touched them in the same way before. He gives me the feeling of being the first and, God, how I need that. If I start thinking now about how normal it is for him to have women in his room, to be touched by them, to be *wanted* by them, I'll get sick. So I don't. I touch his elbow and think it's the most beautiful elbow I've ever seen.

"Paisley, look at me."

I look at him. His room is dark, but even here there's a string of lights at the window dappling his face in gold. He kisses me between my eyebrows, right there where I feel the little wrinkle every time my thoughts begin to control me. My stomach contracts.

"This here is new," he says. His expression is so real. It goes so deep. "This didn't exist before. Okay?"

I nod. My hand is trembling. My mouth still tastes like beer from the party, and I'm worried Knox wants to kiss me but will be disgusted. But maybe he tastes like beer, too, and beer plus beer will be okay.

"Don't think so much," he whispers. "Just feel."

His lips press themselves to mine, and I think anyway. I think: *And how I can feel everything, Knox, and how.*

"I love this," he says hoarsely, a breath between two kisses. "The way it feels kissing you."

I don't know how much time goes by, but we kiss for a long time and in every way possible. Quick kisses hounded by hot desire. Warm, slow kisses, and with every touch a small meaning, heated, wild, urgent. He can feel that I want *more*, need *more*, and I can feel that it's the same for him. If I had a camera that was made to capture the special moments of my life then, right now, I would hear it snapping *click, click, click.*

Our lips move in a familiar rhythm as if they had known each other a whole lifetime already, in perfect symbiosis, as if they had only waited for the right moment to find each other. With every breath I smell vetiver, smell Knox, and it's crazy how much his smell and his kisses drive me nuts, along with the feeling of being wanted by him. My hands wander up his taut arms, across his wide shoulders, up his neck, across the shaved hair at the back of his head and up through the somewhat longer hair on top. I dig my fingers in, pull, somewhat too strongly, but Knox seems to like it, because he starts to moan again with that strange sound that just makes me lose my mind.

His fingers encircle the hem of my woolen sweater, stroking the individual stitches, and I know he's doing it to stop himself from sliding his hand down and exploring my skin. But I want to, so I remove my fingers from his hair, pull the sweater over my head, feel my hair grow staticky, but it doesn't matter, nothing matters because here we are, Knox and I, and that's all that does.

Knox explores my stomach, moves over the muscles beneath the skin. He caresses my midriff, up across my ribs, traces invisible lines as if I was a map he wanted to study until he knew it by heart. When he begins to move over the curve of my breasts, I take a sharp breath. He stops. Pulls back in shock. I shake my head, violently, intoxicated, grab the fabric of his shirt and bend over him, kiss him again. "Don't stop," I whisper, "Don't stop."

That seems to be confirmation enough. He nudges my head to the side, nibbles at my throat, his warm breath brushes my ear and I swear, *I swear*, I can't go any further. I have never felt anything like this. This insistent throbbing beneath my center, this devouring passion for his touches, this desire for more, so much more, quicker and quicker, nothing is quick enough, and everything is too quick. Every touch should last forever, should echo in my nerves forever because I don't want it to ever stop.

Knox's hands wander on. They move across my arms, my back,

stop at the clasp of my bra. He waits, looks at me, questioningly. *May I?*

I nod. *Do it, do it,* then I'm sitting in front of him, my upper body naked, but in my jeans. I feel exposed, but in a good way, in a way that says: *Here I am, just for you, everything just for you, and maybe you can see the trust I am giving you.*

Knox's lids are fluttering. He moans softly as he eyes my breasts. As if he had never seen anything nicer. As if he had never seen anything more precious.

He strokes my nipples with the ball of his hand, and I can't, can't, can't think straight, bend my back and fall backward onto the bed. Knox's lips mark my body, leaving behind damp impressions, painting the rivers of our map. I tear at his shirt. I'm tired of it, that blue-checked fabric, I want to see more, want to feel more. He pulls it over his head, and I can feel tight, warm skin. I've seen him shirtless before, but never so close. Never so palpably. Looking at him now, a slight gasp escapes me, he is just so *cut*.

Every. Inch. Of. His. Body.

I put my finger to his chest, follow the line down to his bulging stomach muscles. Stroke the defined rib area, count each individual muscle, four, six, twelve, eighteen. Knox, my Lord, how is such a body even possible?

My fingertip reaches this one particular line that blurs every thought in my head into a swirl of colorful streams. All of a sudden, I feel like I've fallen into a whirlpool. The line that leads to areas the waistband of his jeans is denying me. Thanks to the whirling in my head I pull on them before I even realize what I'm doing. Knox laughs, a deep, soft laugh. It is so beautiful, I want to catch it.

He pulls off his pants. Just a few movements, nothing more, then they're on the floor. The mattress sinks when Knox lies down next to me, propped up on his elbows. Not even in this position is there any fat showing, and that's simply impossible. For years I've been training every day, morning, noon, and night, and even *I* have a bit of fat. Everyone does. But not Knox, and that does something to me, gives me a snippet of info I want to take hold of and interpret, but somehow I don't manage, somehow it eludes me. I think it's important. I think it's something I'd like to know, *have to* know. But the whirlpool, the whirlpool just won't let me.

Knox bends forward. Nibbles on my ear and I notice how *wet* I am, wetter than I've ever been in my life. He turns my head, spreads my lips with his tongue and things get wild, fiery, *hot*. His fingers are fiddling with the button of my jeans until all of a sudden I'm lying next to him with naked legs and wet underwear.

I pull away from his lips, look down, down to his gray boxers. There's a bulge. A bulge and a wet spot. I stretch out my hand and touch him there, right at that spot. Knox whistles through his teeth. He digs his fingernails into my waist, closes his eyes, and moans, and that sound downright *forces* me to spread my legs, for if I didn't, I'd explode. One hundred percent.

The look on his face, this agonizing pleasure I feel allows me to go farther. My fingers wander below his waistband, farther, farther, farther until my hand is touching Knox's penis—warm, hard, throbbing against my skin.

I don't have much experience—and the experience I do have was for the most part forced—but this here, I want to do this right. I stroke him; I don't let his face out of my sight so I can read if I'm doing it right, if he likes it.

Knox's lips open, he emits that moan again, two, three, four times, then buries his nose in my hair, bites my ear, my neck. I keep going, I want him to keep going, and he does, God, and how. His hand disappears into my underwear, he puts a finger to my clit, and I think I'm going to die. The tension is making my entire body vibrate. Knox knows *exactly* what he's doing. He makes circles with his thumb, with a little bit of pressure, not too much and not too little, and I get wetter and wetter and wetter. I am so hot it feels like I'm on fire, and something takes control of me. I stop thinking about what's right, what I could do wrong, whether what I'm doing is okay. I simply act. I pull Knox's boxers down, take in what I see, wide-eyed, the skin of my throat aflame. I am so, so hot. I grab his penis with one hand, move it up and back down, hear his throaty sounds. He tries to touch me again, but I notice I am making it hard for him to concentrate, notice that he can hardly do anything as his entire body is trembling. I run my palm across the damp spot, Knox lets his head drop right onto the little image of Pluto on his bedspread before shooting back up and biting my shoulder. Nothing bad, just a love bite, probably thinking it's all he can do to keep from exploding.

"Is this…"

"It's everything," he says. "Everything, Paisley."

I keep going. Touching him I notice the palm of my hand growing damper and damper, I watch him, see the red flecks creeping up his throat, kiss him. Quick, jerky kisses as he's shuddering with desire, with lust. He pulls my hair, just at the edge of bearable, and my groin trembles. He leans back his head, the veins in his neck are throbbing powerfully, so I kiss him there to calm them down, but that just makes things worse. Knox moans again, which causes me to break out in goose bumps, and I want him to do it again and again and again, the whole time, while I continue to stroke his cock. His face is completely open, given over to me completely, his lips, those lips of his, I love them—and then Knox rears and cums—cums right into my hand and all across his stomach. It's a mess, a real mess, but I have never loved chaos as much as ours.

His entire body relaxes. For a few seconds, there is nothing but our wheezing breaths, our stomachs touching each other at every inhale and exhale, our hearts beating for each other.

And then Knox is above me. He pushes my hands over my head, covers the curve of my jaw with kisses, continues down to my belly button. Two seconds, then my underwear is off. But that's fine, away with you! I'm lying beneath him, every nerve electrified, my legs spread, just here, just for him. He runs his warm tongue across my pussy and. I. *Explode.*

My fingers dig into his bedspread, sending waves through the solar system and making a complete mess of it while he presses his lips to my clit, kissing it, sucking it, licking it. *Help, help, help, what on earth is he doing?* What is he *do*ing?

Now I know why everyone is so interested in this, why everyone wants to do it. I dig my fingers into his hair. I need to hold onto something. I can hardly bear it when his full bottom lip sweeps across the most sensitive part of my body.

The whirling in my head intensifies. I can hardly stand it any longer. I can't breathe. I can't see. I can only stretch out even farther toward him and moan and gasp, squeal and everything at the same time with every kiss, until everything inside me builds up, quakes, and I cum. It is so intense, so agonizingly wonderful, so *Knox*, that I feel like I'm dissolving. I am swept away, carried off by vibrating waves. But I decide to simply drift, to enjoy being completely lost and the movements of the waves as they slowly, slowly, slowly diminish.

We push the bedspread away, and Knox lies down next to me. He puts his arm around me and pulls me toward him, my cheek against his chest.

"That," he says, "wasn't normal."

I look up at him. "A good not-normal?"

"Better than good. Give me two minutes, and we'll do it again."

I laugh. "I'm too tired."

"That's good, too. I'm looking forward to that at least as much."

"To what?" My voice is sleepy. I'm almost gone.

Knox's voice reaches me as a warm, distant rushing, but I hear what he says, and carry it with me into sleep, packed up tight within my heart.

"Falling asleep next to you, then waking back up next to you."

35

Christmas Wishes and Mistletoe Kisses

KNOX

PAISLEY AND I ARE LYING ON THE FLOOR IN FRONT OF THE fireplace.

The fire is crackling, and the radio is playing "Last Christmas." She's put her head on one of the sofa cushions and is leafing through her copy of *Skate Magazine*. Her feet are lying on top of my thighs, and she keeps on wiggling her toes. Between us there's a plate of gingerbread cookies. I have to hold myself in check so as not to eat them all within a few minutes, but, man, is it a challenge. Paisley needs an eternity to just eat one of them. She nibbles at it for fifteen minutes and then stops every time she loses herself in an interesting article.

She turns a page. "Could you please stop staring at me like that?"
"Like what?"
"Like you wanted to devour my gingerbread man."
"But you eat *so* slowly!"
"No. I'm just not as greedy as you."

I groan, lean my head against the sofa and grab my phone. It's time I answered some of my messages on Instagram before Dad has a breakdown and finally hangs that content creator around my neck.

Paisley puts her magazine to the side and looks at me. "What time is everything starting tonight?"

I'm right in the process of reading a fan's fucked-up message telling me she wants to give me five children. "No idea. Ask Gwen."

"She's not responding."

"I think around seven."

It's Christmas Eve. For as long as I can remember, it's been a tradition for a few close friends in Aspen to meet at Kate's Diner for a nice dinner. It started with my and Aria's families, because Mom, Ruth, and Kate were inseparable. After Wyatt's parents died, I started bringing him and Camila along. William's been there all along, too, because he's lonely, though he'd never admit it.

"Is Aria coming, too? I'd love to meet her."

I delete another let-me-bear-your-children message and put my phone away. "I'm afraid she is."

Paisley hops over to me, puts her head in my lap, and looks up at me from below. The deejay is talking about increasing snowstorms and drops in the temperature before introducing the next song: Ariana Grande's "Santa Tell Me."

"What do you mean you're *afraid*? I thought you were friends?"

"We are. But it'd be the first Christmas after the whole thing with Wyatt. It'd be the first time they saw each other again. No idea if he knows she's coming. Or how he'll react."

"Oh. How long were they together?"

"Five years. Maybe even six. They got together during high school, they were fourteen, I think. They were joined at the hip. When his parents died, next to me, Aria was the only one who took care of Camila and him. She did everything for him."

Paisley takes my hand and strokes the individual knuckles as if wanting to paint them. "Why'd he cheat on her? Didn't he love her?"

I have to laugh. If Wyatt ever loved anyone, then it was Aria Moore. "He definitely loved her. But, no idea. It was a difficult time for him. His parents were dead, and he and Camila just totally lost their shit. Drank themselves half to death, took drugs, did everything just to not have to think about it. I don't think that Wyatt really knew what the hell he was doing back then."

"That's awful," Paisley says. "And so he lost her, too, without really knowing why?"

"Well, I told him why. But he couldn't remember."

Paisley looks into the fire. "Gwen feels awful about it."

I stroke Paisley's hair, strand for strand. "I know."

"Did she tell you?"

"She doesn't need to. She and Aria had been good friends. All you have to do is look at her when Wyatt's around."

Our conversation breaks off when my father comes down the stairs. He looks at his smartwatch while making his way through the living room, but when he looks up and sees me and Paisley he stops and stares. For a few seconds he doesn't say anything, then he rolls his eyes, lets his head sink into his hands, and emits a dull *umpf.*

"Knox," he says.

"Yeah?"

He raises his head, comes over to us, and sits down on the arm of the sofa. His suit pants are creased. Dad crosses his hands in his lap. "Please tell me this isn't true."

"What?"

His eyes wander to Paisley and back. "She's the best chalet girl we've ever had."

"Yeah, and?"

Dad clenches his jaw. I know that he wants to say something, but not in front of her. He weighs the situation for a moment, then appears to decide that he's going to anyway. "You're going to drive her off, just like all the others."

Paisley peels herself off my lap and sits down next to me. I start to grow warm. She knows that I didn't exactly live like a monk before her but, all the same, my dad's Knox-bangs-every-chalet-girl-before-ditching-her confession is a bit uncomfortable.

"That's not how it is with Paisley," I say. "It's different."

Dad frowns. "Different?"

"Yeah. This time I'm serious, Dad. Really."

I'm not actually saying it for him, but because I want Paisley to believe me. As far as I'm concerned, Dad can believe what he wants. But I don't want to give her any reason to doubt us.

"When have you ever been serious about anything?"

I think for a moment. "Until now? Never."

It is impossible to decipher my dad's expression. He looks at me for so long, it's as if he was looking at me for the first time in a really long time, then he turns to Paisley. She's huddled next to me and looks like she'd prefer to disappear. Dad places his hands one on top of the other and puts on an amused, doubtful face. "Please, *please* stay with us, Paisley. If my son acts like an obnoxious ass, I'll throw him out, no problem, but *you* have to stay."

"Hey!"

Paisley laughs. "It's still the probationary period, but I think he'll make it, Mr. Winterbottom."

Dad smiles at her. "Call me Jack, please."

She bites her lower lip, just like she always does when she doesn't know what to do in a particular situation. "Okay, Jack."

"Welcome to the family." My dad stands up, smooths out his pants, and casts a glance at his smartwatch again. Then he looks at her once more, his face gentler than I've seen it in years, and says, "Knox is a good kid."

Before leaving he points at me. "If you screw this one up, son, I am *so* going to kick your ass."

Please, Dad. Please do that.

Aside from William, we are the first ones to arrive at the diner. Paisley is carrying a bowl of pasta salad, I've got the beets and the cranberry sauce. Dad is bringing up the rear with four bottles of champagne.

Between the booths and the counter, Kate has set up two tables and beer benches, which she has decorated with string lights, tinsel, and fir garlands. The tablecloth is the same as every year: white linen fabric that Gwen painted with reindeer, Santa Clauses, and other unidentifiable bits and pieces as a kid. *MaRRy Christmas* written on top in crooked, colorful letters.

As the jukebox plays "Jingle Bell Rock," Kate puts the turkey down on the table and Gwen arranges the wine and the glasses. When she sees us, she quickly puts the last bottle down and grabs the salad bowl out of Paisley's hands before hugging her. "You look *so* beautiful. What kind of dress is that?"

"A Valentino," Paisley says. She's beaming. It's the dress from the sponsors' evening.

"Maybe I should become a chalet girl," Gwen says. "I mean, if clothes like *this* are just going to appear."

"I asked you three times whether you wanted to work at The Old-Timer, Gwen." William looks upset. He straightens his bright red, oversized Christmas sweater, twirls his mustache, and then rubs his thighs. "I told you: you'll get two bags of popcorn a month for free."

"I don't need a job, William." Gwen sits down next to him and pours herself a glass of wine. "That was just a joke."

"You could clean out the stables."

"I really don't need a job. I help Mom out in the diner here."

Kate raises her eyebrows as she sits down next to her daughter. "Oh, Gwendolyn, really? When was that?"

Gwen casts her mother a glance that more or less says: *Come on, Mom, play along with me for once.*

We sit down—Dad across from Kate, Paisley next to me—we are just pouring glasses of champagne when Wyatt and Camila come through the door. Camila is carrying a big cake box that has to contain her famous apple pie. Wyatt's glance scurries almost in panic across everyone sitting at the table before his shoulders sink back down, relieved. He undoes his scarf and hangs his jacket on the coat hook, then sits down on my other side and gives me a slap on the back. Snow falls out of his hair onto the table. "Merry Christmas, man."

"Merry Christmas."

"Should we make a toast?" Dad asks, and Kate says, "In a second, Jack. We're waiting for Ruth and Aria."

Dead silence. "Let It Snow" sounds so much louder than before. Paisley's knee bumps against mine, her silent way of saying *Oh my God, Oh my God,* and I press back, my way of saying *Let's get out of here. Please, let's get out of here.*

Everyone at the table does their best not to look at Wyatt, but, of course, we *all* look over at Wyatt. He's staring into his wine glass as if weighing whether to drown himself in it while Gwen is staring at the beets so intensely, it's as if she was waiting for them to jump up and hop off. Before any one of us decides to break the silence, the door opens one more time and makes the bell ring. I can hardly look, but then I do because I'm curious.

Ruth is limping a bit. I don't know what she's got, but it's gotten worse since last year. She's holding her daughter's arm, who in turn is carrying a bowl of Christmas pudding.

Aria looks just the same as always. Her long brown waves of hair are spilling out from underneath her wool cap, and her green eyes are sparkling. She rubs her nose, right over the dark freckles, and looks every inch the cheerful, harmony-needing person I've known half my life. Gwen, on the other hand, looks like a cat who's just been shot in the face with a water gun, and Wyatt is as gray as a shriveled mushroom.

"Aria!" William pushes back his stool while Aria is putting the pudding down on the table and takes her into his arms. "How wonderful to see you!"

"Thanks, William." The cold has left red splotches on her face, which reach all the way up to her high cheekbones. "It's good to see you, too. How *wonderful* to see all of you together so happily." She says it brightly, no trace of mockery in her voice whatsoever, but all the while she's looking at Wyatt and Gwen, and, to be honest, her smile's got something psycho about it.

Kate seems overwhelmed. She can tell that things are tense, and I think she heard about the two of them breaking up, but I'm pretty sure she doesn't know anything about Gwen. She pushes the cranberry sauce next to the mashed potatoes and then back between the turkey as if she couldn't make up her mind and says, "Yes, wonderful. Have a seat."

Aria sits down next to her mother, across from Paisley. Half a table and all of America lie in between Wyatt and her, but, God, it is so obvious that that's not enough. Aria can make all the effort she wants, but she is *smoldering*.

Dad is the first to raise his champagne glass, and the others all follow his lead. "Merry Christmas," he says, and we all repeat it in unison and take a sip. Wyatt almost downs his entire glass, Camila does her usual, and Aria appears strangely content.

She looks at Paisley. "You must be the new figure skater. Mom told me about you."

Paisley serves herself some turkey and smiles. "Yeah. Thanks again for letting me stay in your room. Unfortunately, I wasn't able to catch the marten."

"And I had *such* high hopes for you!" Aria says.

"She's my girlfriend," I say, annoyed that she's only been introduced as a figure skater. Now I'm the one everyone's staring at. I clear my throat, take the beets from William who's filled his entire plate with them, and say, "Paisley and I, yeah, well, so, we're together."

Camila chokes on her garlic bread. Kate begins to beam so intensely it's like she'll turn into the sun. For a second, Wyatt forgets that Aria's here and slaps my back, Ruth squeaks, and William jumps up from his chair. It falls over, everyone laughs, and I feel like my relationship status has become the sensation of the century.

Paisley looks almost pleadingly in William's direction as he picks up his chair and sits back down. "Please do not post that on @Apsen, Will. *Please.*"

"Of course not," he mumbles. "I only publish interesting things on @Apsen. Information regarding the new gully in town, for example, or Woody's new rain gutters." He winks at Paisley from across the table, and Paisley is visibly relieved. She smiles.

Aria reaches for the gravy and in the process grazes Wyatt's hand as he reaches for the beans. He pulls back so quickly that he inadvertently hits Camila in the face. His sister closes her eyes and flares her nostrils. She's probably counting to ten so as not to lose her mind.

Aria acts as if she hasn't noticed a thing. "I'm happy to see you've given your bad-boy image a rest, Knox. It never really fit you."

"Oh, I think he did a pretty good job," Ruth says. She's wearing a blue scarf, but it doesn't really cover her wrinkles, which seem to have doubled over the last few months. All the same, her similarity to her daughter is unmistakable. They have the same eyes. Ruth smiles at me. "But next to Paisley, I like you even more. Just don't *mess* it up."

I roll my eyes. "Why does everyone assume that I'm going to mess it up?"

"Because it's in your blood," Wyatt says. "It's a chronic thing with you." He says that in his usual Wyatt tone, that casual-funny tone that gets him every woman he meets.

My eyes drift over to Aria. She's looking at her plate and cutting her turkey but doesn't seem to have noticed that her knife's been scraping the plate for quite a while. Ruth lays a hand on her arm, subtly and discreetly. Aria's hands are trembling as she puts her silverware down. Then they disappear beneath the table.

"How's Brown?" my father asks, and Aria immediately picks up the thread, as if he'd tossed her a lifeline. I can see the relief shoot through her body. "It's wonderful. Really. I love the people there." She casts Wyatt a brief glance. "And with the exception of Mom and the mountains, I don't miss a thing, really, *not a thing.*"

Wyatt's Adam's apple jerks up and down. He just stares at his plate and grinds his teeth.

His sister is looking at him, then Aria, then back to him before clicking her tongue. "We got it, Aria, all right? He understands how happy you are without him. You knew that he would be here, and you knew that he fucked Gwen. Deal with it."

My Dad curses. "Camila!"

But she just grunts, shrugs, and empties her champagne in one go. The legs of Gwen's chair scrape across the floor as she pushes it backward and disappears through the door behind the counter. Paisley gives my arm a brief squeeze then follows.

Kate looks shocked. Her beets fall off her fork. She's sitting stock-still in her chair and staring at Wyatt, who is tensed up next to me, holding onto the tablecloth with all his might. He wants to go, I know that much. He wants to go, but he's holding back because he doesn't want Camila to end up sitting around with him alone on Christmas Eve. He's putting up with this for his sister, and I can feel that it's tearing him apart.

The mood is awful. Gwen and Paisley haven't come back, no one's speaking, suddenly the Christmas music sounds like a funeral march, and William alone is humming along as if he were walking with the bees in a field of sunflowers on a hot summer's day with his soul at ease and a pot of honey in his arms.

For the rest of the evening I count the number of glances that Aria and Wyatt exchange.

Obvious glances: zero.

Secret glances: the number is too high, the champagne too good, and, at some point, I simply can't count anymore.

The next morning I'm woken up by something scratching my nose. I need three tries before I manage to open my eyes. A green ribbon finds its way into my nostril: Paisley's dangling a little present in front of my nose. I look at the clock. Seven. Her eyes are glowing.

"Merry Christmas."

I rub my eyes, sit up, and lean back against the head of the bed. It's too early. I'm still out of order.

"What's that?" My voice is sleepy and hoarse.

Paisley rolls her eyes. "Yeah, hmm, what is it, Knox? Looks like a giant shrimp, don't you think? But I'm not sure. It's really *so* hard to figure out."

I laugh, ruffle her blond hair, and take the package. It is big and heavy. I shake it, but it doesn't make any sound.

Paisley impatiently waves her hands. "Open it already!"

To annoy her, I take my time. I look at the paper and amusedly note that Paisley is terrible at wrapping gifts. She patched the paper together in all sorts of places and used a hundred thousand strips of Scotch tape.

She punches my shoulder. "Come on! Do it already!"

I laugh, then tear open the paper. It's a brown leather shoulder bag. Exactly the kind I wanted to buy myself.

"Now you've *got* to accept your offer to study," Paisley says, bobbing up and down next to me in bed. She is so ridiculously happy about her present that I can't do anything but pull her toward me and bury my nose in her flowery smelling hair. "Do you like it?"

"Just as much as I like you." I can feel her smile against my cheek. "I've got something for you as well." I softly push her to the side, get out of bed, and dig around in my desk drawer until I find the two little packages. "Here." I clear my throat, and start to feel warm, as I've never given any woman other than my mom a gift.

Paisley looks so excited that I have to wonder when the last time she got Christmas gifts was.

In the first is a photo of the two of us that she took with my phone to show me how a story works on Instagram. I saved it, had it printed, and then framed for her. It's just a photo, but Paisley clutches it to her chest and looks so happy that I almost believe it's more than that.

"Thank you," she says warmly.

I shift my weight from one foot to the other and notice my heart is beginning to race. "Open the next one."

She dampens her lips with the tip of her tongue while her fingers strip the paper from the second packet in careful, excited movements and lift the lid of the small box.

Jackpot. Any moment now and Paisley's eyes are going to fall out of their sockets. Every kind of emotion and delight crosses her face as she takes the silver charm bracelet out of the velvet cushion and looks intently at the small pendants. A pair of ice skates, some mountains, a heart, and a little bird. She takes it in her hand.

"Wyatt once told me that birds still sing even when they're sad. That's why there's the little bird there. You remind me of one because you're so strong."

Paisley wraps herself around my neck. She kisses me, and at that moment, I know I want to experience another hundred such moments with her, another hundred Christmases when I can make her happy.

We spend the rest of the day with my dad and a few board games in front of the fireplace. Eventually my dad makes his way to the hot tub and Paisley gets a call from Gwen.

"Hey. Merry Christmas."

I can hear Gwen's voice. She sounds excited and is talking a mile a minute. Paisley is frowning. Then she says, "Hold on. I'll have a look."

"What's up?"

"One sec." Paisley's jaw is tense while she types away at her phone. She looks completely panicked, and I can't bear waiting, so I look over her shoulder. Her phone opens a website, but our internet is a disaster because of the snowstorm, and it takes ages to load. Finally, the front page of the *USA Today* website opens, and there we are, Paisley and I, on the very first post, our hair ruffled, lying on our bed of hay, huge.

Finally Revealed! Knox Winterbottom's Heart Beats for This Figure Skater!

I look at Paisley.
I take her in my arms.
But it's too late, she's already falling.

36

Your Love Roars Louder Than My Darkness

Paisley

My phone slips out of my hands and lands on the parquet with a dull thud. Knox's breath is audible. My knees are wobbly. I stand up, feel like I'm about to buckle, then, do, and stumble over to the sofa. I sit down, listen to my heart, my heart that's beating far too fast, and look at my hands. They're trembling. I knead every single finger, try to calm myself down, but I can't do it. My whole body is shaking.

"Hey." Knox sits down next to me. He takes my hands in his and turns me so that I have to look at him. "Slow your breath down," he says. "You're hyperventilating."

I try but don't manage. Knox places one of my hands over my stomach. "Breathe through your stomach. Against your hand. Exactly. Concentrate on taking long, deep breaths, in through your nose, out through your mouth. Try again, even more slowly. You're doing great."

The tingling sensation in my hands and feet begins to lessen somewhat. I run my hand over my neck and realize I am covered in sweat.

"I'm going to call Jennet," Knox says. "However this happened…

it shouldn't have." He pulls his phone from the pocket of his jeans and scrolls through his contacts. I feel dizzy. I don't feel present. Everything around me is swirling into a blur, and all I can hear in my head is: *I'm done. I'm done. I'm done.*

"Hey. Yeah, this is Knox. Listen, there's… What? I don't care, and even if you were having breakfast with the President of the United States I wouldn't fucking care. You stay on the line. Good. Have you checked your messages?"

I hear a 'no.' Knox stands up and walks back and forth between the standing lamp and the Christmas tree, where he's reflected in the wine-red Christmas balls. His body looks immense, his legs three feet long.

Take a good look at him, Paisley. Take a good look at him. Who knows how much longer you'll be able to.

"You were supposed to take care of the photos that were taken of us, Jennet. Of me and Paisley, yeah. In the stable. You said you'd make sure that every single picture would disappear. Did you? Really? So, how come *that* goddamn photo was published in *USA Today*?"

I'm sitting on the sofa, staring into the distance. I feel like this is it. My time in Aspen is over. That's it with iSkate.

That's it with Knox.

I knew it. From the very beginning, I knew that I wouldn't get that far. By now at Skate America, everything would have come out. All the same, I came here in the hopes of feeling talented *at least once*, of seeing Skate America from inside *at least once*. It was obvious that Ivan would find me. As was the fact that I'd have to go back. I'm not made to accomplish things. I'm made to exist, to suffer, and take what life is willing to give.

How could I have ignored all that? *How dumb*, I think. *How dumb* to believe that I could have a future with someone like Knox. It's time to look reality in the face. Maybe I'll make it to Skate America, so I'll just use this time, enjoy it in order to have memories I can think back on in order to survive somehow later on.

Knox curses. "Then a picture must have slipped through by *accident*? Jennet, are you aware of what you're supposed to do in your job? *Is it clear to you?*"

Jennet mumbles something I can't make out. Knox has run his hand through his hair so many times that it's sticking up all over. "Then make sure that picture gets destroyed *now*." Knox is steaming. "I DON'T CARE HOW DIFFICULT THAT'S GOING TO BE! THAT PICTURE COMES OFF THE WEBSITE OR YOU'RE DONE, JENNET, DONE!" He hangs up, throws the iPhone onto the sideboard next to the front door, and walks over to me. The sofa sinks when he sits down. "Paisley." He pulls one leg up and leans sideways into the cushions, his elbows against the back of the couch. "Tell me. Tell me what that guy's got on you."

I shake my head. "How…"

"You're safe with me. You know that no one can touch you here in Aspen, babe. Unless you're running away from something else."

At the word '*babe*', everything in me tenses up. I can hardly bear the idea that any day now could be the last one he calls me that. The thought that he could call *someone else* by that name steals my breath.

I consider telling Knox *everything*. But then he'd know that our relationship has an expiration date. Then he'd know that, soon, we'd never see each other again. Can I burden him with that? Isn't it enough that *I* have to live with that awareness? I shouldn't ruin his joy about the time we've spent together, really, but there are things that feel so terrible you just don't want to carry them alone. Moments that hurt *so* bad, all you want is to be taken by the arm and consoled or built back up.

I take a deep breath in order to tell him everything, to tell him what I did—then the panoramic window slides to the side, and Jack comes in from the terrace. He is wearing a fluffy bathrobe and waving a paper in the air. I only see the red circle next to the small font, but that's enough. "Did Jennet arrange this?" His tone is easygoing. I think he's happy about it. Of course he is. It's good publicity for his son. He puts the paper down on the island in the kitchen and pours himself a tea that I'd prepared. "William's snow rides and his stable are mentioned by name. I'm curious to see how often he'll bring that up at the next town hall. This must be the best Christmas he's had in three years, when his favorite butter-popcorn topping came back onto the market." Jack blows into his tea and casts us glances over the rim of his cup. We don't react. "Why do you both look like this is round two of Christmas dinner with Aria and Wyatt?"

I don't say anything. Knox doesn't either. Jack sips his tea. The slurping sound drifts through the vast living room. The saucer rattles as he puts his cup back down. "Okay," he says, drums his fingers across the granite a few times and then points behind himself with his thumb. "If something comes up, I'll be in the sauna."

He goes and Knox looks up at me. Waiting for an answer that just a few minutes ago I was ready to give. But in the meantime that window has closed. In the meantime my head was able to get rid of all the emotional ups-and-downs and make a case for rational decisions.

I smile. Put a hand on his arm. "It's all good. It's just...I don't like attention. But if I want to be by your side, I better get used to it."

Hard to say whether he believes me. I don't think so. But he doesn't push it, doesn't force me to talk. Instead, he puts his arm around my shoulders and pulls me to him. I bury my cheek into his chest, enjoying the soft fabric of his knit sweater and the fresh scent of vetiver, and convince myself that everything is going to turn out fine although I know that can't be true.

"We've got to live, Paisley." Knox is making circles on my upper arm with his thumbs. "We've got to live, no matter how many times our world threatens to go down."

37

Happy New Year

PAISLEY

"Eggnog?"

"Oh, yeah. Thanks, Gwen."

She plops down onto the bench next to me. The pom-poms of her cap are dangling to either side of her face. It's New Year's Eve. It's been a few days since that photo of Knox and me was published, and every morning I wake up in a panic that it could be my last.

"Okay. It's New Year's, Pais. We're all here together. What's going on with you?"

I take a sip of my eggnog and swallow a clump of cream. "What do you mean?"

"For days you've hardly been reachable. At iSkate, you hardly give me a chance to talk to you because you're training nonstop like you're obsessed. No offense."

"Of course."

She pulls up her legs. Snow trickles off her boots onto the bench. Her eyes dart in my direction. "Sooo?"

I look over at Knox who is standing next to the fire while William attempts to explain that he shouldn't hold his marshmallow directly in the flame. In his mad gesticulations, his marshmallow lands on his shoe. Knox laughs, the fire lights up his face. I have rarely felt so warm.

"Have you ever felt that you are so happy, happier than you've ever been, but you know that it can't last? And then your whole body quivers with fear, and every one of your nerves is tense—right about to snap—because you're waiting for everything to come crashing down, for everything to be over, and you can accept that, but beforehand you're so afraid you can hardly stand it?"

Gwen stares at me. "Umm. No. Honestly, Paisley, what's up?" She looks over at Knox. "Things between the two of you are working out, right?"

I shrug. "Yeah."

Gwen sighs. She leans back and observes Aria, who is letting herself be served a mulled wine by Dan, the owner of the little ski hut, before spilling half of it on the snow when Wyatt walks past.

"He won't cheat on you, Paisley. Knox isn't one of those types. He wouldn't have gotten together with you if he wasn't serious."

"I know."

She frowns. Her thick brown eyebrows come together, and a dimple appears in her cheek. "You're not going to tell me what's up, are you?" When I don't answer, she nudges my shoulder. "Listen." She pushes up the sleeve of her jacket and pushes her glove down a little. The woven bracelet from Malila is bouncing on her wrist.

I smile and show her mine as well.

"Look, you and me, we're a team, Paisley. You can tell me everything. Whatever it is, I'm there for you."

God, my heart is bleeding. I want to so bad. I want to tell her what I did, how dumb I was, and then I want to cry on her shoulder while she brushes the strands of my hair out of my face. But I feel so awful, so ridiculous, that I simply can't. My days here are numbered, why should I ruin the little time I have left in Aspen?

"It's all good," I say, just like I did to Knox, and nudge her back.

"Let's go over to the others. I'm freezing my ass off on this bench. For real."

We get up and stomp through the snow to the fire. The fireworks will be set off from one of the higher points of Aspen Mountain later on, and we have a great view from where we are. I put myself next to Knox. He stretches out his arm and pulls me into his puffy jacket in order to kiss my forehead.

"Everything good, Snow Queen?"

"Super. I just wanted to talk to Aria a second. We didn't get a chance at the Christmas dinner."

"Sure. Go for it. Look for her wherever Wyatt isn't."

Smiling, I bump him with my shoulder and go off to find Aria. She's standing under a large fir tree, half-empty mug of mulled wine in her hands, looking like she'd rather hide.

I go stand next to her. "Hey."

Her hair brushes her cheeks as she looks at me. "Oh, hey. Did you have a nice Christmas?" When I make a face, she laughs. "What? Not a friend of publicity?"

"Not at all," I say, take a sip of my eggnog and look over at Kate, who's grabbed her daughter and is dancing to Justin Bieber's "Mistletoe." Gwen tries to escape, but Kate is as persistent as a whole tube of adhesive cream. "Up until the photo in *USA Today*, everything was lovely. More than lovely. Really. I really like being here."

Aria smiles. It looks sad. "Yeah, I understand you."

"I know what you said on Christmas Eve, but suppose I were to ask you whether you missed Aspen and suppose you were to tell the truth, just between the two of us, what would your answer be?"

"You like to read between the lines, huh?"

"Oh, I'm a natural talent."

She smiles and looks back out in front of her. The flames of the fire are reflecting in her eyes. "I would tell you that I miss it *terribly*." She looks over at Wyatt. I follow her glance. He's talking to Knox and keeps letting his eyes dart about.

"And him? Wyatt?"

Aria takes a sip of her mulled wine and clutches her cup. She's wearing gloves with the Gryffindor emblematic animal. I resolve to like her a little bit more. "There is no expression for how much I miss him. But sometimes things happen; sometimes things really go to shit, Paisley, and there's no going back. Doesn't matter how much I'd like to. It just doesn't work."

The smell of roast apples drifts into my nose. Ruth, William, and Kate prepared them yesterday at the diner, and now all the red-gold apples are on the stones around the fire and bathing the cold winter air with a heavenly scent.

"How can you stand it?" I ask. My glance lingers on Knox. "Letting someone you love go?"

She pulls off a glove and scratches her cheek. Her white painted nails leave behind red weals. "At the beginning, not at all. It was bad. Worse than anything I'd ever felt. But at some point..." She scrapes an X in the snow with her winter boots. "At some point I simply let the pain in and thought: *Let it hurt, Aria. Let it really hurt until no one and nothing can hurt you anymore.*"

"I understand that."

She looks at me, on her lips the hint of a smile. "Yeah, I thought so."

"Why?"

"You have such a presence. Looking at you, the first thing you see is that you are way broken but also strong." I want to say something, but Aria points to Knox. "Strange."

"What's strange?"

"I've never seen that expression on his face when he's looking for someone."

I look over at him. He is turning his head in all directions, clearly looking for me; when he sees me, his face brightens.

Aria's smile is soft. "I've known Knox all my life and have never seen him look at someone as if only just now realizing that there really is such a thing as love." The speakers are now playing "Rockin' Around the Christmas Tree."

"Come on, go over there before he comes over here, bringing Wyatt along with him. I can't handle that today."

I hesitate. I don't like leaving her alone beneath this sad fir tree. "Come with me."

She tilts her head. Above us the snow is dripping off the pinecones and falling onto her cap. "In a sec. I need a moment to finish this wine and allow my body to accept being in the same radius as Wyatt."

"Okay."

I go over to the others. Levi gives me a wide smile over Aaron's shoulder, whom he's holding tightly from behind. They are sharing a baked apple on a paper plate right by the fire. Gwen comes over to me before I reach Knox. She jumps through the snow and stops herself by clawing her fingers into my upper arm. "I thought you'd taken off already."

"Why would I do that?"

"No idea. You've got to try one of these apples. They are *so* good." She takes my empty glass of eggnog out of my hand, puts it down in the snow, and pulls me over to the fire. With two gloved fingers, she rolls an apple off the stones that have been arranged around the fire in a circle onto a paper plate, crushes the soft stuff with an already dangerously charcoaled plastic fork, and looks delighted when she hands it all to me. To be honest, it doesn't really look that good, but it smells divine, so I try it and, no kidding, I melt. It is so good that I just can't.

"What I wouldn't give for you to look at me like you are that apple." Knox hands me a flute of champagne. I quickly shovel another bite of the baked apple but manage to burn my tongue. All the same, it was worth it. I smile at Gwen. She takes a glass of champagne herself from the trolley next to the fire.

"Maybe you should invest in a bottle of baked-apple cologne. Then I'd look at you like that. Not to mention constantly sniff you."

Knox laughs. "You're constantly sniffing me the way it is."

"Not in the least."

He kisses my temple. "Okay. Try to convince yourself."

William's arm appears in front of us, and before I can understand what he's doing, he's pushing us with his back. He does that to everyone. He circles the fire with outstretched arms and pushes everyone back.

Aaron cocks an eyebrow. "What's this all about, Will?"

William looks fantastically concentrated. The fire is lighting up every wrinkle on his face while he makes his rounds. I've got to say he really does look like the horror-movie version of Rumpelstiltskin a bit. "Don't get any closer than around three feet, or you'll get burned."

Ruth sighs. "Will, *please*."

He shakes his head, his expression severe. "No exceptions. It's important,"—*wheeze*—"—that no one,"—*wheeze*—"gets hurt." WHEEZE.

Wyatt lifts his leg with an amused gleam in his eye and pushes it back and forth, closer and closer to the fire. William sees it, hurries over, and then Wyatt stops. But as soon as Will creeps off, Wyatt starts up again. It drives the old man absolutely crazy, over and over he keeps running through the snow towards Wyatt, looking just like an Oompa Loompa, and I get *such* a laughing fit that I have to bury my face in Knox's jacket.

When I raise my head back up, my glance wanders over Knox's shoulder and into Aria's face. She's still under the fir tree, looking like a ghost that is simply observing proceedings. For a second, my chest contracts when I see that she's looking at Wyatt—at how he's laughing, how he's raising his hand and patting William's shoulders—and her face is so distorted that I swear I am confronting pain in its purest, most open form. It hurts, it hurts *so much*, because I know that all too soon I'll be going through the same thing.

I don't have any more time to think about it, because at precisely that moment Gwen grabs my arm. I look at her, her lovely face lit up by the sparkler she's holding in her hand, and then things go off:

"TEN." William burns his bottom out of pure fright.

"NINE." Jack is looking up to the sky, and I think I know why.

"EIGHT." Levi is wiping Aaron's face with a snowball.

"SEVEN." Aaron laughs and pulls Levi's hat off his head.

"SIX." Kate hops through the snow over to Gwen, raises her arm, and waves a sparkler back and forth.

"FIVE." Gwen laughs and lays her head on her mom's shoulder, and I can feel a longing, just a little bit, but a little bit too much.

"FOUR." Ruth drags Aria out from the shadow of her sadness-tree and over to the fire.

"THREE." Wyatt looks at Aria as if he had never seen anything more beautiful in his life.

"TWO." Aria's jaw is clenched; I think she wants to cry.

"ONE." I feel joy and think that everything I have is right now.

"HAPPY NEW YEAR!" Knox's lips on mine, snow-drunk, the flash of fireworks behind my eyelids, laughing hearts all around me.

How beautiful life is.

How beautiful it would be if it could always be like this.

How *beautiful*.

38

I Wasn't Worth the Truth

Knox

I'M STANDING IN FRONT OF THE RIDERS' TENT, THE PLACE where all the X Games participants hang out. It's already dark, but the whole place is ringed with spotlights and lit up. I can hear the audience's calls as well as the commentators' observations through the speakers all the way over here. My heart is hammering against my chest. But not because I'm nervous. It's the steroids I just shot. Pearls of sweat are forming on my neck and running down into my jacket. Maybe I should've taken a lower dose. Maybe I shouldn't have taken *anything*. But I've got no choice. Shit, I've got to be the best. I've *got to*.

It's the fifth time ESPN's invited me to the X Games. Not for one discipline, but two: superpipe and superpipe session because I'm known for landing awesome tricks and coming off as cool and easygoing. That's my thing.

I nod to security out in front of the tent, and they move to the side. They know who I am. I pick up my gear in the fore tent at reception and move on to the riders' tent. It's nice in here, warm and full. A buddy of mine is sitting between two skiers with a pair of recovery boots on, which are supposed to massage his calves. He flashes me a peace sign. The kind of peace dude who goes and gets baked after every contest.

I take a Monster Energy out of the fridge when I realize that Jason Hawk is staring at me. He's sitting in front of a mirror while a hairstylist is flitting about him in an attempt to tame his hair. I open the can and return his stare, expressionless, until he looks away. We both do superpipe, and last year he just crushed me. I can't stand him, really, his big mouth freaks me out, but, shit, can he *rock* the half-pipe.

I sink down onto one of the couches, drink my energy drink, and look at the livestream on one of the TVs. A Canadian snowboarder is attempting a double cork but doesn't manage and takes a pretty bad fall. "Oh, shit," someone filling up their plate at the buffet says while another whose hip is being massaged by a physiotherapist says, "Dude, he's out."

I pull out my phone to write Paisley a message.

You here already?

Yep. With your dad and Wyatt in the front row.

Brief pause, then:

A cameraman keeps sticking his finger into his nose. It's so gross.

I have to laugh, then my name is called, and I'm told to get ready. I polish off my drink, put the can to the side, and stand up.
I'm up next.

She sends me that GIF of the pig in the sequined dress. This is what I look like when I cheer you on. Go, Knox, uh, uh, go, Knox.

God. I *love* this girl.

My hands are sweaty with nerves. The audience would never

notice, of course, but before every ride I get butterflies. It's a great form of nerves. I like it. A tingling excitement. If my life as a star snowboarder weren't filled with so many uncomfortable things, like the pressure, all the time required, the publicity that digs into every aspect of my private life, I'd never want to change it.

It's so bright that it feels like I'm going to go blind. Lights are dancing before my eyes and, thanks to the snowmobile, it stinks so bad on gas that I think my lungs are going to give out.

"Knox!" the audience calls as I make my way past them. "You're going to rock this, Knox!"

"Oh my God, I love you!" a sandy-haired blond yells before breaking out into tears when I walk past. Another guy bellows, "Yo, you're the best, man!"

I smile at everyone as I make my way to the snowmobile, my board pressed up tight against me. The snowmobile will take me up the slope to the pipe, where I'll get out behind the huge blue X Games banner. From there, everything else looks unspectacular, like working backstage at a festival as a scaffolder or something. But I can hear the crowd going nuts, and I can hear the speakers egging them on by saying my name and asking everyone whether they're ready to see me.

Security steps to the side and lets me up the stairs. There's a lot of them, like walking up to the third floor of a building, and when I come out at the top, a woman with a headset comes up to me immediately. Gesticulating wildly with one hand while the other is on her headset, her eyes are narrowed as she listens to all the instructions. "Just a sec," she says. "They're still running a commercial. We've got to wait for the cameras. Okay. You can go out now, strap in, but wait until I give you the go-ahead."

I do what she says and step out in front of the scaffolding and the crowd *goes wild*. The spectators are calling out, screaming, and yelling with all their might, but I can't see a thing due to the glaring lights. It's so loud my ears are ringing. Thankfully I know that as soon as I hit the pipe, my head will block everything else out. Then all that's left is me, my board, and my jumps that I've been perfecting all year long. All there is is my heart slamming against my chest and this moment.

The woman with the headset gives me a sign with her index finger. "Go!"

I push off, jump, and feel that feeling in my stomach as I hit the pipe. For a few seconds I'm weightless, then I think: *What an awesome feeling.*

I kick off with a frontside double cork 1260° followed by a double backflip that looks like a corkscrew. My snowboard lands perfectly, inside I'm cheering even louder than the spectators, then I do a backside 900°. I shift pressure to the front right, shoot up the right wall, jump off on the edge of my heel and in the first half turn I'm back to the audience. Then I do a frontside and cab, land flawlessly, and get ready for my last jump: the frontside double cork 1440°. It's a tough one, and last year I almost didn't land it, but I trained all summer long and am praying that it'll work out this time, praying, praying, praying, and...

I land it. *Holy shit.* The adrenaline makes me laugh out loud. I ride into the middle of the pipe, push up my goggles, and wave into the cameras with an ear-to-ear grin.

Top that, Hawk.

I snowboard past the front row on my right and see Paisley laughing, cheering, and beaming, and my heart just opens. She is just so beautiful. *So beautiful.*

Dad looks happier than I've ever seen him, and Wyatt is roaring.

There is only a small passageway between the front row and the main area, behind it the spectators are waiting. I sail between them, there's not much space, barely three feet, and the crowd reaches out for me. I give people high fives, stop for photos and autographs, and know that this is what I want forever, even if I decide to take another path.

At this very moment I realize that changing something doesn't necessarily mean having to give something up. When I think about it, I am happier than I have been in a long time, and I think that in my heart, Mom's smiling at me.

I grab hold of it and don't let go.

It's shortly before three. We were at the riders' party in some old villa, sponsored by some brewery or other, and everyone was celebrating my having taken first place. Jason Hawk was *some kind of pissed*, and that made me *so* happy.

Now, I'm drunk, and Paisley, too, and we're stumbling into my room. She falls onto the bed, runs her hand across my bedspread, and giggles. I kiss her laugh away and take it inside me. I've kissed a lot of women in my life—a lot—but there's no one like Paisley. Not a single one kisses like she does. It's hard work holding back and slowing down every time she touches me. She just does that to me, makes me so *impatient*, and I don't know why, but I love it. I love every single tension-filled second she explores my body with her lips, with her fingertips.

Paisley is more. She's enough forever.

Her hands tear at my sweater. I help her pull it over my head and like how she explores my abs, how her lips move along the sides and my penis pulses in reaction. It takes me three goes to get her jeans open, then everything becomes a whirlwind of kisses, pulling off her pants, and tossing the whole thing into the farthest corner of my room by the dresser.

I push her shoulders down until her back is against the bed, then bend over her, my hands to the left and right. I scatter kisses, feel her warm skin, hear her panting. Her hands grab my hips, pull me on top of her while she pushes and rubs against me. *Shit, this is heavy.* I have to pull away otherwise the whole thing will be over in two, maybe three seconds.

"Knox."

She can't go any further. I can see it in the width of her pupils, feel it in the heat of her body, the way she lifts herself up. I wander down, run my finger along her collarbone to her breasts. She's wearing a lace bra with the clasp in front. It must be new—it's nice, real nice—but I don't want to see it now, I just want us. Just skin on skin. I undo the clasp and kiss her soft skin beneath, kiss the fine curve of her breasts, take her nipple in my mouth. Paisley grabs my hair and makes a sound that causes me to break out in goose bumps. She digs her nails into my scalp. It burns, but not in a bad way, just one that makes me want *more, more, more*. I pull down her panties, she spreads her legs, whimpering with desire, and I run my tongue back and forth over her most sensitive area. She writhes beneath me, her hands on my shoulders. Her hold is so strong I know she can't hold out too much longer. Her legs begin to tremble. I like seeing her face from down here, her fluttering, closed eyelids, her pursed lips right before they open again and give off that bright, *beautiful* sound that drives me crazy.

"Knox," she says again when I stop, and it's a pleading, an "*I can't do anymore*." I like the sound, like knowing how much she wants me. With my hand, I pull open the drawer of my nightstand, blindly dig around, gum, pens, the broken alarm clock from last year and then, finally, a condom. I nibble her ear while I peel off my pants and boxers and notice the way her skin reacts as I let my breath brush her ear. I tear open the package and slide it on while Paisley lies beneath me, burning, as if she had a fever. *I* have this effect on her. *I* can make sure that she feels good, that she feels *loved*.

"Paisley," I say, quick and soft, husky and fraught with meaning, because this moment *is* fraught with meaning, *is* everything.

Then I let myself sink into her, find the warm, moist part of her body that still separates us, and give her what she wants, what I want.

What we want.

It's stunning. Slow and tender, then faster and urgent, a *you-are-everything, you-are- everything, you-are-everything.*

Her lips open, we look at each other while moving in time, and I know that we're both thinking the same thing: *How is this possible?*

How is it possible to want someone so much that sex can feel this way? How is it possible that our feelings can be *so strong*, so *all-encompassing* that I think I'm going to explode out of happiness?

It's possible by loving. Truly loving. I didn't realize that before, but now I know. And Paisley, too.

I kiss her, caress her face, look at her, look into those big blue eyes that recognize more about me than I do. I lay my forehead against hers. She's breathing quickly. Irregularly.

"Everything okay?" I whisper.

Her grip on my hips grows stronger. She closes her eyes. I can feel her lashes brushing my skin. She nods against my forehead, laughs against my lips.

I kiss her everywhere, her neck, her ear, her mouth, brush my hands across her soft breasts, enjoy the effect I am having on her. Paisley pushes against me, wrapping her legs around my body tighter, and everything starts to move harder, quicker. I let go of all my self-control and let myself be guided by my feelings, give her back everything she is giving me. Her body tenses; she presses her heels into the mattress and holds her breath. I can't describe it, can't believe this feeling at this moment—it's so agonizingly beautiful it's almost unbearable. We are moving, heading toward something that is more than we ever thought possible, more than anything we know. She and I, me and her, together here, now. Until we gasp and breathe, forget to breathe and gasp again.

We claw at each other and let go, my heart is beating against my chest as if it wants to dig its way out.

I sink down and begin to breathe more heavily. Our glowing bodies are slick with sweat. It takes forever for me to stop feeling dizzy so that I can roll back off her. I interlock my fingers with hers and kiss her beneath her now messy hair.

"I wish you knew what I was feeling right now," I say.

She turns toward me. "I feel the same way."

"I don't think it works that way."

She laughs. "Wanna bet?" And then, "I'm sweating, and it's cold. I don't want to catch a cold."

"Wow. You are *so* romantic."

"My fear of getting sick is stronger than the after-sex-romance moment."

Laughing, I bury my face in the crook of her neck. "If I give you a sweater, can we cuddle some more?"

"Yeah."

I roll away from her and give her space. "In the dresser. Last drawer."

Paisley crawls off the bed. Her naked feet make their way across the parquet. I close my eyes and wait. Hear her opening the drawer. Hear her hold her breath. I'm wondering why until I hear another noise. The sound of glass on glass.

I sit up straight. I want to do something, something to reverse this moment, but it's too late.

Paisley turns around. She's looking at me and there is nothing, absolutely *nothing* left of the bliss we just shared.

Her expression is one of pure disgust.

39
Gunpowder Is Feeding Your Monsters

PAISLEY

"You can't be serious, right?" The glass vials are heavy in my hand. They weigh next to nothing but feel as if they were pushing me down. "Please, Knox, tell me you're not this dumb. You simply cannot be serious."

Knox doesn't move. He's sitting straight up in bed, the bedspread a huge ball between his legs, staring at me open-mouthed.

I look back into the drawer, dig through his socks and boxers, and can't believe how many ampules and syringes there are. "You're insane. Completely insane." I hold the little bottles under my nose as if I didn't know what they were. "Testosterone. Androstenedione. Are you crazy, Knox? *Are you crazy?*"

The shrill tone of my voice seems to tear him back out of his state of shock. Knox jumps out of bed and pulls on a pair of jogging pants. Then: heavy steps across the floor, grabs the stuff out of my hand, tosses it back in the drawer. The sound it makes as he closes it echoes through the air.

"That's got nothing to do with you."

I laugh. "Oh, really? Really? Am I supposed to say: 'How lovely,

Knox, that you're taking the illegal route to success! How lovely that you're experimenting with your health!'"

"I'm successful because I'm talented."

"And because you're chemically enhanced."

Knox snorts. "That's bullshit, Paisley. As if none of the others would take steroids. Not everybody plays by the rules when they want to win. That's how life goes."

"That's how *your* life goes," I correct him. "Snowboarders don't engage in doping, Knox. Did anyone ever tell you otherwise? That any of the others shoot that shit?" The answer is written on his face. "No. No one. And you know why? Because none of them are that dumb. Snowboarders have got to be in tune with their body and mind; they've got to be completely concentrated on what they do. Bigger muscles might bring you some strength, but this stuff *weakens* you overall. One false move on the pipe, just one slip in your body, and your whole career is shot. *You'd* be shot."

He's grinding his teeth. At first I think he's not going to answer, but then his nostrils flare and his mouth opens. "Dad wants me to be the best."

Dad wants, Dad wants, Dad wants...

"Yeah, Knox, but what do *you* want? Do you really intend to do this kind of harm to your body, maybe making it impossible to have kids or causing a heart attack or something else *just to please your dad*?"

"You have no idea, Paisley. I've got to."

"You're right, I really don't have any idea why you're *so goddamn dumb!*" With every word I punch him in the chest, but Knox doesn't move an inch. I am so angry that I'm starting to feel hot. "But I'm pretty damn sure your dad doesn't want you to dope!"

"He doesn't care as long as I win."

"Sure, convince yourself of that. Keep on finding new excuses for why you can't give up your *oh-wow-I'm-a-superstar* life although you don't want to live it at all. But really, Knox, if you don't start living the life you want to live, then you're going to go down."

"Paisley, stop. Please. I need you."

"*You could die, damn it!*"

"I could die landing badly, too."

"Yeah, that's exactly right, and that will happen one day when you shoot your body full of unnatural stuff!" I take a deep breath and grab his hands. "Knox, please. Please. I'm begging you, please leave this shit alone."

"My dad…"

"Oh, stop with that crap. Stop with your dad, Knox. You're not a kid anymore who can't make his own decisions. Your mom is dead, and that's awful, really, it's terrible. But you can't spend the rest of your life trying to distract your dad. You all have to come to terms with it. Both of you. And that will never happen as long as your dad keeps on distracting himself by living through you and you by living your dad's dream just so neither of you has to face your thoughts."

Knox just stands there, he looks like he's got a full-body cramp, then he collapses like a balloon with all the air let out. He slumps down onto the side of the bed and buries his head in his hands.

"Knox," I say, softly this time, gently. I sit down next to him and place my hand on his back.

He exhales as if he were tired, dead tired, and runs his fingers through his hair before tilting his head and looking up at me. "You're right. I know that, Paisley, I realize everything you're saying. I feel like shit because of it all, I wish I could just throw it all away and buy my books for college, dig my nose in them, and read until it's dark and I have to close my eyes in the dim light of the lamp on my nightstand. I want all that, absolutely, but I can't, okay? I simply can't because I don't know how. How should I explain that to my dad? How am I supposed to handle his disappointment when I take away the only thing that's made him happy since Mom died? How am *I* supposed to be happy when my only remaining parent is sad? *How?*"

"By simply talking with him. He'll understand, Knox. He's your father, he *loves* you, and he'll understand."

Knox's eyes rest on me. His pupils are big, the green around them dull, not like the ones I love. Then he shakes his head. "It won't work. If I give up the steroids, I'll be done. I'll have hormone disruptions, my performance will suffer, my muscles will shrink. I'll never be able to prepare for the World Cup."

"You can taper off your dose," I say. "Of course you shouldn't go cold turkey. Increase your intervals in between, and when you're at seven days, start taking down the dose step by step. There are estrogen blockers, too. You can make it, if you want to."

Knox looks at me, his forehead wrinkled.

I shrug. "I know some folks from Minneapolis who used to dope and then weaned themselves off it. It's not impossible to do it and remain competitive."

He takes a deep breath. "Paisley, what do you want to hear? 'Of course. Absolutely, I'll start right away?' I can't promise you that. I'm sorry, really, maybe we can work on it, but I just can't swing it right now."

Maybe it's a start. It definitely is. But I can't stop myself from getting angry because he's playing with his health and for something he *doesn't even want*. I remove my hand from his back and dig my fingers into my thigh until red half-moons appear.

"Hey." Knox moves to take my hand, but I stand up in order to find my clothes and put them back on. He turns to face me, leaning an arm on the bedframe. "Paisley, please don't be like this."

"It's fine," I say, pulling my hoodie over my head. "All good. It's just that right now...it just really makes me mad, okay?"

He sucks in his lower lip then lets it back out. Then he nods. "Sure. I get that."

He doesn't say anything else. Just: "*I get that.*" Not: "*We'll manage. Just stand by as I deal with this. I want to stop taking this shit.*"

The knot in my stomach is growing, running wild and cramping.

In reality, I don't want to go. In reality, I want to keep on standing here and yell at him before kissing him. Shake him before I sit on his lap and enjoy the feeling of his lips moving down my throat.

I don't want to be angry at him, but I am, and I'd rather leave than keep talking, driving him into a corner, and making him feel closed in and harassed.

40

Bibbidi-Bobbidi-Boo

PAISLEY

I ATTEMPT A TRIPLE AXEL AND LAND ON ALL FOURS. For the seventh time. I scratch the ice with my fingernails and kick my skates against the side of the rink. I avoid looking at Polina because I already know what kind of looks she's been giving me all morning. Training today is an absolute catastrophe.

I hear the sound of blades slowing down and then a shower of ice spray against my arm. Gwen offers me a hand and helps me up. "If you keep up like this, Harper's going to be out of a job."

I wipe my palms off on my training dress. "What?"

Gwen walks next to me with her Choctaw steps. Forward, outside edge of right foot, backward, inside edge of left foot, before she continues to walk normally and looks at me. "I mean, it's Harper's job to screw up jumps. What's up with you, Paisley?"

In reality, I should be going through my program as long as it takes until the axel lands, but it does me good to take a breather and walk a few steps with Gwen. It's easy.

I pull aside my dress's turtleneck and scratch my neck. "Yesterday Knox and I had a little…difference of opinion."

"Over what?"

I can't tell her. I would like to just to be able to talk to someone about it all, but this isn't the right time.

"His future."

We circle around Aaron and Levi who are practicing a death spiral. Aaron is almost touching the ice, his arms outstretched, and is being held by his hands while they spin around their own axis.

"You are always *so* cryptic when you're in a bad mood. I never get even a snippet of information out of you."

Before I can answer, Polina's voice echoes through the hall. "Paisley, what is that? The axel won't thank you for walking across the ice!"

I sigh, cast Gwen an apologetic glance, and make a mohawk turn, a foot change from forward outside edge to backward outside edge to skate in backward for the axel. I succeed twice, but Polina seems anything but content, and I know that she has every reason not to be. Skate America is just a few days away and we'd made it *so* far, I could actually land my triple axel, wobbling a bit maybe, but land it. But now I feel that the thing with Knox has thrown me off *by weeks*.

I try again. And again, and again, and again, but it just doesn't want to work out today to the degree that I—and Polina—would like it to. After another failed attempt, her forehead is a sea of wrinkles. She pushes off the side and calls out, "Okay, Paisley. That's enough. Let's go through your program."

Harper zooms past me from behind Gwen to continue training on the other side of the rink, so that I have room for my program. Maybe I'm imagining things, but I swear I caught a sympathetic smile on her face.

I get into position, one leg straight ahead, the other bent and my arms stretched out so that my crossed hands touch the tip of my skate. It's not long before Polina reaches the rink and Ed Sheeran's "I See Fire" begins to ring out through the hall. I set myself in motion, stretch my arms into the air, and begin with elegant changes of direction and big loops. As the notes of the first verse fade, I shift my weight to my left leg, lunge with my right, hit the ice with my skate blade and do a double axel. I land on my right and use the momentum of my left to push the edge into the ice again. My left arm and bent right leg follow before I jump off from my left foot and do a triple counterclockwise turn—a triple toe loop.

The instrumental sounds of the song begin, and I move fluidly, dancing—the ice and I in perfect symbiosis. I glide backward across the surface, shift my weight to my left leg and plunge into the ice with my right, jumping off the left at the same time. I manage to pull my arms up quickly and get enough height—a successful triple Lutz. The melody leads into the chorus. I slow down, move along a low edge, lower my body, and shift onto my knees. My legs tremble with strain as I push my back parallel to the ice so that, during the deep turn, the back of my head almost touches the ice. Every muscle in my body is on fire, but I manage to straighten up and continue skating on steady legs. Sweat is pouring down my neck while, with a mohawk step, I switch from forward inward to backward inward on my other leg and am now standing on the inside edge of my skate. In a big lunge, I pull my right leg around, making a half turn on the ice, before jumping off for the triple Salchow, followed by a triple flip turn on the left foot, jumping off on the right. The song's bridge begins, and I begin the dance I showed off at the Christmas party at Silver Lake. I repeat the Lutz and the toe loop, turn in a spread eagle—arms and legs outstretched—and transition into an Ina Bauer by placing one foot on the forward edge and the other backward on a different parallel edge while bending backward.

And now for the climax: an explosive chorus right as I stretch out my right leg, jab the edge into the ice, and jump off—the triple axel, one turn, two, three, and there, the half, oh my God, I land it! *Holy shit*, I think the whole time, the whole jump, in fact, and am still thinking it when I land on my right leg. A bit wobbly, like a small foal, but I land it.

My heart is racing and the muscles in my legs are trembling as I continue to skate in circles, smaller and smaller until I reach the center of the ice for my Biellmann spin. I lift my right leg back, bend back over my shoulders, grab the skate, and turn around, facing the ceiling. The last notes sound. A dramatic bass blows across the ice, and I drop into a sitting spin with my leg outstretched, spinning around myself twice, three times, before the song begins to fade and I straighten up in an elegant, fluid movement to finish in a flying camel spin: right leg straight on the ice, left leg lifted back, righthand fingers clutching the blade and pulling to the right, parallel to my upper body as it, too, bends to the right. I spin, spin, spin, breathing in the cold air, feeling freedom in my lungs, in my soul, feeling everything, *everything*, life and love and joy in every breath.

I stop and shift into the final position. I stretch my left leg backward, pitch the point of my skate into the ice, right leg bent forward, head thrown back, hands in my hair. The song ends. My pulse is thundering, and I can feel my heart banging against my ribs over and over. I let out a gasp and open my eyes to look at Polina.

She is smiling. And nods. And right then, with the Olympic medalist staring at me with that look on her face, that you-got-what-it-takes-girl look, it becomes clear.

Paisley Harris, trailer-park roach from Minneapolis, daughter of a crack whore, take a look at yourself, *take a look at yourself!* You can do it, damn it, you can *really* do it, this whole Olympics thing.

During the break I am up in the lounge with Aaron, Levi, and Gwen, nibbling an avocado sandwich.

"The problem is that you don't build up enough tension in your back," Levi tells Aaron. "If you could bend more, I could spin us more quickly."

"Nonsense." Aaron lifts his forkful of salad to his mouth. "You don't switch blades quickly enough. My tension is *tutti-frutti*."

Levi wants to reply, but Gwen puts her hand across his mouth. "Stop! If you say one more word about your death spiral, I'm going to lose it. My feet are throbbing, my legs hurt, and my thighs desperately need a seed pillow. Can we let our break be a *break* for once?"

Levi pushes her hand away and leans back in his chair. "Gwen, you're aware of the fact that Skate America's just around the corner, right?"

Gwen groans, throws her arm over her head, and undoes her bun. "Yeah, I'm aware of that. My Lutz still isn't clean, Paisley's triple axel is the living image of 'London Bridge Is Falling Down,' and all the same I'm sure we can find other things to talk about. So, please, boys, *please* talk about how awesome your salad tastes or something."

Aaron stares at Gwen while he chews. He swallows. "That little piece of cucumber was amazing. Velvety going down. Clean in consistency."

Levi rolls his eyes with pleasure. "You should've *tasted* my tomatoes. A moist and spicy explosion of flavor."

They manage to bring a smile to my face. All these little stupid conversations with Gwen and these two mean so much to me I *swear* every word has helped to stitch my soul back together. Piece by piece, piece of tape by piece of tape.

The rest of the day I manage the axel more and more often than I'd thought possible and listening to 80s love songs during fitness class following the end of training that are full of unconditional love, of sticking together and doing it all together, my anger toward Knox vanishes. Hard to believe that he has that effect on me, but I still want to go back to the resort and take him in my arms, tell him that I understand and am there for him. Tell him that he can count on me, just like I can count on him.

Gwen frowns as she watches me stuff my things into my bag and gather up my things in record time. "Was there speed in your avocado sandwich?"

I pull up the legs of my skinny jeans until my feet poke out the bottom. "Just say no."

My sleeves land in Gwen's face. She swerves and rubs her eye. "Seriously, what did you take? Does that help you land a triple Lutz? If that's the case, then later on I'm going to break into the lounge and steal every single avocado sandwich there is. Please imagine me in Donatello's purple *Ninja Turtles* outfit. Or, well, in reality, Michelangelo because he's the party turtle and all, but, anyway, orange doesn't suit me at *all*. So, purple bandana, a bag full of avocados, and…"

"Sorry, gotta go. You'll be an *amazing* Donatello. See you tomorrow!"

I sprint through the hallways, cross the entrance, and pray that Knox is going to pick me up after our discussion, but once I get outside and the cold air slams into my face, I see him. He's not waiting in his Range Rover as usual but is standing right at the bottom of the stairs, his hands in his jacket pockets, and I know immediately, *immediately*, that something isn't right. The way his jaw is building a stiff, tense line. His eyes dark and joyless. No trace of the easygoing cheerfulness Knox usually gives off. No trace of *my* Knox.

"What's wrong?"

He takes a deep breath. His front neck muscles tense up and protrude clearly. He's scaring me.

"Did something happen?"

"Guess, Paisley. Just guess what happened."

"No idea." I start to panic. He should simply tell me what's wrong. My heart stumbles and begins to beat more quickly. "Tell me already."

"Hmm, strange." His face twitches. He fakes a smile, a snide one that doesn't fit him at all and distorts his beautiful features. "I could have sworn you'd be more self-satisfied."

"Shit, come on, Knox, *what do you mean?*"

"No doubt you had a good training session, huh? I can just

imagine how your whole body must have been trembling in anticipation of siccing the anti-doping folks on me."

I feel like I'm falling. "What?"

"Stop playing dumb. That was precisely your goal. Congratulations, Paisley. It worked. Are you happy now?"

"Do you really think I informed the Anti-Doping Agency?" The strap of my sports bag slips off my shoulder, and it hits the ground. "Really, Knox? *Really?*"

"You are the only person who knows. Yesterday you found out, and today, what a coincidence, the authorities are standing in front of my door demanding that I piss into a cup while *staring at my fucking dick*."

For a second I am unable to respond. I stare at him, unable to comprehend that he really thinks *I* ratted him out.

I try to stay calm, but it's not easy. "These doping controls are standard, Knox. You're a world-famous half-pipe snowboarder. You won first place at the X Games and are now preparing for the World Cup. Did it really never cross your mind that the ADA might pay you a visit?"

He snorts. "They don't just simply show up."

"*Of course* they simply show up! Knox, my God, are you serious? You *know* that much as an athlete!"

Knox turns away. He looks at the snowy sign on the wall of iSkate and seems far too far away. I could stretch out my hand and touch him, he's standing right there, but it wouldn't be Knox because Knox isn't there. My heart sinks into my boots. I take a step forward and really do want to reach out for his hand, but he moves away and stretches out his arm to keep me at a distance.

"Knox, I swear, I was…"

"Stop. Just stop, okay?"

He goes. The sound of the slamming car door echoes in my ears. I start. My eyes follow the car's rear end as it moves off. The snow swirls.

I feel a hand between my shoulder blades. It's Gwen. She, too, looks after the car until it's gone.

"You wanted to know what kind of emergency I was saving my strength for at the X Games, remember? This is one of them. Come on, I'll take you." She picks my bag up off the ground, looks at me, and takes my hand. "*Bibbidi-bobbidi-boo.*"

41
What If You Fly?

PAISLEY

IT'S BEEN FOUR DAYS SINCE THE USADA PAID KNOX A visit. Four days since Knox has spoken a word to me. I've been keeping busy with the tourists, going to training, and torturing myself with the triple axel. In the mornings, I get up, make breakfast for Knox and Jack, then wait until I hear a door open and Knox comes down the stairs in his running gear. Most of the time, his hair's still messy and standing up in all directions. I like that. It looks bold. I'd like to run my fingers through it, every time, but he always hides it beneath a gray Vans hat. When he opens the door and gets going, I take off behind him.

It's always the same path: Into the Aspen Highlands, shortcuts through the firs, dark all around us. I don't listen to any music, as the sound of our steps on the snowy ground and our irregular breathing is music enough. Knox knows that I'm jogging behind him, but he never talks to me. He hears me, and sometimes, when the rise of the mountain gets to me, he slows down. He acts like he's catching his breath, but I know it isn't true. Knox could run this stretch without a pause. But he always slows down when I do, and if things between us were over, he wouldn't do that.

Gwen said I could stay with her and work at the diner. I refused. This here is everything I want to fight for until our time together is over. As long as I can fight, I will.

By the time I make it to the resort, Knox is already in the shower. Normally I take a long shower myself so that he can eat breakfast in peace without having to see me one more time before heading off to training. I want to give him time so that he can sort out his thoughts and recognize that he made a mistake. I want him to apologize and for us to be Knox and Paisley again. *Knox and Paisley.*

But not today. Today I shower in record time and am downstairs with wet hair and two different socks on by the time he's mashing his eggs into his quinoa-spinach bowl and mixing it all together. He always does that. Mashes everything together.

"Hey," I say and sit down across from him. I pour myself a coffee and add some milk.

Knox doesn't answer. He shovels a mountain of quinoa onto his spoon and doesn't look at me once.

I rub my feet across the parquet. "I love your heated floors."

Knox takes his bowl and his coffee, pushes back his chair, and stands up. He sits down on the couch with his back to me. Quinoa drips onto the cushions.

I follow him. "Have you spoken to your father already?"

Knox fishes a tomato out of his bowl and shoves it into his mouth. Of course he hasn't spoken with his father or else he wouldn't head off for training so quickly and act like everything was normal. It's not. He was doping, got tested—which is going to turn out positive, of course—and can forget all about the Snowboard World Cup now. He'll be suspended for several months. The press will get wind of it. Knox will get taken apart as soon as the results come out, and from one day to the other will be seen in a completely different light. Of course he hasn't told his father yet. Of course not.

"He'd rather hear it from you than from the press, Knox."

"Tell him yourself." These are the first words he's said to me in four days, and I could puke. *I could puke.* "Tell him that you narced on me so that it'd be a lesson. Then you can tell me how he reacted. It interests me *immensely.*"

"Knox, enough. It was your fault, you know it, but because you don't want to accept it and feel like shit, you're using me as a scapegoat. *Cut the crap.*"

Knox turns so red I'm afraid he's going to explode like a piñata at any second and it's going to snow quinoa all over the place but then he simply gets up and leaves. I can't believe it. The jangle of keys. The front door closing. The sound of tires moving down the driveway.

My pulse starts to speed up. *How could he?*

I go into the kitchen, fish the hidden Cheerios out of the cupboard, and throw them into the trash. Then I take every single bag of chips, gummy bears, Pop-Tarts, and Twinkies out of the linen closet and throw them in, too. Knox loves junk food and sweets. I am so angry, so furiously angry—he can take his guilty pleasures and stick them *where the sun doesn't shine.*

Gwen texts to tell me she can't pick me up. Her mother has a doctor's appointment, and she has to help out in the diner, so she'll be late to training as well. I go downtown on foot to take the Highland Express to iSkate. I'm early, and close to the bus stop there's a sports shop. Just two blocks away, I see the festively decorated shop window flanked by two field hockey sticks. A bell rings as I enter the store. It smells like sneakers fresh out of the box, just after you've pushed the wrapping paper aside.

A young woman with a long black bob is standing behind the counter, bent over some document or other. She looks up and smiles. "Can I help you?"

"Do you have any figure-skating things?"

She nods. "Over there in the corner, by the changing room."

"Thanks."

I look at two dresses that are so beautiful and so expensive that they will always be my *I'm-just-going-to-look-at-you* pieces. There are a couple of E-spinners with a forward-shifted pivot point and integrated rubber band for bounce safety on sale. E-spinners look like shoe soles and are made for practicing take-offs and spins when you're away from the ice. I grab a basket and put them inside, shortly thereafter a pair of knee pads. Thanks to all the unsuccessful axels my legs are full of bruises. The pads are followed up by a pair of beige gloves and two new pairs of tights and leg warmers. It's wonderful to be able to spend the money you've earned yourself. It makes me happy.

Just as I'm about to turn around and head to the register, I feel a hand on my bottom. It grips tight. Real tight. I freeze. Warm breath brushes my ear. It smells of licorice candy and herb-flavored booze. I know that smell. I know, I *know* who's behind me and die before I even hear his repellent voice.

"You've gained weight, Paisley." More pressure on my bottom. "Do you think you can afford that?"

A tingling sensation in my hands causes me to drop the basket. The things spill out over the floor. I look for the saleswoman. She's disappearing with her papers into the back room. *No.*

I don't want to turn around. I don't want to, if I do, it'll all be real. *He* will be real. But when his hand begins to move upward, I have to. Turn around.

I knock his hand away and look into his face. *Ivan Petrov.* He laughs. Thin lips. Straight smoke-yellowed teeth. An unkempt beard and dark eyes where hate has made its home.

I don't say anything. I'm paralyzed. All the thoughts I've been thinking over the last few weeks—I'd be stronger than Minneapolis Paisley—all of those thoughts were lies.

Hi, here I am: small.

Full of fear. With quaking legs and the terrified face of a doe.

Ivan takes a pair of skates off the shelf and runs a finger along the blade. "Did you think I wouldn't find you?" He puts the skates back and laughs as he strokes a sequined dress. "Did you think you could hide behind that snowboarder? I'll always find you, Paisley. Always."

He lets go of the dress and takes a step toward me. I think I'm going to die. There's no way I can stand this, standing here, right in front of him, listening to his voice. I thought I had left it all behind me, had left *him* behind me, but when you realize that your throat is prickling and you want to cry, then you know it's still an issue.

Ivan Petrov is an issue for me. He always *will* be, because I cannot forget what he did to me. The scars on my skin will always remind me of the pain. My life is not a piece of paper full of marks where you can just erase the terrible pictures. What happened, happened. And that remains.

He bends down toward me, his lips close to my ear. I dig my nails into my thighs. "Do you think he'll still want you when he knows how hard, how often I *fucked* you? Do you think he will, Paisley?"

After all the beatings, all the abuse and courage Ivan took from me, this line is the humiliating crown. I feel disgusting. I feel used.

"I didn't want that," I manage to say. "I never did."

"Oh, Paisley." He runs a finger down my temple, twirls a strand of my hair. "I know that. But do you think that plays any role? Who's interested in what *you* want?"

Me.

His hand lands on my crotch. I struggle for air and push him away. He bangs into the mannequin with the skating dress. It falls over, and the saleswoman comes out of the back room.

Her glance lands on the mannequin, before she moves from Ivan to me. "Is everything okay?"

I don't respond. I run. Past the tables, past the hockey sticks and ski poles. Out the door and straight down the street, past Vaughn, the guy who sings about reindeers and Christmas elves, two, three, four streets, straight downtown. Past the bell tower, past The Old-Timer, past William, who wants to tell me something, but I'm too quick, and onward, ever onward, past the last houses until I'm completely alone. I run until I'm out of breath, I run until I can hear the tall fir trees whisper my name and can find a place to hide beneath them. I sit right down in the snow, my back against the trunk. My bottom becomes wet. I take heavy, quick breaths and only now do I recognize where I am.

In front of me, the icy sheen of Silver Lake glitters in the sun. My heart wants to weep. I was so happy in that store, was smiling while placing all those beautiful things in my shopping basket, was just so happy that I could buy them for myself. Now they're on the floor and I'm sitting here, hardly able to catch my breath. I'm panting, slamming my palms against the snow and screaming. The scream echoes through the mountains.

I don't want it to be over. My life in Aspen. My life with Knox. I don't want it to be over. My life.

But I don't have any choice. I know that Ivan won't give up. I know it because there's a legal basis he can use against me if he wants. Even if I simply wanted to stay in Aspen, he could *force* me to go back to Minneapolis. He would take the matter to court, and he knows that I don't stand a chance. Not me. Because, let's be honest, who am I?

I'm Paisley. Paisley, the trailer-park roach. Paisley, the daughter of a crack whore.

My fingers are numb as I claw at the zipper of my sports bag. The laces of my skates escape me, but I grab them a second time and manage. They land in the snow, right next to my tears. I pick at the knots, slip inside, and tie them back up. It doesn't matter where I am, it doesn't matter how I feel: as soon as my feet are stuck inside of a pair of skates, I am home.

The ice crunches beneath my blades. I absorb the sound and store it in my imaginary jam-jar. Or wait, no, in my peanut butter jar. Peanut butter because Knox has that memory of his mom— *"Did you polish off my peanut butter?"*—and I think it's so warm, so sad, so precious that from now on, it will be for my most beautiful moments.

I take off into a triple axel. I land it and laugh. I laugh, then cry, both at the same time. How ironic that I land it right now, right here. One day before Skate America. How ironic that I managed to do it, but that Ivan could manage to stop me *once again*.

I don't know how long I spend out on the ice saying goodbye to my life in Aspen, but at some point, it's dark and the lights in the surrounding lanterns snap on. I skate to the end of the lake, change direction with a mohawk turn, but come to a backward stop when I make out the shadow of a person I know beneath the fir tree.

"Did he find you? Is that why you weren't at training?" Polina's hands are stuck deep into the pockets of her fur coat. "Ivan?"

I'm starting to feel dizzy. "How..."

"You think I don't inform myself about my students?"

I'm like a deer caught in headlights. Polina pushes off the trunk and comes out to me on the ice. She's not wearing skates, but her movements are sure. She stops right in front of me and sits down. Her hand grabs mine, pulls me softly down next to her. It's cold. She's sitting on her coat; all I've got are my wet jeans. All the same, I stay put.

"I know where you're from. I know that you can't really be here. I've known it from the beginning."

I think I'm going to freeze to death. Her words are worse than the ice. "Then why did you train me?"

Polina looks at me. Then she reaches into her coat and pulls out two little bottles of booze. Jägermeister. "Here, drink this. It's cold."

She hands me one. I look at her and wonder if she's serious, out here on Silver Lake with our numb butts, but she's already unscrewing the top, so I do the same. We toast each other and down the shot in one go. My throat is burning. But I start to feel a little warmer, not much, but a little, as I'm already frozen.

"I trained you because I knew that you were passionate about what you do. When you skate, you are *on fire*. You shine. I knew that you weren't happy. However, I knew that you weren't sad either. You're simply empty. And then I saw how, little by little, Aspen filled you with life. I was certain that, sooner or later, he'd show up. But you know what?"

"What?"

"You've got to keep going, Paisley. You didn't come this far just to get this far. You can do it. You're stronger than he is."

"What if I'm not?"

"Oh, Paisley." Polina presses my upper arm. "What if you are?"

Then she stands up and leaves.

I thought I'd frozen to death, but maybe I'm still alive.

42
Deep Inside, We Always Hope

Knox

Twenty-four missed calls. Eighteen messages. Every single one of them from Cameron. I grab my iPhone, take a sip of my beer, and watch his name blink. I put the bottle back down on the table with a smack. I lunge and toss my phone into the snow.

I didn't go to training. What's the point? It's pointless now anyway. No idea what scares me more: the fact that everything's over or my feeling of liberation.

Paisley was right. It wasn't her. Four other snowboarders I often train with wrote in the WhatsApp group that they, too, received unannounced visits and piss tests. All of them right after the X Games. I feel like shit. I'm an ignorant dumbshit. I was so deluded that I thought those kinds of tests didn't just happen. Now I'm sitting under a blanket on the sofa outside, next to the fire, waiting for Paisley to come back from training so I can talk to her. I wanted to raid my candy, but she'd thrown everything out. I had to laugh when I saw it. That's Paisley.

I tear the label off the beer bottle and toss it into the fire in pieces as the terrace door slides open. My eyes wander across the floor, see gray Panama Jacks, black jeans, a Canada Goose parka. Dad's hands are stuck in his pockets, and he's looking down at me. He's just come back from the hairdresser. He's had his salt-and-pepper hair shaved on the sides and styled up on top, like me. I take one look at him and know he knows. He and Cameron are old friends.

"Is there something between you and Paisley?"

I turn my head and look into the gray sky. "Nope."

"Knox," he says. I don't react. "Knox, look at me." The couch's rattan fabric scratches my neck as I turn my head. Dad leans against the sliding door, looking like some kind of film star. "Why weren't you at training?"

I go through a thousand excuses in my head, but Paisley's voice winds through every one of them. *You've got to tell him, Knox. He should hear it from you. Well, get on with it, tell him.*

I sigh, sit up, and wrap my hands around the beer bottle like it's a life preserver. My heart is racing, and that's rare outside of cases that have to do with Paisley. "Something happened, Dad."

"Between you and Paisley?" He pauses. "Please, tell me she's not pregnant."

"No. God, no. Not with Paisley."

My father seems to recognize that he has to be serious because he pushes off the window and sits down across from me in the chair. Snow falls off the soles of his shoes as he puts one leg over the other. "What happened, Knox?"

I can't look at him. I simply can't, so I watch the hypnotizing flicker of the flames instead as they grow smaller, then larger, then smaller again.

"The USADA was here."

Dad removes his leg from his upper thigh. He bends forward. "When?"

"Four days ago."

"Four days ago. And you're just telling me now?"

"Yeah."

"Why?"

I look up. "I didn't know how to tell you."

"You didn't know how to tell me that the USADA had been here?"

"No." I'm holding onto the brown beer bottle so tightly my fingers go numb. "I didn't know how to tell you that the tests will be positive."

He finally opens his mouth. "Are you kidding me, Knox?" Pause. "*Are you kidding me?*"

"No."

"What were you taking?" His voice is soft but in an unsettling way. As soft as the ocean at night, still and black, right before a storm breaks.

"Testosterone. Androstenedione. Now and again Tren."

"Trenbolone." He speaks the whole thing out, as if there were still a chance he'd misunderstood.

He didn't. "Yeah."

He takes a deep breath. Then he jumps up and bangs against the sofa. I start and grab my bottle so tightly I'm worried it might break. Dad comes to me, rips it out of my hand, and throws it through the air. It shatters against the trunk of a fir.

"Why, Knox? Why?"

"I wanted to be the best."

"You would've been without the stuff!"

"No."

He grabs the arm of my jacket and squeezes my upper arm. "Do you have any idea what you're doing to your body with this stuff? Snowboarders don't dope, Knox. They just don't!"

"It doesn't matter. You wanted me to be the best."

"I wanted the best *for* you! I never wanted anything but for you to be okay and to be happy. Your mother is dead, Knox. You're my son, and I love you. I idolize you. And then you go and shoot yourself up with some shit and risk dying so *I have to lose you as well?*"

My throat tightens. "I'm sorry, Dad." I have to say it one more time because my voice breaks. "I'm sorry."

Dad cusses. He lets go of my arm and begins to pace back and forth in front of the fire. He taps his fingertips against his nose in a steady rhythm. For a long time, I don't know exactly how long, but it seems like an eternity before he casts me a glance and says, "We have to wean you off this right now. After we get you off this, I don't want you to ever touch it again."

"Yeah." I was planning on doing that anyway.

Dad nods. He sits down on the arm of the chair and folds his hands in his lap. "You're going to be suspended for a few months. At the very least. You can forget about the World Cup. But, with luck, you can be at the Burton US Open. I'm going to call Jennet. She can straighten it all out with the press and…"

"Dad."

"…certainly get something going so that it doesn't go public. We'll have to pay back all the sponsors' money, but that's not a problem, and…"

"Dad."

"…I'm sure the sponsors you still have will stick by you. I'm going to call them all in a minute and explain…"

"DAD!"

He looks at me. I miss my bottle. My whole body is shaking, but I've got to do this. I take a deep breath.

"I want to stop."

He blinks as if he misunderstood me. Then he laughs. "No. No, you don't."

"I do."

His smile dies.

"Listen, Dad." I rub my thighs through the blanket and knead my hands. My chest hurts, this discussion is that difficult. "Snowboarding, that's…that's *your thing*, okay? I like it, it's fun, but only in the way of things that you do every so often. Like climbing or, I don't know, baking Christmas cookies. I wouldn't want to be a professional baker. And I don't have any interest in being a star snowboarder. I'd like to keep on going, but without any pressure. Just so that I don't stop enjoying it and do it the way I want to." I hesitate a second, then add, "Colorado Mountain College accepted me. I applied to their psychology program, and they…they accepted me. That's what I'd like to do."

My father looks at me as if I'd just pushed him into a crevasse. He swallows. The fire illuminates his bouncing Adam's apple as he turns his head and looks out to the Aspen Highlands.

"Dad," I say carefully.

But he shakes his head and stands up. "Excuse me, I need a bit of time."

"Yeah. Of course."

He walks out into the evening, and I am once again alone.

When he gets back, his cheeks are glowing red. I can tell immediately that he's had something to drink. It's late, almost ten, and Paisley still isn't back. I'm starting to get worried.

"What a load of shit," Dad mumbles, closing the front door. His keys land on the floor after he misses the bowl. "A dirty fucking load of shit."

A dirty fucking load of shit?

I put my book down and walk over to him. He collapses onto a chair at the dining room table and starts tapping around on his phone.

"Everything okay?"

Dad snorts. Drops of mucus land on his display. "These motherfuckers."

"Ah." I take a seat across from him. "I know that you're angry, Dad, but if you want to insult me, you don't have to do it in the third person."

He looks up and squints as if he was just noticing me. "Why would I insult you?"

"Hmm. No idea. Because I just tossed all your future plans for me out the window?"

"Doesn't matter."

"Huh?"

Dad sighs. He puts his phone down on the table and looks at me. "Psychology, you said?"

I nod.

"You think that will make you happy?"

I nod again.

He shrugs. "Then do it. I want what *you* want."

I can't believe what's happening. "Just like that? No scene?"

"Knox, please. Why should I make any scene?"

I spread my arms wide because the answer's so obvious. "My being a professional snowboarder was always your dream."

"Yeah. Because I thought it was *your* dream."

"It wasn't."

"Maybe you should've told me, Knox."

Yeah. Yeah, I should have. I'm sitting here in my chair like I've turned to stone, I simply cannot believe this whole situation is real. To be on the safe side, I pinch my arm, but instead of waking up, my skin starts to turn red.

"But I hope you realize you won't get off so easily."

I let go of my arm. "What do you mean?"

"You don't owe the USADA any more tests, but you owe me. You are going to go and see Dr. Sherman regularly and have your blood taken. He's going to keep me informed. If I find out that you are shooting that shit again, Knox…"

"I won't," I interrupt. "I'll go to Dr. Sherman. Promise."

"Good." He starts typing on his phone again.

"What are you doing?"

"I'm getting in touch with a few folks."

"Because of me?"

"Not everything has to do with you."

"Why are you getting in touch with people?"

He takes off his jacket before responding. "Ivan Petrov is here in town. I saw him at the ski hut."

An ice-cold shiver runs down my spine and all I can think of is Paisley.

Paisley.

Paisley.

PAISLEY.

I choke back a gasp. "What's he doing here?"

Dad looks surprised. "You know him?"

"Yeah. He was Paisley's trainer in Minneapolis. He…" I don't know how much of her background I'm allowed to share. "She ran away from him. That's why she's here."

Dad's eyes widen, then he jumps up.

I follow his lead. "How do *you* know him?"

He purses his lips. His face grows firm. "Your mother. They were a figure-skating pair when young. He was a fucking pig."

What the…?

"Where's Paisley?" he asks, still typing into his phone.

"I don't know." Saying the words makes me feel sick. I don't know where she is, and her psycho trainer is in town. My body is ice cold.

Dad looks at me. "You don't know *where she is?*"

"No."

"You *always* know where she is."

"Not now," I say while pulling my jacket out of the closet. "But I'm going to find her. No idea what that dude is looking for here, Dad, but it can't be anything good. We've got to get rid of him."

He raises his phone and casts me a glance as if I were slow. "What do you think I'm doing?"

Paisley doesn't see me as I walk into The Old-Timer. She's sitting in a green cord chair from the 70s with a wool blanket around her legs and a pair of old, retro headphones over her ears that's connected to the record player next to her. Her eyes are closed, and her head is leaning back.

I close the door. William's face peeks out from behind a bookshelf in the middle of the room.

"How long has she been there?"

"Hours. She's been listening to one record after another and doesn't want to talk. I even tried offering her a cheese sandwich."

"She doesn't like cheese, William."

"That explains why she always looks so sad. She should eat some. Cheese makes you happy."

"I'm going to go talk to her."

"About the cheese?"

"No."

He looks disappointed. "Okay. But I'm closing up in fifteen minutes. Remember. If I'm not in bed on time, my stress levels go up. My acid-base balance gets all mixed up, I start to get tense, can't look after my horses, and…"

"We'll be out of here on time, Will."

I walk over to Paisley, sit down on the arm of the chair, and take the headphones off her ears. She starts as if she'd seen a ghost, but then sinks back down in relief. "It's you."

"Yeah. What are you listening to?" I put the headphones on, smile, then take them back off. "Simon and Garfunkel. Of course."

"What are you doing here?"

I put the headphones to the side and tuck a stray strand of hair behind her ear. Her hair is so soft. "I wanted to ask you the same thing, Paisley."

"I'm listening to music."

"For hours," I add.

"Yeah. Nothing wrong with that, right?"

"No." I sigh and take her hand. "Come here."

Her hand is so small. So delicate. Her fingers slip through mine if I don't hold them tight enough. She is cold, as if she'd been standing out in the snow for hours and not under a blanket next to a crackling fire.

We sit down on the couch, me cross-legged, she with one leg tucked beneath her. There are dark shadows below her eyes, which stand out strongly from her light skin. She hasn't slept well over the last few days. I could hear her footsteps above me, almost the whole night long, moving back and forth across the creaking wooden floor. And it was all my fault.

"I'm sorry. I am *so* sorry, Paisley."

She looks at her fingernails. The one by her ring finger has two white flecks. She scratches them. "I'm angry at you, Knox."

"I know."

"You hurt me."

"I know."

She looks at me. Her stare goes deep. My stomach contracts.

"How could you think that I would *ever* do something like that to you?"

"No idea. I don't think I thought at all. It surprised me. From one moment to the next, my life was packed up as if it were a box full of odds and ends and turned upside down. I couldn't find anything anymore. Everything was all over the place. Absolute chaos in my head."

She nods. "I know something about that."

Silence envelops us. I cast my eyes through the store, considering the best way to bring up the topic. William peeps out from behind another shelf. He points his finger at his watch. Then he performs a pantomime, first contorting his face, then making waving movements with his hand, and, in the end, pretending to vacuum. *Acid-base balance.* I roll my eyes and turn back to Paisley.

"Listen, Paisley." Once again I reach for her hand, trace the lines on her knuckles. "Ivan Petrov is in Aspen."

She doesn't react. Her fingers become rigid, her whole body, I think, but not a single word crosses her lips. She stares at her lap.

She knows, I think. *She already knows.*

And that means that she must have seen him. I feel sick. Her fingers slide away from mine. They land on the cushions. "He found you." She still doesn't say anything. I start to panic. "What did he do, Paisley? *What did he do?*"

This is the moment her dam breaks and the waters flood her center. She doesn't simply cry, she completely collapses. I hold onto her, her delicate body pressed close to mine, her tears damp, salty tracks on my throat.

I want to kill him. Right now. I want to find him and kill him for hurting her like this.

It takes forever for her to quiet down. William's no longer there. Only in passing did I notice him place the keys on the counter next to the popcorn machine before softly closing the door behind him.

At some point Paisley moves away and looks at me. Her face is spotted red, her blue eyes swimming in tears. "I have to go back to him, Knox."

There are things in life you hear but that are so absurd they don't want to reach you. This is one of them. She says it and I hear it, but, somehow, it just doesn't reach me.

"No," I say. "Why should you?"

She grabs her throat. The lump is most likely stuck. "I have no choice. I have to go back to Minneapolis."

"You most definitely do not. Listen, Paisley. Dad's going to take care of him. That pig is going to leave Aspen and never bother you again. You don't need to be afraid, okay? My dad has clout and knows the right people. He's going to take care of this."

"He *can't* take care of it." Her voice is broken by sobs. It's hard for me to understand her, she's crying so hard. "He may have clout, but he's not above the law."

I blink. "Above the law?"

She takes a deep breath as if what she's about to say will demand everything of her. Everything.

"I am bound to him by contract. I simply took off and signed myself up at iSkate, although I'm still under contract with Ivan."

Her words slam into my solar plexus with the strength of steel. I can hardly breathe.

"I was so dumb," she sobs. "It was so dumb of me to come here. I messed up my whole life, yours, too, although I knew from the beginning that it wouldn't work out."

I have no idea what to do. I'd like to tell her that we'll figure it out, that everything will turn out okay, but I'd be lying. I desperately look for a way out in my head, but there aren't any, not a single one. My lungs are burning. They need oxygen. I breathe in but it doesn't feel like I'm getting any air. I feel like I'm suffocating.

"Okay," I stammer. "You're under contract with him. But that doesn't mean anything, Paisley. If you go back, I'm coming with you. I'll protect you from that motherfucker until your contract is up and we can come back to Aspen."

She shakes her head. "Your life is here, Knox."

"*You* are a part of my life now."

Whoops. I shouldn't have said that because she just starts to cry even more. I stand up, take her hand, and pull her up. She's wobbly, as if she's just run a marathon. "Come on. Let's go home." She's still looking at the floor. I lift up her chin and look into her eyes. "You know what, Paisley? I want you so bad it scares the shit out of me. But here I am, freaked, maybe a bit cracked, and I want you all the same. That means that I'm behind you no matter what happens. All you have to do is turn around and you'll see me. All you have to do is say a word and I'll listen. I'm not going away, got it?"

She nods, and I think she really understands how much she means to me. But I also think that *she* thinks that her past is something she needs to sort out on her own. Something that she doesn't want to do to me because it hurt her.

And that scares me more than everything else—it means that I could lose her.

43

That Dream Grew in Your Heart for a Reason

PAISLEY

KNOX'S BREATH BRUSHES MY CHEEK. HE CAME TO BED late. I lay under his deep-space bedspread half the night listening to the muffled voices of him and Jack coming up from downstairs without understanding what they were talking about. But I didn't want to hear them, anyway. For me it's clear: Knox is not going to leave his hometown for me and lose his place in the program. There is no way I'm going to allow that to happen.

Just a little bit longer, I think, as his chest rises and falls against my back. He's holding onto me tight. *Just one more minute.*

I've been thinking it for half an hour now. But time is running out and when I stretch out my hand to type something into my phone, I know that I can't stay in bed much longer.

I have to let go.

My legs are trembling. My whole body is trembling. Everything within me is screaming to stay in bed. Knox's hand falls off my arm as I sit up. He shifts onto his back, opens his lips, and keeps on sleeping. The moonlight has found its way between the curtains and is casting a gray shimmer across his body. His face looks so peaceful, but I just can't. It's like life hates me. First it dragged me through the dirt, then it gave me the greatest joy on earth only to take it away again, and leave me with the memory of how beautiful things could have been.

The bed creaks when I stand up. I hold up my phone and take a picture of Knox so that I can look at him whenever I want. It's dark, but I can make out enough of his angelic face, and I'm going to need it.

For a while I just stand in the middle of the room, Knox's far-too-large Hilfiger hoodie wrapped around my body, listening to the tick of the alarm clock.

It's terrible. Terrible letting go of something you'd rather hold onto forever. Letting go of something you love.

My heart is pounding against my ribs as I take a deep breath and leave. I go upstairs to my own room, over to the huge triangular dormer window and look out onto Aspen Highlands. A winter wonderland. Everything is white. Snow, snow, and more snow.

I see myself in the reflection of the glass. I look different than before. Bigger somehow. I'm standing up straighter. I'm not as thin. My time in Aspen changed me. I think I am more myself than I ever was. The next few months are going to be the worst of my entire life, I'm sure of that. But I've survived it before. I'll make it again. And then I'll be free. As soon as the contract is over, I can do what I want.

The Paisley from back then doesn't exist anymore. I am stronger. More self-confident. I won't let anyone do anything to me. My body belongs to me. *I* belong to me. My decisions belong to me. I am enough and always will be. After all this time, after all these years, I have finally understood that the only person I have ever needed, the only person who's got to have my back, the only person I lost but *so desperately needed*, was me.

I know that now. I'm going back because I have to, but it won't be the end of me. It will be the beginning of a long story that I myself can write. *I'm* the one with the pen in my hand. *I'm* the one who can erase and edit—even write new things and make it better—if I want.

The curtain slips out of my fingers and covers nighttime Aspen again. As I make my way through the room to gather my things, my steps are no longer wobbly. They're sure.

I make my way downtown on foot. It takes a long time, but I enjoy every step, every crunch of the snow beneath my boots, every cold breath of air, every white snowflake that falls onto my tongue. The first houses are coming into view, and I move way too quickly through the streets that have become so familiar to me over the past number of months. The streetlamps are shining dimly down onto the sidewalks. There's a light on in The Old-Timer, and for a second I wonder what William's doing in his shop already but then I remember: *it's William*. He looks up as I make my way past his window. I quickly look away and walk faster. At some point the corner building with its winter-themed shopwindow and butter-yellow string lights appears. *Kate's Diner.*

Kate was the first person I got to know here. I can still remember how she smiled when she brought me her pancakes. I can remember the sad look on her face as she looked me up and down and her glance caught the blue spots on my face. I gasp for breath; it is *so* painful thinking about all these things. I wipe my gloved hand across my runny nose, look up the side of the building, and recognize the old stickers on the slanted windows. Most of them have been scratched away and now only suggest what they once were. I think about Gwen who, at this moment, is asleep on her yoga mat beneath the window, think about Bing Crosby sprawled out in his house, pressing his damp nose against the plywood. It hurts. Really bad.

I think of my mother being left by one of her endless boyfriends. They'd been together a few months, and I thought that they were happy because they laughed so much. But once it was over and Mom was cooking and humming, dancing and smoking her cigarettes in front of the old beaten-up TV, I asked her if she was sad. She just flicked ash on the trailer's nasty floor in response, blew out a big cloud of smoke, and said, "What, *because of him?* That wasn't even real." I asked her how she knew whether something was real, and she said, "When it hurts like you was going through hell. When it tears at you, and you think you're going to burst into flames because of the pain—that's when it's real."

I didn't know what she meant. But now, looking up at the scraps of stickers on the windows, now I do, and the hot tears stream down my cold face.

This here is real.

"You getting on, or what?"

I slowly turn around. The bus driver is a lanky guy with three-day stubble and dark circles around his eyes. He's chewing gum. A cup of coffee in his hand. Disgusting combination. Nodding, I have to force myself forward and not turn around.

One step after the other. Just one more. And one more after that. Just keep on moving.

There are four other people on the bus. A couple around my age, way in back; a man around thirty; and an older woman who is knitting and reminds me of Ruth. She watches me as I walk past and casts me a smile full of wrinkles. It's the most beautiful thing I've experienced so far this morning, so I stop next to her and shoehorn my bags into the space above the seat. I arrived with nothing but a jute tote, now there are two big sports bags, stuffed to the brim. The doors close as I sit down, and the bus moves off down the street in the direction of town square. Not a soul about.

Leaving Aspen, it's like my body is paralyzed. The whole time I'm thinking, *It's all good. I'm still here, no reason to be sad*. But then we're on the highway, and I feel like someone's ripped my heart out of my chest. Now there's no going back. The most beautiful time of my life is behind me.

I undo the laces of my boots, slip out of them, and pull my legs up beneath me. I lean my back against the dirty window so as not to see the spots on the glass, and because I can't handle the fact that we've left Aspen.

On my phone, I open the photo of Knox and play with the pendants of my charm bracelet. The bird glides through my fingers.

"Sweetheart," the woman across from me says. "Why do you look so sad?"

"Because I *am*."

Her knitting needles clack against each other. "But why?"

I shrug and lean my head back. "Because I had to leave people behind who I love."

"Are you sure that you had to?"

For a moment, all I do is listen to the crackling of the radio. "It's not that simple."

"Nothing is simple," she says. Her ball of wool falls out of her handbag and rolls across the floor. She doesn't pick it up. "The gardener sows his seeds, but do you think everything's easy peasy until harvest comes?"

"That's something else."

"I think it's the same. First you sow, and then it's up to you to see what happens."

"Sometimes that doesn't work," I reply. "Sometimes a wild animal shows up, or people who don't care about your harvest at all, and they destroy everything."

She shrugs her bony shoulders. "And? Then what becomes of your harvest is still up to you."

"How so? It's been destroyed."

"Just because something's destroyed doesn't mean you can't plant new seeds."

I don't know what to say, so I close my eyes and inhale Knox's smell that's still on his sweater. My tears trickle into the fabric.

"Don't cry," the woman says. She starts digging through her brown bag. "Here's a tissue."

"Thanks." As I speak, all I can taste is salt. I take the package, and it doesn't take long for it to be empty.

"I don't have any more," she says.

"It's okay." I'm probably going to spend the next sixteen hours crying in this bus. No one's got that many tissues.

The bus rattles on, the radio tuned to some techno station, the woman's knitting needles clacking away. At some point my eyes grow heavy with exhaustion and I doze off.

No idea how long I sleep, but when I wake up, it's bright outside. I immediately feel a lump in my stomach. If it's light outside, it's got to have been hours. Hours separating me from Aspen. Hours separating me from Knox.

I rub my eyes with my knuckles and notice that older woman is staring at me. She's still knitting but her job has definitely grown in proportion. The end almost reaches the floor.

"What time is it?"

She looks at her slender wristwatch, the veins beneath her skin clearly visible. "Just about ten."

"*Ten?*" How long did I sleep? "That can't be!"

"Sure. Whether you believe it or not, I've known how to read a clock for fifty-eight years. I'm fairly certain that it's ten."

"Oh my God." I slept for over six hours. That has to be the exhaustion. And the desire to block everything out. To simply sleep and forget what's happening. I squint and look outside the window but can't make out the signs. "Where are we?"

"Close to…"

She's interrupted by the bus driver honking his horn, cursing, and slamming on the brakes. I'm thrown forward but my seatbelt keeps me down and pulls my body back into its seat.

The bus driver yells, "FUCKING ASSHOLE!"

Everyone in the bus raises their heads to see what's going on.

"There's a car," the guy in the back with his girlfriend says.

She agrees with a nod. "Yeah, an SUV type thingy."

"How brave," the older woman says. I am relieved she didn't stab herself with her needles.

I crane my neck to see through the window and see a white SUV blocking the road.

And then Knox gets out, just like that, right in the middle of a snowstorm, six hours away from Aspen, in his black Canada Goose jacket and without a hat. Snowflakes land in his hair, which is shooting out in all directions, on his shoulders, his lips. He walks up to the bus and knocks on the door, as if that's just something you did. Cut someone off and then just knock on the door all friendly like just to say hello.

"Oh my God," I mumble. And again, "Oh my God."

I hear the girl behind me let out a breath. "That's Knox Winterbottom, right? Shit, yeah, I think that's him. Take a photo, Lane, quick!"

The bus driver considers whether to let Knox in or not, but then appears to conclude that the dude won't drive his car away beforehand anyway.

Press the button, press the button, do it, ohmyGod, ohmyGod, ohmyGod, press the goddamn button, open the door!

He does. The door opens. Knox steps in. He looks down the aisle. He looks toward me. My heart stops. This second we're looking at each other isn't a second. It's an eternity, that's what it feels like. When it feels like this, it's real, right?

He starts walking toward me. My face is burning. He stops next to my seat. His breath reaches me. It's cold. From the air outside. His fingers dig into the seat in front and behind me. He lowers his face until it is just a few centimeters away from mine.

"Don't. Ever. Do. That. Again."

"I had to."

"You're getting out."

"I can't."

"You can."

"Why are you here?"

"Why are *you*?"

"I had to."

He growls. "I just drove 150 mph for hours to catch up with this fucking bus after William called me. You've got a choice, Paisley. Either you get off the bus, listen to what I have to say, and come with me, or you stay here, continue on to Minneapolis, and accept the fact that I'll be there when you get off and will not leave. Either way. You're not getting rid of me."

"That won't work."

"You'd be amazed by what works when you let it."

The old woman's face slides past Knox's lats. "Go on. Otherwise the guy's going to die of longing."

"Yeah, go with him," the girl says from in back. "You're that figure skater, right? From the news? You two are *so* cute together!"

Knox's lips curl into a self-confident grin. "You see?"

The bus driver clucks. "Come on, girl, I want to get home."

I'm not sure how this is supposed to work; how Knox imagines us though we don't stand a chance. But now he's standing in front of me with his birthmark, with those eyes of his, and I can't *not* go. I managed to leave him once today, but I won't be able to do it a second time.

Knox's grin grows wider when he sees that he's won. He pushes off the seats, takes a step backward, and pulls my bags down with an ease that'd make you think they were simply filled with cotton.

The old woman casts me a mischievous smile as I walk past. "And then there are always people who *save* their harvest; it's a good thing he's one of them."

I don't think I'll ever forget this woman.

Knox and I get into the Range Rover. He turns it on. The seats get warm in a second and everything smells like Aspen, like Knox, like *my life*.

He steps on the gas and speeds off like it's a race against time.

"Knox…"

"Listen," he says, his eyes on the road. He seems keyed up. Completely out of his senses. "Ivan is gone."

"What? Where?"

His hand finds my thigh. "No idea. But your contract is now null and void."

"*What?*"

Knox passes a truck. "Dad did some research, Paisley. The guy is disgusting. He's been that way for half his life. Mom and him were pair skaters back in the day. Did you know that?"

"How on earth could I have known that?!"

"No idea. I didn't know it, either. Long time ago, back in her hometown. But she told Dad about him later on. We did some research. Dad's got a few contacts at the criminal investigation department."

"At the *criminal investigation department*? Knox, you're talking in riddles!"

"Yeah, yeah, let me explain. It's actually illegal, but there was a guy there who owed my dad a favor, so Dad said, 'Hey, get ahold of his record for me.' Guess what was in there."

"Tell me."

"Multiple reports of sexual harassment. Stalking. Blackmail. To be honest, I don't understand why the dude hasn't been behind bars for years."

"Yeah, okay, but what do *you* all get out of the info?"

Knox types an address into the GPS before continuing. "The reports all came from a girl from your former association, Paisley. Before Minneapolis. Dad got in touch with them and lost his mind. Truly *lost it*. I don't think I have *ever* heard him yell like that. He asked how it could be that multiple skaters were harassed by their trainer, yet they didn't report him. They were pretty intimidated, and he said that if they didn't deal with your former association on the spot and demand that Ivan be fired for his actions, then he'd report both associations for not having a safety net in cases of harassment." Knox looks at me. His eyes are big and open, *so open* I could lose myself. "It didn't take long for them to call us back. Ivan was officially out. The contracts were rendered invalid. You're free, Paisley."

You're free, Paisley.

The words race through my head, over and over, so quickly that I become dizzy.

"It's over," I whisper, just to hear it, as otherwise I wouldn't believe it. "It's really over."

I feel weightless, in this moment, in this car, with Knox next to me. And I think the bravest thing I've ever done was simply to keep on going, to keep on going even when I wanted to stop, even when I wanted to die. If I hadn't gone on, I wouldn't have believed in hope or in life and I never would have experienced what joy in its purest form feels like. It's a beautiful feeling. Everyone should keep on going just to feel what I'm feeling right now.

Knox tilts his head. "It should be obvious to you by now that you're not going to get rid of me, Snow Queen."

I look at him for a second, two, maybe even ten, then laugh with all my heart. I have never been as free or as happy in my whole life. I laugh for me, for Knox, for this life, and for all the others who have forgotten how to laugh in the hopes that they won't give up until, at some point, they learn again.

Because laughing can be so wonderful.

Knox beams at me, tugs at my ear, and gives a number to the hands-free system.

A few moments later I hear Polina's voice. "Where are you?"

"Six hours," Knox says.

"You'll *never* make it."

"If you knew the way I drive, you wouldn't say that."

"I don't care, kid, just make sure she's *on the ice on time.*"

"We're driving to Skate America," I mutter. So much is happening at once I can hardly keep up.

"Of course, we are. Do you think I'd let your program go unseen? You're nuts, Paisley, *nuts.*"

"We're never going to make it," I repeat Polina's words.

Knox rolls his eyes. "I hate that expression. 'We'll never make it.'

Please. We're Paisley and Knox, you forget that already? We can do everything."

And then he really steps on the gas. He's driving so fast the other cars are just a blur, all the way to Las Vegas. Everything is so bright, so colorful, I'd love to have a look around, but we don't have any time. My sports bags in tow, we rush into the building. It takes ages for us to figure out where we need to go and feels like we've gone through a hundred hallways. I've never been here before and have no idea where the backstage area is. At some point, we reach a door behind which we can hear a large babble of voices. Knox rips it open, shoos me through, and when I see all the skaters in their various outfits, an enormous weight falls from my shoulders. We're in the right place: the green room. Several of them are going through their programs on the dry ground, while others are sitting on stationary bikes to warm up, but I don't have time left for any of that. Knox and I storm through until we reach the black curtains that are blocking off the rink. Panicking I look for Polina and the others, but then I hear the audience, hear the commentator's voice calling my name over and over.

I freeze, right in the middle of the green room, everyone staring at me. My boots are dug into the ground and Knox bumps into me.

"I'm too late," I whisper. "I won't make it."

"Stop saying that. Stop. Get changed. Hurry up, get going."

We dump the contents of my sports bag onto the ground until I find my dress, the one Gwen gave me. My pulse is thundering in double and triple time as I climb into my tights and Knox pulls the dress over my head. I quickly make the ugliest bun ever, though, at the same time, it's the most beautiful bun ever as I'll never forget it.

"I think I'm going to puke."

Knox pins up my loose strands of hair. "Good. But not right now. Now you've got to skate, Paisley, okay?"

"Okay."

He takes my face in both hands, looks deep into my eyes, and says, "Show them what you can do, Snow Queen."

My name booms from the speakers. I feel hot and cold, cold and hot. I take my skates and run through the lobby, run like I've never run before, past the black curtains, and am suddenly blinded by light, so much light and so many people. I'm in the area right off the ice that allows skaters into the rink. It's overflowing with press, and they look up from their cameras to stare at me. I wave my arms furiously so that the commentator at the long table next to the jury sees that I'm here and doesn't disqualify me. I have no idea where Polina is—no idea where Gwen, Levi, Aaron, and Harper are—but I know they're somewhere here backstage, watching and smiling as I lace up my skates and glide out onto the ice, right into the center, right on top of the giant Skate America logo.

I move into position. Everything is as quiet as a mouse. I take a deep breath but no one can hear me because the rink is huge, and I mean *huge*. And as I hold my starting position, legs crossed, arms outstretched, head lowered, I think: *This here is my moment.*

The music starts. Ed Sheeran's voice drifts out over hundreds of heads. My veins are tingling. I have never felt as ready as I do now, taking the first step of my program. At this very moment, I know it's going to be flawless. I simply *know* it because my head is free. I am free.

I am skating.

I am dancing.

I am in love, and I am *alive*.

Afterword

"You wanted it."
  "Don't make a fuss; it'll be quick."
  "It's your fault when you dress like that, you whore."
  "You deserve this."

These sentences are just four of many that victims of sexual violence are subjected to while undergoing abuse that hurts not only physically, but also especially psychologically—and for a long time afterward.

Every year in Germany, there are over 10,000 reported cases of rape or sexual coercion, which is likely not even a fraction of all the unreported cases.

Dear girls, dear women, dear boys, dear men, dear *people*, this afterword is my way of standing up for you and is here to serve as a reminder of what horrible, inhuman, and cruel suffering this kind of violence inflicts upon the victims. In my story, Paisley had the good fortune of being taken up and empowered by loving people—but not everyone is so lucky. And that is why it is so important: all of you, keep your eyes open. This kind of violence can take place anywhere, maybe even happen to people you know, a mute cry for help in their eyes, but with silent lips, for wherever one person wields power over another there is fear, even tormenting, all-consuming panic. And this is why I am begging all of you: be alert, pay attention to any signs that make you wonder.

Symptoms of violent crime can vary. Some people, like Paisley, have physical wounds. Others display them in behavioral patterns. Maybe, as if out of the blue, they don't have time to meet friends anymore, or maybe they can't make any decisions anymore, or respond haltingly and stress the fact that they need to see what their partner has to say first. Generalized anxiety and panic attacks, eating disorders, and noticeable issues of substance abuse can also be warning signs that all is not okay. Be ready to help, to ask whether everything is all right—sometimes all the person needs to take the brave step to leave and to open themselves to a helping hand. Show understanding, take disclosures seriously, and discuss what kind of help is available.

What I have written about here is a profound, important topic and the fact that victims of sexual violence are still being told that *they* are the ones who are at fault hurts me deeply. The fact that, by being ignored or trivialized, people are made to feel that they cannot talk about what happened and/or that they are somehow lesser makes me angry, indeed furious.

Let me say this right now: It's not your fault. In any way whatsoever. You are wonderful and incomparably strong. The people who generate such pain are the ones at fault. They alone.

For those of you who feel caught, who don't know what to do, how to get free from the pain, or where to turn, I would like to share the number for the National Domestic Violence Hotline in the USA: (800) 799-SAFE (7233).

To all the rest of you: be alert, keep your eyes open, and offer help whenever necessary.

Playlist

Ava Max—"Kings and Queens"
Billie Eilish—"Bad Guy"
Billie Marten—"Bird"
Coldplay—"Fix You"
Daniela Andrade—"Crazy"
Ed Sheeran—"I See Fire"
Fink—"Looking Too Closely"
Gary Jules—"Mad World"
Harry Styles—"Falling"
James Arthur—"Naked"
Lewis Capaldi—"Bruises"
Lord Huron—"The Night We Met"
Ruth B.—"Lost Boy"
Sasha Sloan—"Dancing With Your Ghost"
Sia—"Breathe Me"
Simon & Garfunkel—"The Sound of Silence" (acoustic)
The Gardener & the Tree—"Rebel of the Night"
The Gardener & the Tree—"Wild Horses"
Valentin, caravan—"The Scientist"
Valentin, caravan—"Somewhere Only We Know"

Acknowledgments

This book means the world to me.

I never would have believed what it could become one day. All of Aspen's inhabitants are so close to my heart that I don't intend to ever let them go. The fact that the story became so lively, heartwarming, and *big* is in no small part due to several wonderful people whom I would like to thank here.

My deepest thanks to the Thomas Schlück Literary Agency and, above all, my dear agent Kathrin. By the time I applied with this story, I had already collected years of rejections for several manuscripts and no longer believed in myself. You gave that belief back to me, empowered me, and recognized my potential. Without you, there would be no book, and for that I will be eternally thankful.

Another, equally important thank you is due to Penguin Books, especially my editor Laura. From the very first you were passionate about the story, welcomed me so affectionately to the team, and were always by my side with help and advice. I think your wave of praise catapulted my self-confidence into the Aspen Highlands, ha ha ha.

I would also like to thank my editor Steffi Korda. You extracted immense quality out of the text, discovered errors I never would have noticed, and examined every line so thoroughly. I have nothing but the greatest appreciation for your work.

A heartfelt thank you to Gesche Wendebourg for believing in my story and making it possible for it to reach readers across the globe. Your dedication and guidance opened the door to an English release, and I'm endlessly grateful for your support on this journey. And most importantly, thanks to Sourcebooks for making this dream come true by publishing my book in English. It means the world to me!

Thanks to my charming husband Jannik, who without fail dropped everything to support me. It wasn't always easy, you had to put a lot of things on the back burner, and be both houseman and nanny—who knows, maybe you're even a superhero.

Thanks to my dear mother—you unbelievably powerful woman! Thank you for being my biggest fan, for taking care of Valerio every day, and for giving up your day-to-day life so that I could meet my deadlines. You're the best.

A big shout-out to the talented snowboarder André Höflich. Thank you for taking the time to talk to me on the phone so that every snowboarding scene and the chapter on the X Games would be realistic and truly come to life. The same goes for figure skater and *Disney on Ice* Snow Queen, Sydney. Without you the figure-skating scenes would not have been nearly as professional—thank you!

A huge thanks as well to my beloved #Schlücklich-Kolleginnen and to my writing crew Mirka, Lexie, Lily, and Bianca.

And to you, Sandra, for being my best writing buddy for so long now and simply my friend, I love you, and thanks to Tine for believing in me and my story. #veganpower.

At this point I could go on forever, so I would just like to offer a general thank you to everyone who has believed in me, and especially to my readers—none of this would be possible without you.

About the Author

Bestselling author Ayla Dade was born in 1994 and lives with her family in northern Germany. She has won the hearts of her readers with her new adult romances, each of them a *Der Speigel* bestseller that remains in the top ranks for weeks. She studied law but spends every spare minute she has writing. She is a popular book blogger, and fills the pages of her novels with tumultuous feelings, secrets and intrigue, love, and spice. When she isn't dreaming about the world of her books, she spends her time playing sports and snuggling up in front of the fireplace with a good book.

Instagram: @ayladade
TikTok: @ayladade.author

LIKE FIRE WE BURN

He's finally back on the ice. But can he melt her heart?

Aria Moore thought that two years and two thousand miles would be long and far enough. But when she returns to Aspen to help run the family B&B while her mother is ill, her feelings for Wyatt Lopez come surging back.

If she's honest with herself, she'll admit she still carries a torch for the charismatic ice hockey player who once broke her heart. Aria swore never to see him again—which proves impossible when Wyatt is forced to move into the B&B.

Aria begins to feel hopeful when she finally meets someone new—and she makes it clear to Wyatt that they can only spend time together as friends. But on a trip into the snowy mountains, they can no longer ignore the chemistry between them, and Wyatt seems intent on convincing her that friendship will never be enough.

"A gripping story and an irresistible setting!"
—Anna Todd, *New York Times* bestselling author, for *Blackwell Palace*

For more info about Sourcebooks's books and authors, visit:
sourcebooks.com